HER TWISTED SINNERS

HER TWISTED SINNERS

THE SEVEN SINNERS OF HELL'S KINGDOM. BOOK FIVE

by

GINNA MORAN

SUNNY PALMS PRESS

This book took a damn devilish miracle to reach you, dear souls. And damn it! Kase, Dante, Micah, Zade, Elias, Andre, Lucian, and Cass-hole, it might be your fault for wanting to include the Great Coming! The soul blasting climax. The eternal fountain of pleasure.

Yeah, that's right. I'm calling you devils out. Everyone expects to face your brand of delectable punishment, so have at it. Get those appendages to work. Find some new ones. Let's give Raven and her legion of gorgeous souls what they crave...one helluva wild ride, good time, and unforgettable finale. They all deserve it! Well, okay. Throw in some torture, too, I guess. They've been naughty.

Oh, and give Noel and Missy their rewards for being good minions. But don't let them lick you. That's how they claim things. Crap. You guys like that. They're all yours.

Power Struggle

RAVEN

"THE LITTLE ANGEL spawn is a lot feistier than my boy," Dante says, resting his big palm on the side of my stomach. He trails his fingers across my skin with the twins' movements, chuckling as they each kick him.

Forcing myself to smile, I play with Dante's hair, combing my fingers through the soft tresses. We've been sitting on the couch for hours with the TV blaring for background noise, but I haven't been in the mood to watch.

I stare at the bulge shifting under my skin, the cooler spot a clear indication to me of which baby it is. I haven't thought about names yet. I haven't really thought about anything. I know my devils grow anxious, and my lack of feelings doesn't help any, but I don't know what else I can do. Faking the excitement is pointless. They know it's not real, so they do their best to show it for me. If I allowed Dante to adhere his hands to my belly, he would. I never knew someone could be so obsessed. His waves of affection never grow old. I remember enjoying it even if I'm numb now.

My heart should swell with the thought of his adoration and love for the twins. I should be ecstatic by how thoughtful my devils are. Things like smiling only come out of habit now. I'm just a vessel to these two beings of power. An empty shell.

My time on the Mortal Plane is almost over. I can sense it deep in my bones. It's as if each passing day will bring me closer to my soul, but with my soul comes an eternity without my devils. We've failed humanity. I've failed the men who love me. Who I know I love despite the absence left behind by Heaven's bastard warriors.

"Come on, baby boy. Give Daddy a power kick. Show me your strength." Dante pokes his fingers to my belly, trying to summon a reaction.

I tap his forehead. "You don't even know if it's a boy. Maybe she won't respond because she's female," I say, patting the hotspot on the left side. I decided the less I know, the easier it would be when the time comes. If I think about those things, it'll make it more real. I don't want this to be real. I want this to be a dream that I can wake up from.

I should find comfort in knowing what my future entails, but knowing that the birth of my twins will end my life...it's the worst thing in the world. How can I prepare to bring life into this world knowing that it will kill me? How can I prepare never to know my children? I can't. I don't like having this sort of knowledge. I thought I wanted to know everything about the universe, but some things are just best left to the unknown. It would make it easier.

"Tell that to Kase. He swears to the end of time that he can only produce a little dude. Our swimmers are definitely all male, and together, we've created a power in our image." Dante leans in and presses his lips to my belly. "Isn't that right, baby boy? You probably have two cocks and everything."

I tip my head back and laugh out of pure exasperation. "You're ridiculous."

"I'm happy. Excited." Dante's face lights up with a smile, and he shifts closer and grasps my chin, guiding me to kiss him. "Your laughter helps. It sounded natural. I think the babies might be influencing you more. We've all noticed."

The smile vanishes from my face, and I flick my eyes to stare at Dante. The diamond-shape of his pupils expands and retracts, and he rubs his thumb over my bottom lip.

He traces my jawline until he tucks my black hair behind my ear. "Have you realized it? We think that you've been so numb to protect yourself. Without your soul, it's a bit harder, but these babies bring so much more. You just have to—"

"Stop, Dante. I don't…I don't want to feel anything. I prefer this. I know it bothers you that I've changed but look at me. Look at all of this. You've given up Hell, and things haven't changed. We are no closer to finding answers. The only thing we are getting closer to is my end. If I feel it, it will destroy me. Heaven has done enough already. Just let me live." With my words, a swell of unbidden emotions blasts through me, cracking the wall protecting me from myself. But they're not my emotions. They belong to the power I carry inside me. The twins react to me, and it's as if a part of their beings possesses mine. I can't control it, and it forces me to feel things that I forgot.

Tears burn my eyes, and my mouth trembles, my whole body turning rigid. Fuck.

"Raven, hey. Pretty soul, look at me." Dante cups my face, leaning in so close that he fills my vision. His fangs peek from beneath his lips, and he releases a soft hiss. "Don't fight it. This is a good thing. If you can summon the strength to handle this, then maybe we can use it. The babies know a part of you is missing. I know they can feel it the same way we can. Let them in. Let them help you feel. If you do, we might be able to pinpoint where they're keeping your soul."

I blink a few times. The heat of my tears splashing my cheeks burns trails over my skin. "We've been looking for months. This isn't going to be any different. I can't have this kind of hope."

Dante growls, his eyes flashing green. Scooping his arms under me, he flips me off the couch and bends me over his knee, managing to hold me just right, so I don't lie on my stomach as he keeps me up with his arm under my boobs. I don't even have a chance to react before he flips up my dress and spanks me hard on the ass. My whole body tenses with the sting, and I gasp. It's been a while since he's surprised me. He's been far more gentle the last month or so since I look as if I'm about to pop now. My pregnancy feels a lot more real now that he can see it with my changing body.

"Don't think I'll go easy on you because you are carrying our babies. I need you to know that this isn't hopeless. We will get through this, even if I have to break through Heaven's protective shield, burn my fucking cock off in the process, and fly into that shithole paradise to get your soul. I'll do whatever it takes. I mean it." Dante swings his hand again, smacking my ass harder this time. "I'll even kidnap Cassius, chain him beneath me, and ride him like a damn horse into the light to make it happen. He would deserve it. I bet he would even like it."

I open and close my mouth, sucking in deep breaths as my body slackens with a wave of lust. This cute fucking bastard.

I can't believe this. It's like he awakens something inside me, and I can't ignore or deny it.

Pulling me across his lap, he forces me to hold myself up with my palms, and I squeeze my legs together as he sinks his fangs right into my ass cheek, biting me. My body buzzes with his actions, and I moan. Warmth pools between my legs, and Dante hums deep in his throat. I expect him to pull me back to his lap to fuck me, but instead, he gets to his feet and forces me on mine.

He towers over me, a drip of my blood splashing on his lips. "I think it's time we prepare. I've just ensured that you can't comfortably sit on your ass and watch TV now, so it's time to let me take charge. I don't want to ever hear you say this is pointless again. Do you understand? I love you, Raven. I need you to trust me and the rest of the devils to take care of you. I know everything has been a shitshow, but life is always a fucking shitshow. Eternity is always a fucking shitshow. We just need to adjust and evolve and make it our bitch."

I can't stop a smile from crossing my lips, my body still humming from his unexpected punishment. It gets me in a good way, and it takes everything in me not to tease him.

Fuck it. I'm not going to just ignore things I want to do any longer.

Shoving my hand into his chest, I push him back a foot to give myself room, twisting away from him. I peek over my shoulder as I lift up my dress and bow forward as far as I can before it turns uncomfortable with my pregnant belly. "I need you to take control of me. I've missed you like this. Come on, Dante. Show me who you are as a devil. I think your disconnection from Hell has made you soft. Where's my sexy dominating man?"

His eyes flash green again, my words getting to him how I wanted. "Careful, pretty soul. I can still open the damn portal to Hell."

"Then do it." I shake my ass, nearly certain I look as if I'm waddling in place, but I don't give a fuck. Dante's never made me feel anything less than beautiful. "Open the portal and bring out one of those damn traitors. I'll feel better if I can fuck something up."

Dante hisses under his breath, curling and uncurling his fist. His chest rises and falls as he thinks about my words. The devils had agreed never to open a portal to Hell until they were ready to take it back, but I think the sudden mundane lifestyle has taken a toll on all of us.

"Kase is going to fuck me up for this," Dante mutters, stepping closer. "You do realize that, right? He won't only fuck me up. He will fuck me hard in the ass. You know that I prefer it be you now."

I turn back around and glide my tongue over my lips. "I bet I can convince him to let me do it," I tease, striding closer until

I can rub my hand over his hard cock. "Come on, Dante. I'm dying to see what kind of trash the angelic army turned the place into. I'm dying to see you beat someone up for it."

Dante flares his nostrils, his muscles flexing with my words as I continue stroking him through his pants with my hand.

"If you don't give her what she wants, then I will. I'm not afraid to be the big bad devil she craves. Isn't that right, Ray? This fucking place is boring, and I'm getting impatient waiting around. My dickhead brother is taking far too long with his investigation." Lucian stands in the hallway. It's Dante's time, so he's been staying out of the way. Because there's always two devils with me at all times now. They tend to flip a coin to see who will babysit who, and Lucian lost. They have a weird agreement that Kase can't always be the one with Dante and the same goes for Andre and Zade. They are less likely to be distracted when they're not together.

It's only when everyone is out, though. They tend to all return to watch me eat either breakfast or dinner. I don't know if it's just because tension is high, but the devils do like to get out more. It also helps with Cassius and Elias. It's harder for them to ignore what they describe as a summons. Because it's as if Heaven knows that its army has betrayed them, but there's also nothing we want to do.

The angels have upset the balance, and we want to show them exactly what happens because of it. We need to make a point. They have been so off with their thinking that they will have to come begging for help. And by they, I mean those who aren't guardians. Those who keep Heaven in order. But they're not quite there yet. The angelic call is intended for angels. It's intended to try to bring them back from Hell. But it's too late for that. Once Hell gets to them, it won't release them. We've insured it. They're the ones anchored now.

I push my thoughts away and swivel to look at Lucian. I curl my finger, motioning for him to come closer. "See, Dante. Now we can blame it on this asshole. He wouldn't mind a little punishment."

"Fuck no. I would like to see any of those bastards try. Let's go fuck some shit up." Lucian grins, tugging me toward him, but Dante remains flush against me, and I find myself sandwiched between their two hot bodies.

"Damn it. Fine. I will text Kase and let him know. You know that we have an agreement, and as much as I want to bow down to that sexy ass of yours, pretty soul, we need to all agree as a team." Dante tugs his phone from his pocket and taps the screen a couple of times.

I shift in anticipation, bouncing on the balls of my feet. His phone chimes and I expect to be denied, but Kase only says to give me what I want. He says to bring someone home for him to destroy when he gets back as well.

I laugh and bounce some more, bumping my belly into

Lucian's hard abs. He automatically steadies me by pressing his palms flat to the sides of my stomach, and I smile at him.

"We were right," Dante says, tilting his head to kiss my neck. "The babies' powers grow stronger, and they give our girl some semblance of normalcy."

Lucian wags his eyebrows at me, leaning in and brushing his lips to mine for a second before sliding his tongue into my mouth and kissing me harder, deeper, letting me feel exactly how much he enjoys being with me.

"I love being right. Cassius is going to have to bow before me again. I can't wait to clock him in the face with my dick." Fire lights Lucian's eyes, and he eases away from me and strides toward the summoning circle that hasn't been opened in months. He moves the table and drags the rug covering it out of the way. It was better for them to hide it to help keep it off their minds. But it's mostly for my benefit. I really doubt the lingering presence of it helped them. It was just a constant reminder of what they gave up.

"I'm going first to make sure there's no fuckers there to try and stop us." Lucian closes his eyes and summons hellfire in his hands, the gesture enough to shake the world around me.

My heart races, and my stomach flips and flops as the babies react to the sudden cracking of the plane. Dante lifts me into his arms and cradles me, my belly making it hard for me to hug him with my body. But I don't mind having him hold me as if I'm the most precious thing in the world to him. Because I know I am. I'm the most precious thing to him and the rest of the devils in the universe. I feel it in this moment. I forgot how amazing it felt.

As quickly as it comes, I shove it away. My fear keeps me from allowing my body to play on the babies' emotions. Because I know it's not me. I have to keep reminding myself that what I'm feeling comes from them.

Lucian reveals his devil façade, and I stare in amazement as his horns graze the ceiling. I know that the devils don't like to show off who they are to Hell now that they are no longer connected to its power, and it feels so good to see. I never knew that I would miss seeing them in the form they feel the most powerful. But I do.

Whoa. I don't think rising emotions belong to the babies. Seeing Lucian stomp his massive hoof to crack the foundation of the realm zings through me. It's as if my body knows where I belong despite not having my soul. Hell calls to me. It has never been more apparent that it's the place I belong.

Lucian vanishes in a cloud of smoke and fire, and Dante adjusts me in his arms and shifts on his feet, preparing for whatever shit might unfold.

"It's all clear," Dante says, brushing his lips to my ear. "Are you sure about this?"

I bob my head. "I'm more certain than ever. It's the strangest thing. I don't know if it's because of the babies or what, but I feel I need to go. I feel as if I'll somehow be okay as long as I'm there."

His eyes sparkle green. "You're going to be better than okay. We all are. You'll see."

Stepping forward, Dante doesn't wait for me to respond and jumps into the ring of fire. The world spins and darkens around me before flames light up my vision. The rancid smell of rotten eggs assaults my nose. I breathe in deeply regardless, as if just the fragrance of Hell can unleash something dark inside me strong enough to conquer Heaven to get my soul back.

My stomach clenches and one of the babies kicks, most likely my little devil spawn, and I inhale another deep breath, now craving the scent of sulfur. It doesn't smell the same as it had. A tinge of sweet florals blends with it. It's different.

And then I realize why.

The souls aren't where they belong. They roam around, trying to find a way out. The angels here aren't strong enough to control them. They're breaking Hell down.

Oh fuck.

Lucian stands a couple of feet away, staring at what remains of his kingdom. The lava pits no longer glow. The fires have burned out, and only black rock remains in its place. His towering palace lies in a mountain of rubble. All of his work over the millennium wastes away in such a short time because of the angel invaders. The energy that used to zing through here is gone.

"What the fuck?" Lucian asks, crossing his arms over his chest. "These fucking bastards. I'm going to destroy them all."

Screams rip through the world, and I stare in shock as a cloud of smoky darkness swirls through the air, twisting and spinning around the blips of light. Not light. Angels.

"Help!" a masculine voice calls out. "Heaven help us!"

Silence greets him.

There is no help coming for him.

I watch from Dante's arms as the darkness crashes over the specs of light in the distance, devouring them all.

Satisfaction should course through me, but then the shadow spins in our direction. A tidal wave of inky black souls comes crashing toward us, and there's nothing we can do.

Without the devils, Hell is as unbalanced as Heaven. It seems as if the universe might collapse.

This is no longer about Heaven or Hell. It's about humanity.

It's about the power of the souls.

Power that yearns to break free.

"Fuck! What the fuck!" A blinding light erupts in my vision, and I squeeze my eyes shut as a wave of pure white steals the darkness of the souls. "Give her to me!"

It's Cassius. What is he doing here?

Dante tries to toss me to him, the light stinging and burning his skin, but I clutch onto him. It's as if Cassius's light repulses me, and I can't get my body to comply and agree to go with him. Dante grunts at my strength.

"I'm not leaving," I snap, grinding my teeth. "I need to be here."

"Raven, please—"

The ground shakes, causing Dante to stumble a few feet before he regains his balance. Heat ignites inside me, and I tense and arch my back, feeling fire course under my skin to shoot out of my palms. The flames devour the light and the shadows of Hell-bound souls, leaving us standing in a strange haze.

"I need to be here," I repeat, resting my cheek on Dante's shoulders. "Please. Just for a bit. The souls won't hurt us."

Lucian and Cassius stare at me with slackened jaws, their reactions making them look more similar than I've ever seen them.

"I'm sorry, pretty soul," Dante whispers, his voice shaking. "You can't."

I fist my hands to fight, to force him to let me down, but Cassius snatches me away. Dante doesn't intervene.

"Cassius!" I scream, bucking my body. "You fucking bastard!"

Fire swallows Lucian and Dante, separating us. Whirlwind emotions crash through me, stealing my breath.

"Hold on, Raven. This is going to hurt." Cassius summons angelic light in one of his hands.

Agony burns through me at its closeness.

I scream.

Soul Searching

RAVEN

AS QUICKLY AS the pain slices through me, it vanishes.

"Raven, please trust me. Hell is not where you should be right now." Cassius's voice comes everywhere and nowhere as his heavenly light fades.

"I'm going to cut your wings off and slap you in the dick with them, you fucking bastard. You don't know what is right for me. I felt whole there. You better take me back." I smack my hands, hitting nothing but air. My body tingles everywhere, and I can't tell exactly where I am. I think Cassius holds me from behind.

The fucking coward.

"You don't understand what I saw. Your body was turning into a void. The darkness of the souls was trying to fill you up as a vessel. I was afraid that they would hurt you. The devils can't see the darkness like I can. They are too close to it. They probably felt the same thing you did by being home. They should've never taken you there," Cassius murmurs in my ear, and I can finally grasp that he holds me by my hips, resting his chin on the crook of my shoulder.

"You only ever see things as bad. The darkness is not your enemy. It's all a part of the balance. You should know this, Cass-hole. Take me home. If you're not going to return me there, then I just want to go home. I want to go lie on my ass and watch another month's worth of trash TV." I reach behind me and manage to lock my fingers around his soft hair, yanking the strands.

He jerks his head back, trying to escape my grip, but I only yank his hair tighter. Growling under his breath, Cassius swears in my ear. "Stop being such a pain and just let me handle this right now. You need some grace. You need my light."

I shift my fingers and manage to pinch his ear. "I need you to fucking—"

Spinning me around, Cassius lets me freefall a couple of feet before he catches me in his arms and cradles me against him. I don't get a chance to prepare myself as he plants his lips to mine and kisses me, silencing me and any argument I might have. I suck his bottom lip into my mouth and bite him hard, but he doesn't yank away. I think he likes it, because he growls deep in his throat and shifts his hand to squeeze my hip.

Easing his head back, he tries to break away from my mouth, but I don't let him. If he wants to try to silence me with the fucking kiss, he's going to give me a kiss that lingers for the rest of time. My anger toward him pushes me, and I finally release his bottom lip only to slide my tongue into his mouth. He tastes of citrus and something sweeter as if the light he carries embodies everything I love tasting on the mortal plane. I hate him. I hate how he tries to shift my emotions and distract me from the fact that he pulled a dick move. I want to be in Hell. I don't want to be close to anything involving Heaven's grace. Heaven's light has only fucked everything up for me. The angelic army has nearly ruined the universe. Cassius needs to get his shit together and realize that he's doing no one any favors by clinging so desperately to his broken path as an angel. It's as if he can't see the cracks and debris in his way. He can't see anything because the light shines too brightly. He doesn't allow any of us close enough to balance it out.

Things have to change.

"You need to turn your fucking back on Heaven already, Cassius. I'm tired of waiting for you. You need to drag Elias with you. I don't know why he resists so much. You've been hanging out with us for months now. Just let the fuck go."

I nip him again, not letting him speak as I crash my mouth to his once more, trying my best to cling onto him with my pregnant belly between us. I want him to fill me in a way that he has never allowed. I want him to know what it's like to be close. I want to know what it's like to be with him in a way that he resists. It's infuriating. It's as if it's gotten easier for him because I no longer have the light that drew angels to me like a moth to a flame.

"I can't. Please don't demand such things again. I know you're scared so you just want Hell to have its kingdoms, but you need to accept that it will not happen unless things change. Someone needs access to Heaven, and even though Elias has his wings, the angelic army has part of his soul through you. He is less likely to do what needs to be done, because no matter what, you guys are bound together. You know that." Cassius rests his forehead to mine, and the world stops with a jolt as he lands. Haze envelops us, but I don't look around. I know we're not on the mortal plane. We're in his personal sanctuary that he manages to keep separate from Heaven and Hell. The only one able to access it is Lucian because of their bond as brothers.

"I don't give a fuck right now. You're just pissing me off. Take me home. I don't want to be here. I need to be with the others. They understand me." I try to keep my voice strong. "This is too much."

Cassius furrows his brows, his amethyst eyes sparkling from

the light radiating from his very being. Reaching up, he strokes his fingers across my cheek, smearing a tear away. And damn it. I didn't want him to see this. I don't want him to know that the babies are shifting something in my being.

"You're crying." He shifts his jaw.

"No fucking shit," I snap, flicking his hand away to scrub my own cheeks until they dry. "Why do you think I wanted to stay in Hell? It was as if I felt like me again. I felt almost whole."

"But you weren't. It was all in your head. It was probably the familiarity of it. The unruly souls of Hell were getting to you, making you think that was where you belong. Let me prove it." Cassius rubs his lips together as if he tastes me on his mouth still. I wonder if he wants to kiss me again as much as I want to kiss him. I know it's not going to solve anything, but I like the distraction. He is such a stubborn dickhead that he won't take me anywhere until he's good and ready, no matter how much I beg him. So I just need to get to him another way.

"If I let you prove it and do that angelic asshole bullshit that you swear by, will you take me home then?" I purse my lips, narrowing my eyes on him.

"If you still want to go after." His eyes lock on mine as his sharp features soften the longer I capture him with my stare. "There is a chance you might not want to."

I roll my eyes. I can't help it. He's so full of himself to assume that anything he does will get me to want to stay in this blah, goody, shithole of a sanctuary full of light and bland nothingness. I know we don't see the same thing, and I know we don't feel the same thing either, which I'm pretty sure he is aware of, but it's as if he thinks he can just convince me otherwise. He can't. He's stubborn, but I'm worse.

"That won't happen unless you decide you're going to allow my devils in. For one, I doubt you can cook anything that I ask for. You don't know how to take care of me like they do." I whack him in his chest, his hard pec flexing under my touch.

"But you can take care of yourself," he says, smirking at me. "Isn't that what humanity wants? Independence? To do everything themselves?"

"Fuck that. I've been spoiled, you angelic bastard. I'll let the devils worship me as much as I worship them. And if you haven't realized, I have a damn watermelon attached to me that makes things harder to do." It was weird at first to give in and allow the devils to basically do everything for me, but I enjoy it more than I realized. Dante helps me do things I can't like paint my toes and shave my legs. He finally gets to do whatever the fuck he wants without me putting up a fight. He loves it as much as I do.

"You never fail to surprise me, Raven. I hate it." Cassius ruffles his feathers and finally sets me on my feet, but he laces his fingers through mine as if he's worried about letting me go. I purposefully squeeze his fingers, testing him, but he's a master of not reacting.

"I hate everything you do, so we're even." I lift a brow as something strange crosses his face. I struck one of his nerves.

"You're a terrible liar." This asshole. He calls me out just like Lucian does.

"I'm not lying. I can't stand to be around you and your light." I glower, hoping I look like a bitch. I don't want him to know that he gets to me. But I do tolerate him. Maybe even more. I like kissing him when he's not such a dick. I've already accepted the idea that he will fall from grace, and he will be one of my kings. But he's going to have to work hard to make up for everything he's done. If he had just cooperated to begin with, I would never be in this situation. The angelic army would be doing whatever the fuck they did before, watching over humanity instead of growing psychotic about Hell.

"You love my light. Especially now. You can't deny it. You are practically devouring it this moment. You know it can cleanse you from the darkness of those rotten souls." Cassius bows closer, his mouth only an inch from mine again. All it would take is for me to stretch just a little, and we'll be kissing. Fuck. Now that's all I can think about. I shouldn't want him this much. I shouldn't want to push the boundaries, considering he keeps rejecting me. I know it's not because he's not attracted to me. I don't think it's my giant belly either. He's just too full of himself to really let his guard down. He wants me to let him in, but he won't let me in.

At least, not yet.

"I'm just starving. It's been an hour since I've eaten." I smirk with my words. "I'm horny too. It's gotten worse."

"Don't you dare start asking for orgasms, Raven." His lips stretch into a smile. Before he started hanging around us, realizing what the angelic army was doing, he would've been shocked. He wouldn't have teased me about orgasms or sex or anything like that. That's how I know he's changing.

If only it wasn't too late.

"You would be the last one for me to ask that from. I have to be extremely desperate and also unable to touch myself." Damn. My words ignite something dark in his eyes, and if I didn't know any better, I would think he was now Hell-bound. But a little teasing won't accomplish that. I don't even know what will anymore.

I bite my lip between my teeth, knowing that he's thinking about me masturbating. Slowly unlinking one of my hands from his, I reach out and pat his cheek, grinning wider at the lust weighing his eyelids, turning them heavy. He doesn't react or says anything, so I continue my way down, and I touch his muscles through his shirt, traveling my fingers lower until I reach the ridges of his hard abs. His jaw flexes as he swallows, and I keep my eyes locked on his. He doesn't stop me or put up a fight. He remains hypnotized and lost in his emotions. I don't know exactly what he's thinking about me, but I know it's something dirty. Something probably filthy as fuck.

I continue exploring his body until I reach his hard-on. Cupping it with my hand, I inhale a slow breath. "But you are free to ask me," I add, drawing my fingers lower until I caress them over his balls through his pants.

He finally breaks, grabbing my ass and lifting me back up into his arms. Light explodes from him, the shock of heavenly power sizzling over my skin but not burning me. It feels as if it eats away at the negative emotions whirling through me in a wave of darkness.

I gasp, the sensation lighting me from the inside out. The babies react, moving and shifting inside me, turning my insides into a punching bag, and it startles Cassius. His eyes widen, and he drops his gaze down between us, and he opens and closes his mouth. But no words come out. He doesn't know how to express exactly what he feels in this moment. I know he's been caught off guard.

"Raven, make them stop." Cassius reaches between us and touches my stomach. "Please, stop. You need to settle down."

I realize his second comment isn't intended for me. He's talking to the twins, and I wonder what he sees. Because I don't see anything except for his light.

"You're cracking the plane. I can't stop it. Take a breath, Raven. You're not going back to the Mortal Realm. Please."

Cassius trembles with his words, his eyes flicking from my belly and back to my face. His hands tighten around me, and he clenches his jaw, his light brightening even more.

I squint, my vision dimming as he continues to glow with heavenly light. My body hums, and pain zaps through me as if I'm being torn apart. But it's not me or my soul. It's Cassius trying to hold onto the power within me, keeping us grounded. But he's not strong enough. Whatever the twins are doing shifts the world around us, and then Cassius's hold vanishes along with him.

I screech out as I drop a couple of feet and land on the strange cool ground of the foggy plane. It's the place created by the twins, and I haven't been here since losing my soul.

I swallow and inhale a deep breath, trying to settle my nerves. Usually Cassius would follow me in, but it's as if he's been purposely pushed out. The twins didn't allow him access as they pulled me from his plane and into theirs.

My stomach bounces as the babies move, and I press my hand to the outside and feel them pushing against my skin as if they're trying to escape.

"Take me back to the mortal world now. We can't be here." I keep my voice low, a bit nervous about being in this foggy world alone.

Closing my eyes, I concentrate on trying to listen for signs of the mortal world in the shift between planes, but nothing happens. The babies keep me chained to this world.

And then I feel it.

Snapping my eyes open, I peer through the haze, watching as a figure spreads golden wings wide, angelic light drawing my attention as it reflects off the mist.

Oh fuck.

I push to my feet, holding onto my belly as if just feeling the babies move from the outside helps keep me calm. Because whatever they've done, shifting me into this world, brought me close to Heaven. I can sense it. It's not just Heaven. I feel as if I'm whole again. I think my soul is nearby, guarded in a place that not every angel can touch. It's the same place they had kept Elias when they had taken him from me.

Anger rushes through me, and I clench my fingers into fists, gathering my strength and bravery. The twins used Cassius to do this. It's as if they know that I need my soul to survive giving birth to them, and they're helping me. I feel more than anger in this moment. Because under my rage lies something warm and inviting. Something pure and balanced. It's unconditional and unending. It's love.

And I know what I have to do. I can't waste this chance. I don't know when I'll get it again or if I ever will. How do I rescue my own damn soul? I guess I'll find out.

Striding forward, I close the space to the angelic figure within the fog. The light grows brighter, and I realize it's not coming from the angel. It's coming from a spot in front of them. I don't know what I was expecting in finding my soul, but it freaks me the fuck out. I see myself standing before the angel, translucent and made of pure light. Except I'm not smiling like I would imagine someone to do in Heaven. Glittering tears splash on my cheeks, and my own soul looks to be silently screaming as if Heaven is the new Hell for me. And it is.

My chest tightens, and I raise my hand, preparing to touch the veil separating me from the one thing that will give me forever with my devils. Tingles course over my skin, and the babies tumble in an acrobatic performance in my belly. Their excitement radiates through me as if they know what this means.

I hold my breath, expecting the world to explode around me, but it's as if I'm caught in a magnetic pull. I can't take my eyes away from my soul, and I feel as if I know what the devil saw in me to begin with. It has been hard to understand the significance of an angel-kissed soul. I've always just felt like me. Like a mortal. But now? I feel as if I'm staring at a source of power far more significant than anyone's comprehension. I'm so close to reuniting with something I had no idea how much I love. Is it vain to love myself? Absolutely not. I just want to be whole again. I want to fix the damage caused by the righteous assholes who can't see past their bigger picture.

And I plan to do so now.

Swinging my arm, I use the strength of the twins and punch the veil as hard as I can. It cracks under the force, but it doesn't shatter.

The angel whips around, and our eyes meet. Unfurling his wings, the angel gathers light in his palms.

I don't have a chance to brace myself.

His power collides into me, knocking me away from the veil and my soul. The world shifts, and it feels as if my heart climbs into my throat, trying to escape me.

A void swallows me, stealing away the pure goodness of being near my soul. It's as if the angel ripped me apart once more, leaving a hole in my being.

The bright light fades, and the horn of a car honks.

I gasp. I'm no longer in the plane created by the twins. I'm back in the Mortal World.

A car barrels right toward me.

Apocalypse

RAVEN

STRONG FINGERS DIG under my arms, dragging me up as the angel takes flight. Car tires screech, and I jerk my arm and punch the angel in the face as he dangles me off the ground. He drops me without a care. The bastard. I shriek at the freefall, my muscles tensing. Swooping down, he grabs me by my hair, stopping me from crashing to the sidewalk. My scalp bursts with pain, and I kick my leg behind me, doing anything I can to escape the angel. He lets go of me, and I stumble forward and land on my hands, scraping my palms on the sidewalk.

"Raven, be careful. You're going to hurt yourself." The musical voice stabs at me as if it's the most annoying sound in existence. I hate when angels try to tell me the obvious. I damn well know that running away from him will end with me hurt. I'm mortal, after all. It doesn't stop me though. I'm willing to risk hurting myself to escape.

"Stay away from me!" I yell, pushing back to my feet.

My body reacts to the sudden threat, and fire ignites in my palms. I whisper a silent thanks to my babies and spin around, staring down the righteous bastard.

His eyes widen, and he startles at the Hell power growing in my hands. I bet he wasn't expecting as much. I bet the angelic army didn't tell him what he'd face if he ever confronted anything that wasn't my helpless soul. But now, my body is a vessel to unimaginable power, and I have a desire to pluck feathers. Knock off halos. I crave the destruction of those against me.

"Heaven, please calm down. You're going to cause a scene. You've just broken my shield with that abominable power." The angel strides forward, lighting his fingers with angelic light.

I thrust my hands forward, shooting Hell power at him. There's no fucking way I'm going to let him get close to me. I can already see it in his eyes that he believes he has a right to control my existence.

"I said, stay back." I flare my nostrils, my body tense and ready to fight. If only it wasn't so difficult to move. My scraped hands and knees ache. I haven't done anything extremely physical apart from sex, and even then, I rarely do a lot of work in this state. The devils are very considerate when it comes to me. They truly are the most selfless beings in the universe. It's what makes me want to give them whatever they want. It makes me want to fight hard for them. It makes me want to destroy Heaven.

"I can't. This is the first opportunity we've had to speak to you. Please, let me have just a second of your time. I don't want to fight you. I only want to reason with you. I know it's difficult in this...state, and you're feeling quite deviant without your soul, but I know that you're smart. Hear me out." The angel drops his hands to a side, allowing his angelic light to dissipate.

Confusion scrunches my face. It's not like an angel to want to have a conversation. Maybe it's because they think they've won. I'm not exactly a huge threat...at least, that's what he thinks. And maybe this will be my chance. If he doesn't think I'm going to continue to fight, he'll let his guard down. When he lets his guard down, I can fuck him up. I can show him what it's like to ruin the forever of the devils' love.

Inhaling a slow breath to settle my racing heartbeat, I nod my head and shake my fingers, putting out the hellfire. I know that my little demon spawn will ignite it again if I'm threatened, and I trust the babies to take care of their mama as much as I take care of them. It's a bond unlike anything I've ever known, and it's all purely emotional. I can feel it. It's the only thing I can feel. I don't feel any of my own emotions, but I can feel goodness the babies bring.

"You have two minutes." I place my hands on my hips and straighten my back, even though I don't feel threatening with my bulging belly.

Closing his wings, the angel offers me a smile. It's far more twisted than he probably realizes, and I can't stop the goosebumps from prickling over my skin. "Two minutes is all I need. I know that the devils have gotten to your mind, but you must think of yourself, your children, and your soul. I know you saw the state of it. Your soul is facing such despair. I'm sure you felt it being so close. But it doesn't have to be that way. Your soul is distraught because it knows that you are resisting. All it wants is to help Heaven. It wants to help cleanse the mortal plane of the darkness. And you can help us accomplish that by finally seeing the truth."

Rage simmers below the surface of my skin, preparing to overflow. I want so badly to jump at the angel and clobber him. I want to rip every damn feather from his wings and tell him he knows nothing about my soul. But the more reasonable, cautious part of me knows that I shouldn't touch him. I need to keep space between us if I can. At least, until I'm ready to fight. I just need to buy a couple more minutes of time. Cassius would've gone to the devils to let them know what happened, and everybody will be on high alert and looking for me.

"I know the truth. I saw what the angelic army has done to Hell. You've let the souls get out of control, and they're devouring everything. You've upset the balance of the universe. The only way you will be able to help is if you give me my soul back." I shift on my feet, a part of me hoping the angel thinks over my words and realizes the truth to them. But I can't hold my breath over it or I'll die. I can see in his eyes that he thinks I'm ridiculous for saying as much. He is too lost in the light to see how dark his being has become.

"That was purposeful, Raven. Hell was growing too strong, and it's time that we start again. Humanity needs to be reset so this plane can survive. We expect the souls to destroy Hell first and then return to the mortal plane. Once that happens, we can destroy the darkness and rekindle the light and the Higher Power's good grace. You can help. You just have to come with me. It'll be best for everyone if you comply." The angel flexes his muscles, his body shifting and tensing, and I can tell that whatever I say in this next moment will lead to one or two things. He will either attack me and drag me away, or he will keep his guard down so I can destroy him when he turns his back.

"You want the apocalypse to happen." It's not a question. I knew that it was coming. I knew what the angelic army was doing but hearing him say he wants to destroy the universe and start over freaks me out. That's not how it's supposed to be. Souls make mistakes, but they're not all bad. There are far fewer Hell-bound souls that deserve to be punished for eternity. The other ones just need guidance. They need to work through their mistakes to go to a more level plane. They need Purgatory. They don't need to be annihilated.

These fucking righteous bastards. From the gold of his wings, I know he was once human, and he knows what it would mean. He doesn't even care. This is why Cassius still fights. I couldn't grasp it until this moment why he wouldn't abandon Heaven. He still believes that his purpose is to save souls. But I don't think he realizes the only way he's going to be able to do that is if he jumps from grace. It is his path. I know it now more than ever.

If only his pride wouldn't get in the way.

"Yes, in a way. It would just be eliminating the darkness. Humanity will thrive in peace after that. The mortal plane will no longer have to be a test. Humanity won't have to worry about such a dark evil." The angel's jaw twitches, and light begins to glow from his skin once more.

It takes everything in me to nod my head. I'm a terrible actress, but this angel is so self-assured and full of himself that he can't tell whether or not I'm lying or pretending.

"It'll be a better place for my children." My heart hurts to say the words because I know it's not true. Only the devils and I can make such a perfect place for our family.

"Yes. You will be able to reunite with them eventually. It would be a sacrifice that will give you what you need to have peace. So please, come with me." Stretching out his hand, the angel waits for me to take it.

This is it.

It's now or never.

Closing my eyes, I summon my strength and bravery to slap my hand against the angel's. Hellfire ignites in my palm once more, and I lock my fingers around the angel's wrist and burn him, yanking him closer until I can strike him in the balls with my knee. He doesn't expect my move and screams out in pain.

But he doesn't stay down for long.

Charging me, he envelops me in his arms, trying to launch into the air. As if a bomb detonates inside me, hellfire shoots out from my core, knocking the angel away. I crash to my ass, and pain swells through my body. The angel hollers with his rage and pain, and he expands his burning wings, threatening me with his sheer size. But he has nothing on the devils. I'm used to people towering over me.

"If you will not come willingly, then I'll take those precious gifts from you. You're far enough along for them to survive. It didn't have to be like this, but I can't let you leave. I can't let you do this." Angelic light gathers in the angel's hand, and he summons a sword. It crackles with his power.

The sight of the blade strikes fear inside me. He's going to try to cut me open to take the twins. What a fucking monster. I can't believe he's going to try. I need to get out of here. I need help. Hell, help me.

"No!" I shout, gathering more hellfire in my palms. I thrust it at the angel again, praying it keeps him back. But I'm not praying to the Higher Power. I'm praying to the universe. I'm praying to my devils to save me. I'm praying to the two precious beings growing inside me to help me.

The angel grinds his teeth as fire licks over his skin and devours every inch of him, turning him into a monstrous beast. He has turned his back on Heaven, choosing to swear his loyalty to Hell to be able to fight against the dark power escaping me. His features morph, and I stare in shock at the demon now standing before me. The ground rumbles around us, and he manages to absorb the shock of my hellfire.

Fuck my life. Fuck this bastard. Fucking fuck fuck fuck. It's all I can think right now in this moment as he aims the blade, planning to kill me first. If I die, it's over. He will have won.

The hellfire streaming from my palm sputters out, and I gasp as the hot energy fades and ice erupts through my veins. My whole body refuses to give in. It refuses to give up. Pure light explodes from me next, and the angel's eyes widen in shock. He underestimated me. He believed I was too close to

Hell to realize that I also have the light of Heaven within me through my angelic spawn. The twins complement each other and work together, and they're the perfect balance to protect me. He wasn't wrong about them saving the universe. They will help. Their existence alone is enough to help me, which will help everyone. I've never felt so proud in this moment. It feels so real now, and I can't believe I've wasted so many months already just accepting defeat. The twins prove to me that it's not over. We can still win.

"Raven!" the angel yells, his body igniting with the fires of Hell as the world trembles around us.

I don't stop. I savor the sound of his screams and watch as the foundation cracks beneath his feet and a Hell portal opens up. He tries to flap his wings to come at me, but they disintegrate into bones on his back. The ground explodes between us, and he jumps and misses, falling into the gaping crevice leading to Hell.

My body kicks into action, and I close the couple feet of space and stomp my feet on his fingers until he releases the edge and falls into the pits, his voice vanishing as the portal closes and leaves me alone on the sidewalk.

I heave a couple deep breaths and drop to the ground, exhaustion getting the best of me. My whole body aches, and I can't stop the tears from pooling in my eyes. I can't believe all of this just happened. I sent another angel to Hell, but I also know what the angelic army plans. We can use this.

I just have to find my way home.

Pushing to my feet, I rest my back against the wall of an old, abandoned building. I rub my hands over my stomach, feeling as the twins settle down and stop trying to flip out of my pregnant belly. I shudder at the memory of the angel and his sword and how he wanted to cut me open and steal my babies. It pisses me off and makes me hungry for revenge. I swear if I see another angel, I'm going to fuck them up.

"Fuck, Raven. How did you end up here?" Cassius skids to a halt in front of me, and a gust of wind from his wings blows my hair from my face.

Is this fate that he happens to land right in front of me?

Swinging my hand, I smack him upside the head, still want-ing to fuck up an angel. He probably regrets that it was him who showed, and he doesn't even know why I'm reacting this way. I'm just so angry. I have no other way to express myself. It's as if my emotions keep flipping on and off, but I know it's just a reaction. It's the babies.

"This is your damn fault! You never should've tried to cleanse my being or whatever the fuck you were doing. I just sent a damn angel to Hell. He was trying to kidnap me, and when I didn't agree, he was going to try to give me an angelic C-section before murdering me!" I can't stop my voice from rising in pitch, everything that just happened crashing back on me. I swing my arm and smack him again. He doesn't even step back out of my way.

"I'm sorry. I'm so sorry." He stands firm in his place, not even trying to block me from hitting him.

So I swing out again and punch him in the nose. I just want to beat him up. I want him to know exactly the pain I went through because of his actions. I never needed to be cleansed with his light. I just needed to stay in Hell with my devils. I don't care if the souls are out of control. I know that they would've gotten them under control.

Except if he hadn't have taken me away, I would've never seen my soul. I would've never found out what the angelic army plans.

Damn it. There's no way I'm going to tell him. I'll leave it up to the other devils. I will not give him that kind of satisfaction. It'll only make him do this kind of bullshit more often.

"Just take me the fuck home!" I yell, grabbing onto his shoulders. I attempt to climb him, but my belly gets in the way, and I dig my nails into skin. "Pick me up and take me the fuck home!"

My words finally knock some sense into him, and he lifts me up by my waist and adjusts me in his arms. We don't stay on the sidewalk a moment longer as he bends his knees and launches us into the air, the wind whipping around me, freezing the still damp trails from my tears on my cheeks.

Cassius flies us in silence as if he doesn't know what to say. And I know if I speak, it'll be a long string of swear words. It'll probably be followed by another punch. Maybe I'll bite him. Maybe I'll blast him with hellfire. I don't know. All I know is that I'm so over today. I just never want to leave the damn couch again. It's not worth it.

Except I know that's not possible.

I know I can't continue living as if it's over.

I need to fight. I need to do it for my babies. I need to do it for humanity and for Purgatory. I need to do it for my future and the future of my devils.

If the angels want a war, they're going to get a fucking war. They're going to get a fucking apocalypse. I'll do whatever it takes to see them fall to their knees. I'll be the reason the universe resets, but not to destroy humanity. I'm going to destroy the angelic army and put things back in order how it should be. I'll gather the strength for my devils to see this through. It's the only way.

I'm so lost in my thoughts that I don't realize Cassius lands and opens the door to our house. It's the fifth one we've lived in since my devils abandoned Hell, and I can't help looking at it as if it's just another roof over our heads. It's not really a home.

"Dante!" I yell, wiggling in Cassius's arms until he sets me on my feet. "Kase! Micah! Zade! Andre! Lucian! Someone better fucking be here! Elias! Please, I don't want to be with this asshole for another second. I need you to kick his ass and get him out of here." I glower at Cassius over my shoulder, and he remains firm in place with a frown scrunching his features.

And the fucking pouty angel. Why does he always get to me?

I purse my lips and try not to give in to his sullen face, but it's as if the light of my angelic spawn inside me reminds me he couldn't have known what would happen. He couldn't have predicted I would end up near my soul and in the path of a deadly angel.

"Angel-girl, what did the fuckhead do now?" Kase strolls from the hallway with his arms crossed over his chest. "We weren't expecting you back for another hour."

I blink in confusion.

Spinning on my feet, I glower at Cassius. "You didn't fucking tell them what happened?"

Cassius straightens his back. "There was no need. I was following you."

What the actual fuck? He didn't even let anyone know that he lost me? And claiming that he was following me? Total bullshit.

My body tenses, my anger igniting the depths of Hell inside me. "Then why the fuck didn't you intervene when that fucking asshole tried to—"

Lunging forward, Cassius silences me with his hand, stopping me from shouting out that an angel wanted to kidnap the twins right from me.

I fist my fingers and punch him in the cock, trying to bite his hand at the same time. He grunts, but he doesn't pull away.

Kase growls and whips Cassius with his tail, twining it around his neck and squeezing until he lets me go. Shoving him away for me, Kase unleashes his devil façade and roars with his anger.

"Don't you fucking put your hand on Raven like that again. I will cut it off next time." Red Hell power ignites across Kase's skin, and he slams his massive paw into Cassius's chest, sending him sprawling across the floor.

Spinning, he faces me, using his tail to pull me closer to him. I rest my hands on his big head, staring into his red-glowing eyes. He doesn't release his devil form as quickly as usual, and I can tell that he wants to stay in it as a precaution against Cassius. Even though the angel has been with us for a while, Kase doesn't trust him. Neither do I. I don't think any of us truly do. We can't trust him until he makes the right decision.

"Tell me that you don't want me to disembowel him," Kase says, the words guttural and deep coming from his monstrous fanged mouth.

I crinkle my nose. "But what if I do?"

"Fucking fine. I'll tell him. But keep the bastard away from me. He can't see as clearly as I can, especially when it comes to you and your spawns." Cassius rolls his shoulders, ruffling his feathers. "I messed up, and I'll accept the proper punishment for my mistake. Disemboweling me is quite extreme though, considering that Raven is safe."

Kase heaves a fiery breath, finally managing to suppress his devil nature. "Disemboweling you is always the proper punishment, you fuckhead. And what do you mean Raven is safe? She should've been safe the whole time. Now what aren't you telling me?" Pulling me closer, Kase gathers me in his arms and hugs me as if I'm the only thing keeping him from following through with his threat. I shift around and wrap my arms across his back, snuggling my face into his muscular chest. It feels so good being in his arms again. I can tell the babies love being near him because they make sure he knows that they're aware of his presence as they kick and wiggle, pressing against my belly.

His stern expression breaks, and a smile crosses his face. He automatically reaches down and rubs his warm hand across my belly, taking a moment to feel each of the babies. I know he can see them in a way I can't, spotting their essences, so he knows exactly where to touch.

"Get on with it," he says, jerking his attention back to Cassius, who remains silent as he watches Kase shower me with affection.

"Raven got upset with me when I was trying to purge the darkness from her, and she walked between planes and somehow managed to find herself close to Heaven. I couldn't get through to her until an angel banished her to the Mortal World, and there might have been a fight. But you know how powerful she is. She took care of it before I even had a chance to intervene." Cassius shakes out his hands, bouncing on his feet as he prepares to run. I wouldn't put it past him. He's a fucking coward after all, hiding behind his light and morals and his inability to see the true greater picture. He still thinks there's a chance for him to return to Heaven as normal. He needs to accept that his place is with us, and when he does, things will be so much better. I just know it. I can feel it. It's one of the few things I'm certain of.

Kase doesn't respond, and he continues to smile at my belly, moving his hands and tapping the spots that protrude from my skin. I don't think I'll ever get used to seeing my stomach look as if a demon is about to explode free, though I know it won't. There's nothing demonic about my devil spawn. It's a baby. It's half-mortal and the ultrasound proved it. I don't have to worry about some horn poking through.

Small miracles. I won't lie. I was a bit concerned about having to give birth to something that had horns. I don't care if I occasionally ride on Kase's. It's completely different.

"I'm truly sorry. It was quite a shock." Cassius shuffles closer, risking his bowels by trying to show he's being earnest. "Please, forgive me."

Again, Kase doesn't respond. He ignores Cassius completely, dropping to his knees to kneel in front of me. He lifts up my dress, exposing my belly to him, and he brushes his lips over my skin a dozen times. I play with his hair, my anger and anxiety settling and shifting as joy explodes through me. It feels incredible. It feels as if I'm still close to my soul but without the pain and heartache I felt when I saw myself outside my body.

Cassius stops behind Kase, towering over him. "Will you—"

Kase growls, swings his arm, and punches Cassius in the balls hard enough to send him off his feet and crashing to the floor. "Just shut the fuck up and let me take care of Raven. If what you said is true, then she needs me right now. Your apology bullshit can wait. I just need a moment to make sure she's safe and to make sure that the babies are safe too. The only way you can ever make up for that bullshit is to retrace your steps and find Raven's soul."

Cassius releases a breath. "I tried. They're really concealing the location of it with all the power of Heaven. That's what took me so long to get to Raven when she returned to the Mortal Realm. I was trying to get to her soul."

I turn my gaze to him, finally meeting his amethyst eyes. "You were?" I don't know why it surprises me.

He bobs his head, his frown softening his usually hard features. "Of course, I was. I want you to have your soul as much as the devils. I know you don't believe me, and I know we don't see things eye to eye, but the last thing I want is for you to experience an eternity of grief. Because that's what your soul is going through right now. It's as if you're bound to Hell. Heaven is your Hell."

Blinking his eyes, Cassius clears his glassy vision. I can't stop myself from reaching out my hand to him. Now that I know what he was doing, I don't feel so angry. I just feel sad. I feel as if no matter what we do, it might never be enough.

"I still don't give a shit. You lost Raven, and she almost got hurt." Kase summons Hell power in his hand. It's not as bright or volatile as if he were connected to Hell but still strong enough to make Cassius inch back. "I'm going to fucking burn my mark on you for it."

I cup his face, getting him to turn his attention away from Cassius. "That's not necessary. We have something else we need to talk about. I know what the angelic army's plan is."

Kase cocks head. "You do?"

I swallow, the thought chilling me to my core as I think about the bastard angel's words again. "It's worse than what we thought. Call the others. They need to know this too. The angels aren't just starting a war. They're starting the end of humanity's existence as it is altogether."

"Fuck. I must go. I need guidance." Cassius expels a wave of light, not giving me or Kase a chance to demand him to stay otherwise.

We stare in silence at his sudden absence.

I don't know where he went, but I know he's going to confirm what I fear.

This battle is going to be brutal.

I'm not sure either side can win.

Bundle of Joy

KASE

"SHE'S FINALLY ASLEEP," Andre says, standing in the hallway.

I know it's his night, but I want nothing more than to shove past him to join Raven in bed for a cuddle session. There's just something about cradling her from behind and resting my hands on her voluptuous, beautiful pregnant belly that just gives me the sort of peace I never knew I'd get again.

"You make sure she has a glass of water and a snack at her bedside?" I shift on my feet and turn my attention to Dante sitting on the edge of the couch. He wants to run to Raven as well. I'm nearly fucking sure all of us do. She probably wouldn't mind a devilish cuddle pile, but we have other shit to deal with first. And I fucking hate it. This should be the time where we can just cuddle and love up on angel-girl, and I want to destroy the universe far more than the angelic army does because I can't.

"I even put her special vibrator on the pillow beside her in case she wakes up and can't wait the few seconds it takes for us to come running." Andre smirks with his words, and I can't help chuckling. Dante went all out with that custom piece of a pleasure weapon. Raven doesn't have to even stretch to get off, the length and curve of the bean buzzer tailored to her pregnant body.

I whack him on the shoulder. "Good man. Always looking out for our girl's endless appetite."

"Forever. I made her a promise just as you have. Plus, I think I might be a bit responsible for her desire and never want her to get frustrated because of it." Andre strolls past me, striding across the living room and to the couch where Zade sits and stares at the ceiling. The fucker still doesn't take a lot of initiative, and it drives me crazy. He's lucky that he has Andre on his side or else I'd be constantly whipping him with my tail, treating him like my little bitch.

"Only a bit responsible?" Lucian smacks his hand against the wall, standing just outside of his room. "We all live with constant boners, and I'm pretty sure Raven hasn't had a dry pair of panties in who knows how long...not that I'm complaining. She's so hot."

He's fucking right about that. I didn't know she could get even sexier, but she does. I love seeing her like this. I love knowing that she grows life from us. It's not something I ever thought about as a devil. It's almost as if she gives us the chance to feel what it's like to be mortal. If only the angelic army didn't make it feel like shit half the time. I could do without their righteous attitudes.

"Damn. Let's get this over with so we can spend some time with her. You know she's been all over the place emotionally. We should've already had this shit taken care of." Dante rubs his hands on his knees, shifting forward without getting up.

"He's right. We need to evaluate what's going on with Hell and the mortal souls being unleashed to wander that plane." Micah speaks up from his spot leaning against the wall. I'm surprised to see Elias isn't with him, but I know he left to follow Cassius. I can't trust the prideful bastard, but I know that Elias will make sure he doesn't turn things to shit. He feels he has to find redemption with Raven and wants her to survive as much as me. He doesn't want our children losing their mother to Heaven. To anyone, really. Cassius was right about the grief holding Raven's soul hostage. He wouldn't want her to suffer like that. I know that some of the others are concerned that he will betray us because if we fail, he still has

Raven. He still can access Heaven and be with her. But I know he's not as greedy as he sometimes acts. His greed falls in line with himself, but he has a weak spot for our woman.

"All right, Micah. You do the honors. Everyone get the fuck up. Keep shit together. I'll make you watch me fuck Raven for a week and deprive you assholes of her if any of the commotion wakes her up. Andre shouldn't have to put her to sleep because she's too stressed to do so on her own. It isn't good for our spawns." I clap my hands together and motion to the others to get their asses up to surround the summoning circle. We're only going to crack it open a bit to get a better view. Dante warned me earlier that it was a shitshow, so as much as we'd rather ignore it, we need to do something even if it's temporarily.

The heavenly bastards that have tried stealing Hell only to let it implode don't stand a chance against us. We can set all the souls straight and return them where they belong. We will need to act fast, but it'll at least settle the balance a bit until we get Raven's soul. Because it seems as if the angelic army is going to hit hard and fast, and not even at us. They're just going after humanity. The fuckers. Don't they realize that's how everyone gets their powers? They think they can just reset everything, but they're going to destroy it completely. They're not all-knowing or powerful. They haven't been around forever like we have.

I guess the Higher Power needs us to do its work after all. It's going to fucking owe us. We don't do shit for nothing anymore.

Lucian cracks his neck, unleashing his devil façade first. It's about to get really fucking hot in here. Stomping his massive hoof, Lucian sets the summoning circle aglow in a ring of fire. Micah growls deep from his chest, the sound vibrating over my body and down to my balls. Son of a bitch. I shouldn't like it, but the sensation entangled with the arousal of Hell gets to me in a good way. And now my hard cock wants to fuck something. If I didn't think Raven would pout about not getting to watch, I'd bend Dante over just for relief until I can get my angel-girl.

"Shit, grab it." Lucian whacks Micah between the shoulder blades, forcing him into the circle for him to summon the tether. We need him to connect to it just long enough to tap into our kingdoms.

Micah growls again, revealing his hellish form, and he bows forward, forcing the portal open wide enough to snatch the tether, connecting us to the plane. The floor rumbles around us, and Andre reaches out and braces himself on my shoulder. He's lucky he's on my good side or else I might knock him in the nuts for making it harder for me to snatch the power from my kingdom to whip my souls into submission.

"Okay, done. You all have five minutes. I'm not as strong

as you. My body wants to return to my kingdom." Micah unleashes a wave of orange fire from his palm, using it to keep him grounded to this plane.

Whipping my tail, I lasso it around his waist. "You heard him. Go!"

The world darkens around us, and we shift planes while still anchored to the Mortal Realm. Micah not only keeps his focus on linking us to Hell, but he also keeps his mind open to Raven, ensuring no bullshit happens in the next five minutes.

Screams screech through the air, and I land in a crouch on the middle of the onyx path cutting through my kingdom. Shadows flicker around me, the souls of the damned running wild. I don't see even one of my goddamned minion demons, and I roar, shooting a ball of Hell power toward the nearest soul tree, smoldering vibrant red electricity across the branches. It's empty. The tree no longer contains a soul facing eternal punishment. The battles of the wrathful no longer litter the ruby fields either.

"You piece of shit! You're going to regret returning. This isn't your kingdom any longer." The annoyingly familiar voice erupts from behind me. "We've been saved!"

Fucking Hell. This shitbag can't seriously think he can—

A scrawny, rancid-smelling soul crashes into my back, trying to knock me off my feet. I reach behind me and snag the fucker with my claws, ripping it over my shoulder to throw the bastard in front of me. Raven's ex-fiancé materializes from his shadowy state, his arm still severed from where I bit the thing off. His eyes widen for a split second, but then he gathers his confidence and attempts to get to his feet.

I slam my paw onto him, crushing him into the ground until he screams. "Who the fuck do you think you are?" I ask, snarling and spitting red Hell power at him. "I might've left my kingdom, but Hell still belongs to the devils. Humanity isn't strong enough to handle such power. We will be back, dickhole. Consider my absence as paternity leave."

I grin with my words, watching as Joel processes and realizes exactly what I said. "I knocked Raven up, and we're about to start a fucking new generation of power unlike anything the universe has ever seen. This little shitshow you've started here is about to end. We're cleaning house. I plan to start with you."

Swiping my claws, I strike Joel across the chest, ripping at his very being. He screams, his voice high-pitched with agony, and I savor the sound of his torture. It feeds my power and my devilish nature. I will devour his energy until he is no more. He deserves a fate such as this. I thought eternal torture would be best, but now I have my heart set on ensuring he never exists again.

"Wait! Wait! I want to make a deal. I can lead you to the bastards who freed us." Joel holds his hands up, trying to block me. The chickenshit bastard trembles, his solid form shifting to a shadowy haze and back as he attempts to run. The fucker isn't going anywhere though.

I decide to humor him but only because it'll make his obliteration far more satisfying if I allow Raven to see. I know she'd want to. Punishing souls has turned into one of her favorite pastimes, and it's been a while since she's been able to. What better soul to fuck over and destroy than the man who tried to steal her light? The man who fucking abused her and treated her as less than human. I get angry just thinking about it. I want to rip off his other arm and whack him in his tiny dick for it. Fuck. I can do both. I'll punish him and then act as if I'm giving him mercy.

"Let me think...no." Jerking my head forward, I snatch his hand in between my jaws and bite down, crunching it with my power. I might plan to humor him, but I also plan to torture him and make him beg. He's my little bitch.

"Wait! Please!" Joel struggles to pull away, and I release him without taking his hand clean off. He tastes as foul as the smell permeating around him.

I swipe my claws at him, scratching his gut next. "Give me a good reason."

"The angel is here. She's in your palace right now," Joel says, locking his hand around one of my claws as if he can even stop me from impaling him.

I close my long toes, snapping his index finger right off. "Not good enough. I don't have time to start a proper battle with the bitch."

"Then what do you want?" He screams as tears trail down his face.

"You to eat the ass of my shittiest demon minion." I drag my tongue across his cheek and savor his pain and anguish. I wish I could bottle it up so Raven could have a taste of his torment. "Only then, will I consider letting you exist another minute longer." I sense Micah trying to take me back. He's losing his strength. Not his strength to hold onto the tether, but his strength in resisting it.

Joel sobs. "Please—"

I slam my paw into his face, shoving him down and silencing him. Micah calls my name, forcing me to turn my attention to him and away from the Joel. Rage ignites inside me, my connection to Hell filling me with the need to dish out punishment.

"Twenty seconds. Raven woke up. I'm trying to keep her back, but she's acting as if she's hypnotized." Micah's voice rumbles through my mind as he speaks through our connection.

Damn it. I need to get my shit together.

"You better fucking keep her back, Micah." I roar, blowing a breath of Hell power in Joel's face.

"Then somebody else take the damn tether!" Micah's desperation rings through my mind, and I know it's serious if he's swearing. It takes punching him in the nuts to get him to speak like a devil. Cassius is far worse than he is.

"Lucian," I say, trying to reach out to him through our kingdom link.

But it's too late. Micah shouts Raven's name, and it's as if her being comes to one of the places most familiar to her because I watch as she freefalls from above toward the frozen ruby lake. I launch away from Joel and charge in her direction, whipping my tail out and snatching her from the air before she can hit the plane. Her soul radiates with light, singeing my skin, but I don't let her go. Her hair veils her face, her muscles tighter than her sexy ass.

She screams and bucks her body, swinging her arms and shouting as if she doesn't know what's going on. She yells for help, acting as if she doesn't realize I have her. My whole body reacts, and I roar, shouting in her face, trying to snap her out of her trance. Her eyes stare off at nothingness, and I watch as light and dark radiate from her core.

I touch her chin. "Raven. Look at me. Focus on me." Resting my paw on her belly, I growl deep enough to send a rumble through her. "Little spawns, don't take your mama away. I know you want to protect her, but you're safe. Daddy has you." I lean forward and snuggle against Raven, feeling as her body finally relaxes as she stops fighting.

She gasps and curls her arms around me, yanking my horns as she tries to orient herself to what happened. "Kase…"

"Everyone, finish up. I got our woman. She's safe." I inspect every inch of her to be sure. Her eyes lock to mine, glassy with tears, and I lean in and lick her. "She just needs a minute, and we'll be right back."

Raven snuggles her face against me. I transform back into my human façade completely, showering her with a dozen kisses. She smiles as I work my way down and blow raspberries into her cleavage, her tits glorious and plump, and enticing me to want to give her a warmup to show her what she's in for with those spawns of ours. Desensitize her to getting bit on the nips on occasion.

"Thank fucking Hell you caught me." Raven's voice shakes, and she clutches my head, easing me away from her tits. "I hadn't realized I entered through the portal. That was fucking freaky."

"Micah is going to want to punish your ass later. Why don't you let me prepare you? I can love you up for a bit. Help calm that racing heart." I sneak my tail around her, teasing her ass, feeling her pucker.

She gasps a laugh. "You know you're just going to make my heart beat faster."

"As long as it's for the right reason." I grin and lean in, kissing her forehead. She groans and hugs me tighter, savoring my affection and silently begging me to just hug her and cuddle her. I'll give her whatever she wants.

"I knew you were an unfaithful bitch, and it's so fucking satisfying to see that you screwed over the devils." Joel's voice slashes through the air, his sudden appearance tensing Raven's muscles.

This dickhole. How dare he speak to my angel-girl like this.

I snarl, gathering Hell power in my palm. Raven snatches me by my wrist, not letting me shoot a wave of fury at the bastard. Her eyes light with the fires of Hell around us, and she heaves a breath of agitation. I love how confident she is in this moment. There was a time that she was so afraid of this rotten soul that she'd have panicked. But now? She's embodying the glorious wrath of my kingdom.

"You're a psychotic, stupid, shitface, murdering bastard! You have a lot of fucking nerve coming and accusing me of cheating on my devils. I've never cheated on anyone in my life." Whipping her attention around, Raven tries to confront Joel. I loosen my hold just enough for her to face the asshole.

"You're a liar." Joel jerks his eyes to mine. "She's a fucking liar. A bitch. I know she was sleeping around on me."

His soul is about to be obliterated.

I don't even get the chance to react as flames burst from Raven and swallow Joel, sending him to his knees. He screams and writhes in pain, arching his back. Raven wiggles in my arms, and I finally let her down. I know she wants to tear the fucker another ten assholes for the demons to play with, and I'm here for it. I find her need to put him in his place so fucking sexy. I feel like I want to fuck her brains out while she does it.

"You have no control over me here! Your words mean nothing. You can't manipulate my devil. He knows me, and he knows you as the scumbag, douche canoe you are. You will pay for all the pain you put me through. You will pay for your sins. You will never, and I mean fucking never, find peace. You'll never reach Purgatory. You'll suffer. Forever."

Raven strides forward, the Hell power in her palms turning into brilliant light. Her body sets a glow with the heavenly power, and I squint as heat radiates across my skin. I've never seen her summon so much at once. Hell doesn't even stand a chance against it. My kingdom rumbles around us, and I lace my tail around her belly, keeping her steady as she moves forward through the quaking world.

"Raven, please! Please, I'm sorry." Joel's pain and agony waft through the air, the scent like sweet vanilla. I inhale a deep breath, savoring it even more.

"It's too late. Your soul cycle is over forever. You will never hurt anyone again." Raven thrusts her arms out, shooting the heavenly light at Joel, and his body explodes like a bright white firework. Hot wind whips around her, sending her hair blowing, and I gawk in surprise as Joel's very essence turns into a tornado and swirls around her. The energy left behind by his soul's annihilation funnels itself into Raven, and for a second, I glimpse glorious horns protruding from her head. Bright wings sprout from her back, and she flaps them once before her new image vanishes, leaving her on her knees in her mortal state.

She hunches over and clutches her stomach, and I drop down, bowing over her. I've never seen anything like this before, and the power radiating from her gives me a massive fucking boner. She encompasses what I remember of being with the Higher Power. It's as if she has now been made in its mirror image. She carries both light and dark, and it's not only because of the babies. It's her. She might not have her soul, but the power she got from Joel is as if she managed to create another from nothing. She is the ultimate creator of life, and she's the ultimate destroyer.

"Unholy fucking Hell, angel-girl. Look at me. Let me see your eyes." I tilt her head up and search her gaze, seeing fire light one of her blue irises while the most beautiful silver flicks in the other. "Are you okay? What about the babies? You fucking devoured him. You changed his very energy."

Raven doesn't speak. She continues to cup her stomach while staring at me, her pouty mouth breathing in and out as she puffs her bottom lip.

Fear strikes me in the chest, and for the first time in a long time, I'm afraid. I'm not afraid of Raven. I'm afraid for her. She might embody a wicked amount of power in this moment, but she's still mortal. She looks as if she might break or shatter at any second. I can't allow it. I won't allow it.

I gather her into my arms and send power around us, shifting us from my kingdom and back to the Mortal World. She gasps at the sensation of falling through the planes, and I steady myself, grabbing on to Dante's shoulder as I return to the summoning circle.

Everyone surrounds us, but the intensity of their emotions, aroused by Raven, leaves her panting harder. She needs space. I can see it in her eyes,

"Give me a second," she whispers, her voice hoarse. "Kase, please take me to the room."

I follow her orders, pushing past the others even though I know they want to follow behind. I threaten them with a growl and strut down the hallway and to our king bed, setting her on the edge to kneel before her.

"Breathe in and out, angel-girl. You just absorbed energy incomparable to anything you've ever experienced. That's some devil and angel shit right there." I massage my fingers into her shoulders, shifting her legs to be able to get as close as possible.

"I feel weird. I feel like I have a soul, and everything is a million times more intense." She bows forward and rests her head on my shoulder. "I feel as if I'm going to explode. Everything hurts."

I lean forward and press my forehead to hers, sharing her breath, encouraging her to breathe in and out with me. "You can release it. I want you to hold out your palms, and I want you to focus on that sensation crawling through you. I want you to imagine it flowing through your body from your heart and into your hands. Will it to form in one central location."

Bobbing her head, Raven closes her eyes. "I don't want to let it go. I don't want to return to how I felt before. I just...I feel so out of control."

"You don't have to let it go. You just need to be grounded." I close my hand around hers and summon a stone, using my Hell power. She wiggles her fingers and opens her hand, revealing the black rock. I rub my finger across it. "Try it on this first. I know that you aren't familiar with how to shift energy, so I've made this for you. I want you to channel it into the stone. Once that's complete, we'll ground it in your plane. Okay?"

"Okay." Her voice barely comes out a whisper.

I release her hand and touch my palms to her belly, feeling the babies shift and move in anticipation for her to tap into power. "Help your mama out, little spawns. She needs you."

A soft smile crosses Raven's lips, and I lean forward and brush mine to hers, showing her that I'm here for her on every level she needs. I know I'm a horny fucking bastard, and I can't help it with how sexy and irresistible she is, but I can be more than her pleasure devil. I'm ready to be so much more.

She eases away from me and sucks her bottom lip into her mouth as if she wants to taste my lips for a moment longer. And damn it. My fucking cock throbs and my balls tighten. I hope that I'm a good enough teacher to get this over quickly, so I can bury my damn face between her thighs and reward her for being such a good angel-girl. She needs some orgasms. It'll uplift her more than anything else.

"Close your eyes again. Do exactly what I say. Imagine you're pushing the energy through your body and working it toward your palms. Feel the stone in your hand and squeeze it if you have to. Use your mind to channel the power. Imagine that you're winding a cord around the stone, growing it in size but also leaving an end open that we can tie up." I stroke my hands along her stomach, encouraging her while enjoying the closeness of the babies.

Energy hums from Raven, and I close my eyes and feel it pulsing through her. She whimpers under her breath, and I shift my hand from her belly to cup it around her fingers. She relaxes as I imagine helping her guide the power through her veins. I know it's uncomfortable for her. No mortal has ever contained such power, and I hope my presence is enough to get her through. Actually, I know she's strong enough to get through. She doesn't need me. But I need her. I need her more than anything in existence. So does the universe. Heaven and

Hell.

"You're almost done, angel-girl. Do you feel it? It should feel as if you're holding something incredibly heavy and powerful in your palm." I rub my thumb across the side of her wrist.

"You mean like your cock? If that's the case, maybe. I think yours is a million times mightier." She releases a breath, her beautiful face smiling with so much love and appreciation that I could live right here, watching her for eternity. She brings out the romantic side of me, and I know how much she loves it.

"Fuck yeah, it is. Nothing can compare...well, except maybe Andre's gigantic pussy pulverizer. It still amazes me how tough you are. I clench my ass every time I see him spread you open." I'm only teasing, but I would say anything to make her continue to smile.

Tipping her head back, she laughs loudly, her voice echoing through the room. She doesn't even realize the onyx stone in her hand turns red, and I carefully ease her fingers away from the heavy rock to show her just how incredible she is. Her eyes widen, and I place my hand on top, sandwiching the soul stone between our palms.

"Now let's get rid of this fucking thing so I can reward you for being so brave. I plan to lick your clit until you beg me to give you a break. I can't wait. I need those thighs locked around my face. I need you to ride me so hard that you could possibly send me back to Hell."

Raven moans at the thought, and I graze my free hand over her eyes, getting her to close them again. I whisper to her belly to check that they're playing just a little, and I watch as light and shadow weave around us as the veil thins.

"I feel so strange," Raven says, loosening her hold. "Do you think this plane could possibly be Purgatory one day?"

I wish I had the answers, but I don't. I don't know exactly what the angel and devil spawn can do, but I can't wait to fucking find out. They amaze me so much already just like Raven does.

"No idea, but whatever it is will be absolutely powerful enough to contain souls just like Heaven and Hell. So let the stone go. Just drop it. It will ground itself and still allow you to connect to it."

Raven turns her hand over and drops the stone. It sparks as it connects to the other plane. The veil thickens, cutting us off, and I engulf Raven in my arms and hug her, showering her with a dozen kisses.

"I did it," she says, awe in her voice. She didn't think she could, and I hope this proves to her that she's capable of anything and everything.

"Fuck yeah, you did. Now give me your fucking delicious pussy and sit on my damn face. I feel like letting you ride my horns for a bit." I climb onto the bed beside her and pull her on top of me, dragging her to my face by the backs of her knees.

She laughs and squirms, playing hard to get but also teasing me by stretching back to stroke her fingers over my cock through my pants. I tear the side of her panties and let her dress billow over my face, cutting the world off to where I can just have my way with her body.

Using my tail, I slide it just under her tits and lift her up, forcing her to turn around until her ass plants right on my forehead. I tease her with my lips, tasting her skin as I adjust her and unleash my devil side enough to where she can sit on my horn, the blunt middle one perfect for her to bounce on while I use my demon tongue to taste her how I want.

Raven pulls at her dress, lifting it over her head, and she contorts her body, trying to see me under her pregnant belly. I love teasing her. I know it frustrates her not being able to see past the bulge, but it's a whole new level of surprise.

"You better fucking ride me hard, angel-girl. If you do so, maybe I'll let you watch in the mirror." I growl, sending vibrations through her body.

She moans, wiggling and using her knees to bounce. "I need Dante's fucking swing. This is getting harder to do." She stretches the best she can, trying to grab at my pants, and I can't stop smiling at her effort. I continue to lick her and use my tail to lift and drop her until I know she'll squirt on my face because of the curve of my horn rubbing just right against her G-spot.

"You can tell him that. I have you the way I want you. Now relax. Enjoy everything." I flick my tongue, licking her pussy as if it's what I need to survive on. Her murmurs turn into gasping moans until her body clenches, and I feel her spray across my chest, soaking my shirt. And damn. It's so fucking hot. She has no idea.

I lift her off of me, and she trembles and gasps, her pouty mouth looking so fuckable, but I plan to fuck her how she wants instead. Even the spawns are going to feel the power radiate through her, and they will be reminded of how they came into existence through such passion.

Raven would smack me upside the head for even thinking it. I'm just so damn proud of our creation. It might be a little twisted, but I am a devil after all.

"It's your choice tonight. Do you want to be on top, pressed against that wall with me carrying you, or maybe a little pounding from behind on all fours?" I yank off my shirt and unbuckle my belt. Raven crawls forward on her hands and knees and grabs at my pants, doing the honors of pulling them down until she laces her fingers around my cock. She bites her lip as she rubs her hand along the length, thinking over my question.

Silently, she turns around and gets on her hands and knees, shaking her ass teasingly. I growl and crawl forward, loving seeing her answer me this way instead of having her just tell me to do what I want. I know she loves to give me control, but sometimes I just feel like taking care of her how she desires. If she's in the mood for me to fuck her from behind doggy style, then I'll do it so hard that she gets slapped by my balls too.

Swiping my belt off the bed, I fold it in half and spank her with it once, loving how she gasps and looks at me from over her shoulder with heavy eyelids. I align my body to hers and massage my fingers into her ass cheeks, savoring the view. I tease her with the tip of my cock and use my tail to play with her clit, slickening it with her desire. She wants me to fuck her ass too. I know it. I can see that star pucker just for me, and I can't wait to feel how good she is in this moment. I'm going to fuck her until she can't think any more about Heaven or Hell, the planes or souls, or any of that damn bullshit. I'm going to fuck her until all she can think about is my cock and my body and how I make her feel.

Raven moans as I glide into her until my hips smack her ass cheeks. I shift my hands from her hips and lean forward, cupping her belly to keep her in place and comfortable. I will support her completely physically and mentally in any way I can. I just want her to enjoy it.

"Hold on tight, little spawns. Things are about to get bumpy." I thrust deeper with my words, grinning as Raven cracks up, her voice so light and beautiful that I can listen to it forever. She feels so hot and wet. I can't get enough of her. I rock my body, holding her and keeping a good rhythm, losing myself to the sound of our moans and pleasure. Using my tail, I slip it into her ass, just teasing her and stuffing her with everything I know she loves. The pressure does incredible things, and I feel my Hell form break free.

Raven arches her back, looking so incredibly sexy, and she glances at me in the mirror in front of us. She loves watching herself get fucked as much as I love watching her. It's been her thing for a while. She loves to be watched as well.

I bet all the devils are hovering right outside the door listening, and I nearly shout for them to just crack it open and peek in. Because they should see just how damn sexy our soul is.

But I don't have to tell them.

I catch sight of Dante standing in the doorway with Andre behind him. I bet Lucian is about to lose his shit because he can't get the best view as Zade stands in his way.

"I hope you fuckers are jealous." I grunt with my words, thrusting and picking up speed.

Raven can't even speak because I fuck her so hard, and she stares at me, never taking her gaze away from our reflections. I love how in this moment, her mind focuses on the pleasure between us and nothing else.

I feel like more than a devil. I feel like a fucking God as I pump the Hell into our woman until she screams out in bliss, her pussy tightening so hard around my cock that I'm not sure she'll ever let me go. Not that I want her to.

Her pulsing body is enough to strike me in the balls, and I groan as I come, the force of our passion rumbling the bed. Raven shoots fire from her palms, smoldering the comforter, and I holler in approval and smack her ass once more before flipping us over to have her lie on top of me. I grab her thighs and spread her legs wide, showing off how fucking hot her body looks with me inside her to the other devils.

"Bow down to her beauty, assholes," I say, panting and gasping into Raven's hair. "Whoever does so first can have the next taste."

A flash of light radiates in the hallway, drawing everyone's attention. Elias's arrival puts a stop to the fun we are about to have.

He flaps his wings and pushes past Dante, entering the room. "Damn it. You guys can fuck me up later for this interruption, but shit is going down. I need you to see this."

I growl and slide my tail out of Raven just to whip it in his direction. "It can't wait?"

Elias shakes his head. "No. Now fucking hurry. We don't have time to waste."

5

Redemption

ELIAS

I CAN'T TAKE my eyes off Raven. I haven't been gone for long, but it's as if she's completely changed. Her figure is fuller in the best way, and I'm dying to wrap her in my arms and kiss her belly. I yearn for just a moment alone with her. But I know I won't get one. Not yet. I have to earn it, and I won't stop trying to figure this bullshit out until her soul is safely back in her body. Heaven's warriors are out of their damn minds thinking they can get away with this.

"You better give us something to prepare for, Jizz Master," Dante says, unfurling his wings and opening his arms for Kase and Raven.

I shouldn't be jealous that they carry her, but I can't help myself. She always flies with them. I don't think it's intentional—more out of habit for her. They just know exactly how to handle the shitshow of the world and keep her safe. Even though I envy their closeness, I appreciate it as well. Raven deserves it. She deserves having the happiness she finds with each one of us. I just feel as if I need to do more. I blame myself for the state she's in. I was only trying to help her and look at what happened.

"The angelic army is fucking with the veil. They're trying to connect the planes and release those who have sacrificed themselves." I couldn't believe it when I felt the tremor of power. Mikail wants to get his companion back despite the consequences. I didn't know it was possible, but they are trying anyways. We have to stop it. I need everyone to help. I can't do it alone.

"These fuckheads are going to be obliterated. I'm so damn tired of them messing with shit. Raven needs to rest. She needs to enjoy this damn pregnancy." Lucian grumbles as Andre locks his hand around his side. He lifts both Zade and Lucian off their feet.

Micah scrubs his fingers into the back of his neck, making his way closer to me. He's the only one who doesn't constantly glower at me. He doesn't blame me like I blame myself over the situation. He knew that I was doing what I thought was right.

He even reminded me he had been in the same place, trying to figure out what to do.

I grab him, hugging him against me. It should be more awkward than this, having him hug me back, but all I feel is the familiarity of our bond from being companions long ago. He was there for me and forgave me for all the bullshit I put him through. If Micah wasn't here, I don't know how I would handle all of this. He is a true friend, and I wish I could just turn my back on my grace and join him. It's not that I don't want to be a ruler of Hell. It's just that I can't figure out how to be. I've tried nearly every day since the moment Raven lost her soul to jump from Heaven. Every time I try though, it's like a cord yanks me back up, and I bungee between the two places. I hate it. I hate these wings and this light coursing through my veins. I despise myself more than I ever have in my existence. The angelic army can use us against each other. I just want the Higher Power to give me answers. The silence that surrounds my thoughts and prayers leaves me anxious. What the angelic army is doing is against everything in my entire being.

"Where is Cassius? Shouldn't he be with you?" Micah murmurs, keeping his voice low as I launch into the air, leading the way. The angelic army picked a demonic hotspot a couple miles away from here, tapping into what was once an active Hell portal before the devils cut themselves off.

"I haven't seen him. I thought he was with you guys." Fucking shit. I don't trust Cassius and his righteous ways. He tried to convince me to stop attempting to jump into Hell. He thinks that I'm not supposed to claim a kingdom and that Raven needs me to hold onto grace for the sake of the twins, which is wrong. Raven needs me by her side and stronger than ever. I feel weak as a celestial being. Especially seeing how strong the devils are even if they aren't tethered to Hell.

Micah doesn't get a chance to respond, because I nosedive toward the dark energy radiating from a crack in the plane. I can hear the damned souls screaming for help. A dark cloud hovers over a building. It's grown much larger even in just the last hour, and I can't stop myself from gathering light in my palms. They shouldn't be here. That cloud isn't only made of darkness. It's made from the negative energy of souls cast into Hell. Souls unable to find redemption because there's no place in between for them. Purgatory doesn't exist yet.

"Are those what I think they are?" Raven asks, her voice echoing over the whistling wind blowing through my hair.

"Fucking shit. We've got to split up. There's a couple featherheads on the ground, and they're already preparing to blast us with light." Lucian growls and transforms into his devil façade as Andre glides next to me. Lucian has far better vision for soul spotting than I do, and it takes me a moment to realize what he's talking about.

He's right. There are at least a dozen angels summoning

heavenly power in their hands, protecting their crack as a fiery figure stands beside it, pulling the souls from where they were intended to spend eternity in Hell's kingdoms.

"We will circle in close. Don't let any of them go. Lucian, you need to focus on sending the souls back to Hell. Kase and I will take care of Meri. The rest of you separate and send those blasted angels to the pits. Secure them there. We can't have this bullshit right now." Dante hisses with his words, expanding his wings to slow down.

I flare my nostrils. "Raven should stay out of—"

Micah covers my mouth with his hand, cutting off my argument. "She needs to do this. Don't worry. She can handle such things. You must allow her to channel her power. It's the only way she will learn to have complete control. She needs to be able to fight beside us instead of having us stand in front of her. I know it's hard because we all want to protect her, but the best way to do so is to let her find her strength."

"I'm all here for it but not until after she delivers…" I let my words trail off. I can't think about it. I struggle with keeping hope when the world around us seems dark even though it's just because the light of Heaven tries to devour everything. When Raven delivers the babies, things can change. I don't even want to think about the consequences of her giving birth to the twins without a soul.

Micah groans and shakes his head. "The twins make her

more powerful. They give her a reason to fight harder. Let her."

I sigh and nod my head despite my innate need to do everything I can to see to it that Raven never has to throw a punch or stab with a blade, gather hellfire, or blast some monster away with heavenly light. I just want her to be able to enjoy sitting in her favorite spot with her legs curled to the side watching her favorite shows.

Fuck.

But the only way that will ever happen is if I get shit under control. I'm a fucking savior, for Christ's sake. I should be able to get the angelic army in line. I should be able to beat them down and get them to see how off-path they are acting. I should know. I turned my back and fell from Heaven before. I don't even truly know why the Higher Power returned my wings to me, but I know it has something to do with this. It has something to do with Raven and our children. And not just my angelic child. I will accept the devil spawn as mine too. These precious gifts will unite all of us as a unit. I've already accepted it. The others have too. It doesn't matter whose blood runs through their veins. It just matters that we love and care for them. We will do whatever the fuck it takes to ensure they have an amazing future. An incredible eternity. We will not let the angelic army destroy their chance.

"Drop me low, and I will clear a path for you," Micah says, twisting in my arms so that his back presses against my chest.

He shifts into his devil form, and the sudden change of his weight causes us to freefall faster. He doesn't yell or complain as I let my wings glide us toward the earth.

"I got your back, man. Just fuck them up for our girl." I grind my teeth and flatten out my wings, slowing down our descent enough that Micah can jump from my arms and land on his giant hooves without stumbling.

I launch back into the air and spin, shooting blinding light at the angels focused on the crack, the force enough to turn their attention toward me.

They don't see the devils arriving around them, and Andre drops Lucian and Zade next. I protect their backs, blasting a wave of heavenly light at a fallen angel who now carries the fire of Hell over his being. He hisses and growls, whipping his attention toward the sky and at me. Andre lands in front of him and whips his giant tail over his shoulder and stakes the bastard, throwing him a dozen feet into the air.

I allow Andre to cover Zade, Micah, and Lucian and I fly toward where Dante and Kase land with Raven. I haven't seen her look so magical in a while, and the air around her radiates with fire and light and everything beautiful she summons. Her hair blows in the breeze of the angel wings, but Kase and Dante let no one near her. They let her channel her energy into her palms, and I can't stop being distracted by her presence. It takes her whipping her attention up to me and pointing for me to realize someone heads toward me.

"Mikail!" she screams, thrusting her hands out and shooting a wave of hellfire in my direction. I freefall to the ground and land in a crouch as Mikail yells as Raven's Hell power collides into him.

I jerk my head up and stare at the bastard, fury rolling through my very being. He's a dead angel. I will destroy his very being, and he'll never exist again.

Bending my knees, I launch back into the air and unsheathe my heavenly sword. He averts his gaze from Raven and the other devils and glowers at me.

"You are an abomination. You traitor! You know what must be done!" Mikail gathers heavenly light and tries to blast it in my direction.

I duck and fly under him, jerking my sword up and slicing it across the back of his calf. "You're right. I do. It is my path to cut your fucking head off in the name of the Higher Power, the universe, Hell, and my soulmate!"

Mikail releases a loud whistle, and flashes of bright light come from every direction, smacking into my body. It's as if he called all of the angels away from the crack of Hell to bring them toward me. It's now that I realize what the fuck he's truly trying to do. He's given up on tapping into Hell for a moment to try to end me. I still have a connection to Heaven, and I can use that. He wants to stop me from being able to tap into heavenly power. Even if it means...

"Protect our girl! I have to go!" I yell, dodging out of the way of another blast of heavenly light.

It hurts my very soul to abandon Raven and the devils like this, but if I can get them to chase me for even a couple minutes, the devils can get things under control and stop the souls from seeping out. It's a risk, but I don't have a choice. I don't know what else to do.

Gathering heavenly light in my palms, I blast it at the air and break through the Mortal Realm to access Heaven. The world shakes around me, and I fly as fast as I can, flapping my wings until they blur and I can dive into the portal.

Something strange happens, and one second, I feel the peace of being in Heaven and hear the battle cries of the angelic army around me as they circle me, and in the next, shadows swallow me whole, and Raven's voice envelops me a second before she jumps into my arms, forcing me to catch her.

"You better kiss me before I smack you upside the head for that move. Micah told me what you were thinking and trying to do. You know the risk you face going to Heaven. They could imprison you again." Raven groans, resting her forehead to mine.

I obey her command and kiss her, adjusting her to straddle me even with her bulging belly between us. Molding my lips to hers, I don't let her pull away and savor her closeness and the taste of her mouth. I savor her body touching mine and what it feels like having two incredible beings moving and shifting between us, reacting to our presences coming together. Raven might not have her soul, but she can still touch mine in a way that leaves my body buzzing. It leaves her breathless.

Something washes over me, and I snap my eyes open and see a strange halo of light surrounding Raven. It's not the heavenly light of our baby together, but it carries the same energy as if her soul returned to her body. But it's different. It's not hers. I don't know what it is, but it mimics a mortal soul enough that it leaves me confused.

"Darlin', what the fuck have you been up to the last day? Something light has gotten into you, and I know it wasn't me or Cassius." I tilt my head, searching her stunning blue eyes, wanting to drown myself in the depths of her irises.

She lifts and drops her shoulders. "I don't know how to explain it, and it sounds really fucked up to put it into words. But I kind of obliterated a soul in Hell and somehow absorbed it."

I blink in confusion. "That soul is pure. How could it be from Hell?"

She sighs. "Do I look like I know? You are the angel. Why don't you give me some answers? It was as if I turned a piece of shit into a diamond. I don't know. I don't care. All I know is that the energy is now mine and it's grounded to this plane."

"I don't even know what to say except...you are fucking incredible. Please tell me that you managed to obliterate someone who should've never existed." Without even having to ask her, I know exactly who's soul it was. She must have had a confrontation with her ex-fiancé, and I wish I were there to see it. She is right about turning a piece of shit into a diamond. Mortals think that turning water into wine is cool, and sure, it is, but it's nothing compared to turning a blasted, foul, irredeemable soul into pure good energy.

Whoa.

She slowly nods her head. "Yeah. I want to do it again and again. I feel like myself when I do. I feel close to my soul even. I saw it, you know. It was by accident, but I know if we look hard enough, we can find it. I saw it through this realm. I just don't know how to truly work it. Everything seems to be instinctual and not on command. It drives me crazy."

I open my mouth to respond, but a flash of light cuts into the shadowy haze of this sanctuary for Raven, and I see Cassius materialize before us. He would be able to find both Raven and I because he's been here before. He's aware of our presence and is a master at manipulating different planes.

"Which is why I have returned. I have prayed on it and listened to everything around me. And no matter what I think, my thoughts continue to shift back to you and those precious twins. Every time I close my eyes, I keep seeing you guys on this plane. I believe it is my duty to train you how to manipulate the realms. It shouldn't be possible for a mortal, but you are far from being one anymore." Cassius steps closer, his ethereal light radiating from him brighter against the shadows. "Will you let me?"

Raven looks from me to Cassius. "I'll do whatever it takes."

I raise my hand and motion to Raven to hold on before she agrees with Cassius. "We need to discuss this with the devils first. I know what you would have to do to train her, and I'm not sure they will agree."

Raven furrows her brows. "I don't understand. Why can't you ever just fucking tell me everything, Cass-hole? If Elias is hesitant, I know I'm not going to like it."

Cassius flexes his fingers, the muscles on his arms rippling with the movement. "I have to take you somewhere holy. Somewhere the devils can't follow."

Raven groans and shakes her head. "I'm fucking weeks away from popping out these babies. I'm not going to spend them away from my devils and with you. There has to be another way."

"There's not." Cassius rubs his fingers through his dark hair. "If there was, you know I would go with that. But right now? Getting your soul is the most important thing. You're the one who will be capable of doing it. Please, Raven. Be reasonable."

She whips her head back and forth, sending her hair sweeping around her face. "No, I—"

I touch your shoulder. "Why don't we have a meeting? We can discuss everything first. I think Cassius might be right. If he can train you to properly manipulate the planes, Heaven won't stand a chance. They can't keep your soul forever."

Raven sighs and looks Cassius over. "Fine, I'll keep an open mind only if the others agree. We're a team. We're a family. I don't want to waste time unless I have a guarantee that I can fix this."

Cassius tightens his jaw, his light dimming with her words. Her sudden grief stabs into me, stealing my breath. I hurt on a soul-deep level. I wish there was more that I could do. Raven doesn't deserve to talk about how everything might end with her bringing a new life into this world.

"I know we haven't always gotten along, and I know that I have fucked up. I also know I don't deserve to be in your presence. I get that, Raven, more than you know. But I want to earn it. I want to help you and humanity. Things are clearer now. Please, trust me. Trust that I will help you. I won't let you down. If I let you down, that means I let the Higher Power down, and I would rather jump into Hell than do that." Cassius reaches out and touches her cheek, caressing her skin in a way I crave to do. She leans into his hand like she can't resist the weight of his skin, his closeness digging into her.

Raven sniffles and cups his hand, her emotions swelling

through the world around us. "When this is over, I need you to promise me that you will stay by my side, Cassius. I need you to agree that this isn't about Heaven or Hell anymore. This isn't even about me. This is about the balance of the universe."

"You're right. It is about the balance. I'll do anything to see this through. You have my word, Raven. I promise." Cassius twists his hand, gathering light in his palm. He touches both me and Raven and shifts us from the plane and back to the Mortal World.

The ground shakes under my feet, and hellfire rips from the earth.

I tense as a wave of dark souls breaks free from Hell.

They burn everything in their path.

6

The Price of a Soul

RAVEN

CASSIUS LATCHES HIS fingers to my shoulders and yanks me against his chest, shooting heavenly light toward the sky at the shadowy souls escaping Hell. The sunlight above disappears behind the dark cloud, and it's as if Hell comes to Earth. My vision dims, and I dig my fingers into my palms. I can't believe this is happening. I can't believe so many souls have escaped. What does it mean? What happens now?

"Seal it off! Now!" Lucian roars with his words, gathering hellfire and shooting it at the crack.

Cassius engulfs me with his wings, shielding me the best he can as Elias stands in front of us, continuing to blast his heavenly light at the souls trying to come after me. They swirl through the air, creating a funnel, and my heart pounds so hard in my chest that I feel as if it might kill me any second.

"Someone tether them. If they escape, they can possess mortals." Andre jumps into the air, trying to create his own wind to contain the cloud of dark souls. But it's not enough. A few of them break free and vanish.

Oh fuck. Did he just say that they can possess humans? My stomach twists at the thought. I have been possessed before, and it was the worst thing in the world.

"Micah, you have to take the tether. You must bind yourself to Hell. It's the only way. We have to claim what is ours." Dante hisses and throws green liquid at a growing entity escaping from the crack. It's an angel trying to pull itself from Hell. But he doesn't let it.

"We need more power!" Kase whips his tail, knocking another angel through the crack. The devils force their power at the fissure, but it only slowly closes. If they hadn't cut themselves off from Hell, they would be able to do it without a problem.

Fear clutches me, radiating through my being. I have to do something. But what?

Cassius digs his chin into the crook of my shoulder. "Raven, listen to me. I have an idea about how to control the souls. I want you to open your plane again. If you can open it for me,

I can manipulate it around enough to keep the souls within a bubble."

Shifting his body, Elias looks at me from over his shoulder. "You can ground them to your plane and cut off their soul cycles. It must be done. I know that it might be painful, but you will get through this. We're here for you. It might be our only chance."

My chest rises and falls, the anxiety of completing such a task overwhelming me. I don't know how to control my plane. It just happens on a whim, based on what the twins feel I need.

"I don't think I can." I lick my lips and watch as Dante and Kase blast their power at another growing shadow forcing its way out of the shrinking crack to Hell.

"Anything is possible, darlin'. You know this. Come on, have some faith. I know it's tough and this all seems so hopeless, but it's not. You're the most powerful being in the universe. You're powerful enough that you scare the angelic army. Look at what they have done because of their fear of you. You need to prove them right." Elias blasts his light toward the swirling souls again, keeping them back once more.

I puff a breath through my lips and slowly nod my head. I don't know how I'm going to do this, but he's right. I must have faith in myself. It's only ever been my devils and me to see things through in my life. I can count on myself. I know it. I just have to be brave.

I shift my hands and rest them on my belly, feeling the babies kick and move, more active than they have ever been. It's as if they're trying to escape, or maybe they're just exhilarated by the power blazing around them. I just hope they can sense what I need help with.

"Okay, you two. Help your mama out, will you? We need to help your daddies." I rub small circles, closing my eyes and imagining their power coursing through my very being and filling me up. My body buzzes and hums, but it's not the brilliant warmth I get from my twins. It's darker, tainted by the Hell-bound souls. They are getting closer. There are just too many of them, and it's taking Micah too long to grab the tether and bind himself to it.

"You can do it, Raven. Envision it in your mind. Open the door. Imagine you being able to turn the doorknob and see another world. Think about what it feels like entering the realm. Think of the hazy air and the perfect balance of light and dark. Manifest it with your mind. You can do it. Use your senses. What do you see? What do you smell? What do you feel?" Cassius rubs his hands up and down my arms, the gentle wind from his wings stirring my hair.

My closed eyelids flash red as more heavenly light erupts around us. I squeeze my eyes tighter, afraid if I open them then I'll lose my concentration.

"You got this, darlin'. I see the veil. Break it open," Elias says, his voice growing deeper with his unending blast of heavenly light. I wonder if he has a breaking point.

I wonder if the world does.

Something shatters, and the world shakes under my feet. The air cools around us, and the bright light fades from my red-tinted eyelids. I gasp as energy zings through me, and a heavy silence blankets the world.

"Oh, unholy Hell! Raven, you're fucking brilliant." Dante's voice booms through the quiet world, startling me.

I snap my eyes open and stare around at the foggy air. All nine of us stand within the haze, and I gawk at all of the dark souls peppering the air, frozen and unable to move. Three fiery angels stand frozen outside of the crack to Hell, no longer able to move. And as for the Hell portal? It's as if a sheet of impenetrable glass covers it. I can see into it, but nothing can go in or out.

"Everybody circle around her. We need to give her our strength to obliterate these fucking bastards. They're the worst of the worst. Only the darkest souls are strong enough to escape the Hell plane. There's no redemption for them." Kase rushes toward my side and holds his hand out to me. "Remember what you did to the fucking bastard in my kingdom? Channel that rage. You need to end their soul cycles completely."

I swallow, my whole body aching. I don't know if it's because of the amount of power I had to use to create the shift in the planes and bring all my devils and cover the crack or what, but I feel as if I might blackout at any second. I don't think I'm strong enough for this.

"Hurry the fuck up. Lock the tether to her." Lucian bounds closer, his hooves shaking the ground. He summons his fire chain and lashes it at me, but it doesn't hurt me. All it does is wrap around my other hand as he channels power to me.

"Little hellion, we have you, okay? You're strong enough. You're capable of doing this. Don't be afraid." Andre steps beside Kase and rests his big palm on my shoulder.

"He's right, heathen. Open your mind to me completely. I will build a mental wall for you. We will fix this together." Micah stands within the crack a few feet away, but he doesn't come closer. He can't. He holds the tether to Hell.

I want so badly to touch him, and it's enough to shift the world again until I stand within his reach, hovering on the weird glass keeping the souls in Hell.

He reaches out and touches my other shoulder, and Zade and Dante complete the wall around me. Dante expands his wings, shielding us. Cassius and Elias join him, keeping the devils within their glorious wings, the mixture of light and dark stealing my breath away. It's a beautiful blend of Heaven and Hell and the ultimate power coming together as one.

"Imagine your light and dark blanketing everything around

us. You can do it, Raven," Zade says softly, his eyes glassing over as they meet mine. "I will absorb as much of your pain as I can."

A wave of cool tranquility courses through me, and I feel myself connect to Zade. He uses the new energy around me, opening up his empathic side to blend our emotions. He doesn't open himself like this that often to me, but when he does, I savor every second of it.

"That's it, pretty soul. Use us. We are yours and our power belongs to you." Dante caresses me with his feathers, and I finally let myself open completely.

My stomach flips as the babies shift and move, and fire erupts in one of my palms while light explodes in the other. Kase and Lucian guide my hands until I press the power together, creating a beautiful fiery light that turns blue in the process. I can't stop staring at it, and then I realize that my eyes are still closed, and I'm looking at the new power in my mind's eye.

I see everything differently. The shapes and darkness around me morph into silhouettes of souls, and they squirm and growl. They fight and try to break free of my control over them. I listen as they berate and degrade me, threatening me with eternal torture the second they escape. It's enough to ignite a rage inside me, and I fling my hands out, sending the Heaven and Hell power through the realm, blasting every unwanted soul in the process.

Colorful light explodes in the air as if I set off a hundred fireworks. I finally open my eyes, looking with my vision instead of my mind. I watch as the energy flickers around us in starbursts decorating the air. The dark souls turn to light, sparkling as if the air itself is made of glitter. The devils shift on their feet and look around, their expressions just as amazed as mine.

I suck in a breath, watching as the glittery light circles around me, and a shock of electricity blasts into my chest. The new energy pours into me like a tidal wave of emotions. I scream out in pain, the shock of absorbing this incredible energy burning me to my very core. My hair lifts around me with static, and the devils react and close in. Zade shouts my name, and I can feel his cooling presence stealing the heatwave. He takes some of the burdens from me, and Micah whispers words of encouragement in my mind, reminding me not to let the power control me. The power is mine to control.

"Raven, remember how we tethered the energy before. Imagine another stone. Manifest it. It must be larger this time." Kase strokes his hand over mine, trying his best to calm my tense body.

I hold my palms together, imagining a giant multi-faceted gemstone in my hands. I imagine the cool and hard texture and how it will sparkle unlike anything I've ever seen before as long as I can manipulate the souls into it.

The density weighs my fingers down as I summon a stone as big as a basketball. The black color shines in the sparkling light, and I force the energy pouring through my veins into my arms and my fingers, setting the stone aglow in rainbow light.

My body trembles and my knees weaken. It takes everything in me to force the overwhelming energy out. My body burns. Hellfire licks across my skin only to have angelic light put it out.

"That's it, Ray. You're almost there. Release that last bit." Lucian places his hands on top of the stone, using his own power to help suck the energy from me.

Ice freezes me, and the light and fire vanish. The world spins. I can't hold onto my consciousness much longer. It's too much. It's as if I just got rid of the one thing keeping me stabilized in this plane.

I open and close my mouth, but only a whimper escapes my lips.

The plane collapses around us, leaving me on the pavement in the Mortal Realm. Brilliant wings envelop me.

I let myself go.

I stare at the dazzling, colorful field of flowers stretching toward an endless blue sky. I don't know how long I've been sitting here, staring, but I know that this isn't the Mortal World. It's a dream that I can't seem to get myself to wake up from.

"Your body needs to rest, little hellion. You're safe and the crack has been sealed. Just let me help you now." Andre's soft voice comes from beside me, and he rests his hand on my bare knee.

I feel bad about not saying much to him. My mind almost made me forget he was even here, but I'm just so exhausted. I can feel it even in my sleep state. He's right about how hard manipulating the planes was on me physically. Mentally. And losing the energy that I had just gained? It feels as if I lost my soul all over again, despite it being grounded to me. It's so strange.

"How are the others? Is everyone okay? What about Micah?" The questions spill from my mouth as I managed to grab hold of my awareness and turn away from the colorful flower fields made especially for me. Shifting, I rest my legs over Andre's and grab his hands, linking our fingers together, just needing to feel him and be close on this level.

"Micah is tough. He knew that he would eventually have to take the tether. He is happy to do so for you. The other devils are currently cleaning up Hell and getting things back in order. Everything will be okay." He offers me a soft smile.

"Why don't you sound so sure?" I pout my bottom lip.

"It's not that, little hellion. I've never been more certain about getting through this." Andre slides his arm around me and pulls me onto his lap. He kisses my shoulder and waits for me to turn to him completely to meet his lips. Even in this dream state, I can feel his hard-on for me. It's never-ending, and the others always tease him about it being completely eternal. I can't help squirming on his lap, my focus re-directing to the lust rising inside me, enchanted by the pheromones he releases.

It's enough to distract me from my worry, but I pull myself away from thinking about it to look into Andre's eyes. "Then what is it? Don't think you can distract me with that massive sex stick you have trying to poke my being." My dream might be seconds away from a fantasy, so I need to get him talking while I still can.

He chuckles, his face lighting up with a smile I've missed. I hadn't noticed until this moment that he hasn't been smiling at me as much lately, but I know it has nothing to do with me. I know it has to do with the weight of the universe weighing heavily on all my devils. This is truly testing their power.

He wags his brows, flexing his cock beneath me. "Are you sure about that?"

I shove him back, straddling him. Grabbing his wrist, I force his hands over his head and lean over, pressing my big pregnant belly into his taut chest. "Yes. Because I'm going to sit here and pin you down until you tell me. I'm not against torturing you, my lustful devil."

He play-growls deep in his throat, and his eyes light with hellfire. "Careful, little hellion. You know you're my perfect brand of torture. I crave it. I crave you. Always."

Hunching forward, I try to kiss him, but he has to meet me halfway because I just can't get over the size of my belly to do so. I laugh against his lips and nuzzle my nose to his. "Nice try. You're going to have to romance me harder than that. Or you can just tell me what's on your mind, Andre. You don't have to keep any secrets because you're afraid of something. I'm here for you. I know how hard things are...well, things that shouldn't be hard." Straightening my back, I reach behind me and stroke my fingers across his raging boner resting on my back.

He groans in his throat. "You are something else. Getting me to open up to you on this level, but it doesn't make me feel vulnerable. I feel stronger."

I bite my lip between my teeth. "Good. So tell me, and then I will reward you."

"You make a hard deal, but I accept. I'm just struggling over what needs to happen and what I want to happen. We've talked to Cassius." Andre doesn't continue, letting me fill the blanks because he knows that I know. Cassius wants to take me away from them to help train me. I don't even know if I can survive hanging around him for more than a couple of minutes at a time.

"Oh." I'm not sure what else to say. I don't want them to feel bad if they agree with Cassius. I know deep down that if he can help me control my new plane, then it's worth trying. But the thought of losing any time with my devils freaks me out. What if something happens and I deliver early? Not being able to have every second possible with them makes it feel as if I die inside already.

Andre massages his fingers into my arm, sliding his hands lower until they rest on my belly. "I hate the idea of not being with you, but I can't stand the thought of losing you to Heaven, Raven. I have faith in Cassius. He's a powerful angel, and I think that he isn't intended for Hell yet because it's his purpose to do this first."

Tears pool in my eyes, and I blink them away. Even in the dreamworld, I feel as if my heart shatters. The blue sky turns dark, and stars glitter above as Andre tries to summon light the only way he can.

My lip trembles. I'm afraid if I speak that my voice will crack, but I know I must say something. "You're right. I know you're right, and I know Cassius is right despite me wanting to be stubborn as Hell and not give him the satisfaction of telling him. But if I can learn to manipulate the planes and access my soul, I can get it. I need to get it. We're running out of time.

I'm so scared that we will fail."

Andre leans up and hugs me close, brushing his lips to my cheeks to smear the tears away. I inhale the scent of his skin, trying to use it to settle my frazzled nerves. His mouth sets me off, and I grab onto the lust radiating from him and use it to suppress my depression and panic. I need something to take the sudden wave of unbidden emotions away.

"Wake me up. Please, Andre. I want to be with you in the Mortal World. I want the reminder that this isn't a dream. I just want to feel you. Touch you. Be with you. I need something, anything to help keep me from losing my shit." I ease away from his mouth and peer into his eyes. "Please."

"Anything for you, little hellion." Andre leans in, and his handsome face fills my vision.

I intake a sharp breath. The world shifts, and I startle myself awake. The dimly lit room smells of coconut and toasted marshmallows, and I groan as I shift and spot Zade sitting in a chair, watching me in Andre's embrace.

The second our eyes meet, I throw my arms out toward him. I need us all to be together. "Come here. I need you too. Please help get my emotions in order. I feel out of control."

Zade doesn't hesitate and stands from his chair, striding across the room and to the bed. His muscles ripple, and I don't even let him kneel for long before I yank his shirt over his head and kiss him. Lust fills every molecule on my body, sending tingles through my body. I need relief. I need someone to detonate the bomb ticking inside me, so I can explode and get through this ache consuming me already.

Zade reacts to my affection with hot passion and slides his tongue into my mouth, taking control. He usually doesn't, but it's like he craves it in this moment. I can feel his need to take care of me. I can feel his emotions suppressing mine just how I asked. He wants me. He wants Andre to help him. I don't think I've ever seen him so reactive to my commands. It's hot.

I reach between us and stroke his cock through his pants. He unbuckles them for me, and I pull his hard-on out. He moans as I rub my fingers over his tip and explore the length of his shaft down to his balls. Andre shifts on the bed beside us and helps undress me, not allowing me to stop kissing Zade in the process. He kisses my shoulder and works his way down, exploring my back while massaging his hands into my boobs, trailing them over my sides until he slips his fingers between my legs.

I moan against Zade's mouth, the sensation of Andre's hands working over my clit sending explosions through me. I wish I could easily bend down and suck him, getting him off with my mouth. I want so desperately to taste him. To give in to his desires, his lust intensified by Andre.

"Stand up. She wants to pleasure you, Zade." It's as if Andre can read my thoughts and hear my fantasy. And who knows, he might. Just like the way Micah can listen to my thoughts, Andre knows my desires so well and how I love working my mouth over my devils. I love pleasuring them and get off on hearing them moan my name. I get off on them watching me and watching each other. It's like I can never get enough.

Zade eases away for me, tilting his head to the side and staring deep into my eyes. He silently assesses me to see if Andre is right, and I flick my tongue over my lips and smile.

"You heard him." My smile widens with my comment, and I rub my hands down Zade's abs. His eyes close with his anticipation. He carefully stands up, dropping his pants completely, and I lace his cock with my fingers, adding pressure as I lick his tip and suck him into my mouth, rolling my tongue across the bottom of his shaft. He combs his fingers through my hair, pulling it out of the way, and Andre shifts on the bed, working his muscular shoulders between my legs until I sit on his face. I moan as he kisses my thigh, slowly teasing me as he works his way to my clit. Sucking it into his mouth, he ignites an explosion of incredible sensations through my body, and I gasp and suck Zade farther in. He takes over for me and guides my head, getting me to deep throat him. I cling onto his ass cheeks, digging my nails into his skin and scratching lightly.

Andre works me over, harder and faster, using his whole face to get me off. I squeeze him between my thighs, the intensity of pleasure building and building until I feel as if I'll explode.

He slides a finger inside me and strokes my G spot, determined to give me an orgasm that will strike my very center.

My whole body clenches, and I scream my pleasure, the vibration of my voice zinging over Zade. He comes in my mouth, set off by our deep-seated connection. Our emotions tangle with each other. I swallow and slow down, trying to catch my breath. I feel so incredible in this moment. I want more. I crave more. The pheromones that Andre releases into the air make everything that much more intense.

"I need you, little hellion. I'm starving." Andre nudges me down lower until my slickness glides over his majestic cock, the size of him still daunting even though I know he can use his Hell power to ensure we have only pure pleasure.

Zade crawls closer and climbs behind me, straddling Andre too. He lifts me up by my ass, positioning my body while helping Andre guide his cock inside me. I wish I could see everything. I want to know exactly what it looks like having the king of lust spread me open.

"Let me see," I whisper, voicing my desires, knowing how much they love when I do so. "It makes me so hot."

Zade uses his purple power and manifests a mirror into his palm, holding it just right so I can see my body connect to Andre's. I can also see how hard Zade is again and how his cock rests so close to Andre's ass that I can't help thinking about whether Andre would like to feel that kind of pleasure as well.

"Careful, Zade. Keep teasing Andre like that, and I'm going to ask you to fuck him as he fucks me." I smile at Zade's reflection in the mirror as he stares at it from over my shoulder. His eyes flash with his power. I just put a thought in his head, and he can feel my emotions and how I want to see such a thing. "Andre, wouldn't you like that?"

Andre licks his lips, stroking his fingers over my exposed clit. "I'd love that. The pleasure of being with both of you feeds my very being. Zade, you can fuck both of us if you want. I'll leave the decision up to you."

Zade exhales, his whole body shuddering behind me, and Andre summons a bottle of lube. I already know Zade wants to give in to both of our desires and his own. We all love each other, and this is more than about sex. This is about the bond we share. Their companionship runs so deeply that I can feel it the same way I feel it with Kase and Dante. They do things that feel good and bring pleasure to all of us. It's not about just one of us individually. It's about us as a whole.

Zade squirts lube across his cock, and I watch his hand slicking his hard-on. I slowly bounce on top of Andre, wanting to give him the most pleasure imaginable as Zade adjusts his body, spreading his legs until he can position himself just right. Andre reaches forward and balances me on him until I plant my feet to the mattress for better leverage. I can control how much he enters me, but I know that the second I slide all the way down, feeling as if my insides rearrange, that I will be here until he gets his fill. The pressure builds as his cock expands and he locks on to me.

I gasp and draw my attention back to the mirror watching as Zade slides into Andre's ass, and both of them moan in unison. Heat builds between my legs. I feel my desire dripping down Andre, making things even more slippery. Pleasure sizzles through me, and I can lose myself in what Zade and Andre experience.

Kissing my shoulder, Zade whispers how good Andre feels. I smile, keeping my gaze on Andre, gasping every time I bounce on him. I love how our passion softens his face, and he moans loudly, enjoying every second of pleasure. Reaching up, he rolls my hard nipples between his fingers, exploring my body as Zade's hips bump my ass as he fucks Andre harder and faster. Pressing into me, Zade draws his hand lower and rubs my clit, increasing my pleasure until my body tenses and I scream out. Andre grunts as he comes inside me, and I see a flash of fire as I feed his power, our orgasms in sync and breathtaking.

"Come on, Zade, fuck him harder. I want to hear him moan. Get him to come again." I gasp with my words, loving Andre's reaction. I practically fall forward and rest my hands on Andre's chest as Zade lifts up his legs, spreading him open wider. Andre stretches and kisses me, sliding his tongue into my mouth, moaning and panting against my lips as we share a breath.

"It feels better than I could ever imagine." Andre kisses me with his words. "The connection I feel, having my perfect woman ensure that I get what I need is the best gift in the universe."

"I love you, Andre. I'll do anything for you." I tip my head back and look at Zade upside down. "You too, Zade. I love you and your loyalty and desire to take care of both of us.

"I wish I could've seen things sooner," he murmurs, continuing to play with my clit as he fucks Andre.

"It was supposed to be this way. I know that now. You had to come at your own time. Had you jumped any sooner, you might have resented us." Andre grunts again, and I feel his orgasm ripple through me, the pressure building again.

Zade nips my shoulder with his teeth, and his body reacts as he finishes. But it's not over yet. Andre isn't ready to let me go.

Zade lowers Andre to the bed and shifts off, watching as I slide up and down Andre, picking up speed, but my body trembles, and it's hard to keep up in this position.

Zade takes over, spreading my legs as he holds me, guiding me up and down on Andre faster and harder until all I can do is scream out my pleasure in bursts. Andre continues to rub my clit over and over again until my body explodes once more. My eyes roll back in my head, and I rest on Zade's pec, just savoring the sensation of pure and utter bliss coursing through me. Zade hardens again, and he helps Andre scoot to the edge of the bed until he can stand between his legs. I rest on my hands and knees, and Andre manages to rock his hips up and keep the pace for me, letting me enjoy the sensation of being fucked by the devil of lust.

"I want you now, Raven," Zade murmurs from behind me, stroking himself and adding more lube to his cock.

I let my hair hang forward and moan my agreement, my words refusing to form. Zade spanks me, massaging his fingers into my ass cheeks as he spreads me wider. He leans down and kisses me before gliding his tongue along my body, slowly using his finger to work me up from behind. Andre groans with a new wave of pleasure, and I know that he will come again.

He slows down enough so that Zade can position himself to my ass, and I gasp and moan as he teases me with his tip, waiting for my body to adjust to his size to let him in. I whimper in pleasure and pain until the ache of getting used to him shifts into ecstasy, and Andre summons a vibrator, the small toy fitting perfectly under my lips to zing across my clit. My body holds it in place, and I scream in pleasure and orgasm again after just a couple of seconds, the intensity of getting fucked in the ass at the same time as Andre remains knotted to me, drinking in his fill of my pleasure so much that my body just reacts.

Heat radiates from my core and courses through the rest of

me, and Zade moans, his voice louder as he enjoys my body at the same time as Andre. I give in to their every desire and lie complacent, letting them have control. It ignites their devilish nature, and I watch as Andre's devil side breaks free. I reach out and grab onto his tail, stroking it as I close my eyes and lose myself to everything that they create in me. Because with them together, I feel as if nothing can get between us. We can take on the whole damn world. We can take on the universe.

But we don't want to take on either. We want to save them. And I know we can.

My body clenches, and my muscles spasm as I orgasm again. The pressure between my legs subsides, and Andre grunts as he comes one last time and manages to slide out of me. I sink onto him, arching my back and keeping my ass in the air as Zade finishes up and moans one last time. The two of them sandwich me between them without squishing me, and we lie in bed in a tangle of arms and legs, kissing and enjoying each other.

"Let me get Dante. I want to make sure that you feel amazing. I know things get a little rough with me." Andre kisses my forehead, ensuring that Zade cuddles me in his arms. "I'll start a bath as well."

All I can do is nod my head. The incredible energy zinging through the room fills me up and makes me feel complete. I feel whole again. I never want it to end.

But then I see Cassius gazing at me from the hallway as Dante enters the room alone, shutting the door in his face.

It's a wakeup call. I know that this can't last forever.

I know what I must do.

I must put my life in the hands of the bastard who has a lot of making up to do.

I have to trust Pride. I just hope this isn't a mistake.

I hope after this is done, he'll see that his path leads to Hell, and he'll jump.

I count on it.

Pride will fall next.

7

Evil Angels

DANTE

I SWOOP ACROSS the treacherous landscape of my kingdom, searching the deep ditches where most of the souls of my territory remain stuck in fiery sand.

"Hey, fucker! You missed one!" Kase grabs a bastard demonic angel from behind one of the rubble piles, squishing a few dozen souls, and dangles the woman in front of him.

It's Meri.

I close my wings and nosedive toward the fiery landscape, spreading them at the last second to glide until I touch my feet to the ground and run to a stop.

"We have to take her to Raven. She wants the honors of

fucking this bitch up." I flash my fangs at the woman and spit venom in her face. It's not the worst thing I can do, but I want Raven to have that sort of satisfaction.

Meri screams and thrashes in Kase's arms. "You traitors! You should've just remained in Hell. The world is falling apart because of you and your lust for a mortal. One that doesn't even belong to you. I don't know why you even try anymore. Raven belongs to Heaven. She will ensure humanity gets to restart like it needs."

Kase growls and locks his tail around her throat, squeezing as he dangles her out. "You know that isn't true. We had a plan. Purgatory is what we need. Starting over won't accomplish anything. It will just end up right back here or not at all. Souls need to learn and grow. It's what the Higher Power wanted with the soul cycles, but it just wasn't effective."

"Don't speak for the Higher Power." Meri locks her fingers around Kase's tail, trying to squeeze. I grab her by the throat and rip her away, spitting venom in her face again until her mouth melts together and she can no longer talk.

"Shut the fuck up. You are done." I hold my hand out to Kase, locking my fingers around him as I launch into the air, flying him with me while I continue to strangle the bitch angel. If I could strangle her until her head popped off, I would. And then I would carry her head and drop it at Raven's feet so she could kick it across the universe.

"Raven is going to be so fucking excited. I can't wait for her to destroy this bitch." Kase ruffles his fingers through my hair, smiling at me.

I chuckle. This psycho is hot as fuck in his excitement over giving our soul such a gift. I love the shit out of him for it. Craning my head, I snuggle against his hand, getting him to rub my head a bit more. Raven's panties would melt off if she saw his affection toward me in this moment. I want to capture his good mood until she can see for herself. She could use something to cheer her up, and if it involves a damn devil dogpile with her climbing on top and hanging a flag on my cock to declare herself as queen, I'll happily oblige.

Kase opens a portal for me, and we fly through and land in the middle of the apartment. Meri's muffled scream breaks the silence. I drop her to the floor and slam my boot into her back, restraining her with my bodyweight.

"What is going on?" Zade peeks his head out of the bedroom he shares with Andre and Raven. His eyes widen, flicking to the fallen angel beneath me.

"Where is Raven? She can't be sleeping still. I know that sexy woman gets horny too often to sleep for days, even with Andre's help." Kase steps from the summoning circle first, crossing his arms over his chest.

Raven's voice sounds from behind Zade, her breathy concern striking me in the balls. They were at it. I don't even have to see her to know that she probably walks funny after spending so much time with Andre. It only feels like hours since we've been gone, but I know it has been days. Hell was a complete shitshow. Micah and Lucian are still cleaning the mess up. Lucian feels the need to control things a bit, thinking that he is still the strongest devil.

"It's best if you stay here. Dante and Kase brought someone." Zade holds his arm up, blocking Raven's exit.

She doesn't let him stop her for long, ducking under his muscular body and managing to squeeze her way through the doorframe, even though Zade moves his body so she doesn't squish her belly.

"Yeah, asshole. We brought this bitch for Raven. Finally caught her hiding in my kingdom. We thought she would want to do the honors of destroying her. She doesn't deserve everything that has been given to her." I twist my foot back-and-forth, making Meri yell and struggle beneath me.

"What do you say, angel-girl? Shall we add to your power? Serve some justice? Really stab Mikail in the gut when he realizes his companion will never be joining him again?" Kase laces his tail around Raven, pulling her to him until he can wrap her in his arms.

Raven doesn't respond right away, looking from Meri to me and then to Kase. Something dark flashes across her face, and I wish I had Micah's power and could hear what's on her mind. I don't know if Andre told her what we had discussed involving Cassius or not, but I wouldn't put it past him. It's fucking torture keeping anything from her these days. It's like she just knows when we're not telling her everything, despite us wanting to protect her.

If she knows, it might make her more volatile and aggressive. It'll make her angrier and in need of revenge. I wouldn't blame her. I don't think I could survive hanging out with Cass-hole for more than a day. He gets on my nerves more than Lucian's asshole attitude does.

"Hold her, Dante." Raven slides herself from Kase's arms and waddles in my direction. And not just a pregnancy walk. I think that Andre and Zade fucked her so good that she's not going to be able to walk normally ever again, especially with her cute belly.

I bend down and grab Meri by her hair, yanking her up to hold in front of Raven. Raven enters the Hell circle, baring her teeth in her fury. Fire light flashes in her eyes, but she doesn't unleash Hell power. Instead, she summons angelic light, making Meri flinch and buck her body. I grip her tighter, wrapping my arm across her throat to silence any noise.

"What? Are you afraid? You shouldn't flinch away from the power you so carelessly sacrificed in the name of ruining the world. Open your eyes and look at me, Meri. I want to make one thing clear to you." Raven jerks her hand out and grabs

Meri by the chin, forcing her to pay attention.

Meri finally stops fighting and opens her eyes, meeting Raven's gaze. "You're undeserving of such power. You claim that it was me to ruin the world, but you need to look at yourself. You are a disgrace. An abomination. We've had to do this because of you."

Raven stiffens at Meri's accusations, and I hiss and dig my fingers deeper into her throat, ensuring that she can no longer respond to Raven. Heaving a couple breaths, Raven gets herself in control. A dozen thoughts flicker with the fire in her eyes, and once again, I crave to know what's on her mind. I just hope she doesn't think twice about Meri's words. They're far from true. Meri is a psychotic, wannabe righteous angel who deserves absolutely nothing.

"Fuck you. Fuck you and everything you have done against humanity. I'll save them. I won't let the angelic army get away with trying to reset the universe. Hell is ours. Purgatory is mine. Heaven will no longer be in control of the souls who manage to escape their cycles for their supposed paradises. Do you understand? This is over. You've lost. You've sacrificed everything for absolutely nothing." Raven gathers hellfire and heavenly light in her palms, her whole body blazing with energy.

My cock hardens at the sight of her power, and I imagine dropping this bitch to grab my pretty soul, lift her up and prop her against the wall to fuck her over and over again the way she likes.

Raven smacks her palms to each side of Meri's face, knocking me out of my new lustful haze.

The bitch screams, flailing and fighting as hard as she can, but it's no use. Raven uses the light and darkness of the twins to devour the angel's very essence until she explodes in a light-show of rainbow color that flashes through the air.

Raven gasps, and the world trembles. I don't get the chance to snatch her before she falls back and disappears.

"Fuck! She slipped into her plane. Can anyone find a crack?" Kase spins on the balls of his feet, searching around the room.

Raven grows more powerful than ever. If she keeps walking through the different realms, she could very well find herself somewhere she can't escape or somewhere none of us will be able to go.

"It's gone. It's completely sealed off." Andre tugs on a pair of shorts, feeling the world around him with his eyes closed.

"We need to find Cassius. I don't think we can wait much longer. I'm afraid we could lose her." Zade scrubs his fingers into his scruffy face in desperate need of shaving. He hasn't done so in a while, and I don't know if it's because he's coming into his devil side or if he just gave up on his mortal appearance. Either way, it doesn't matter. It's as if my thoughts want to distract me from the fact that Raven vanished.

"I'll summon Lucian. He might be able to find him the quickest." Kase shoots red power at our summoning circle, choosing to jump back into the Hell plane instead of calling Lucian to us. It's faster if he just goes to find him.

"I'll see if I can get Micah." Andre strides toward the summoning circle next. "Zade, try to reach Elias. We need to all be here."

"I'll keep trying to access her plane." I hate not being able to just rush somewhere to find Raven. I hate waiting around to see if she returns. It makes me feel helpless and useless. It makes me want to fuck shit up. But someone must stay. I'd prefer it be me.

I pace around the living room, staring at Raven's favorite spot on the couch where a blanket lies half on the floor. Striding to it, I pick it up and fold it nicely. I busy myself by straightening a couple things up, realizing how messy the other devils are. Kase and I have always been clean and tidy, and now that we're all together, they need to start treating our home better. Especially with the twins coming.

Fuck.

There has to be something I can do.

"Dante?" Raven's voice sounds through the air, and my heart jumps in relief.

I spin on my feet and catch sight of her on her ass in the middle of the living room. A small ruby stone rests in the palm of her hand, and I realize that the energy must belong to Meri.

Rushing to her, I drop to my knees and engulf her in a hug. I kiss the top of her head, moving to her temple, and then her cheek before I meet her lips. I could kiss every inch of her. The minute she's been gone felt like an eternity.

"Are you okay, pretty soul?" I ask, leaning back to search her beautiful blue-green eyes. "You scared the hell out of me."

She forces her lips to smirk and reaches up, caressing her index finger to one of my sharp fangs. "Doesn't look like it."

I play-growl and nip her finger, sucking it into my mouth for a tiny taste of her blood. Shit could be falling apart and she'd still find it in her to tease me. I appreciate it more than I realize. Without Raven, I'd go insane. I'd lose the best part of me. It's the fear of it that strikes me in the core. I never knew such emotions until I met her. Until I fell madly in love with her. And now that she carries the twins, I swear it's gotten a million times worse. I didn't know a devil could feel this way. I wish I could just create a bubble for all of us to live in for the rest of time.

Sliding her finger from my mouth, she pokes my bottom lip, her eyes sheening over. I lean closer and brush my lips to hers again, savoring the softness of her pouty mouth.

"Raven..." I let my words trail off. It feels like torture to even try to speak what's on my mind.

She blinks her eyes, clearing her vision. "I know, Dante. You don't have to say anything. Walking through the planes like this and not knowing if I'll be able to return or not freaks me the fuck out. It's not safe. It's not good for the twins if I don't know how to protect us like I should. I'm afraid that if I don't get it under control, I'll fuck everything up for us."

I flick my forked tongue between my lips, unable to keep my devilish nature in control. "You could never fuck anything up, Raven. This isn't your fault or your responsibility. You shouldn't have to carry the weight of our feelings. We should've figured this out sooner."

Raven cups my cheeks, combing her fingers into my hair and playing with the strands. "Don't you dare try to take the blame and keep it all to yourself. We've been dealing with a shitshow. There's no way you could've predicted that one of you guys would've knocked me the fuck up."

I smile, the thought sending a wave of happiness through me. "Tell that to Kase. He is still so adamant that it was his mighty cock to do the job."

She giggles and nuzzles her nose to mine. "You guys are going to be amazing dads. I hope you know that. Just try not to overwhelm them with your sex ed. And you all better not be so overprotective that they don't get social lives. They're part mortal, you know."

Her words stab into me. I know she doesn't intentionally speak as if it's the end for her, but it's like she can't help herself.

She talks as if she's not going to be around to raise them. Strange, hot liquid floods my eyes, and I hiss as a tear splashes on my cheek. What the actual fuck is this bullshit?

Raven gasps and smears her fingers over my cheek, and then hot trails pour from her endless gaze. Her shoulders shake, and she sobs, her sudden emotions stealing the playfulness from her voice.

I suck in a deep breath, getting my shit together. I can't believe I'm crying. I need to be strong for her. I need her to know that whatever happens, I'll not stand by and do nothing as Heaven keeps her soul. I'll break into that plane even if it's the last thing I ever do so that she will be here for the twins. For humanity.

I clear my throat and grab the hem of my shirt, rubbing it across Raven's cheeks to dry her face. "We're a fucking mess. We shouldn't be crying. It's for no reason. Nothing is going to happen. You're basically going to go on a shitty vacation with an asshole angel. You're going to come back stronger than ever, and we're going to kick some angelic army ass. And then we're going to fucking have an orgy to celebrate. Everyone's getting stuffed. I will put together the toy collection while you're away." I force my voice to remain strong. "And you know what? I'm going to give Cassius instructions. If he fails to follow them, you're going to let me know. He will have hell to pay if he doesn't at least try to make your time together pleasant."

Raven laughs in exasperation, her face softening and lighting up as she thinks about my words. "You are ridiculous, but I love you. You're right. I'm sorry. I didn't mean to get all emotional. It's this damn energy rock. I don't know why I brought it back with me. I should've grounded it to the plane. It's just—"

"You're still learning, Raven. It won't be like this forever. I promise. I'll do everything I can to train you as quickly as possible. But we have to start now." Cassius stands in the doorway, his annoyingly bright wings stinging my eyes.

Raven jerks her attention to him. She flares her nostrils, crinkling her nose. I half-expect her to blast him for interrupting our moment, but all she does is hug me tighter. "I'm not leaving until I get to see everyone."

Kase groans under his breath. "Sorry, angel-girl. We're all here already. We need you to get that ass in control, okay? Elias will be able to check in on you, but we need him in the Mortal Realm. He's the only one that can keep an eye on the angelic army while you and Cassius are away."

Raven squeezes her eyes shut. "I swear to Hell, Cass-hole. You better not make us regret this."

Lucian exits the summoning circle, dangling his fire chain in front of Raven. "You should be able to take this with you, Ray. Use it on him if he acts like a dick. He sometimes needs to be put in his place."

I get to my feet and pull Raven to hers, hugging her once more. I don't want to let her go, but I know that the others want her affection too. I nudge her toward Lucian, so she can grab the fire chain.

Turning to Cassius, I summon a sheet of paper and pen and quickly scribble a list down. I hold it out to him. "This is everything you need to know. If I find out that you don't do something on this list and Raven wants you to, you're going to get fucked up the second you come back."

Cassius swears under his breath, but he doesn't comment on my list. I wonder if he'll show Raven what I put. She doesn't even notice as she kisses Kase next.

Folding up the paper, Cassius tucks it away in his pocket. "I expect you guys to have everything in order when we return. I don't want to have to come save your asses."

I flash my fangs at him. "That's the last thing you'll ever do for my ass," I snap, laughing at his reaction. He's going to be fun to fuck with for the rest of eternity. "Just remember. When this is all over, you better fucking jump. Do you understand?"

Cassius doesn't respond to me. He waits until Raven kisses Micah last and flies toward her.

I blink my eyes, summoning my strength as the two of them disappear in a flash of light, stinging my skin.

I scrub my hands down my face and turn my attention to

Kase. He strolls toward me and swings and arm over my shoulders. I squeeze him as he inhales a deep breath.

"Are you ready to fuck shit up?" He summons red power in his palm.

I force myself to smile. "I thought you'd never ask."

8

Godly Power

CASSIUS

"**T**HIS PLACE SUCKS and not in the good way." Raven places her hands on her hips, peering at the pure white nothingness of my sanctuary. I wiped everything I've ever manifested to start with a clean slate for her to work with. It's the only place in the universe that I can keep everyone out of. It's also the one place that she can learn to access different planes purposefully and not by chance.

"I agree, so why don't you do something about it? I'm not here to serve you. I know that the devils have spoiled you, but in my domain, you're going to be doing shit for yourself." I summon a chair and plop my ass into it, kicking my shoes off.

Am I being a dickhead? Maybe. But I know that she reacts best when she's either scared, angry, or horny. Since she's neither scared or horny, I need to piss her off.

Raven narrows her eyes at me. "You are the worst teacher I've ever had." Striding to me, she stands on her tiptoes to add an extra inch of height to her frame in an attempt to tower over me. We're more eye level than anything, because I purposely increase the height of the chair, so she has to look at me straight on.

Fire flashes in her eyes, and I know that we're close to her getting a feel of how to use my plane. I want her to realize what it takes to start controlling the energy without training her with my words. Manifesting is mental. It comes from deep within our beings. Raven must know the sensation first before I can explain to her what it is.

"Let me sit down. I need a moment to process everything." Raven nudges my shoulder with the back of her hand. "Please. My feet hurt. You try carrying around two spawns inside you."

It takes everything in me not to give in to her request. But it's important that I don't. She needs to do this herself.

"No. I made this, so I get to sit in it." I tighten my jaw and stand my ground.

"Then teach me how to make my own, fuckhead. We're going to get nowhere if you're just going to sit on your ass this whole time." Raven jabs me in the chest with her finger next.

Again, I shake my head no. "Get your own chair."

Fire flashes in her eyes, and she shoves her hands into my chest, knocking me out of the chair and onto my back. I hit the floor with a thud and gasp. I should've expected that. I was a dumb shit for not thinking she would just kick my ass and steal my chair.

She looks cute as hell doing so, all smug as she smiles at me and plops down. So I wave my hand and make the chair disappear. She screeches as she falls, but I summon a pillow to stop her from hitting the ground of the plane.

"You fucking asshole. I'm going to—" She summons the fire chain Lucian gave her, pulling it out of nowhere.

I whistle and clap my hands. "Look what you just did. You summoned Lucian's chain. How did you do it? Talk me through it. Go over everything that went through your head for you to pull it into this plane."

Raven glowers at me. "I don't know."

"Think. Come on. You're smart. I know you are a bit emotional because of..." I twirl my finger at her round belly.

She whips the fire chain at me, nearly taking out my knees in the process. "I felt pissed the fuck off. You're such a jerk. All I want to do is bend your ass over, rip down your pants, and see if there's a literal stick stuck in your ass. That way I can yank it out and help you feel better. Maybe you won't be such a douchebag."

I clench my damn ass cheeks at the thought. Inhaling a deep breath, I turn around, knowing that I might regret this. I need to focus, and I know sometimes a distraction from everything going on will help. So I do her one better. Instead of making her wrestle me to follow through with her threat, I unfasten my belt, drop my pants, and bend over.

She gasps with a laugh, her high-pitched cackle echoing around us. I don't even have a chance to move before she slaps her hot palm to my ass cheek, sending me stumbling.

"Damn it, Cass-hole. I don't want to see your fucking ass-hole. I was joking." Raven stands behind me, making me flinch, thinking she might do something Dante would approve of.

I straighten my back and turn toward her, the look on her face priceless. It's better than I expected. She's been so serious lately that I almost forgot what she looks like with a smile. I'm not sure if she's ever given me one, and it stirs something inside me. I can't help thinking about stepping closer to her beautiful smile until it fades because I kiss her lips.

I shake my head and scrub my hands into my eyes. "I was just trying to get you to settle down. Your emotions control every-thing, and you're more connected to your soul here. We're on the same plane as it, and with the added power of the energy you've already collected, I'm sure you're feeling a bit wild. You need to take a breath and calm down."

I realize my mistake immediately. I broke Dante's number seven rule on his list of things that will keep Raven happy. *Never tell her to calm down. Instead, try validating her emotions.* I'm really a fucking idiot. Dante has far more experience with Raven, and mortals for that matter, than I do. Begrudgingly, I can see things more clearly now. I hate it.

I throw my hands up. "I mean, I know you're upset. I know that you miss the devils already, and we are not exactly always on the same page. I can't possibly understand what you're going through, but it's okay. You're entitled to feel out of control and full of rage. You're entitled to hate everything about the situation. I know you think I'm a dick. I know that I'm a dick, and I'm trying to change my ways. It's hard, but I want to do it for you. You are important to me, Raven. You might not believe it, but you are."

I brace for her to yell at me, smack me upside the head, and demand I summon her a couch or some shit, but she doesn't do any of that. She continues to sit on the pillow with her legs bent and rests her chin on her knees. The grief pooling tears in her eyes steals my breath away, and I stride closer and summon another pillow to sit on the floor beside her.

I pat her back, unsure if I should hug her or not. The devils are so open with their affection. I just don't know if such things are wanted or despised when it's me giving them. Yes, we've kissed each other. She's teased me and tested my restraint. But that was a power play. This is more fragile. More raw. I don't want to mess up.

"Why don't we practice some meditating?" I gently rub circles on her back, testing to see if she'll smack my hand away.

She doesn't.

She doesn't speak to me either, and her silence makes me shift, my nerves getting the best of me. I'm a damn savior. I've faced far worse things in this universe. Why am I so chickenshit now?

Reaching over, I brush her hair away from her face so I can see her. "Why don't we start by closing our eyes? I want you to use your other senses and tell me what is going on around us."

Raven flicks her gaze to mine and burns me a look but doesn't protest. She sighs a heavy breath and squeezes her eyes closed, pursing her lips, remaining tense instead of relaxed.

I don't say anything, reaching into my pocket for the list Dante gave me. There is something about getting Raven to relax on here, and I need to look at it more.

Number seventeen: Raven must be reminded to unclench her jaw. Start by kneading your fingers right outside her ears and below her temples, giving her a massage to help her loosen up. If her body refuses, then make her orgasm.

I palm my forehead, reading over the list again. Ninety-five percent of it ends with giving Raven an orgasm. It's as if Dante thinks that is the cure to her problems.

"What are you doing? I thought you were meditating with me?" Raven snatches the list from my fingers, trying to read over it.

I grab it right back and shove it into my pocket, not allowing her to see what a dumbass Dante thinks I am. Apart from his supposed cure to all her mood issues, he doesn't think I'll remember to feed her. He doesn't think I know how to cleanse her in this world either. Obviously, I have a lot to prove to him, so I can't fuck this up.

I snatch her wrist, linking my fingers through hers, stopping her from trying to reach into my pocket. "Control yourself. This is not any of your concern."

She narrows her eyes at me. "Let me read the list Dante gave you. It'll make me feel better."

I meet her glare with my own. "No. He made it for me. I want you to close your eyes again. You need to follow my instructions and use your other senses to tell me what you hear, smell, taste, and feel. I want you to learn to ground yourself to my sanctuary. If you can tap into it, you can access it without me."

Raven ignores my command and shoves me back with her hands, climbing on top of me. I grind my teeth as she spins and sits on my chest, lifting up my shirt to dig her hand into my pocket, trying to grab the paper.

And fuck.

She unintentionally grazes the side of my cock with her fingers, turning me on. We're ultra-close in my sanctuary, our beings merged together as I tether her here. And this doesn't help any. Neither does her ass in my face. It's getting awfully close to where she'll sit on my head if she moves again, and I realize just how much I like the idea.

"Now it's you who needs to control yourself," Raven says, whacking my thigh an inch away from my hard-on. "I'm trying to grab the list, not initiate foreplay. Tell your cock to settle down. There is no action for you until you either teach me things properly or let me see the list. I want to know what Dante expects."

"You have three seconds to get off me and do as I ask, Raven. I'm warning you." I hover my hands just outside her hips, preparing to lift her off me.

"One. Two. Three." She laughs as she says the words, yanking at the paper.

This unruly woman. No wonder the devils love her so much. She just makes me want to punish her.

"Damn it. You asked for it." Flipping her off, I drop her onto a pillow and grab her hands, restraining her by her wrists. My knees rest between her legs, and she squeezes me with her thighs.

Fuck me. Am I going to live the rest of eternity constantly regretting my decisions? Because Raven wears nothing under her dress. I can see every inch of her bare body, her pussy as perfect as my brother described it over and over again.

And I can't stop staring.

Raven stops struggling, her eyes flicking from mine and trailing down my body, watching me watch her. She likes the way I look at her. I can tell by the wetness dripping between her legs and how she wiggles but doesn't yell at me.

"Did his list only include sex?" Raven asks, biting her bottom lip between her teeth as she teases me. "I'm sure at least a couple things say as much, but Dante knows you're a virgin. You're not exactly going to know what to do with me."

Her words are like a slap to my balls. No, I don't know what I'm going to do with her, but I sure as fuck know what I want to do to her. And it takes everything in me not to show her that I might not have experience with mortal sexuality, but I know everything there is to know about a woman's body.

"You want to bet?" I loosen one of my hands from her wrists, bringing it to her knee and slowly trail it across her thigh and toward her pussy.

Raven gasps, squirming as I tease her, but I don't plan to go further than just grazing my fingers across her smooth lips. Not yet. We have to focus.

She releases the sexiest whimper I've ever heard, and she tries to squeeze her legs together, but my body is in the way.

"You fucker," she mutters, trying to break her hands free of my hold, but I don't let her.

I bow forward instead, keeping my body off hers while stopping an inch from her mouth. We share the same breath, her fragrance sweet and irresistible. I can't stop myself from brushing my lips to hers, letting her feel the hardness of my body through my pants between her legs. I'm sure she'll soak me with how turned on she is by my presence. It takes everything in me not to follow through with my word.

"I knew you didn't have it in you, Cassius," she says, her voice husky with the desire coursing through the world around us. "You're all talk."

I ignore her instigation and kiss her deeper, sliding my tongue into her mouth. Easing away, I say, "If you do as I ask, I will show you that I'm not all talk. But unlike the devils, I'm not going to let you just have your way. I don't let my cock think for me either. Consider it a reward. For both of us. If you can manage to complete the tasks I ask, we will go over Dante's list, and I'll let you choose whatever you want. We'll do that until you become a master of manipulating the planes."

She pants a couple breaths, her desire running as rampant as mine. I expect her to push me off and climb on top of me. If she does, I'm a goner. I can't resist her any longer. I don't want to. Being with her in my sanctuary and so open and bare has my whole being twisted around her. I am at her mercy now.

She doesn't respond to me right away, choosing instead to

brush her lips to mine again. I give into her need for affection, listening as her heart finally stops racing and she relaxes. I don't need Dante's list. I think I can handle Raven on my own and in my own way. The only reason I'll even look at his instructions again is purely for Raven. I know she wants to see it. I know she wants for me to do everything on it. I don't even think it's because Dante wrote it. She is constantly belittling me and reminding me that because I'm still an angel, she doesn't completely trust me, but I'm going to change that. Starting here and now.

I've made mistakes. I'm starting to figure out how to find redemption for them. I just have to believe that everything I have faced and everything I have done up to this point was part of my journey. I don't think the Higher Power would purposefully lead me in the wrong direction. My brethren all fell as if their paths were intended to lead directly to Raven, jumping from grace to be damned. As for me? It just doesn't feel right. Not yet. This is why.

I can do something the others can't. I didn't lead the saviors just because. I was gifted with the same ability as Lucian. We can both manipulate planes. And with enough power, we can create them. It's how he started Hell. With his jump, he opened another realm. He led the way for the other devils. And me? It's my turn to lead the way for Raven. For Purgatory. For the rest of humanity. I'm not here to smite anyone. I'm not here to serve what I thought was justice for wayward souls. I'm here purely to teach and to learn things myself. I'm here to grow alongside Raven and the twins. I'm here to stand beside my brethren, regardless of which realm they connect to. We are not so different after all.

"Keep kissing me like this, and I'm not going to be able to do anything until I get off." Raven smiles against my lips. "That will defeat your supposed reward."

She's right about that. I silently pray she does ignore me and pushes me over. I pray she gives me what I want but refuse to ask for.

"Close your eyes, Raven. Tell me everything going through your mind when you do so. Tell me what you feel. What your senses focus on." My voice comes out raspy with lust, and I don't pull away. I continue to kiss her, exploring her mouth, trying my best to keep her focus solely on me.

She hums under her breath, the sexy sound doing nothing for the ache coursing through my body. "It's hard to explain. I feel as if I am everywhere and nowhere. I hear your quick breathing and the thudding of your heart every time I kiss you. You taste exactly how I imagine Heaven to be like if it was bottled into an elixir to drink. It's like sugary caramel and apple. Like rain and sunshine. Like hope. I taste everything pure in this world as if I'm drinking cool, fresh water after having my head shoved into the sand. I never want it to end, but I also want to carry it with me instead of staying."

"Then do it. Imagine you can carry the very essence of this place. What does it look like to you in your mind's eye?" I stare at her closed eyelids, her whole being lighting up.

It envelops around us, hugging me in everything she is, everything she can be, and everything we are together. The light grows brighter and brighter until it's all I can see and the world shifts.

Raven builds her own tether, twining it through mine to connect to my sanctuary. Her fingers light up, and she snaps her eyes open, staring at the glittering diamond in her palm.

"Holy shit. I did it." She gawks at the diamond, shifting her gaze from it to me. "I can't believe I did it."

The world shakes around us, and Raven drops the diamond, shattering it across the plane.

Darkness swells within her, and something triggers her volatile emotions.

Snatching her up, I hold her close, not allowing her to shift between planes without me.

I blink my eyes, my vision hazy. This can't be. Raven somehow managed to pull us both from the sanctuary, snapping my tether in the process.

We stand in a realm of shadows and light.

I see Raven's soul, guarded by a dozen angels.

They turn their swords on me and Raven.

Spreading my wings, I launch into the air, determined to grab it.

But the world shifts again.

I lose connection to her soul.

Pain bursts through my very being.

Everything disappears.

Last Stand

RAVEN

F EAR CLENCHES MY chest. Hovering over Cassius, I plant my hands on his shoulders and shake him. I don't know what happened. One second, I felt unimaginable power with the tether I managed to grab onto in his sanctuary, and then in the next, I find my soul standing before me with a dozen angels surrounding it.

We were so close to my soul that I could feel it trying to reconnect with me deep in my being. But something severed it. And whatever did that, also did something to Cassius. He remains unconscious on the floor of the sanctuary. The tether I clung to yanked us back.

"Damn it, Cass-hole. Wake your ass up. Please." I shake him again, harder this time.

Still, he doesn't move.

Pinching his chin, I turn his face from side to side and then I lean down. "Hey, fuckhead! Wake up!" I scream out in frustration, and hellfire explodes in my hands.

It tumbles from my fingers and smacks Cassius in the chest, jolting him upright. He hollers in surprise, expanding his wings. His eyes flash with his heavenly power, and he unsheathes his sword, sending blue fire dancing across the blade.

"Get it together. It's me." I lock my fingers around his arm, forcing his hand down so he doesn't accidentally stab me.

Cassius's eyes dart back-and-forth, his mouth hanging open. This time, I slap him. I don't know what else to do.

"Cassius! Focus!" Fear rattles me, and my whole body trembles. It's unlike him to have something affect him in a way that he can't get his shit together. And I'm scared. He's supposed to protect me. He's supposed to take care of me.

"Raven, your soul. Your soul. Your soul." He repeats the words over and over again, his eyes continuing to shift until they roll back into his head. He falls unconscious once more, and light blooms from his heart, growing across his skin.

What should I do? What the fuck do I do? "Elias!" I shake Cassius again, trying to get him to wake the fuck up. I know Elias should be able to reach us, but I don't know exactly how to contact him. Or if I can even do it on my own.

Silence greets me, and Cassius glows brighter and brighter.

"Shit. Fuck. Damn it. Cock-sucker." I struggle to get to my feet, the world turning blinding white around me. There must be something I can do. I need to ground myself.

Focus. I can do this.

Closing my eyes, I try to use my other senses to get a feel of the world around me. It's hard to concentrate as my eyelids turn bright red. I don't know what the hell is happening with Cassius, but it's as if he might detonate at any second. Can an angel actually explode? I have no fucking idea. I don't want to find out.

I inhale a deep breath. "I taste berries. Fizzy carbonation. Tingles blooming on my skin. The ground shakes beneath my feet. My heart pounds in my ears more erratically than Cassius's. The light envelops me. I can feel the electricity of it. It shocks through my bones, wrapping around me, tethering to my wrists."

I talk myself through everything as if I'm speaking to Cassius. I hold my hands out, cupping them and imagining the electric, blinding light zapping my fingers and gathering on my palms.

Something icy lashes over my arms, and I stumble forward, landing on my hands and knees. Snapping my eyes open, I stare in shock at the laces of angelic light tangling around me as a brilliant force pulls me across Cassius's sanctuary. I scream and fight, twisting so that I'm not pressed stomach down. Cassius's figure lies motionlessly on the floor, and I buck and wiggle, fighting to move so he can block my path.

"Cassius!" I scream, my voice ripping through the air. A wave of fire shoots from my body, my Hell power taking over. It strikes Cassius in the side, sending him rolling.

He jerks his head up with a growl and whips his attention around the sanctuary. His eyes widen as they land on me, fighting against the light dragging me right toward his legs. Spreading his wings, he launches forward and grabs onto me, lifting me into his arms. He hugs his wings around us and skids across the ground, trying to slow us down.

"Something's wrong. I think they managed to hook you using your soul, because we shifted from my sanctuary." Cassius grinds his teeth, gathering heavenly light to shoot in the direction of the pure electricity refusing to let us go.

"Break the line. Come on. Do something. You can't let them take me." I clutch onto him tighter, biting my nails into his skin and burying my face in the crook of his neck. "Please. You promised to protect me."

Cassius growls under his breath, trying to resist the pull of the tether with all his strength. "I will. I won't let you down."

We continue to skid across the plane until my whole body zings, and I can feel myself closing in on my soul. I can hear the cry of my being shouting for me. I gasp, the swelling emotions turning unbearable as grief, pain, heartache, loneliness, and fury crash through me. I can't believe this is happening. How is this possible?

A dozen silhouettes grow and materialize within the blinding light, and golden wings stretch out, turning the world so bright that it's all I can see. My eyes burn, watering with my tears. Cassius swings out his sword and slices it across the lines of light tangling me, and pain steals my breath away. Agony clutches me, and it feels as if I lose my soul all over again.

"Cassius, it's time. Bring us the heavenly gifts. Do not stand against us. You are not a traitor." Mikail's deep voice reverberates through my bones. "You know what must be done. You cannot fight against us, and you know it."

Cassius hollers, jerking to a halt with every fiber of his being, shaking the sanctuary. "Raven, you need to open a portal. I can't concentrate on stabilizing us and shifting through realms. Do it now!"

I fucking hate pressure.

I hate the angelic army.

I hate all of this.

"Raven!" Cassius shouts again, skidding forward.

I squeeze my eyes shut, saying a prayer to the universe to help me. Fire and light explode from my hands, blasting the silhouettes back. Cassius yanks my being, sending pain crashing through me. I gasp, my body going numb. I lose control over my power, and the angels gather once more.

"Raven, I'm sorry," Cassius whispers, grinding his teeth hard enough for me to hear. "I've failed you so much as a savior. I've failed humanity."

I stiffen at his words. "Don't say that. You haven't failed until this is over, dickhead. I swear, Cass-hole. You need to—"

Crashing his lips to mine, Cassius unfurls his wings, expanding them wide on his back. He creates a wall between me and the guardians, growling as they blast their heavenly light at him. His skin lights aglow, his feathers buzzing. Some escape his wings, floating on the wave of energy humming through the air.

"Cassius! Give her to us. Now!" Mikail shouts, his voice bouncing around the world.

Cassius's grip on me loosens, and he eases away from my mouth, putting space between our faces. The world quakes and rocks, and fissures of darkness break through the world. Setting me on my feet, Cassius rolls his shoulders.

"You've fallen from your path, brother. You've disgraced all of Heaven. This is the right choice. Do what must be done." Mikail extends his hand out, wiggling his fingers toward me.

I jolt forward, the strange light reeling me closer. Screaming, I stretch my arms to Cassius, trying to grab onto him. He doesn't move. He doesn't look at me. The world crumbles around me in flashes of light and dark—not shadows, just absolute nothingness.

"Cassius!" Fire and light erupt from my hands again, setting Cassius aglow.

He launches forward, spreading his wings, wielding his angelic sword. The fire ignites across it, shifting from blue to turquoise, as if a hint of orange explodes from the blade. He hooks his arm around me at the same time that he slashes his sword through the tangle of heavenly strings dragging me toward the angels. The lines snap, releasing me. Mikail and his soldiers kick into action, charging forward as they steal the realm from Cassius. He spins midair, and fire erupts over his arms, licking across his skin and eating away at the tethers of heavenly light the angels try to trap us with.

"You all have failed Heaven. You have failed humanity and the universe. This was not how it was supposed to be. I will not let you take the one who will set things right. Raven is mine." Cassius's voice deepens as his wings spark aglow, turning from white to the most mesmerizing blues and greens and turquoise as a strange new power explodes over his skin.

Mikail tries to blast us one more time. My fury triggers the twins, and another flash of dark and light escapes me, cracking the foundation of the realm.

Cassius adjusts me in his arms and dives through a crack in the brilliant white, and the plane shifts as he jumps from his sanctuary. My whole body screams with unbidden emotions. Grief and turmoil mixed with relief and excitement. It's as if I experience a hurricane within me and I'm not sure if I can withstand the destruction that comes with it. I'm not sure I'm strong enough.

My heart jumps into my throat, and I close my eyes, listening to the sudden roaring flames. Cassius snuggles his face into the crook of my throat as if he doesn't want to look around either. We cling to each other as the world zooms around us, and we tumble through a realm of fire and brimstone. The tortured souls of Hell scream in my ears, and I gasp, realizing what's happening. Cassius didn't leave his sanctuary to return to the Mortal Realm. He turned his back on Heaven. He turned his back on the guardians and their purpose. He jumped from Heaven for me. He chose me. He chose Hell and the devils. But most importantly, he finally realized that it was about neither of us. It was about humanity.

A boom echoes through the world, and I wince at the loud noise deafening everything else. Silence greets us as we jerk to a stop, and Cassius lands in a crouch, his magnificent, vibrant form unlike any of the other devils. His wings glow blue and green as if heavenly fire remains with him but adapts to the Hell plane. His wings no longer glow with white feathers, and I can't help caressing my fingers over the deep sapphire and emerald tones that sparkle with flecks of iridescent purples.

I blink a few times, staring into his shining amethyst eyes, the color the same as the holographic glitter sparkling from his wings. His features shift, and beneath his dark hair grows a crown of a dozen short horns peeking out from his head, wrapping around it completely. The muscles on his body ripple under my touch, and I want to hop from his arms to look at the rest of him. He doesn't let me go though. He squeezes me tighter, burying his face into my hair once more. The act of jumping from grace hits him hard, and he exhales a long breath. We are alone in this new level of Hell that I've never seen before. Souls scream and move, pooling around us as if they wait for their king to control them.

"I feel so lost," Cassius murmurs, his warm breath tickling my skin. His voice cracks, and for the first time ever, his defenses falter. He's no longer the tough asshole angel I just learned to tolerate. He's the ruler of the Pride Kingdom, and I was his downfall... No. I refuse to believe that. I wasn't his destruction. I've helped him rise. He can see past everything now. He knows he's where he belongs, beside me and the other devils.

"I know. I feel lost too, but we're going to get through this together. Now set me down, so I can get a better look at you." I pat his cheek, forcing my lips to smile despite my whole body reeling over the fact that Heaven almost took me.

"We need to find my brother." Cassius ignores my command and shifts me in his arms to cradle me like a blushing bride.

My stomach flips and flops, the twins tumbling around as if they are coming down from the surge of energy we all experienced.

"Cassius, he will find us. You just jumped from grace. You need to take a moment. You don't have to go running. Just breathe." I get him to focus on me, and I bow forward and caress my lips to his, wanting him to know that no matter what differences we've had and how things weren't always great between us, that things are changing. We're no longer on separate sides. He is now a ruler of Hell, and he claimed me. He told the guardians that I was his, cementing my place by his side. I don't even have to question it to know that he was serious. It came from his very being and was the turning point for him, cracking the realms to bring us home. To bring him to the place he will be the strongest. The place that will help us save everything.

Cassius doesn't pull away, devouring my affection as if my kiss awakens something new inside him. And maybe it does.

Tingles rush over my body, and I can't help myself from reaching to feel more of him. I draw my fingers over his shoulders and back to the soft feathers of his wings, wiggling in his arms until he has no choice but to set me on my feet. I stand before him, but he doesn't let me move more than a couple inches, not allowing much space to get between us.

His clothes hang in tatters, the fire burning through them

and exposing him. Muscles ripple over his body, and he lets go of his angel façade completely. I step back, watching as his neck elongates and his nose and mouth sharpen into a jutting point almost like a beak. Sharp fangs glisten in the fiery light around us, and I trail my gaze over his boxy body, bulking up to his claw-like feet, the talons sharper than Kase's claws.

And then I see the most shocking yet fascinating thing in my life. Two thick, rod-like pieces of flesh grow between his legs, pointing in my direction, one on top of the other. I always knew he was a dick, and the fact that he now has two? It proves it. And unholy Hell. My mind can barely wrap around any of this.

I place my hands on my hips, just staring at the two hefty appendages, thinking dirty thoughts that I probably shouldn't in this moment. Cassius just jumped from grace for fuck's sake, and here I am, channeling my conductor position on Dante's Kinky Express. I'd say my thoughts would send me to Hell, but we're already here.

"Say something, Raven." Cassius shifts, his talons cutting into the onyx floor and sending sparks of fire through the air. "Is it bad? I'm afraid to look at myself."

I keep my face expressionless and shuffle to him completely until I wrap each one of my hands around both of his cocks and give him a surprise stroke.

"Depends on who you ask. I think you look intimidating

on every level. Glorious. And double the cocky bastard that grew on me these last couple months. I mean, look at these things. I'm going to take your fucking virginity to find out what these are capable of." I laugh at my own joke, watching as Cassius's eyes widen in surprise only to have my suggestion sink in. His two dicks grow harder, and I drop my gaze to them again, letting him see what it looks like with my hands around them.

He puffs a breath of air, his majestic wings spreading wide, the shape rounder than they were before, and far more expansive too. I'm pretty sure Dante is going to be jealous as fuck, and I'll have to remind him how much I love his black feathers and how he knows how to tickle me and all the right places.

"Cassius, Raven. I felt the powershift. What happened? The others are on their way. Are you hurt, heathen?" The ground rumbles with Micah's thunderous footsteps, and he charges from the swirling souls.

I drop my hands from Cassius's cocks, the reality of what happened setting in now that I can no longer distract myself with his new devil form.

"They used Raven to crack my sanctuary. They forced me to cut my ties to the heavenly plane. It was time. Raven got to experience what it was like to ground herself to a plane that wasn't hers, and she might not be an expert, but she can still manage. I think she'll be able to get into Heaven, even without me. Elias can be her guide." Cassius drops his arm across my shoulders and pulls me into his side as if he doesn't want even a foot of space between us.

"They're going to expect us to try," I say, my voice soft with the words.

"And we will be ready. If you can get into Heaven on your own and tether yourself there, we might be able to join you or at least be close enough to guide you and your soul home." Cassius leans forward to look in my eyes. "We can practice."

The ground quakes, and I watch a portal open up and the other devils come through. I can't stop myself from pulling away from Cassius to run to them. I want nothing more than to have them engulf me in their arms.

Lucian claps hands once. "It's about fucking time. Welcome home, brother."

If only it felt more like home.

Unless I get my soul back, I don't think it will ever be.

This is it. Cassius is right.

I'm already running out of time, and it's time to fight. Even if it's the last thing I do as a mortal.

Heaven can't win. My soul isn't theirs. It's mine. It'll always be mine.

10

Final Wishes

RAVEN

I STARE AT the unfamiliar house—or should I say, mansion—towering in front of me across a sprawling lawn. It felt like no time had passed while I was with Cassius in his sanctuary and only a few days as he grew used to Hell, but in actuality, two weeks have gone by. Two weeks closer to what could possibly be my end.

I shove the thoughts away and smile at Lucian. "You picked this place out?"

"Only if you like it. If not, then it was Cassius." Lucian swings my hand, letting me drink in the sight of it instead of dragging me inside.

His devil façade flashes across his handsome face. "And if that's the case, we'll fucking move. We want you to love the home that we will spend the rest of time in while we're on the mortal plane."

I try to suppress the sadness rolling through me. It's hard for me to think the way he does. I know the devils want to have hope, but I'm just struggling. Cassius fell, and the only one we have left that still has a connection to Heaven is Elias. If he falls now, I'll be alone. I'll have no one and my soul will shatter.

I force myself to smile and nudge Lucian in the shoulder with the back of my hand. "I love it. I love it so much. Show me the inside."

Lucian scoops me into his arms and carries me toward the grand entrance gleaming with polished concrete outside.

"Raven! Hey!" Tamia waves at me from the doorway, her hair pulled up into a high ponytail. She's been taking care of a lot of the demonic business for Lucian, and it's the first time I've seen her in weeks. "Isn't this place fucking amazing? Just wait until you see the—"

Lucian flicks his fingers, sending a burst of power at her, stopping her from finishing her sentence. "Don't spoil the surprise. You don't want to piss off all these devils, Tee."

Tamia rolls her eyes. "I doubt anything will piss them off right now, especially when Raven sees everything. Plus, you know how much she hates surprises."

"This is different. She won't be getting a big fucking cock in her hand until later." Lucian chuckles at his words and Tamia rolls her eyes again. I'm nearly certain she can see her brain matter at this point.

My heart swells with their banter. I appreciate their friendship now that things have settled between Lucian and me. It'll be good to know that she will be safe for all of eternity. She'll also be here to help the devils when needed. She was always here for me, even when Joel isolated me, and I trust her with my children. As much as I love the devils, the twins need someone who knows the Mortal World as a mortal.

I suppress the thought again. I need to stop thinking like that.

"Probably more than one." Tamia holds her arms out, hugging me within Lucian's arms before resting her palms to my stomach. A peel of laughter escapes her at the babies kicking, and I finally find myself smiling in earnest. "Damn. They're already so feisty. Look at them move. Like that alien movie where it rips—"

I reach out and slap my hand over her smiling mouth. "Don't even start."

Kase growls from behind her, hovering in the grand foyer. He blasts a burst of red power at her feet, making her jump. "Yeah, Tamia. Knock that shit off. If Raven can handle fucking all of us, then she—"

"Enough! No more talking about alien babies or devil fuck-ing. I just want a damn tour. You've all seen the place. It's my turn." I shift and graze my knuckles on Lucian's beard. "If you hurry, I'll sit on your face."

Lucian hums and summons his fire chain, whipping it around to get everyone to back off. He dodges around Kase, who attempts to intervene, and I squeal and laugh as I bounce in his arms. Racing toward an elevator, he hits the button, forcing the others to take the stairs. I'll never get used to having an elevator, though with the way all the devils currently carry me around, I doubt I'll ever appreciate not having to take the stairs.

Lucian surprises me, smacking his hand to the emergency stop button, halting the elevator. Propping me against the wall, he bows in and kisses me. I don't know if it's the sudden distraction or because my heart flutters wildly now so full of excitement or what, but I give in to his need to steal me away from the others, even if only for a moment.

"I want to lick your pussy until you beg for mercy, Ray. Get that piercing humming with my power." He slides his hand between my legs, teasing the line of my thong. "And when you can't take another second, I'm going to restrain you to this wall and spank you until you're weak in the knees and beg me to carry you to our new room to fuck you senseless."

Wetness tingles between my legs at his desire, and I nearly

give in. "Not this second, Satan. The tour first."

"We'll see if you say the same thing in a second. You'll beg me to kidnap you for the rest of the night despite it not belonging to me." He drops me to my feet, spins me around, and pulls my hair, tilting my head to the side. His hot mouth caresses my throat, and he slides his fingers into the band of my thong and snaps it against my skin. "You can submit now and make it easy on yourself. Be my good little princess."

"What's the fun in that? I know you like to get rough. You love working hard for me." I stretch my neck, tipping my head back to meet his fiery eyes.

"You wicked queen. Maybe for once I want you to worship me. Go easy on me. Haven't I been a good enough devil?" Lucian grazes his mouth to mine, trapping my bottom lip between his teeth as he stretches it. His hand slides lower until he dips it between my legs, feeling my excitement for him. He eases his finger out and pops it into his mouth, sucking it, watching me watch him.

"A little too good. You should've already started fucking me by now. I know that's what you want." I wiggle my ass, feeling his hard body ready to take mine. I know he might've been waiting for me to give him permission to proceed, but I'm beyond that with him. With any of my devils. I want them to take what they want from me and let me have whatever I need from them. "I think I see some heavenly light shining from your back. Maybe you've followed in Elias's footsteps and now have taken your asshole brother's place. Have you seen him as a devil yet? How are you going to compete with two cocks? You know I can't wait to try him out."

Lucian growls, the heat of his breath scorching over my skin in a way that makes me gasp. He yanks my hair harder, spinning me around, and then he lifts me up by my ass and rips my panties right off me. He leans in close, his beard tickling my chin as he shares my breathing space. "You're going to pay for those words, Raven. There is no competition to win. You're mine. Do you understand?"

"He claimed me too. Did you know that? The second before he jumped, Cassius said that I was his." I hum with my teasing words. He would never admit it, but he likes when I get him riled up like this. He wants to prove that I'm wrong, especially when it comes to Cassius.

The guttural noise that escapes Lucian's throat vibrates across my neck, the sound so sexy that I can't stop myself from reaching between us to grab him by his cock.

"You think I'm going to just let him stake a claim on the woman I've worked so hard to get after everything he has done? Fuck no. He's going to have to prove his damn worth. He can claim you all he wants along with his throne in Hell, but I won't accept it until he shows he's powerful enough to have you. Until then, he's going to know that I had you first."

Lucian unfastens his belt and pulls out his cock, using the tip to rub against my clit.

I moan and wiggle, trying to break his hold, but he doesn't let me. He keeps me trapped against the elevator wall, kissing me deeply, his tongue dominating mine as he thrusts inside me hard enough that his movements force me onto my tiptoes. I cling onto him, letting him bounce me and hit my back to the wall. The whole elevator shakes with our movements, his power exploding through me in wave after delicious wave.

He reaches between us and taps my piercing, sending intense vibrations through me. I scream out in pleasure and my body zings. His cock ring strokes my insides, and I feel my orgasm coming harder than ever. It feels as if I'll implode or explode and take us both to Hell. And I want to. I just want to let everything go and experience what it's like being with Hell's most notorious devil in his kingdom over and over.

I gasp, my body tensing as I come, the shockwave enough to steal my breath. I dig my nails into Lucian's shoulders until he bleeds, unable to do anything accept ride the feelings like a never ending wave of ecstasy.

He thrusts harder, deeper, and faster, and I can't do anything but just lose myself and everything he is. I savor his strength and power, feeling as if I absorb it into me. Lucian's devil form flashes before me, and I reach up and grab onto his horns, using them to give extra resistance to my body. He groans and growls, his eyes lighting with fire until he finally grunts with his release. Flashes of Hell dance across my vision, and I wait for the world to settle. He really can fuck the Hell into me, and it feels like a part of me is home.

"You're fucking so irresistible. Beautiful. More stunning than ever." He adjusts me in his arms, sliding out of me only to cradle me and kiss me again.

Swinging his hand toward the wall, he slaps his palm to the elevator button, sending us lurching upward a few feet until we come to a halt on the top floor of the mansion. Voices murmur through the door, and I know that everyone waits for us. I bet they knew Lucian would fuck me on the way up. I'm sure all of them would've done the same.

The door slides open and I frown, realizing I was wrong. No one waits on the other side. But I can hear them. Their voices echo down the grand hallway, still in need of decorating.

"Why do you look disappointed? You know, we could fuck again." Lucian tugs my attention to him, pinching my chin and getting me to meet my lips to his once more.

"If you fucking try, I'm joining in. And since we'd have to share, you'd be taking my tail in your ass. Dante would want her pouty mouth if he can't have her ass or pussy." Kase leans against the wall outside of the double doors. I can't stop the smile crossing my face, wondering if Lucian would agree to such a thing. He's as possessive and dominating as Kase.

Neither of them seems like the bottom type.

"I'll fucking break your tail off and tie it around your neck if you even try." Lucian strides forward, trying to use his devilish height to intimidate Kase, but nothing Lucian does can threaten him now.

Kase grins wider. "You can go ahead and fucking try. Raven might blast your ass to the pits. You know she considers my tail her most prized possession."

I tip my head back and laugh, the ridiculousness of his words getting to me in a good way. "He's right. And you're lucky I only like to share his tail with Dante." I meet Kase's dark burgundy eyes, flashing with his red power. "You can share me with your tail. When your cock needs a break, your tail can take over. I might need it to play with my clit for a bit. You know I love that."

Kase purrs, the sound feline yet sexy. "Fuck. Lucian get her ass to the room before I take her up on that offer. Her cousin and Gia are here, and I really doubt they want to witness our attempt to give her our devil seed, keeping her pregnant for eternity."

I'm surprised they haven't done so already. I don't know how it happened before, but I would accept a lifetime of being pregnant with devil after devil's children as long as it meant that I never had to face the reality of where my soul rests.

"I'm down for that kind of show. Would be a lot more entertaining than managing our asshole contracts. They're stupid disobedient souls lately. I think they can sense the possibility of what's to come." Gia's voice sounds through the air, drawing my attention away from Kase and my own thoughts. "I heard that you like that kind of thing, Ray. Being watched."

"Fuck no. That's my cousin. If you want to watch someone, you can watch me, babe." Tamia grins with her words, flicking Hell power at Gia, Kase and Dante's first in command when it comes to their mortal ventures.

"All right, save your kinky asses for the guestroom. Now's a time to celebrate and not put on a show that none of us want to see. We are family. There are children here." Dante chuckles with his words, opening his arms and wiggling his fingers in my direction.

"I'm sure they're used to your nasty, boundary pushing, dirty deeds. I'm surprised that they don't blast you away just to stop feeling their whole world shake." Gia laughs, dodging out of the way.

It's so strange to see her and my cousin relaxed...and maybe together. They're companions for sure, and this all feels so normal. I don't know whether I should be happy or scared that we even get a moment like this. I feel as if when things seem to be okay that it's just the world bracing for complete destruction and annihilation.

A flash of brilliant light erupts through the air, and my devils and the demons shield their eyes and stop messing around. Elias spreads his wings, using his heavenly light to grab every-one's attention.

My heart clenches as I see him. He's been more distant, and I worry that it's because of me. Because of Cassius's fall. But I don't have time to think about it for long.

Zade and Andre open the double doors completely, and I spot Micah standing within a summoning circle in the corner of a gigantic nursery. Tears fill my eyes the second I see the twins' cribs, two bassinets, two rocking chairs, and a gigantic bed large enough to sleep all of us. I know that the devils each have their individual rooms with me, but they've designed this one not only as the twins' room, but also as a family suite for all of us.

My shoulders shake as sobs grab a hold of me. I want so badly for this life. I want so desperately to know that once I have my babies that we will be dealing with changing diapers, breastfeeding, sleep deprivation, and everything that comes with being parents without the burden of humanity or the universe weighing heavily on us. I want to be able to decorate more, add pictures of all of us, and just live a mundane life for as long as we can.

"Angel-girl, you're not supposed to cry. This isn't intended to make you feel bad. This is to show you that no matter what, we're going to make the perfect life for you happen. There is no other option except for this." Kase steals me away from Lucian and engulfs me in his arms.

"I know. It's just—" I hiccup and shudder, finding it harder than ever to stop the wild emotions coursing through me. It's everything weighing on me. Even without my soul, I can now just tap into the energy that zings through me. I feel too much. I'm starting to think it was better to feel nothing at all. At least being numb saved me from this pain.

"Being numb would also deprive you of everything you deserve, heathen. It would steal your joy, your love, your hope. You don't truly want that. I know everything is so unfair right now, but it's why we fight, and why we will fight harder, better. We've already regained control of Hell, and the guardians are freaking out. They know we're going to come for them. Cassius's descent solidified it." Micah stands tall within the summoning circle, responding to my silent thoughts out loud for everyone to hear.

With his words about Cassius, I can't help turning to look for my double dick devil. He hovers in the corner of the room and away from the others. His eyes meet mine, and his wings appear only to vanish, reminding me of their mesmerizing change. Should I feel bad that he looks like a rejected devil or an uninvited guest we were too nice to send away? Probably not. But I can't help it. His descent with me in his arms replays in my mind. I could feel him breaking apart to rebuild himself to withstand Hell. I felt his emptiness with losing the grace of Heaven and the pain of refilling his being with Hell power. He still thinks he failed everyone despite him jumping to save me from the angelic army.

As if Zade knows what I'm thinking, he strides the distance to Cassius and drapes his arm over his shoulders. "Which I am so relieved about. I've missed you, Cass. I know you've been around, but it hasn't been the same. Now things will go how they were always intended."

Lucian groans, rolling his eyes, looking dramatic as fuck. "Don't give him a bunch of fucking praise. His stubborn ass could've prevented all of this from happening had he just swallowed his pride and done what he was supposed to."

"He has a point." Dante flaps his wings once, sending a gust of wind through the air.

I sigh and rub my hands over my cheeks, their banter now distracting me enough that I can pull myself together. I sniffle and wiggle until my feet touch the floor. All my devils surround me and encircle me in their muscular bodies, hugging and kissing me as they try to ensure I stay together instead of falling apart.

"If there's something you don't like, we can change it." Kase runs his fingers through my hair, pulling the damp strands from my cheeks. "This is just the beginning."

I swallow and shudder again. "It's perfect. So, so perfect. I love you all."

They each take a moment to hug me again, and then I break away and stroll around the grand suite where the twins will stay. I can't even imagine what life will be like. It's not only because of my worry about what happens if we don't get my soul back, but I just still can't grasp the fact that I'm going to have twins. With the devils. With my soulmate.

With the thought of Elias, I flick my attention to him. My eyes water again, and I hold my arms open, begging for him to come closer. I need his embrace. I need his assurance. This is all so hard. He's the last angel standing, and a part of me is terrified of him falling.

Flapping his wings, Elias closes the distance without touching his feet to the floor. He lands in front of me and embraces me, wrapping his wings around the two of us until all I see is his iridescent, rainbow light. I listen as everyone quietly leaves the nursery, and I'm certain Micah told them that my mind wanders to a moment I need alone with my soulmate.

Elias eases back and stares into my glassy eyes. "Oh, darlin'. Your sadness breaks my heart. I don't know what to do to help. I'm trying so desperately to figure out exactly where the angelic army is keeping your soul, but every time I enter the heavenly plane, they're waiting."

I flutter my eyelashes, clearing my vision. "I know everyone is trying their best, Elias. It's just...I'm so scared. You're the last one connected to Heaven. I'm so afraid that something is going to change, and you might have to jump like Cassius did before I get my soul back. If that happens, and Heaven manages to keep my soul, I'll be so alone. I know it's selfish of me, because you also deserve to be here in the Mortal Realm, but I can't help thinking the thoughts. The twins need you. But I need you too. I need all of you, and it kills me at the thought that I might never get that. And every day that passes is like I'm shoveling another mound of dirt into my grave of eternal isolation."

Elias tenses, his muscular arms tightening around me. Heavenly light radiates from his being, and he scowls. But it's not at me. It's at the situation and everything I'm suddenly feeling in this moment. It has taken months to feel like myself again. And the closer I stand to Elias, the closer I feel to being the same. And it hurts. It hurts so much that I can't ignore the ache burning through me.

"Raven, you will never be alone. Do you understand? We will defeat the angelic army." Elias cups my cheeks, smearing his thumbs across the new streams of tears.

"I want to believe that with every fiber of my being, but I need assurance from you that if it doesn't work out that...I'm sorry. This is too much to ask of you." I bow forward and rest my head to his shoulder, my tears soaking into his shirt as I sob again.

Elias rubs his hands over my spine, massaging circles to loosen my tight muscles. "It is not too much to ask of me. If everything fails, I will be by your side. You will never be alone. The devils agree with me. As much as they hate the idea of not being the ones to enter that plane to ensure your peace, they also don't want you to suffer. We have a backup plan. I promise."

I sniffle and squeeze my eyes shut, feeling the babies shift in me, moving around in my belly, as if they just want Elias to give them attention too.

Kneeling down, he rests his palms to my belly and kisses it through my shirt. I play with his hair, staring over his head as the devils linger just outside, waiting for me to call them in again.

"I will take care of Mama. I promise." Elias kisses my stomach again, and I start crying, the tears never seeming to stop.

I hold my arms open once more, calling the devils to me. Hellfire billows in the corner as Micah materializes into view. He must've remained just on the other side, refusing to leave the entrance of the Hell portal in case he's needed here. I wish with everything in me that he could come closer, but his presence is enough. The other devils shower me with their affection again.

"We're all going to take care of Mama," Dante says, touching my belly. "And we're going to take care of you both too."

Light and shadow radiate from me, hazing the room around us. I gasp as we shift planes, all of us together, as if the twins try to respond.

It's in this moment I realize they make a silent promise as well. We're not only going to take care of them. They will take care of us.

We will make it through this together.

I will no longer accept another option. I can't. Things must change. We must fight first.

And as the world shimmers in front of me, and I glimpse the sight of my soul through the veil, I know what must be done. We must take the war to Heaven.

I will make the whole plane fall.

11

Broken Realm

RAVEN

"FOCUS, DARLIN'. I know you would prefer to have Micah open the portal, but I want you to do it. If you can open the Hell portal every time without hesitation, it'll make things easier to replicate it with Heaven. We're going to have to move fast. We'll have a matter of a minute once I cross through to the heavenly plane." Elias rests his hands on my shoulders. "Think about Micah and remember what it's like in his kingdom. Use that to break through."

I exhale a deep breath, pushing away the tightness of my nerves. Elias hovers behind me, sliding his hands down to rest on my belly with his taut chest against my back. He and Micah are the ones teaching me to move through the realms more naturally now. We won't be practicing with Heaven, so it was the best for Elias to be on this side with Micah in his kingdom because they still have a bond. They work great as a team. The other devils are now out and ensuring that the guardians stay busy. They don't want to give them time to plot against us. Everyone knows that time is running out, and the angelic army would prefer to just wait. So we have to be active.

For my plan to work, I need to be able to shift everyone from plane to plane. I don't even know if it'll be possible, but I hope that if I can at least shatter the veil long enough, we can manage to conquer the assholes and get my soul in time.

"Apart from Micah, what do you like about his kingdom?" Elias keeps his voice low as if he speaks loudly, he'll interrupt my concentration.

"I miss seeing Spike, Sam, and Dean. I want to have some fun hunting with them. It's been too long." I never even got the chance to enjoy Micah's hellhounds. The majestic beasts were incredible and not as scary as I imagined. The thought of their fiery bodies is enough to trigger my power, and fire explodes in my hands. Elias's suggestion worked.

Thrusting my hands at the floor of the basement, I manage to crack the realms and open up a portal to Hell. There's no summoning circle or anything. I can feel the energy of the twins swirling through me, helping me. It's like they now know what to expect, and when they know what I need, they help out. I never knew I could love someone I've never even met, but I do. I love the twins more than I ever imagined. It's knowing that they need me, and the devils need me, that pushes me to focus. It helps push me harder.

"Perfect, darlin'. Now, I want you to cross the plane and pull me with you. Imagine you're binding us together. Don't let me go." Elias kisses the back of my head.

Locking my hands over Elias's arms, I hold him tight and step forward. I don't jump into the portal and instead imagine floating until the floor beneath our feet vanishes. The world hazes and darkens around us, but I don't fall. I manage to ease us into the plane and not crash into it. It has never felt so effortless, even with the devils moving me through the planes. This time, with my control, I feel like I belong and am not catching a ride down.

Flames crackle in my ears, and I open my eyes and stare at Micah towering in front of me. A beaming smile brightens his eyes, turning him even more handsome. His velvety skin glows with the firelight, and I automatically pull Elias forward until I sandwich myself between them.

"I knew you could do it, heathen. And look who's here. They missed you." Micah whistles, calling the three-headed hellhound in our direction.

I laugh and hold my arms open, letting the fiery beasts bow

low so their heads meet my eye level. I scrub my fingers into each of their heads, not even fazed by the black goo seeping over my fingers. "Who are the good boys? You are good boys." I make kissy noises at the hellhounds, making both Elias and Micah laugh.

"Only you would talk to a hellhound like that, Raven," Micah muses and scratches the beasts under each of their chins.

"There's no other way to talk to such big scary boys. Aren't you guys just so big and scary? You keep all those souls in their places, don't you? My good hellhounds. Yes, you boys are." I laugh and finally step back, wiping my hands on my dress, though the hellhound's saliva disappears completely, probably because of Micah.

"What am I going to do with you, darlin'? You're going to tame all of the beasts of Hell." Elias grins and gives me a little shake.

I bite my lip with a smile. "That's the plan."

Elias leans in and kisses me. "And you'll have plenty of time after you're trained, okay?"

Sighing, I tip my head back toward the fiery sky. "That's going to take forever."

"It's a good thing we're going to get it. Promise." Elias eases away, putting space between us. "Now, I'm going to return to the Mortal Realm so you can portal back to me. I can tell that the souls are beginning to gather, and I think you need an incentive to help Micah shift through planes. This one will be a bit harder. He's tethered to Hell, so it's going to take more energy. Tap into the soul stones you've been collecting. Manifest them if you have to."

Fucking manifestation. It might be my least favorite thing to do, considering that I'm still figuring out how to do it. The devils make things look so easy and natural. The planes just bow to their every whim. I don't think I could even summon lube if my ass depended on it.

Chuckling, Micah swats my ass, obviously hearing my thoughts. "Go easy on yourself. We've been doing it forever, heathen. It'll get easier."

"I hope so. I don't want to always have to rely on everyone else." I purse my lips with the words.

"But you can, no matter what. Now, let me help you. I need you to release the tether you've wrapped around Elias completely, so we can start fresh. Let's take a moment to summon your stones to help. You already have one on your ring finger, so feel the energy first." Micah responds to my thoughts out loud, reminding me that we have a deep-seated mental connection. That's another reason why he's helping with this task instead of any of the other devils. If he can tap into my mind, he might be able to guide me better.

Elias kisses my cheek and then launches into the air, creating a light portal above Micah's kingdom. I don't turn back to

Micah until Elias disappears completely. An ache resonates inside me. It feels as if Elias takes a part of me with him, and it's hard to steel my emotions against the pain his absence causes.

Micah gathers me in his arms, brushing his lips to mine. "Release him. You'll feel better. Just take a breath and let me steal your complete attention. The shift in power kills me. I already miss the freedom that comes with being with you in the Mortal Realm." Brushing his lips to mine again, he ignites warmth in my being. His thoughts trickle to me, turning lustful as satisfaction courses through him. He's been dying to kiss me senseless since the moment I opened the portal with Elias.

I give in to his desire and slide my tongue into his mouth, kissing him deeper, tasting him in a way that excites me. The whole re-tethering to Hell was so sudden that neither of us had time to really prepare for it. We haven't had much time to be alone since then either, and I won't rush back to the Mortal Realm unless I have to. He deserves my attention and affection. He deserves to feel my appreciation for everything he's done. Everything he's sacrificed.

Sliding his hands lower, he rests them on my lower back. "I do feel that, Raven. I don't regret being the keeper of Hell's power source. You need to know that. I knew what I was getting into when I accepted it. I wouldn't change things, even knowing what I know now. This is my path. Never feel bad about it. I want to be the one in control when it's time for you to take Purgatory. Our connection strengthens me as your guide. It is my duty and place to be as a devil." Micah speaks to me through our thoughts, continuing to kiss me and push away every ounce of fear and nervousness over the situation. His kiss manages to clear my mind completely as he fills me up with everything he is. "Just as you've accepted your place as my queen, I've accepted my reign as king. Now, use me if you have to. Manifest my power from this realm and open yours to get the soul stones. Envision a door to walk through. Think about a table with a bowl on top. Imagine that bowl filled with the stones you've created. Imagine grabbing them and holding them in your hand. Do you feel the weight? The buzzing energy?"

I gasp and snap my eyes open, staring at the two large stones in my hand. They glitter in the firelight, the energy crackling across their surfaces. That was easier than I expected. Cassius could use some pointers from Micah on being a teacher and walking me through things. Micah might've even used me to summon them on my behalf.

"That was all you, Raven. I was only guiding you along the way," he says, ignoring my thought about Cassius. We both know Pride needs work still just as I do.

I roll one of the stones between my hands. "Which is why you're an excellent instructor. Far superior to Cass-hole."

Chuckling, he says, "Come on and concentrate, so you can

tell him as much. Imagine his expression and focus. I want you to take the energy and envision it growing tethers. Envision wrapping it around me, so you can take me with you when you cross the planes as we meet Elias and face Cassius to mess with him. Imagine hugging me tightly, and don't let me go." Micah strokes his fingers across my hands, helping me envision glowing white lines dancing from the stones. The illuminating tendrils of energy twist and move around him, tying around his hulking frame and suppressing his devilish nature.

The world hazes around us once more, and I gasp as I lead Micah back into the mortal plane where Elias stands in the middle of the basement, waiting for us. He applauds and hollers, pumping his fist in the air. His excitement matches mine, and I wag my ass in a happy dance.

"I can't believe I did it!" I screech, throwing my arms out. "I fucking did it!"

"Yeah—" Micah grunts, his words cutting off. The world shakes, trembling beneath my feet. I can't do anything as the tethers binding us together snap in half. Micah vanishes in a wave of fire, sending him back to Hell.

I cover my mouth, furrowing my brows. "Oh fuck. Damn it."

Elias snatches my hand, turning me toward him. "It's okay. He's just been banished and relocated back into his kingdom. You switched your focus from him to me and lost concentration. Don't stress about it. Micah is fine. You did perfect. We'll do it again."

I could kick myself. I didn't realize how fragile the tethers could be. It makes me worried about my plan. What if I manage to get into Heaven with the devils but then they get thrown right back out because I'm not strong enough to cling onto the tethers?

"I'm sorry." I know I shouldn't apologize, but I feel the need to.

"I don't want to hear any of that. Just try again." Light flickers in Elias's eyes.

I bow my head, focusing on the soul stones I clutch in my palm. I don't want to let them go. I don't need them to pull Elias through with me because of my familiarity with his soul, but I will need them to bring Micah back. I just wish—

Heat burns over my skin, and I stare at the ground as it quakes and opens. Micah flies from Hell and lands on his knees in front of me, the glowing tethers of my energy trapping him. My power tangles around him like I've thrown a net and reeled him back.

My jaw slackens, and I rush forward, dropping to my knees and cupping Micah's face. His eyes light with fire, and his tusks protrude from his mouth as if my bringing him back surprised him. Maybe it did. He was probably expecting us to return to his kingdom, and I somehow managed to just pull him back.

Elias claps his hands, whistling with his excitement. "Now that's what I'm fucking talking about. You caught yourself one handsome son of a bastard devil. I can't even do that shit."

"None of us can. It takes a lot of power to anchor to one realm while entering another. What you've done is amazing, Raven." Micah rubs his fingers over his cropped, tight curly hair. His chest rises and falls as he catches his breath, his expression still stunned.

"How about we try to catch another devil?" Elias gets on the same level as me and Micah, looking at each of us. "If we can get her to replicate it, this might change everything. We can drag angels to us."

I blink a few times, trying to process his words. If I can manage to do what he says, this could change everything. I could bring those imprisoning my soul to the devils on even ground. My heart beats at the thought, racing in anticipation. This could save the universe.

It could save me.

"Who do you think she should try to grab?" Elias asks, looking at Micah.

Micah scratches his cheeks for a moment. "I think either Kase or Dante would be the least resistant. Lucian and Cassius are out of the question. Andre does have another mental connection to Raven through her dreams, so he might be as easy as it was for her to pull me. What do you think, Raven? Who do you want to reel in?"

I don't even have a chance to think about it, my whole body buzzing as energy builds in my hands and the world quakes. Light blinds me, and I realize I might've been thinking too much about Heaven and the bastard angels imprisoning my soul.

A man gasps on the ground before me, spreading out his golden wings. He twists and turns, trying to untangle himself from the tether, but Micah quickly blasts hellfire in his direction, trapping him in a devil circle he won't be able to escape.

Holy fuck.

"Micah, take him now. Don't give him the chance to try to alert the angelic army." Elias wraps his arms around me and lifts me up, scrambling away.

We watch as Micah grabs the angel and drags him through the fire and into his own circle still binding him to hell. The angel screams, but he can't do anything. I watch as fire devours him and Micah, leaving nothing but a ring of ash on the floor.

"Darlin', I need you to try again. Focus on one of the devils. It'll be faster if you reel them to us. You can do it. Think about Kase's tail. I know how much you like wrapping your hands around it. Imagine you snatch him by the tail and bring him to you. Think about how hard that would make him. Think about what he would do to you." Elias's voice grows husky with his words. I'm pretty sure he's now thinking about what he wants to do to me.

"He's going to want to tie me up with it. Fuck me in the ass." I can't stop my racing heart, but instead of fear consuming me, passion takes over and I close my eyes, imagining bringing the devil of wrath in front of me so I can drop to my knees in front of him.

The world trembles, and I watch the light tethers open the world in front of us, bringing a fiery door into the room only feet away. Kase hollers and swears, yelling Dante's name, and I clap my hands. It worked. I can't believe it fucking worked.

Kase stumbles to the ground, but he doesn't hit his hands. His devil form breaks free, and his claws penetrate the wood floors. He wipes his head up and roars, blowing my hair out of my face. The second our eyes meet, he purrs deep in his throat. I realize that my hands no longer hold the tethers. I clutch him by his tail.

"That's one hell of a catch, Raven." Elias stands behind me, wrapping his arms across my belly. "Who are you going to catch next?"

I don't respond to him and close my eyes, knowing that Dante will spank the shit out of me if I don't bring him next. Fuck, he'd probably spank the hell out of me if I do it. I can't help the excitement warming between my legs as I imagine him tying me up in his swing to have his way. He's even more creative now than ever, working around my giant belly.

Once again, the ground quakes and a fiery door opens. It's shocking how tangible it looks. I feel as if the flames create a wooden pattern and if I didn't know any better, I could knock on it before its wings open. Dante hisses, and I watch him grab onto the doorframe, but the flames vanish from his fingers, and he catches himself on his wings. Pushing himself back up, he flashes his two sharp fangs.

"Careful, Dante. I'm the one controlling you now. Don't make me grab my strap on and remind you I can be your boss." I grin with my words, yanking him closer by the tethers tangling around him. He play-growls, trying to spin me around to spank me.

"You naughty, pretty soul. You're in so much trouble. I hope you're ready to feel your punishment for days." Dante adjusts his pants, showing off his massive hard-on for me.

Elias shifts and blocks him with his wings, keeping him from trying to charge me to carry me off to his room. "You're getting faster already. Do it again."

I flick out my fingers, imagining bringing my devil of lust into the plane, knowing that with him comes everything I want this moment. With Andre comes the distraction I need to push away the thoughts that I dragged an angel here by accident. I'm sure the angelic army will freak out when they realize.

"Reel him in by the cock. That's the biggest thing on him

and easiest to focus on, angel-girl," Kase says, sliding his tail around my waist, standing close as if he's afraid he'll vanish from my side if he lets me go. But he won't. I know that I've grounded them to me.

Now that Kase puts the image in my mind, I can't help thinking about Andre's delectable body and how his chiseled abs lead to the V in his hips pointing right to the biggest cock in probably the entire universe. And it's mine. All mine. And now I want to feel it in my hand. The weight of it is enough to ground me to any plane.

A soft moan echoes through the air and something hot, smooth, and heavy as hell plops right into my open palm. I automatically lace my fingers around Andre and stroke him, cackling like a maniac because I can't believe I just dragged the devil of lust through the realms by his dick. If that isn't a gift from the universe, then I don't know what it is.

Dante tips his head back and roars a laugh, sounding just as maniacal as I do. "Do Cassius next. Drag him by his damn balls."

His excitement and laughter is enough to encourage me, and I squeeze my eyes shut, imagining grabbing onto the prideful bastard's double dicks to put him in his place.

But something's wrong.

It's as if something interferes, and my tethers try to pull me forward. Oh, no. I don't open a door for Cassius through Hell.

I've made a mistake.

Silence surrounds me, and I snap my eyes open and realize that I stand in what was once Cassius's sanctuary. He did tell me that once I was familiar with it, I could always find it. And now I'm here and scared. Fuck.

I close my eyes and try to imagine falling to Micah's kingdom. It's still fresh in my mind.

Blinding light flashes across my eyelids, and I gather hellfire in my palms, preparing to fight.

"Hold on, Raven. This is going to hurt." Elias's voice snaps the fear out of me, and I gasp and feel his essence latch on to me.

The light vanishes, but his presence still remains.

"Hurry up. They sensed her." Micah's voice whips around me next.

I see a flash of gold wings.

The angelic army knows what I can do.

I'm not ready.

But I don't think I'll ever be ready. Regardless, this is my fight, and I will win.

12

Deal with the Devils

MICAH

"RESTRAIN HER TIGHTER. I'm going to grab a hold of their attempt to tether her." I stand in front of Raven, her eyes wide with fear.

The angelic army uses the angelic light she carries to link her soul with her mind. A wave of panic and anger bursts through my being. Raven somehow managed to access Heaven instead of Cassius because he had taken her to his private sanctuary before. The place should've been destroyed, but it would have just merged back into the heavenly plane. If it weren't for Elias, we could've lost Raven.

But not only that. It's with absolute certainty, I know that the angelic army realizes our plan. They're going to fight back. We lost the element of surprise we desperately needed.

"Darlin', listen to my voice. I need you to take a deep breath. I know you're confused, but you're safe. We have you. Micah is going to ensure that no one can tug you by the energy you've left behind." Elias pins Raven to his chest, holding her toward me.

I lean in close and stare into her beautiful blue-green eyes. "Heathen, I need you to let me into your mind completely. I can untangle the lines they try to wrap around you. Imagine letting go of your own tethers. I know you don't want to, because you feel more powerful this way, but you need to trust me. They'll take me and not you. They will regret even trying." Because the second Raven releases her grip on the energy, I plan to snatch it. It's never been done—dragging Hell's power source from its plane, but it doesn't stop me from trying. I will take the pain of being blasted with Heaven power as long as Raven is safe. I'd do anything for her.

Raven's mouth trembles, and she slowly bobs her head, finally comprehending what I'm asking of her. "I'm afraid they'll try to hurt you."

I smile softly. If it were any of the other devils, they would threaten her with punishment for questioning their power. A punishment she would enjoy, of course. Me, on the other hand? I didn't even know it was possible to love her even more.

She cares so much about me that she's willing to risk herself to protect me from pain.

"You can tie one of your tethers to me. I promise that I'll be back. They can't keep me...not that they'll want to when I'm through." I brush my lips to hers, getting her to finally release a deep breath. And with the relaxation of her muscles, she loosens her mental grip on her power enough for me to grab a hold of the angelic line as if I am taking the reins and controlling an unruly beast.

Pain shoots through me, and I grit my teeth, but I wrap the tethers around my wrist and let the angelic army pull me. They're going to have one massive devilish surprise when I show up to their summons. I brace myself to hit the heavenly veil, but the burning light swallows me only to drop me onto the concrete floor of a dimly lit warehouse. It's an old hunter's safe house, completely protected by different holy runes and sacred artifacts.

I explode into my devil form, stomping my big hooves into the ground, knocking the angels surrounding me off their feet. Summoning hellfire, I create a wall around me, protecting myself from their attempt to blast me back with their heavenly light. Their obvious lack of power, unable to summon Raven from one plane to another fills me with satisfaction. My connection to Hell remains strong, and they'll regret even attempting to take Raven from us. They're fighting a losing battle.

I snarl, spitting hellfire at the angels. "How dare you lock your binds to Raven. She will never belong to you. You might have her soul in your possession, but it won't be forever. You've failed, and it's time you recognize it. Heed my warning to you," I say, my voice guttural as it escapes my monstrous mouth. I narrow my eyes, trying to glimpse the features of the angels but they remain hidden in their light. "You've declared war on Hell, and you will get it. This is your last chance to surrender and accept my offering for mercy. If you don't take it, you will be destroyed. You might think you're superior to us, but you've underestimated our power. We will not allow you to reset the universe. You have gone against the path set before the universe by the Higher Power, and it is my duty as Hell's power source to ensure things go as planned. The miraculous gifts given to my queen have proven it."

"She has proven nothing but being the perfect vessel to power, Micah." Mikail expands his golden wings, stepping closer to stare at me over the wall of flames. It's the first time he dimmed his power, and it takes everything in me not to thrust fire at him. "You are mistaken to believe we would want to reset the universe by choice. That is not the case. We want balance. We want to ensure souls remain on the proper cycles. But the gifts Raven possesses will lead to the total annihilation of everything Heaven has spent eternity creating. All we want is for you to leave things as they are. If you agree and allow us to keep Raven's soul, we will end this war immediately. You can also keep her spawn until their mortal lives end and then they will ascend into Heaven's ranks. If you agree to those terms and bow to Heaven, taking the place where you belong, then we can just move on. If you do not, you will leave us no choice. We will set things right."

I purse my lips, thinking over his words. He expects me to agree with this nonsense. But angels aren't capable of making proper deals. That's my job, and I know exactly what I need to do. I need to lie to Mikail to give us some time. I need to act as if it is a better deal than risking the universe. If I can convince the angelic army that we're afraid they'll succeed, we can hit them harder and faster. They're lying to themselves if they think that they have a chance at winning this war. The only reason Mikail offers such a shitty deal is because he knows that Heaven can't beat us. Not with Raven and the twins. Not with the devils all uniting. They don't stand a chance. It'll be so satisfying watching them burn.

I lick my lips, catching Mikail in a staring contest. I want him to squirm under the heat of my power. Sweat glistens on his forehead, his body reacting to the Mortal Realm. Shifting on his feet, he breaks my gaze to look at the others quietly waiting for his command.

"I'd also like to offer visitations to Raven's soul for Elias in exchange for Meri. You can't keep her." His jaw twitches with his words.

All I do is smile, baring my teeth in amusement. He has no idea that Raven managed to destroy his companion Meri and reset her completely, keeping her energy. I'd love nothing more than to throw it in his face, but I'll wait and give Raven the honor of telling him.

"Hell will consider your proposal. As I am not the sole devil, I'll have to discuss it with the other kings. The twins are ours. We're not going to let you take them at the end of their mortal lives. As for the other stuff, we'll see." I don't mention Raven specifically for the sole reason that if I do, I'll blast all of them off their feet and give myself away. I want to destroy them for even thinking that we'd just give her up. They are out of their minds.

Mikail unsheathes his sword. "The decision must be made now. You were always a good soldier for Heaven. You found yourself in an unfortunate situation, and I know you'll do the right thing. So agree now or face the consequences."

Anger explodes through me, and I gather hellfire in my palms. "You need to give me time."

"No." Mikail grinds his teeth and blasts heavenly light at my protective ring. The other angels take his command, joining him and trying to knock me out of the mortal plane.

I close my eyes and use Raven's tether to drag myself back to her plane and into the basement of our new home. The angelic army hollers and shouts, but their voices silence as I find myself standing in front of Raven and Elias.

She jumps at me, and I scoop her into my arms and snuggle her close, careful not to hurt her in my devil form. She's much smaller, and I know her mental state is fragile. I'm afraid to add to her stress by mentioning what happened.

"I'm going to take Raven to my kingdom. I need you to find the other devils. The angelic army knows what Raven is capable of, and they will come hard and fast at us. They'll do whatever it takes. We need to get everything set. This is war." I stomp my hoof into the ground, opening a Hell portal to my kingdom.

Without waiting for Elias to respond, I jump into it, taking Raven with me. It takes everything in me to keep calm. All I want to do is build a protective wall around her and return to the Mortal Realm to fight. I want to destroy every angel I see, but I can't. I'm anchored to Hell.

Raven clutches onto my tusks, dragging my attention away from the onyx walls growing even taller around us. I summon souls to circle the place, ensuring that if an angel tries to infiltrate my kingdom by falling from grace by choice, I'll be ready.

"Tell me everything that happened, Micah. Did they hurt you?" Raven runs her fingers over my tusks and to my cheeks, waiting until I get my act together to suppress my devilish nature.

Her eyes shine with tears, and I force my darkness away, returning to the form she fell in love with. She caresses her fingers over my short, curly hair, tracing her way to my orange eyes, glowing with the fire of my kingdom. She draws her way down, mapping my body until she presses her hand over my heart, feeling the power radiating from me.

"Please, Micah, I know you're afraid of stressing me out, but your silence is more harmful than you just telling me what the fuck is going on. You weren't gone very long." Raven leans in, kissing my mouth, waiting for me to react to her closeness.

I shudder, my muscles rolling with the fury still clinging to me over the situation. "The angelic army wants us to make a deal with them. They said that if we allow them to keep your soul without a fight, they'll end the war and not reset the universe. They'll not come out for the twins when they're born, and if we bow to them, they will keep things as they were before."

Raven's mind races, a dozen thoughts swirling through her head. She thinks about my words and also the universe. Unlike me, she's not selfish. She has been wanting to protect humanity and create Purgatory since discovering her place. She wants to ensure the safety of the twins regardless of what it means for her. She wants Hell to be able to rise, and she wants us devils to unite. She wonders if complying with the angelic army is the right thing to do. She can't stand the thought of them destroying everything because of her. She carries the weight of their actions on her shoulders.

"Micah..." Her voice hitches as she says my name.

I shake my head, fire erupting around us and stretching toward the ceiling. "Don't even consider it, Raven. It is not your responsibility to make such a sacrifice because the angelic army is trying to test our power. They know we are stronger than them, and they realize they are about to face defeat. That is the only reason they have tried to make a deal. Angels do not ever make deals with devils. It is absolutely unheard of. This is to save themselves, not the universe. Not the world. None of us. They are selfish, and I will not let you be a martyr. Do you understand?"

Raven opens and closes her mouth, her body tensing as she groans and bows forward. I feel her pain as if it's my own, and I hug her tighter.

"This is so fucked up. I just want a future with you. I want to be able to raise the twins. I don't want to leave you. But—"

"But nothing." I jerk my attention to where the other devils enter my kingdom. Raven follows my gaze, and she starts bawling the second she sees them standing before her.

I stride closer, holding her out. Zade breaks away from the others first and gathers her into his outstretched arms, tapping into his kingdom and his connection to Raven to try to steady the intense emotions crashing through her.

I meet Kase and Dante's eyes in silence before looking at Andre and then to Cassius and Lucian. Blinding light flashes as Elias uses his connection to Raven to portal here.

Raven's crying fades after another minute in Zade's arms. No one moves or speaks, watching our queen break before us. This is pure torture. This is what I imagine the souls of Hell experience. Even the ones that don't deserve it. Just like Raven doesn't. Anger swells through all of us. I can feel our rage growing by the second as we all stand together.

"Raven, I need you to do your best to keep faith in yourself. The angelic army is trying to get to you. They are trying to destroy your confidence so that you don't progress in learning to control your powers." Cassius breaks the silence first, and I watch as he steps closer and finally meets Raven's eyes after what feels like days avoiding her.

"I hate fucking admitting this, but Cass-hole is right. They are chickenshit bird brains, and they have nothing to save them. They are no match for us. And we still have Elias's connection to Heaven. He will help you pluck every last one of those bastards from the safety of their plane. Starting now. They'll regret fucking with us. Now be my good little princess and follow my instructions." Lucian stands beside Cassius, flashing his impressive horns as he summons the power of his kingdom into his being, setting his heart aglow. I realize in this moment that he tethers himself to the plane.

He looks at Cassius next. "Your turn, brother. You need to access all the power possible."

"I will do the same," Kase says, gathering his red power in his hands. "We only need one of us with access to the Mortal Realm. Who is it gonna be?"

"I'll do it," Dante says, expanding his black wings. "The legions bow to me and will fight to keep control over humanity's domain."

I nod my head, gathering more hellfire in my hand until I set the palace aglow in a ring intended to cage in celestial assholes.

Raven runs her fingers through her hair, calming down and wiggling in Zade's arms until he sets her on her feet. She straightens her shoulders and turns her gaze upward as if she says a silent prayer. But not to heaven. To herself. To the universe. To the twins. It's taking all of her strength to face what is about to come. And I plan to give her all of mine.

I close the space to her and lift my hand, pressing it over her heart. "I want you to take part of my tether. You need to ground our beings together in your realm."

Kase strides forward and rests his hand on top of mine. "You need to connect to all of us, Raven. It's going to take every ounce of power in Hell to crack the heavenly plane."

She slowly nods her head. "Do whatever you have to do. I can handle it." But she doesn't look so sure. Reaching down, she pets her hands along her belly, closing her eyes as she feels the babies move inside her.

But I know she can handle it. I can see the light and dark radiating from the twins to lace up her arms to meet at her heart. They attach to my power, and for the first time, I can truly see their strength. They are unlike anything I've ever experienced, and it sends a zing of energy through me.

Raven gasps, arching her back as braids of light and dark whip from her and wrap around each of us, creating a circle around us with her and the twins in the center.

The world changes around us, and I stare at a new realm. It's Raven's plane, but something is different. It's no longer just haze and shadows and light. It's now full of brilliant color.

It's full of hope and power. It contains all of her emotions and her desires.

As quickly as I see it, it fades.

"Fuck, angel-girl. That was incredible." Kase steps closer and rests his hands on her belly. "Daddy's impressed. You gave us a vision."

Raven smiles with tears in her eyes. "It was an answer to my prayer. It was a reminder of what we're fighting for."

Elias gathers heavenly light in his palms. "So let's get this done now. I heard the heavenly call. We have no time to waste."

13

Eternal Torture

LUCIAN

"**J**UST KNOWING WHAT you can do gives me a raging fucking boner, Ray. I had no idea when I first saw you that you would be the one to bring me to my knees. Let me lick that sweet pussy of yours while you destroy this bastard." I adjust my hard-on, watching Raven shift from foot to foot, standing just outside the fiery pits where I like to keep the fallen angels who refused to bow to me. "If I could even just taste a little bit of your power, I'd be the happiest devil."

And this beautiful, courageous woman is the epitome of power. I have never seen anyone manage to force a being into pure energy instead of completely obliterate it as if it has been recycled, and not like the soul cycling over and over through the planes. This is different. If we could have managed it before, I'd have cleaned fucking house already. I get bored of torturing those against us. It's fucking awesome that I can finally silence their eternal prayers for salvation that will never come without losing power from annihilating them.

Raven shakes her arms out, staring at the broken angelic bastard on his knees before us. He could make it simple and bow to me, accepting his place among my legion, but he refuses to give up whatever dumbass idea he clings to. He was obviously Mikail's little bitch, because if he wasn't, he'd see good reason in what we're trying to do. Instead, he calls out to the Higher Power to save him as if it's even listening.

"Control yourself, Satan. It's hard for me to focus with you pointing at me like that. I'm still figuring out how to do this shit." Raven licks her lips and bounces on her feet, her dress swaying with her movements.

All I can think about is dropping lower to watch from beneath. Maybe she'll let me just crawl between her legs and wait for her to get tired enough to sit down on my face. "Distractions are good. If you could do this with my fucking distraction, you'll be unstoppable. I will worship you as you deserve. You're my queen, but I want you to be my goddess. Show me your power. Let me touch it, taste it, savor it. Let me see you put this fucker down. He's not going to comply."

Raven closes her eyes, and I can tell that a part of her wishes the fuckhead would just bow. Unlike me, Raven still has a soft spot despite how fucked up this guy's mission is. She doesn't like to destroy things. With the twins, she now understands the amazement of creation. And that's what she wants to do. She will create a place for wayward souls to learn to get their shit together before they can have eternal peace. And damn it. I want that. I don't like being tethered to this shithole again. I want our kingdoms to rise.

"This is your last chance. I don't want to have to obliterate your ass, so you need to make your decision now. You either bow to my fucking sexy king or you'll get to be another little bling of energy on this pretty chain he gave me." Raven dangles the fiery, yet dainty, chain that she wears around her neck as a reminder of how to anchor herself to not only us, but to her new plane that will be Purgatory. We all saw the vision ourselves. And there's nothing I won't do to ensure that happens. I'm willing to pluck every damn angel from the pits until there are no more. It's going to take a while, but I think we will be able to gather enough power to do what we need if we make it at least a quarter of the way through.

The bastard clasps his hands together, turning his head upward. "Your Almighty grace, give me the strength to—"

I whip my fire chain, lashing it across his chest and sending him to the smoldering ground outside of the lava lake. "You will not get any more strength. Bow to me and pray to Raven."

The man expands his burning and broken wings. "I will never pray to a false god or idol."

I puff out a breath of smoke through my lips, striding forward to kick him onto his stomach. I stomp my hoof into his chest, crushing him to keep him silent for Raven. Screams don't push her forward like they do me. And he doesn't do anything that pisses her off in this moment, so it's going to take her more time to gather her rage and power to obliterate him.

"Come on, Ray. It's time. Think about the power you will get from this abomination. With his power, we will be closer to breaking the veil to get your soul." I hold my hand out to her, coaxing her closer to me. "I will help you through it."

Raven bobs her head and waddles closer. I can't help but smirk at how she looks as if I've been fucking her hard for days though I haven't had the luxury of that kind of time with her. It's just her beautiful, glowing pregnant body.

"Just keep him quiet, please. And get ready to drop to your knees for me. I'm going to need the distraction immediately." Raven puffs out a breath of air between her lips and looks at me with her blue-green eyes, glassing over with unshed tears. I want to spank her to clear her gaze, but I know this is hard on her. She needs me to be her strength and her power. She needs me to keep her steady. I will do whatever I have to and do whatever she asks of me to get this done.

I scoop her in my arms and hug her, kissing her softly on the lips without getting carried away despite my throbbing balls just wanting me to sink my cock between her legs. "I got you, Ray. Always."

"And I have you, Lucian. I have you and the other devils." Raven kisses me again and then untangles herself from my arms. She lets me help her squat until she rests on her knees. I pin the angel down, taking pleasure in stabbing my sharp nails into his shoulders. Raven concentrates on her hands, and I watch as she gathers hellfire and heavenly light between her palms, filling the energy into an orb the size of a basketball. She hesitates, studying as the power swirls, but then the angelic bastard bucks his body and shouts that he is going to destroy her. His mistake is my pleasure, because I gape in awe as Raven throws the rest of her power at the angel, setting his body aglow before absorbing him into herself.

She screams out as a rush of energy crashes through her, and I rest my hand against her heart, whispering in her ear to ground it.

"Don't let it control you, Raven. Remember what you were taught. Pour it into your very being and manifest it. If you prefer to change the shape of the stone to make it easier, then do it. That guy deserves to be a dick for the rest of existence." I move my hand from her heart and cup her fingers between mine, silently encouraging her with the warmth of my power to do as I say.

She squeezes her eyes shut. The power drifts through her body and into her palms, and the world around us shimmers as she moves us between planes. She releases a deep breath, and I tilt my head back and roar a laugh at the sight of the small dick shaped stone in her hands. She actually did what I said. That stubborn little sexy woman of mine is actually acting like my princess.

"Good girl," I say, combing my fingers into her hair to guide her mouth to mine. "Come here and sit on my face. You get a reward for that."

"Mind if I watch, darlin'?" Elias materializes in Raven's plane, stretching his annoyingly blinding wings out. If we didn't need him to be a fucking angel right now, I'd use my power and cut off his wings to spank Raven with. I know she likes that kind of reward. We've all seen Dante's angel feather pillows. Fuck, I've gotten burned by them before when they were ripped open.

Raven taps her finger to her chin, faking as if she's thinking about Elias's words. And right now? I don't give a fuck. If he wants to watch, he can watch. Raven loves that kind of shit. He could even jerk off and come all over her, and she'd probably drench me in the process.

"If you watch, I'd want you to join. And if you join, the three of us aren't going to get anything done but each other. Can I take a rain check? From the both of you?" Raven bites her lip, smiling with her teasing words. A part of me wants to deny her and demand that she sit on my damn face like I have requested. Another part of me wants to do whatever I can to keep that smile on her face. And fuck. I haven't been close to Elias in a while. I wouldn't mind bonding with the bastard over Raven. I know he's done some dickish shit but I can't really talk.

"Hell yeah, darlin'. I'll take it. You can light us up with good grace and see how powerful Lucian really is." Elias chuckles with his words.

"Don't test him, Elias. Lucian has a thing for pain. He'd probably let me pinch his balls the whole time I give him head. Maybe even bless them with a little heavenly light so they zing." Raven reaches out and grazes her hand over my now throbbing cock. I feel as if I don't relieve myself of this ache, I might go crazy. I need to fuck some shit up to get my mind off it.

"Careful, Ray. You're poking a devil. I poke back. Hard." I snap my teeth at her and spin her around, spanking her with enough force to make her jump.

"What's the fun in that? I'd love to see you try." Raven rushes and jumps at Elias, trusting that he'll catch her before he's even prepared to do so. I try to snatch her away, but the fucker closes his wings around her protectively, and the realm shifts, bringing us back to the fire pits in my kingdom. Her plane shifting is getting smoother the more she does it. My heart beats faster, and I want nothing more than to steal her away from Elias even for just a couple minutes to tell her how fucking proud I am. She just never ceases to amaze me.

I whip Elias with my chain, getting him to set Raven on her feet. I close the distance and place my hand on each of their shoulders, grinning like a fucking lunatic on a mission to fuck shit up.

"Damn, Ray. Are you sure you don't want your reward right now? You have me so fucking hot. Hell feels freezing because of it." I wag my eyebrows at her, nudging Elias again. "Tell her, bastard. You know she deserves it. That was incredible."

Elias offers her a smile. "I hate agreeing with this asshole, but he's right. That was amazing."

Raven plants her palms to each of our chests, pushing us back as she laughs. It takes everything in me not to just lift her up and have my way. Elias might even help if I start. And if I start, I know Raven won't make me stop. She wants this just as much as I do. She is damn proud of herself too, as she should be.

"I promise the wait will be worth it. I need to practice more. Let's grab another angelic bastard. The more I do it, the easier it becomes. So go fishing. Catch me a crybaby." Raven swings her hand, smacking me in the ass.

I play-growl and shake my hips, getting her to do it again before I strut forward to the edge of the lake. Flicking my arm out, I cast my Hell chain into the lava pit, using my Hell power to pull an angelic bastard from the deepest part. The lava shifts and moves, bubbling as I reel an angel to the surface. Raven and Elias stand next to me, watching as if I'm about to bring up the best catch. And it better be. Raven deserves what she wants.

"Feels like a big one," I say, teasing as I gather my chain in my hands, winding it around my wrists. "He has small dick energy, though."

A holler rips in the air as a flaming figure pops up at the surface, swinging his arms and attempting to swim. Souls move around him, entangling him and trying to drag him back down. I loosen my chain a bit to allow them to do so, enjoying this tug-of-war. If I'm lucky, the souls might rip his dick off or something. Sure, his cock will grow back, but it will hurt. Everything is painful here. Over and over just how I like it.

"I think you're right. He looks like one big ass asshole for me to obliterate." Raven slides her hand across my shoulder blade and gives me a little shake.

I laugh and yank my chain, dragging the fallen angel from the pits. This one came by his own will in an attempt to overthrow Hell. He regretted his decision the second we caught him, begging the Higher Power to save him. He's a fucking idiot. Brainwashed. And now, Raven will sort of give him what he wants. He should be thankful. She's going to stop his suffering while giving us more power. Unless he decides to bow.

"I don't want to give them a choice. The last one ruined it for everyone. We don't have time." Raven exhales a long breath, turning to me to see if it's okay.

Damn. She's sexy when she's ruthless. What am I saying? I think she's sexy and irresistible all the time.

"Do it. I don't want this fucker anyways. I have enough souls around here. The angelic army doesn't deserve a second chance of power. Look what they've done the first time. Let's save my best spots for the naughty souls that prove their worth." I stride toward the angel, pausing to let him push to his feet in an attempt to run from us.

I transform into my devil form and swing my fist, knocking him so hard in the back that he flies a dozen feet and lands on his stomach. The ground explodes with flames around him, and he shrieks, his voice turning high pitched with his agony. I lash my chain at him again, wrapping it around his neck to yank him back. I drop him in front of Raven and stand over the bastard, stomping my hooves into each of his hands to pin him down.

"Be quick," Elias murmurs, his heavenly power glowing brighter by the second. This fucking bothers him, and it annoys the shit out of me. I know it's not his fault that he's an angelic bastard, but he should see how much joy Raven gets from summoning Hell and getting justice against the guardians that tried to ruin everything.

I growl at him. "She can take as fucking much time as she wants. Let her do her thing. Don't pressure her."

Raven rubs her hands together. "Both of you shut up. I will do what I want."

I scowl and blow a breath of smoke at her. "You're asking for punishment, Ray."

She tips her head up and looks at me, a smile parting her pouty mouth. "Maybe I am."

"All right. This traitor is going to wait." I kick him into the lava pit, allowing the souls to drag him back to his eternal prison.

Raven screeches and laughs, trying to rush toward Elias again for his angelic protection. I lash out my whip, snagging it around her wrist, and spin her back toward me. Elias summons his heavenly light, shooting it at my hand and attempting to get me to drop the chain. We all laugh, and I can't help how fucking good it feels to mess around with Raven like this. I'll even give Elias a little credit. He's not always a fucking bastard. He knows what Raven likes and has always been good at going with the flow of things. No wonder he can fucking keep crossing back-and-forth between Heaven and Hell and across the Mortal Realm with soul cycles. He easily adapts. Unlike me. My ass is forever a devil. There's no fucking way I'll ever sport wings again.

I'm so focused on trying to keep Raven with me that I don't see fucker angel crashing into the realm until it's too late. His wings blaze with fire as he falls like a meteor toward my palace. He smashes into the onyx wall of my palace, shattering it and sending flaming pieces around before I can even react.

I roar, my rage taking over the playfulness Raven aroused in me, and I nudge her toward Elias and charge toward the angelic infiltrator before he tries to fuck shit up. They still cling on to their light for a couple seconds after entering my kingdom.

I close the space and grab the guardian by the front of his torn shirt and haul him into the air, smashing his back to my palace wall. "You are going to fucking—"

He bares his teeth. "Wait, Lucifer. I have a message."

I swing my fist and punch the angel in the face, breaking his nose. "We punish messengers in my kingdom. Obliterate them. There is nothing any of us wants to hear from the angelic army."

"Elias! Elias! Stop him. This involves you. I have come with a bargain. Please, hear me out." The bastard angel shouts in pain and struggles, ignoring my threats and trying to get Elias's attention.

And fuck.

It works.

Elias comes up behind me and grabs me by the shoulder, getting me to drop the forsaken bastard to the ground. I don't let him go anywhere though, smashing my foot into his leg and pinning him. He hollers and tries to blast me with heavenly light that doesn't come. The satisfaction at his realization courses through me. It's like a fucking drug getting me high. I love when they realize they've made a mistake. These kinds of sacrifices aren't worth it. His self-sacrifice doesn't get him a ticket back into Heaven. Not like Elias had gotten. The angel had selfish motives with his descent.

"You have two minutes. Tell me what this is about, and I will make your end quick." Raven gets in front of Elias, not letting him speak to the angel.

I groan deep in my throat, loving how she just grabs the situation away from the both of us, taking control. I'm not one to be a switch, but I might try just for her.

Maybe she can call me her good boy.

Raven nudges the angel with her foot, getting his attention. "You're wasting time," she adds when he's not quick to respond.

The fucker purses his lips and shifts his gaze from her to Elias. "This is for him. Not you."

Raven tenses with her rage, and she summons angelic light and blasts it at his chest, burning his shirt and pecs in the process. "He's mine, which makes it for me. You have one minute."

I reach down and slash my claws across his chest, making him scream out. "I advise you listen to our queen."

The angel releases a breath, his face twisting in annoyance, but he doesn't argue. Looking at Elias for a second, he silently makes sure that he's paying attention, still not giving Raven his complete focus.

I glance at Elias, and he shakes his head at me. He doesn't want me to hurt the bastard anymore, because he does want to hear what he has to say. It just pisses me off that he speaks to Raven like that. I'm kind of curious too, but I'm not going to let on.

"I've been sent by Mikail. He realizes the error of his last deal and would like to offer another one. He realizes how obsessed Hell is with Raven, so he is willing to give you her soul as long as it does not return to her mortal body. You must also return to Heaven and remain there. You are not to access any realms. Hell will not rise with the seven sinners. If you do not agree, the purging will begin. The universe will be reset, and there's nothing any of you can do about it." He flicks his gaze from Raven and back to Elias, being a little shithead and purposely talking to him instead of telling Raven what Mikail wants.

"You're saying that Hell can have Raven's soul if I return to Heaven?" Elias asks, his voice softening. "Just like that? What about the twins?"

"They will go wherever their Higher Power intends for them." The angel once again looks to Raven.

Silence falls between us, and Raven's eyes fill with tears.

I blow fire from my mouth, fury rolling through me. "No deal. They can fuck off."

Elias grabs my shoulder, forcing me to look at him. "You can't make this decision on behalf of everyone, Lucian."

Fire crackles in my palms, and it takes everything in me not to blast Elias back. "The fuck I can't—"

Raven screams, pain and anguish lacing her voice, and I wince. Neither Elias nor I have a chance to do anything as Raven gathers Hell power and angelic light in her palms, creating a giant orb in her hands. She thrusts it at the angel, disintegrating him with power from both realms, turning him into pure energy.

Sparks flicker across her body, and I watch as the energy rolls through her veins, and she concentrates on manifesting it into her palm. I grab onto her in case she shifts realms, and Elias sends blinding light around us. He's following her wherever she leads, and I was right. The world shifts as we enter a new plane and Raven throws the small stone into the abyss of haze. Spinning, she faces the two of us, tears burning her cheeks as fire lights her eyes.

"We're not talking about this. We're not even considering it. I'll not lose any of you guys. Do you understand?" Raven asks, grabbing both me and Elias by the fronts of our shirts.

The realm changes again, and we end up in the Mortal

World, in the basement of the mansion.

"Raven, please. You have to think things through. None of this should be happening to you, and it's my fault." Elias softens his voice even more, knowing that she will explode at any second.

She spins and jabs him in the chest. "I won't lose you. We'll figure this out. Now, don't bring it up again. We need to practice. We're going to break into Heaven before it's the last thing I ever do."

14

No Deal

RAVEN

I would think by now that my tears would run out. I almost wish I was numb again. I'm exhausted from my negative feelings toward everything. I didn't think it could be this bad without my soul, but I no longer have balance. Things hit me more intensely with the power I've stolen from the bastard angels, and I feel as if I will drown in my sorrow and despair. I can't believe Heaven. I can't believe fucking Mikail decided to offer a deal that makes the devils hesitate. That makes Elias question his entire existence. He will do anything for me. All of the devils would, and they expect it. If Elias accepts the deal, we will have insurance that Heaven won't keep me imprisoned.

But at the cost of losing my soulmate and one of the dads of my babies? It's too high. I refuse to let anyone pay that price.

"I'm willing to give up the rise of Hell to get Raven's soul back. The twins need their mom more than anyone. I cannot fathom living the rest of eternity without her if we fail." Dante scratches his fingers through his soft hair, keeping his gaze trained on the floor. It hurts me to hear him say the words, but I understand where he's coming from. He just wants a foolproof plan for my soul. He wants to ensure our forever, even if it breaks my forever with Elias. But it's more than that.

"We have spent forever trying to build all the levels of Hell. Humanity needs Purgatory. You say everything as if you don't think we're going to succeed, Dante. Knock that shit off or I'll fuck you up." Kase fists his hand, punching Dante in the shoulder.

I hate that they disagree over this. I know Kase doesn't want to lose me, but he knows how important Purgatory and humanity are. He knows that I don't want to be the reason they fail. He carries all of the confidence in the universe that we won't.

"I don't want to risk it. It's been a shitshow. What if something happens and Raven goes into labor in a fucking hour or something? We can't bring down Heaven in such a short amount of time." Dante hisses and flashes his fangs, looking as if he's about to spit venom at Kase.

I should get between them. I should plant a palm to each of their chests and tell them to knock it off. But I can't find it in me to do anything but sit in the recliner with my hands resting on my belly, feeling the twins tumbling around like they're also fighting each other.

"I believe this should be Elias's decision. It's his soul and eternity after all. It's a sacrifice he has to make. He is also a father to the twins." Andre flexes his muscles, preparing to protect himself if anyone decides to attack.

"No. Elias tends to act irrationally and bases his decisions on what he feels is right in the moment. He might feel this is right for Raven right now, but in the long run? She will be a soul in Hell. He would be stealing her chance at taking Purgatory's throne." Micah crosses his arms over his chest, glowering at Elias. Elias refuses to look at Micah, and I know it's because they also have different opinions over the matter.

"We can still make changes to Hell. We can structure things differently. We don't need all of us. We just need Raven. She brings humanity to us and helps us see things we wouldn't normally as devils. Elias should go. We don't even know if he can jump from grace. He's tried over and over again. Losing Raven on the chance that he might be able to join us isn't worth it to me." Zade keeps his voice low, and I turn my attention to him. He frowns and glances away, unable to hold my stare for long.

It probably doesn't help that I burn him a look and push to my feet, summoning Heaven and Hell power in my palms. I just can't stand the arguing anymore.

"Raven, please take a breath. We will figure this out." Andre steps closer to me. "We all just need to discuss things and work out the best option for everyone."

I snap, my vision turning red. I don't like being in this position in the first place. Thrusting my hands out, I release my power at the floor, sending the earth beneath the house rumbling. Everyone takes a step back from me, and I don't think I've ever seen them look as fearful as they do in this moment. A part of me breaks inside. Another part of me is relieved that they don't try to trap me in their muscular bodies. I need time to think. I need a moment where they're not arguing and discussing matters that I want a complete say in. I'm not allowing Elias to go to Heaven. And I'm not allowing Heaven to keep my fucking soul either.

"You guys have an hour to speak your minds to each other, but just know, it's not going to change things. We're going to proceed with this war." I heave a breath and stride past them, listening to their absolute silence as I march away—or more like waddle my ass toward the elevator.

They all stare at me as the door closes, and I smack the button, taking me to the second story. I'm not sure whose room I'm going to, because I don't have one for just myself, but it's going to get locked. I need the hour of peace. At least, just to think without hearing them fight with each other. We're supposed to be a team.

"You know, nothing's going to change in an hour. There's nothing to be worked out. It's your soul. Elias is your soulmate." Cassius leans on the doorframe to his room. I don't think I have even seen it.

"Well, they need to fucking get it out of their system, and I can't stand listening for another minute about whose soul is worth more." I close my eyes, forcing my wild emotions to remain at bay. I'm tired of my body reacting to them.

"Why do you think I'm here? I know it's not my place. I've done a lot of reflecting over the last few weeks, and I've decided to just give my fate to the universe and the Higher Power. It has been so very long since I've truly received answers, except for now. I got an answer the moment I jumped from Heaven. I knew that you were the one to lead me now." Cassius offers his hand out to me. "Whatever you feel is right will sway me. I don't need the devils to bash what they want into my head."

I should just walk past him. I'm tired of hearing all the possible outcomes and how we lose no matter what if we can't break into Heaven and get my soul back. And I'm not about losing.

"I just want to destroy the veil, drag you guys all into Heaven, and show the guardians who they're truly dealing with. I just want my soul. I don't want to make any fucking deals. I don't want us to act on desperation or sacrifice." I keep my gaze locked to Cassius's, staring into his beautiful amethyst eyes, the purple color flashing with streaks of indigo as his blue fire buzzes through him.

He offers his hand to me once more, wiggling his fingers until I finally take it. "Why don't you hang out with me for a bit? We don't have to talk about any of that bullshit. I can keep them away for at least two hours if you need. You can soak in the tub or take a nap. If you want to practice manifesting shit, we can do that too. Or I can take you to Hell and we can do whatever you want."

I tilt my head up, my brows furrowing. "How the fuck is it possible that taking your kingdom in Hell turned you into an angel? This is what I imagine you should've been like with your white wings." With my free hand, I stretch over his shoulder and caress my fingers to his turquoise and emerald feathers. "Though these ones are so much prettier."

"Just what I always wanted to be called. Pretty." He smirks with his words, his usually sharp features softening.

"Would you prefer me to call you...a showoff? Because really, what kind of devil are you?" I stretch up, standing as tall as I can, silently begging for him to bend a bit closer.

He chuckles, closing the distance until only millimeters of space remains between our lips. "An awesome one. I have two dicks now, don't I? I think that gives me an advantage."

I laugh in exasperation, his comment pushing the negativity right out of me. I never believed I'd be standing in front of Cassius, appreciating his ability to make me smile and laugh as he makes fun of himself...or I guess, acts like the true cocky bastard he's always been. I know it drives Lucian crazy that Cassius now has two very impressive large cocks in his devil form. Cassius doesn't say anything, but I know he loves the hell out of it. His pride still lingers. He thinks he's the shit, and I bet he'll strive to be even more notorious than Lucian given the chance.

"Yet you haven't even let me play with either of them. You're sitting here, mentioning me taking a nap or a bath...but I don't need that. You should be offering to give me orgasms and other fun entertainment. A better distraction. I want to see them again." I reach between us and stroke my fingers over his pants, wondering if he still has two cocks in his human form or if they only come out to play when he's a devil.

Fuck it. I'm going to find out for myself.

Cassius groans in his throat as I press my palm to his chest and push him back, keeping my other hand over his growing hard-on, and I feel around seeing if I can tell. He must know exactly what I am trying to do, because he grabs my wrists and pulls my hand away, trapping it to his chest.

"Not so fast, Raven. I'm not easy like the other devils. I'm not a toy to be played with." He leans in and snags my bottom lip between his, sucking it into his mouth as he lifts me off my feet. "You're going to let me play with you for a bit. You're not the only one who's curious."

Damn. He did not just say what I think he did. And I'm fully prepared to let him have his way. I don't know what it is about this moment, but if Cassius wants to finally progress things beyond kissing, then I will let him do what he wants. How can I resist a devil with two cocks? I can't even resist a devil with one.

I let him lift me off my feet only to set me on the edge of his bed. He gets to his knees, looking as if he's just going to burn my clothes off, but I snatch his wrist this time, stopping him.

"You talk as if you know what you're doing. Shouldn't I be the one in control? You can call me daddy." It takes everything in me to keep a straight face.

My comment shocks him senseless, and he opens and closes his mouth. He goes from lusty to flustered in a matter of seconds, and I devour every second of his uncertainty.

"Or if you prefer, you can just be my sub. Let me tell you what to do. And once you have been a really good boy, we can switch." I graze my fingers along his jawline and down his neck until I grab the front of his shirt. Lifting his arms, he lets me pull it off of him.

"You would love that, wouldn't you? Which means...fuck

no. I'm not going to be your good boy. I'm a fucking devil of a man, and I plan to prove it." Cassius grabs my knees, easing my legs open, and stares at the flesh of my body.

He drinks in the sight of me without any panties. It's a hit or miss whether or not I wear them these days, depending on if anyone helps me. It's easier to just tug a dress over my head. I don't have to worry about if the damn stretchy pants fit.

"Then prove it. You're acting as if you don't know what to do. Do you need me to show you what I like?" I shift my knees until I plant my feet to his chest and kick him hard enough to send him on his ass.

He play-growls, flashing his devil form at me, but I hold my hand up and get him to stay in his spot. Scooting back on the bed, I rest against his pillows and bend my knees, reaching forward to slowly graze my fingers over myself. I'm not as good as one of my toys, but this isn't about bringing me pleasure. It's about showing Cassius what he really wants to see. It's about getting him all worked up until he can't control his devil any longer. He's already claimed me as his vocally. I want him to do the same physically. I want to claim him too.

"I want to learn for myself. That is my job from now on. I don't need you to tell me. You will just let me discover every inch of you on my own." Cassius steps forward, resting his palms on the edge of his bed, still not climbing onto it. He's waiting for me to agree and invite him to join me. But I won't.

"No. Sometimes a woman just has to do things for herself." I smile, my cheeks hurting with the gesture. Sucking in my lip between my teeth, I trace circles over my body, following the seam of my lips until I reach my piercing. "Plus, I already have a little decoration to show you the perfect place to start. So you're just going to have to wait. Watch and take notes. I'm sure Dante will test you."

Holy shit. The low grumble of a growl escaping his lips turns me on more so than him watching me. It zings right to my clit, sending shockwaves through me.

Cassius tugs off his pants, standing at the edge of the bed. I watch as he pulls them down and shows off his impeccable body to me. He remains in his human form, and I'm a bit disappointed not seeing the double stacked cocks. But still, he's huge, sexy as hell, and surprisingly smooth. He must've taken notes from Dante first. Maybe Kase. I doubt he would've listened to Lucian.

I glide my tongue across my bottom lip. "Come lay next to me."

Cassius finishes stripping completely, but he doesn't join me. He shakes his head and smirks at me, continuing to stand at the edge of the bed. "Not until you finish teaching me. I'm better at observing first. I want to see you make yourself come."

He's about to prove that I'm all talk. Now I can't let him. I have just as much pride as he does that I'm not going to back down. If he wants me to masturbate to completion in front of him, then I'll do it.

"I need some entertainment. I'm used to toys. They're the only thing that can compare to the pleasure ignited in me by the devils." My breathing comes in pants, and I close my eyes, listening as Cassius shifts and puts his weight on the edge of the bed.

"What about a little power instead?" The bed bounces under his weight, and Cassius surprises me by giving a little shock of power to my ring, sending it vibrating.

I gasp and grab the blankets, the sensation stealing my breath.

"Open your eyes. You asked for entertainment, so let me entertain." Cassius's voice deepens, the huskiness new and inviting. He's never sounded so alluring and hypnotic before. The Hell that got into him has really done something magical. We've always had a hot and cold relationship, but now? I feel as if I'm on fire. My whole body craves him on a level I've been denying.

I do as he asks, fluttering my eyes open to see him kneeling on the edge of the bed. He summons lube in one hand and slicks it over his cock, gliding his fingers in quick, desperate motions. It's like he doesn't want to drag it out. He wants to experience pleasure. He wants to experience me, but he's just as prideful as I am. We're going to torture each other until we can no longer take it.

"Show me both of them. I'm not afraid of your devil form." I continue to wiggle, shifting my hips as the vibration continues, making it hard to speak without moaning.

"Are you sure? I know it's not...mortal." Cassius swallows, his Adam's apple popping with his nerves.

And there is nothing I love more than making a devil nervous.

I open my mouth to respond, but an orgasm shocks through me, and I arch my back, falling against the mattress with a scream of pleasure. I gasp and pant, trying to focus on Cassius. It's useless as I'm trapped in vibrating bliss, my mind turning to mush.

I set Cassius off, and he comes, hitting me across my legs. If Dante were here, he'd tease him for bad aim. If the devils aren't in me, they usually love squirting across my boobs or ass.

Cassius grunts, quickly picking up the blanket to clean me off. "You get to me too much. I couldn't—"

Reaching out, I grab him by the dick and pull him closer. There's no fucking way I'm allowing him to apologize for getting off by watching me get off. I love it. I want to see him do it again and again. Wouldn't be the first time a devil made it rain in such away.

"Stop your power. I can't take it anymore. I want you. I want to see your fucking double dicks. I want them inside me.

Show me." I moan with my demand, inhaling a sharp breath as Cassius rubs his fingers over my jewelry, stopping it from vibrating.

Tingles rush through me, and I push him over and climb on top of him, wanting nothing more than to take control. It's not often that I get the pleasure, and I don't think Cassius will argue. Not now. Not when I rock my body on his and stare into his beautiful amethyst eyes.

Without waiting for him to show me his devil façade, I align our bodies and sink onto him. He groans and arches up, lacing his fingers around my hips to bounce me on top of him.

"You feel so fucking amazing. I had no idea your body would be this incredible." Cassius closes the space to me and kisses my lips, sliding his tongue into my mouth as if he just wants to devour me.

"Shut up and fuck me harder. I want you as you were intended to be. Don't be shy." I smile with my teasing words, running my fingers through his hair and allowing him to take over completely, guiding me up and down until pressure builds even more between my legs.

I can't see his body beneath my belly, but it sure feels as if he now glides both of his dicks inside me, penetrating me in a way that makes me scream in pleasure. He moans along with me, voicing how much he enjoys my body and how he craves for this forever.

I plant my lips to his, silencing him. "Don't get all romantic on me. I need you to just fuck me senseless. I don't want to hear any promises. I don't want any expectations except that you'll get me off."

He growls his agreement, bouncing me harder and faster while using his free hand to reach between us to rub my clit. My muscles spasm, and I bow my head, resting it to his shoulder, riding the intensity of pleasure.

"I'll fuck you until you beg me to stop if that's what you want." Cassius nips my shoulder, the sensation sending another wave of ecstasy through me.

"That's all I want. Just fuck me until I forget." I lose myself to Cassius, savoring his strength and power as a devil.

The world shifts around us as we fuck our way into my plane before Cassius fucks me until we enter his kingdom.

I lose count of how many times I orgasm, and I let Cassius carry me into his palace and to his bed. He lets his devil form completely free, his power radiating over me until he slows and stops, finishing with another orgasm that rocks the bed.

"You're mine. Always. You are my path that I'll follow and my destiny set forward by the Higher Power. No one is taking you from Hell. I know you don't want promises, but this isn't a promise. It is a fact. Do you understand Raven?" Cassius asks, running his fingers through my hair, our bodies tangled and still buzzing from our fucking.

I lick my lips, my mouth dry from my moans.

He presses his fingers to my mouth, stopping me from answering. "I'll take that as a yes. Now come here. I'm going to fuck you until the devils drag us back."

I bob my head, kissing him again.

I never knew I'd find such passion and peace with Cassius. That he would find the same with me.

If only I didn't feel that it's temporary.

If only I knew it would last.

15

Broken

RAVEN

“IF YOU GUYS aren’t done arguing, leave us alone.” Cassius’s voice tugs me from sleep. I don’t know how long it’s been, but I know I’ve been with him for far longer than an hour.

My body aches in the best way. I savor the soreness aroused through me. My legs are so weak from all of our adventurous positions, him acting as if he has an eternity to catch up on fucking me, leaving me barely able to move. I just want to sleep in his arms a little longer. I don’t have to think about anything while I’m in his embrace. We haven’t even left his level of Hell.

“It’s been five days. I think you’ve had Raven for long

enough. We are done arguing. We just want you two to come home." Lucian's voice booms from the arched doorway leading to the grand throne room of Cassius's palace. I haven't gone beyond the room. Everything I need is here. He manifested food, extra pillows and blankets, the best tub I've ever seen in an amazing bathroom with a waterfall shower. I never knew he had a taste for such a luxury, and I enjoy getting to know him as a devil. I can't stop teasing about someone pulling the stick out of his ass over the last two weeks, and I tell him that when I find out who it was, they will be rewarded heavily. I don't think I've ever seen him laugh so hard.

Just the thought makes me smile and pull the blankets over my head.

"Go away, Satan. Your brother has double dicks and I can't get enough. I'm not ready to return to the Mortal Realm. I'm fine here." I brace myself, gripping onto the blankets as the room shakes.

Growls and snarls echo in the air, and I peek from beneath the blankets to watch Cassius explode into his devil form, expanding his beautiful turquoise wings to block Lucian. Lucian swings his whip around, trying to threaten Cassius, but he doesn't back down.

I sigh and sit up. "Lucian, chill out. Just come lay with me. It looks like you could use a rub and tug."

Lucian growls again, but he shakes his devil form until he

returns into the handsome mortal man I'm in love with. He shoves past Cassius and obeys my command, climbing onto the bed beside me.

"I want more than for you to jerk me off. I want to fuck your face until your throat is sore. And then I want to hear you rasp my name and beg for mercy as I spank you until your ass is the same shade as Kase's Hell power." Lucian grasps my chin, holding me in place as he kisses me with hot passion, his mouth searing me in a way that leaves me gasping and my lips swollen.

"You say that like it's some sort of punishment." I shift and get on top of him wiggling my way back until his hard cock taps against my ass, but I don't let it stop me. I stretch up and over it so it rests between my legs and I can unbuckle his pants and pull it free.

He grins at me, adjusting his arms to rest his hands behind his head. Cassius plops on the bed beside us, unfazed by the fact that I pull Lucian's pants down even though we were just fucking not that long ago. He's already accepted that I'm not his alone, and I think if anything, it has brought Lucian and Cassius together.

"Do you plan to watch or are you going to participate?" I ask, peeking at Cassius.

"Fuck no, he's not joining. It's my turn. We have some catching up to do. He can watch and help position you how I want. Nothing else." Lucian dares Cassius to say anything, his eyes flickering with firelight. And the cocky bastard looks hot as hell. I love hearing him boss Cassius around. There's just something about his aggression and charm that gets me good.

"Damn it. I told them it should've been me to get her. What the fuck do you think you're doing, you bastard? This isn't bringing Raven home. This is you taking advantage of the situation." Elias's sharp words stab through me, stealing the warmth and desire away.

My lip quivers, and I can't focus on Lucian anymore. I thought I was past this. I haven't thought about angels since coming here, but now with my soulmate blinding me with his angelic light and looking at Lucian and Cassius as if he plans to smite them, summons sadness from within me. I feel as if I siphon it from my grieving soul even though it's not on this plane.

Lucian summons his fire whip, sliding me off him. Popping up, Cassius gathers blue fire in his palms, beating Lucian, and he chucks it in Elias's direction, getting him to fly back and out of the way.

"You're the reason she abandoned us. Now go the fuck back to the others and wait. I'm not going to drag Raven there kicking and screaming despite how hot she looks putting up a fight." Lucian grabs me and cradles me in his arms. He touches my cheek, smearing a stray tear. "You hear me, Ray? You don't have to go back until you're ready. If you want to suck my cock for a week, I'll gladly allow you. You have to let me bury my face in your damn pussy at the same time though."

I groan and rest my head to his chest, imagining what such an adventure would be like.

And as much as I want to experience it, I can't help looking at Elias again, seeing my sadness reflected at me and his eyes. His ethereal, iridescent wings sag behind him, and if I didn't know any better, I'd have thought that I already died and was taken to Heaven. His heartache resonates through me as if we share one body in this moment.

"Do what you feel you must, darlin'. Just know that I've made my decision. I'm not going to abandon you even though it kills me every second thinking that I could lose you. But you're right. I should never doubt us. We're soulmates, and I will never leave you again." Elias combs his fingers through his hair, shifting on his feet, waiting for me to respond.

My heart thuds in quick beats, and I blink my eyes, forcing my tears away. Knowing how much it hurts him tortures me with a new kind of agony I never knew existed. Because I know that only half of my devils agree with my decision. They love me too much. They can't stand the thought of losing me as much as I can't handle the thought of losing even one of them or losing the chance to raise our children.

Which means failing isn't an option.

It can't be.

And it looks as if Elias knows that now. He wanted to take the easy way and sacrifice himself like the angel he is, but in doing so, it will only hurt more than it would help.

I wiggle my way free of Lucian, and Elias steps closer, obeying my silent command to pick me up. I stretch my arms out and let him pull me to him for a kiss. I had no idea how much I needed to feel his closeness.

Swiveling in his arms, I glance at Lucian and Cassius remaining in their spots on the bed. "I think it's time to go home."

"I'm sure Micah will appreciate not having to hear you guys fucking around the clock. He's been waiting in his kingdom for days." Lucian rubs his hand over his bald head as he gets to his feet.

I frown. I should've known that Micah returned to Hell and wouldn't have remained in the summoning circle for who knows how long. I was so selfish in my grief over the situation. Yet another part of me knew I needed this. This short reprieve helped refill my energy and my desire to fuck over Heaven.

"Don't be jealous," I tease, wiggling my fingers at him.

"Impossible. I've never been more envious of this bastard than I am right now." Lucian whacks Cassius between the shoulder blades, getting him to follow us. Grabbing my hand while I remain in Elias's arms, Cassius does the honor of opening a portal to the Mortal Realm.

I expect the rest of the devils to be waiting for our arrival, but

Elias strolls into the empty basement. I frown, trying not to show that I'm hurt. I don't know what I expected. I thought that maybe the other devils were just waiting in anticipation instead of going about their business as if I didn't run away with Cassius to his kingdom. Childish? Maybe. Immature? Absolutely. I just needed time to think instead of having to deal with the constant fighting.

"Can I have a moment alone with Raven?" Elias adjusts me in his arms, refusing to set me on my feet. "The others are waiting upstairs. They don't want to overwhelm you, Raven." Elias kisses my temple, answering my silent question.

"Don't take fucking forever. We need to work on our battle plan now that your ass isn't getting tossed back to the light." Lucian grabs Cassius by his T-shirt and drags him toward the stairs leading up.

Elias doesn't set me on my feet until we hear the door close, and he drops to his knees, clutching my hands in his while resting his head to my belly. I comb my fingers through his hair, playing with the soft strands. I don't say anything as he hugs me and kisses my stomach, his love and affection exactly what I need from him in this moment. I'm still upset, but it helps. I know he had good intentions despite how I felt. I'm willing to do the same thing for any of my devils and my soulmate.

"Darlin', I love you. I love you more than my very existence, and I hope you understand why I considered such an offer. It kills me even to think for another second that Heaven could claim you and take you away from the devils. From our children. I thought that my sacrifice would be worth it if it brought you peace and happiness for the rest of your life and eternity." Elias sighs and rests his head against my belly, not meeting my gaze. "I also assumed that's what everyone else would want."

"You can't just make assumptions. I love you, Elias. I've loved you from one life to the next and the universe brings us together every time. When you died, it still managed to bring you back to me. If it were intended to be any other way, don't you think that things would be different? You wouldn't be given to me just to be taken away over and over again. I don't think the Higher Power is cruel enough to do such a thing." I continue to play with his hair, just wanting to absorb his affection into my very being as if I can take part of his soul again.

"You're right. Our paths align perfectly. Even when they deviate from each other, we still reunite. It's just hard. I'm so afraid, especially with the babies coming anytime. And the hostility from the angelic army doesn't help. They're not going to give up." Elias finally tips his head back and meets my gaze, his eyes watering with his swelling emotions.

"Which is why we have to make them. That's why we must keep trying to break the veil. We need to work together to get the devils to cross back into Heaven despite everything. We need to learn how to stabilize our existence in Hell. When the angelic army grows desperate enough, they will do some fucked up shit, and you know it. So instead of just giving in to them, we need to show them exactly who they're dealing with. They're not the Higher Power. They are not the gatekeepers of souls. They were supposed to have one job, and they've deviated from it. We need to get them back in line." I straighten my shoulders and tilt my head up toward the ceiling as if I can see into Heaven despite it being on another plane.

But I feel as if I'm being watched. I feel as if I need to make things clear and say them out loud for things to work in my favor. It's my prayer but it's also my demand. I haven't been put through everything to just end with me alone in Heaven. I refuse to believe that was always to be my fate. My fate is Purgatory and humanity. My fate is keeping my devils in line and raising two powerful beings that carry a piece of me and a piece of the love I share with some of the most powerful beings in all of existence.

"Then what are we waiting for?" Elias pushes to his feet, linking his fingers through mine. "Let's get our battle plan in line before Lucian fucks it up."

I smile. "The only thing he'll fuck up are angels. So watch out."

He chuckles. "Fucking Satan doesn't stand a chance against me. Do you know why?"

"Because you're the Jizz Master?" I crack up, my voice sounding through the air. "You know, Cass-hole managed to at least aim at my legs."

Racing away from him, I stride forward toward the stairs, knowing that he's going to grab me.

He snatches me up. "Now you're in for it. Teasing me like that. Come on, the devils are waiting. And before we do anything, I'm going to see to it that they punish you how you like."

Nothing has sounded better.

"As soon as he opens the portal, connect to him. Understand? You have seconds." Andre stands beside me, his muscles rippling in preparation. This is the first time he's worked with me on shifting planes, because I can't seem to focus with Cassius and Lucian. So they remain prepared and ready alongside Kase and Dante. I don't know if it's because our emotions remain wild, but I try not to think more into it.

Zade rests his hands on my shoulders, staying close by. "Take a deep breath. In and out. Don't think about the time. Think about us and how the connection makes you feel. You got this, Raven. Think of the reward Andre promised."

Heat pools between my legs at just the image of getting complete control over Andre the same way Dante lets me dominate him. I never knew how much I'd enjoy using a strap-on, but it's exciting. I love fucking them. Getting to control their pleasure and needs and desires.

Andre hums under his breath. "You love the thought, don't you, little hellion? I can smell your lust. Use your desire to push you harder." Glancing to Elias, he adds, "If she doesn't connect with you within ten seconds, return. They won't sense a disturbance that way."

"And if they do, I'll be ready to shove them to Micah." Zade stretches his arms in front of him and then over his head. I savor the sight of his shirt pulling up to show off his delectable abs.

"After we cut their wings off, first." Kase cracks his knuckles, speaking for what feels like the first time. He stands beside Dante outside the portal circle, prepped and ready for Micah to put any angels into the pits if we're caught.

"Save me a souvenir." My voice cracks as I say the words, but the devils don't point out my nerves. If anything, I feel the room heat up with a swell of their power as they channel it into me, our tethers still in place.

"You got it, pretty-soul. I'll fill the duvet cover." Dante swallows hard, his eyes blinking with his green light.

Lucian claps his hands once. "All right. Enough talk. Everyone who isn't Andre and Zade stabilize your tether to Hell.

You'll need every ounce of power from the kingdoms if this works."

I bounce on my feet, rubbing my palms over my belly. "Please, help me. Mama needs you," I whisper under my breath.

Andre rests his hand on Elias's shoulder. "Remember, ten seconds."

Ten seconds. I repeat his words in my mind, steeling myself for Elias to open the portal to Heaven.

Ten seconds. It's all the time it could take to have the army attacking at full force. They could try to use the heavenly portal to get to me.

Ten seconds. Fuck, it doesn't seem like enough time.

"Darlin', have faith. You can do it. Summon power now. Get ready to break through." Elias presses a kiss to my forehead. "Everyone else, get ready. Raven's going to succeed. We're getting through now."

His confidence fills me up with strength to believe in myself. I've been moving through realms more naturally with every passing day, and now that we have our plan set, this is it. It's going to work this time. It has to.

"On the count of three, Ray and Jizz Master." Lucian holds his fire chain between his hands, stretching it out.

"One," Cassius says.

Kase purrs with his anticipation. "Two."

Andre rests his hands on my shoulders, expanding his sexy wings. "Three."

Blinding light erupts in the room as Elias summons a portal to Heaven, lighting the world in front of me with angelic light. Fire and heavenly power explode in my hands, and I squeeze my eyes shut and imagine being close to Elias's soul. I envision breaking a wall down to get to him, feeling the wave of emotions crashing through me by his presence alone. I manifest a basketball-sized amount of power, thrusting it at the wall in my vision, sending the world shaking.

"Holy fuck! She did it!" Kase shouts with a roar.

"Go, go, go!" Lucian demands, heat lacing his words.

Silence falls around me, and I snap my eyes open.

Elias stands in front of me, bathed in heavenly light. Darkness swirls through the world around us, and flames blaze in my peripheral vision.

A warm hand slides into mine, and Andre pulls me in close. "Let's get your soul back."

We did it. I can't believe it.

I'm about to be whole again.

I've won.

Hell Rising

ANDRE

It takes everything in me not to lift Raven into my arms and kiss her for her amazing break through to Heaven. We don't have time to celebrate because the entire angelic army would have felt the crack of the plane, especially with the heat of Hell following us in.

"Bring the others. They'll fight while we find your soul." I lean in, keeping my voice low as if that will keep the army at bay.

Raven puffs out a long breath and closes her eyes again. The world shudders around us, and I groan at the sensation of her yanking at my very core as she drags Zade, Kase, Dante, Lucian, and Cassius through. Only Micah will remain in another plane.

"I fucking hate this place. I forgot how much until this very second," Lucian mutters as he materializes beside Raven. "It's even worse now that I can't manipulate shit. What do you see? I'm just burning in the damn light."

I caress Raven's shoulders, massaging my fingers into her tense muscles. "Let us see what you see."

Raven shivers at the sensation of my breath tickling her ear, and she manages to manifest a vision before us all. I stare at a familiar meadow stretching out across the plane. She used my sanctuary in Heaven to create this world around us. It summons a blip of comfort inside me. I might be a king of Hell, but Heaven was once my home. It doesn't just disappear from my mind. Unlike Lucian, I don't hate it. I just felt as if my purpose changed with Raven. I evolved into something better. Something stronger. Something worthy of standing beside the most beautiful woman I've ever laid my eyes on. I won't lose her. Not like this. Not to those who forsake her.

"Ray, this isn't fucking better." Lucian stomps forward, his devil form towering above us as we remain in our mortal façade.

Dante growls and punches him in the shoulder. "Shut up. This is Raven's vision and you will not talk shit about it. It's perfect. Now let's go. I can sense the bastards already ruffling their feathers and gathering light."

I turned to Elias, staring at him as he peers around. "You ready? You're the one who must lead the way."

Elias nods and holds his hand out to Raven. "Come on, darlin'. It's easier if I touch you."

We create a chain with Raven in the middle of me and Elias. Zade holds my other hand, and together we trudge through the realm not intended for us. The further we get away from the crack in the plane, the more painful it becomes. My skin burns, and I struggle to hold onto my human façade. My devil side wants to break free and battle the heavenly light scorching over us.

"Keep your eyes open. I have to concentrate. Her soul is far. Might be even in the furthest corner of the plane where we were supposed to jump with Lucian." Elias flicks attention to me, his wings flapping lightly on his back, not helping any as his heavenly breeze washes over us while it plays with Raven's hair.

"We're going to the highest peak?" Raven frowns at the idea. "I'm scared. It has to be a trap."

"Even so, we must face it. The angelic army has gone too far. If they persist, they're going to destroy humanity." Zade gathers power in his palms, his mere presence helping to extinguish the pain coursing over me. If we stay close, we can bounce our Hell power back-and-forth to ease everything heavenly around us.

Raven bobs her head, slowing down even though Elias doesn't. Her arm stretches out, but it's as if her body quits working. She doesn't even move her feet, and Elias drags her a couple steps before he realizes she freezes in fear.

"What is it, darlin'?" Elias stops and turns to face us.

Raven opens and closes her mouth, her body glowing more intensely with heavenly light. She doesn't find her voice and instead darts her gaze to me and Zade.

"Someone's coming." Zade unsheathes his Hell sword, preparing to fight against anyone who dares try to test us.

I summon my own blade, tensing as I let go of Zade. He steps forward protectively, his hand filling with purple light while he positions his feet for battle.

Elias spread his wings, creating a wall around us on one side, and I join him, helping to close Raven off between us. We stand with our backs toward her, keeping our view of the world. She hovers flush against me, practically trying to climb up my body to look over my shoulder.

"We can't stay. Keep moving. Just keep Raven safe." Zade circles fast, acting as our first defense if any of the angels reach us.

"They're going to head to the crack to try to seal it. The others should keep them distracted long enough to allow us to put some distance between us and them." I nudge Raven, getting her to shuffle along as I stroll back to back with Elias, his wings brushing mine and mine brushing his, but neither of us complains about the pain of our bodies being so close.

"Something's wrong." Raven gasps with her words, the fear in her voice stopping me in my tracks.

I stretch my neck and look at her from over my shoulder. "That's just you feeling the angelic army coming. It's probably messing with all of the tethers to Hell."

She audibly swallows, her voice whimpering with her gasping breath. "You're probably right. Let's hurry."

"Slow breaths, Raven. You're panicking." Zade cuts between mine and Elias's wings, meeting Raven face-to-face. I tense, not liking that I feel horrible without him circling us, but I understand what he's trying to do. He can tap into Raven's emotions and help balance her out. And right now, she's probably experiencing a rush as we grow nearer to her soul.

"I'm trying. I just feel sick. The babies are flipping around and beating the crap out of my insides. I think they can sense danger coming." Raven's voice shakes, and I try to suppress my anger that she has to go through this. This shouldn't be a time of fear and worry. It should be a time of joy and love and everything good in the world. She shouldn't be facing a war like this. But it was her decision, and despite my feelings about it, I will stand by her regardless.

"Zade, carry her. We have to move." Elias glows brighter,

trying to use his angelic light to shield us the best he can. With the light, it's harder to pinpoint our darkness.

Zade lifts Raven into his arms, and she buries her face in the crook of his throat, breathing against his neck. My whole body aches at the sight, and all I want to do is join him in a cuddle fest, ensuring Raven is okay.

"Just hold on. We're almost there." Zade whispers his words, keeping his voice low. I don't think we're as close as he says, but whatever helps Raven.

"Fuck. Up ahead. Get ready." Elias folds his wings as he wields his sword, getting ready to fight against the three angels materializing in front of us. It's as if they knew we were here, because they should've gone to the others first. We should've had more time.

Raven gasps, her voice echoing through the air. She thrashes in Zade's arms, igniting fire and light in her palms. The world quakes around us, and Zade swears under his breath. My mouth falls open at the sight of Raven lighting up the world around us. The ground rumbles under our feet, and I watch as the three angels fly across the plane in our direction. But they're not doing so by their own freewill. It's as if Raven snakes out tethers and latches onto them, yanking them to us.

No, not Raven. The tendrils of light whip from her stomach as the twins react to everything happening. It makes me question how much they're aware of. They know whenever Raven feels as if she's in danger, but this time it seems different. It seems as if they use offensive power and not defensive power.

"Release us!" A masculine voice booms through the air as heavenly light shoots in our direction.

I expand my wings, preparing to launch forward. Elias joins my side, and we create a wall between Raven and Zade and the angels coming our way.

I'll destroy them before they even get within reach of Raven.

"Fuck," Raven whispers, her voice softening. "You have to move. I have to do this myself."

I dig my nails into my palms, wishing with everything in me that I could ignore her demands. I don't want the angels getting close to her. I don't want to risk her safety and have them try to kill her mortal body right here and now.

"You have to trust her," Zade says, tugging my shoulder to get me to move. "Look. She's going to take their energy. Look at the power."

I gather my nerve and peek at Raven, seeing the light and dark swirling around her just as I've seen a dozen times when she opens the plane to her private world created by the twins. It's the same world she anchors the energy of souls to. But this is different. These are angels and not those forsaken and damned by Hell.

"We have to trust her. She has never failed us. Not like we have her." Elias folds his wings and rubs his lips together. He speaks more about himself in this moment, but he's right. I failed Raven the moment I ignored her pleas for help. I ignored her when she asked for redemption instead of being in a contract with Lucian. But all of my mistakes and feelings led to this moment. It has been my path to follow, and I still believe we are being guided. Just not the same way as before. I don't have the same intuition. All I know is that wherever Raven goes, I will be beside her. I will never abandon her.

"Stop! You are going to destroy everything!" A man skids across the plane and tumbles until I jab my sword into his wing, stopping him from crashing into Raven.

He hollers in agony, thrashing and shooting heavenly light in every which direction, searing it over my skin, but I don't react. The only pain I feel is the pain risen inside me by the thought of losing Raven.

Raven pushes past Elias, and Zade manages to pin the other two angels by their wings. He crunches the bones beneath his feet, using his devil form to restrain them.

Raven heaves a couple breaths, the Hell power and heavenly light coursing over her and sending static through the air. Her black hair blows around her face, blocking her beautiful features. I stand ready to lift her off her feet to make a run in the direction I think her soul remains captured.

"I never wanted to do this," Raven says, peering down at the angels. "You have failed humanity. You have failed your duty to Heaven. I'm here to set things right. You will serve a better purpose."

With her words, Raven thrusts the huge ball of energy at the three angels, setting them aglow. The world quakes around us, and the beautiful meadow she manifested blinks in and out of existence, turning the world fiery and then to shadows and back to white. She arches her back as she absorbs the angels' very essences into her being, sending her body floating a foot into the air unlike anything I've ever seen.

I grab her hand, afraid that she might float away, and it snaps her out of the powerful hold created by the twins and grounds her back to the plane by my side.

"That was incre—" Blinding light steals my vision, and I growl and cover my eyes, trying to ignore the wave of pain cascading over me.

Zade roars and his hand links through mine.

Raven screams our names, but the world disappears around us, and I stand beside Zade in a flaming circle in the Mortal Realm. Something sent us back here. But alone. Raven and Elias remain on the heavenly plane.

My ears ring, and the world spins around me again, dropping me into a wave of blinding light. As quickly as we were thrown from Heaven, Raven pulls us back. A dozen voices hum through the air, and it takes me a minute to gather my bearings.

"Do whatever it takes. Grab the mortal. We need those gifts now." The comment comes from an angel and blinding light shoots anger through me. Where are the others? They should be here to help us by now.

I unleash my devil power, swinging my massive tail over my shoulder and staking it through the blurry angelic light trying to keep me back. Fire explodes through the air with a deafening crackle. Dark fissures crawl through the light, forming figures before me.

I jerk my tail over my shoulder again, penetrating the being of another angel. Fire explodes from the spot as I send the bastard through a Hell portal and to Micah. The world shudders as the planes connect. The angels continue to shoot heavenly light at the weakest points, trying to seal off the plane. Raven cries out, her sob stealing my breath away. I still can't see her among the figures, but I know she's nearby. Elias had better be protecting her. If I find out she gets hurt, he will have my Hell to pay.

"You're doing amazing, Raven. Pull their tethers again. I know it hurts, but they're not all the way through." Elias's voice snaps in my ear, and I realize what's happening. Raven fights against the angelic light to bring us through completely. That's why the world is shuddering and shaking and darkness creeps in through crevices leading to the Hell Realm.

"Andre, Zade. Help me. I need you to follow the line. It

hurts so bad." Raven's voice cracks with her words, and I look to Zade.

He presses his hand to his chest, igniting his purple power across his heart. I close my eyes and manifest my own power, imagining a braided cord connecting me to Raven. I don't tug on it though. I don't want to risk pulling her from Heaven and getting her hurt from the sudden crossing between planes. She's only mortal after all and there's only so much her body can bear.

"We're coming, little hellion. Just hold tight." I follow Zade as he uses the line as guidance.

My skin burns and blisters, crackling with lava-like lines as we push completely through the veil and into the one place we don't belong.

The light fades and the figures materialize before us. I grind my teeth and swing my tail, staking another angel right through the top of his head. He has no time to prepare, so caught up in trying to cage Raven with angelic light. His body explodes in flames, and the world shakes again. Opening Hell in this moment shocks the plane of Heaven, and our world wavers, flashing from light to dark and back to light.

"You are banished from this realm." A stream of heavenly light shoots into my chest, aiming for that light tether connecting me to Raven.

Raven screams, and she drops to her knees with Elias beside

her. He feels her pain as if it was his own, and I swing my fist and punch the angel trying to get to them out of the way. The heavenly light grows more intense, and I'm afraid Raven will lose connection.

"Go find her soul. I'll protect her." Zade growls and whips his long tail knocking away another two angels that manage to get through the power crackling around Raven and Elias.

He's right. As much as I want to stay here and fight, I need to get to her soul. This might be our only chance, and I can't let Raven down.

Spreading my wings, I launch into the air and into the light, pushing through the pain and heading toward where Elias thinks her soul is being held captive. The angels split up, half of them chasing me, and I spin and fling my tail, staking them and tossing them away. I slice my sword through the air, cutting wings of angels enough to keep them away. The farther I get from Raven, the more aggressive they become, shooting me over and over with heavenly light. My vision dims, and my energy begins to fade. I slow, my wings struggling to hold my weight. But I can't stop. I won't stop.

"Please help me." The words sound like a whisper from my mouth as I try to connect with the Higher Power on this plane. "I know this was never your intention. Please help me get to Raven's soul. I will serve you well as a teacher of the souls if you give me the strength to fight."

"Your prayers will never be answered." The sharp familiar voice of Mikail stabs through me at the same time as his heavenly blade cuts through my back.

I roar and spin, flinging the blade away from me. I was too focused on reaching the highest peak of Heaven that I missed him stalking me.

I drop from the sky, the world blurring around me. My wings refuse to expand, the heavenly light taking a toll on my body. I crash to the ground, sending flames rising all around me. Mikail lands beside me, towering over me, wielding his sword and preparing to slice it through me. If he sends me to Hell, I don't think I'll be able to get back here. I won't be able to save Raven.

Jerking my tail, I swing it at Mikail, trying to knock his sword away. He slices it across my stinger, cutting it clean off my body. I holler in agony, watching as lava-like liquid pours from my body.

"Andre!" Raven screams, her voice slapping me as if she's within my reach, but I can't see her anywhere. "Andre! Return to me. I can't hold on any longer."

"Take my strength!" I shout, forcing my body to cooperate despite my agony.

I push to my feet and spin around, looking for Mikail. He will be the one who can take me to Raven's soul.

But he's gone.

The world quivers around me, and my chest explodes as Raven tugs on my tether, dragging me back to her. I have no choice but to allow her to pull me. Her hold on me is far stronger than it has ever been, and it feels as if we are one being. Her pain and grief are mine. My agony belongs to her.

I skid across the ground and land beside Raven. Fire burns around us, and I watch the flutter of wings fly above.

"I'm so sorry," I say, reaching out to stroke her glittering face, her tears reflecting off the light around us.

"Take them now." Mikail's voice shocks me, and I whip my attention as he materializes above us.

I can't move as he bends down and touches Raven's belly.

Whipping my injured tail, I use all my force to stake him through the shoulder blades, ripping him away from Raven. She screams as light and fire explode from her, enveloping us in pure love and protection. The heavenly light snaps off, leaving us in pitch darkness.

"Fuck!" Raven screams. "Fuck!"

"Oh, no. No." Zade's voice wraps around me, pulling me from the darkness.

I snap my eyes open to find us lying within the summoning circle on the basement floor. Elias kneels beside Raven, combing her hair from her face. I search over her body, afraid of what I might find. But her stomach remains bulbous, and I reach out and press my hand to it, feeling the twins moving.

"They brought us back here," Raven says, her voice shaking. "They brought us back too soon."

"Darlin'..." Elias turns to me, his eyes watering with tears.

Raven jerks up, watching her belly. It's now that I realize why. "This can't be happening. We haven't gotten my soul yet. Where are the others?" Raven sobs as she begs the twins to hold on.

But there's only so much any of us can do. Her water broke and she's in labor. The twins are coming.

Elias holds out his hand to me. "The heavenly plane is still open. Come on. I need you to help me. We're getting her soul."

Raven cries again. "Hurry. Please. I don't want to die."

Her words shatter my heart into a million pieces.

"I will not fail you, Raven." I turn to Zade. "She needs you here."

Closing my eyes, I allow Elias to guide me back to Heaven.

For the second time today, I pray. If I fail, this is over. The universe will be lost. I will never be whole again.

Last Stand

ZADE

"**H**OW LONG?" I clutch Raven's hand, my whole body rippling as I struggle to control my devil form.

Raven's obstetrician pulls off her gloves and tosses them in the trashcan next to the bed. Sweat beads on her forehead, and I know we must frighten her, but she remains even in tone and professional despite the presence of Hell heating the air.

"She's dilated six centimeters. It could be hours. It's hard to tell, but I will continue to monitor her. The twins are doing great. Nice strong heartbeats." Her doctor swallows, flicking her gaze to Micah as he remains in the Hell circle. His mind is pulled into different directions, but we both need him here. If he can't fight alongside the others, he can do his best to keep Raven calm alongside me. Our connection to her mental state will bring her peace during this terrifying time for all of us.

"Can you slow it down?" Micah asks, his voice booming through the air and startling the doctor.

"I've done all I can. She's too far along." The doctor shuffles back as if she's afraid of one of us lashing out.

Raven sobs again, her fear and grief stabbing me and cutting me open. I wave the doctor away and climb onto the bed beside Raven. Enveloping her in my arms, I stroke my hand over her back, trying my best to sooth her.

"This can't be happening. You two need to stay put. It's important. I know you want to come exploding into this world, but Mama needs you to stay in a little longer until your daddies get my soul." Raven hiccups as she says the words, rubbing her hands over her stomach. She cries out, her body tensing with a contraction.

"I'll get the doctor again. She can give you something for the pain." I try to get up, but Raven grabs my hand.

"No. I need to feel this. I need the constant reminder of what's coming." She sniffles and buries her face into my shoulder.

I grasp her cheeks, staring into her red-rimmed eyes. "Breathe with me. In and out. Take my strength."

Raven's pouty mouth quivers as she inhales a deep breath and exhales again. I know it takes everything in her not to scream, and I try my best to push as much of my love into her as I can.

"Why don't we distract her? Bring her here." Micah stretches out his arms, silently begging me to listen to him.

"This is not the time for orgasms." Raven groans and laughs with her words.

I force myself to chuckle. It takes everything in me to try to lighten the mood and to laugh at her joke. "We will definitely plan for that later. I think Micah wants to just talk things through. You know, we haven't discussed any names. Is there anything you like?"

Raven shudders with another sob, and I lift her from the bed and carry her to the summoning circle where Micah waits. He manifests a pillow on the ground and helps Raven get on her hands and knees as another contraction hits her hard.

"I bet if they are boys, some of the others are going to demand that they be their juniors." I don't know why I say it, because I'm nearly certain that Raven doesn't want to talk about this. She probably doesn't want to think about it either.

"Micah is a nice name," Micah says, grinning with his words as Raven heaves a breath, her contraction subsiding.

Groaning, Raven says, "I love your name, Micah, but I think the twins need their own identities. And I don't want to hurt anyone's feelings. I definitely don't want to name one of the twins after Lucian. He's going to have to live with his bad reputation."

I smile at her comment. "That's fair enough. But perhaps if they're girls...I've always liked your name."

She laughs. "We're not naming either of them after me."

"What about Hope and Grace?" Micah asks, his word soft as he brings up Raven's past life where she was named Grace and her sister was Hope.

"Yeah...I don't think so. My past life has a bad reputation as well. I mean, Grace took Elias from you." Raven crinkles her nose. Blowing a breath, she tries and fails to move the sweaty strands from her face.

I do it for her, remaining silent, trying my best to push a wave of calmness into her.

Our change in conversation works on Raven, and her tears finally stop. I hope it's enough to keep her from falling into grief again. I need her to keep her faith.

Micah pulls her hair up and summons a clip, pinning it in place to stop it from veiling her features. "But that was to ensure you came to me. It was our destiny to meet in this cycle with you as Raven. Had it been earlier, things could've been far different."

"At least I wouldn't be dying." She squeezes her eyes shut with her words and clutches her belly. "Please, babies. You're supposed to be comfortable in there. The world is too scary for you to come out just yet."

"Listen to your Mama. You have plenty of time to disobey her in the future," I say, forcing my voice to stay light and teasing. "All your daddies too, but especially Daddy Andre. He doesn't call your mama little hellion for nothing. I'm sure it's because you take after her, but right now...please. Just listen to your mama."

My voice shakes with the words. I don't even know if they can hear me or if they only react based on Raven's emotions and sensing threats. Maybe if I can connect with her on an emotional level and try to reach them with urgency, it'll slow things down. I'm willing to try anything. Do anything.

"Listen to me or you're going to be grounded in Hell," Raven snaps, her anger getting the best of her. She yells out, swearing at the universe for putting her in this position. Her rage and fear collide into me, igniting Hell power in my palms. It comes so naturally, brought on by Raven, that I accidentally release it, smoldering the back of her shirt.

"Almost over. Deep breaths." I remind her to breathe as her contraction peaks and steals her ability to do anything but grind her teeth.

"Fuck, that hurt. Damn it!" She gasps with her words, baring her teeth. "I'll take that orgasm now. Where are the others? Goddamn, son-of-a-bitch. Dante! Dante! I need you. Get your fangs here with that venom. Now!" Sobbing, Raven slumps forward, crying.

My chest tightens at her desperation for relief. "He's coming. They're all coming." Except I'm not certain if that's true. It hurts me to even say the words, but I can't stand hearing Raven in so much unrelievable pain.

"Take her to the tub. That might help a bit," Micah says, his terror over being unable to do anything to help Raven's pain as clear on his face as it is mine. "Or the ball. The doctor said that movement helps. You can take her on a walk around the house."

"The only thing that will make me feel better is fucking shit up. Bring me an angel. Let me beat the Hell into them until they give me my fucking soul." Raven groans, her labored breathing heavier with another contraction. They're getting closer and closer together.

I scoop Raven up into my arms. "Let's try a shower. If it doesn't help, then I'll find someone for you to torture, okay?" We both know I'm only humoring her because there is no way I'll let anyone outside the doctor, the other devils, and Elias get within her reach.

She growls, her voice deepening with a flicker of fire in her palms. "Micah, call Tamia. Have her find someone and keep them on standby. I mean it. The devils are taking too long. If they're not here soon, I'm going to need to find them."

"You will do no such thing," I say, tightening my jaw. I carry Raven to the grand bathroom, hoping to get her mind off destroying Heaven for at least a couple minutes. "I will handle it."

"We'll give them ten more minutes, and that's it." Raven tenses in my arms.

I rush to the shower and flick on the hot water, setting her on the shower seat. She hangs her head, and I stroke my hand over her spine, waiting until her contraction passes before I remove her sopping wet, half charred shirt.

Adjusting the shower spray to hit her back, I undress myself and kneel in front of her. Raven clutches onto me, moaning at the heat of the shower. I exhale a breath of relief. I still feel her fear and pain, but it doesn't hit me so intensely. Something primal awakens in me, and I think about all of the things Andre and Dante taught me in great detail to bring Raven pleasure. Is it going too far to suggest such a thing? No. Nothing is too far when it comes to easing the stress of the woman I love the most in the universe.

"Fuck, I just want it to stop, but I know if it does..." Raven groans, stabbing her nails into my shoulders.

"Breathe with me." I massage my fingers into her thighs, kneading deep circles as I work my way up her legs. "I'm going to try something to bring you relief. Do you trust me?"

Raven bobs her head, the shower steam dripping water

down her face. If tears leak from her eyes, it washes them away. It's what helps me focus.

"Good. Dante once mentioned that he desired for you to have an orgasmic birth." I lick my lips, my muscles rippling as I gauge her reaction.

Her lip quivers. "He was supposed to be here for that."

I wish with everything in me that he could be here alongside me and the others. Raven needs the support of all of us.

"But I'm glad you're here with me, Zade," she quickly adds. I know her disappointment lingers in the circumstances and not with me. Regardless, I will do everything I can to help her. To give her the best labor I can with the weight of losing eternity with her crushing me. I'm not going to just wait around and pray. I refuse to stand by and hope for the best or for things to work out. I'm going to get Raven through this.

I offer her a smile and stretch closer, grazing my lips to hers at the same time I summon enough power to set off her clit ring. I don't do it right away, slowly rubbing my fingers over her body, listening to her breathing quicken.

"How does that feel?" I ask, channeling tranquility with my ragged breaths. This moment isn't about sex or getting off. It's more primal, natural, and I want her to feel powerful and content. I want her to know pleasure instead of pain. This moment should be nothing short of bliss as she brings the twins into this world.

Raven moans and covers my hand with hers, guiding me to add more pressure to her body, stimulating her in a way to distract her enough from another contraction that she doesn't scream out in agony. She wiggles and squirms, her moans from pleasure instead of pain, and I ignite a blip of power, buzzing her body in a way that makes her orgasm.

She gasps and grabs me, silently begging me to move closer until I sit beside her, allowing her to slide onto my lap. I nuzzle my nose to her wet skin, kissing her softly as I rest my hands on her belly, just silently savoring her first moment of peace since her labor started.

"Why doesn't anyone ever talk about this being an option for pain relief?" Raven asks, her voice breathy. "It felt so...it's hard to explain. It's not sexual like I imagined when Dante mentioned it. I mean, you don't even have a boner." She giggles with her words, shifting to look at me. "Though I can't blame you. I'm a fucking mess."

I chuckle, kissing her again. "You're beautiful. Stunning. It's taking everything in me to keep myself in control because I know you, Raven. You'll try to bring me pleasure, and I'm not going to allow it. This is about you. Your pleasure. Your happiness. Your—"

Her body tenses, and I glide my fingers between her legs, massaging her as she stretches, trying to get comfortable through another contraction. I strum her clit, sending power vibrating through her again. She yells out in pleasure, her back arching, and I inhale a breath.

"Fuck, that was more intense. I feel weird." Raven shifts on my lap, her eyes widening. "Take me back to the bed."

Standing up, I turn off the water and grab a towel, striding from the bathroom. Micah faces the wall with his fingers behind his head. His stiff posture gets to me. Something is wrong, and it's not with Raven.

"Micah? Micah, what is it? I feel strange," Raven repeats, her breathing quickening. "What's wrong? Tell me."

Micah turns his gaze to mine. "I know you want to stay here, but I think you need to go find them," Micah thinks to me, voicing his concern silently. "It's taking too long. I haven't felt another angel passing through the Hell portal."

"Micah." Raven wiggles in my arms, not giving me a choice but to set her down. She bows forward with another contraction, and I do the only thing I can think of, getting on the floor to try to relieve her pain again.

Heavenly light bursts from Raven's palms, startling me. I shield myself, blocking my naked body the best I can. I know she doesn't mean to burn me, and I try not to grunt as my skin sears.

"Fuck. Micah come on and tell me what's happening. Something is wrong. I know it deep inside me. It's setting off the twins. I think they're coming."

Panic steals my breath. "I'll get the doctor."

Raven reaches out and snatches my wrist, wincing at the sight of my charred skin. "No, you need to get the devils. You need to go. They have to be here. I don't want to die without them."

I growl and whip my attention to Micah and then back to her. She knows whatever Micah sensed. And I hate that fear steals away everything that I worked to put in her. This is not how things should be for such a miraculous moment.

"You're not going to die. We won't allow it. Micah will get the doctor, and I will get the others. I will get your soul." I manifest clothes and quickly dress. Summoning a few weapons, I strap them to myself. Pulling Raven into my arms, I kiss her, pushing my determination into her very being. "Hang on. You better hang on."

As if the twins know what needs to be done, the world shifts from one plane to another, and I find myself standing in the middle of a war zone.

Screams and hollers echo through the air, and I spin around, afraid that Raven might have brought herself too. But I'm alone among dozens of souls. Not just any souls. Good souls that have found peace in Heaven but now call out in despair as if they're now facing punishment.

But it's not Hell.

It's the angelic army.

In their desperation to fight the devils, they have tapped into the energy given to Heaven by the souls that cycled to eternal paradise. In doing so, they have interrupted their peace. They have done more damage than good. The angelic army weakens the entire heavenly plane. It feels as if it might collapse at any second.

If that happens...

"The ruler of Sloth. You're exactly who we need. You have more reason than any of the forsaken. Show the others that you are willing to bow. If you bow, we will end this now." Mikail's voice booms through the air, igniting rage inside me.

I unsheathe a sword, spinning around to face him. I catch sight of the devils surrounded, the angelic army trapping them with heavenly light and using the souls to cage them in, their skin burning and blistering.

"Elias, grab him! Get Raven's soul. He can break through." Kase's voice echoes through the air, and I jerk my head up, watching as Elias spins above me, blasting heavenly light at the dozens of angels chasing him.

Summoning power, I chuck it at those following him before manifesting a throwing knife and jerking my arm out, sinking it into Mikail before he has a chance to even charge me. Transforming into my devil form, I buck on two legs and spin, kicking my back hooves out and knocking Mikail into some of the angels trapping the other devils in the heavenly circle.

It's enough for Lucian to whip his chain, knocking another two out of the way. It's all they need to break the circle. Without having to protect themselves from the agony of heavenly light, the devils can summon more power to fight.

"Zade, give me your hand!" Elias shouts, diving toward me.

I stretch my arm up, using my towering height as a devil to give me an advantage. The second his hand wraps around my wrist, I transform back into my human façade. He throws me into the air, catching me by my waist, and I throw more power, clearing a path for him. Hell power hurts the angels more than getting blasted with heavenly light that simply shoves some of them out of the way. But my power can drop them like the bugs they are.

"Go back to Raven. She needs you!" I shout, bellowing through the air, hoping that the devils hear me below. "They're coming. We will get her soul."

"She belongs to Heaven!" Mikail yells, gathering the angels below us. They call upon the souls of the plane, turning the world brilliant white with heavenly light.

My skin sets ablaze, and Elias hollers as I burn his arms, his body not immune to the hellfire created by the pure souls.

"Push through. We have to get her soul back." I shield my face with my hands, sending a silent prayer to the Almighty, hoping that this isn't it. This can't be how things end. The Higher Power would not bring Raven to us only to rip her away so suddenly.

Something tugs at my very core, and I gasp, losing my breath.

"We're being summoned." Elias's voice rises in pitch, his fear crashing into me as if it's my own. I can feel Raven as well. And something else. Something unexplainable.

"Resist it," I say, grinding my teeth. "Her soul can't be far."

Elias doesn't get a chance to respond to me. The plane shifts and dark fissures crack through the air. It's not Heaven or Hell calling us. It's not even Raven.

It's the twins. I can sense it on a deep-seated level, feeling the energy and power they carry.

"No! Stop!" I shout, my voice ringing through the air. "Stop!"

Raven's sobs call out, and my vision restores. I find myself in the middle of a brand-new summoning circle next to the one Micah stands in. And I'm not alone. Everyone is here with me. There is no one left in Heaven to get Raven's soul.

"We have to go back," I say, spinning around. "Raven, you have to send us back. The twins—"

"Baby B is crowning!" the doctor shouts, turning my body cold for the first time in what feels like forever.

It's too late.

We have failed.

18

Destiny

RAVEN

THE PURE LIGHT in my vision fades, and I find myself sitting in a rocking chair in the nursery the devils designed just for our family. A smile crosses my face, and I rock back-and-forth, staring at the two bundles in the bassinets in front of me. I can't believe I'm here with my babies. I don't know what happened, but one second, I was screaming in pain, praying to the universe to give me the strength to make it through, and then in the next, I'm here. Peace fills every inch of me, and I push to my feet.

"Have you thought of any names yet, angel-girl?" Kase appears next to me, the warmth of his skin crawling over the coolness of mine. Draping his arm over my shoulders, he stands beside me and stares at the brilliant light shining from the bassinet with the lavender blanket of my own little angel girl. She shines so brightly that I can't see her features, but I don't mind. I don't need to see her to feel the love and power radiating from her, blessing me in a way that I never knew possible. Not since Elias had given me his light. Now she carries it for me.

"I was thinking Arabella." A soft smile crosses my lips, the name just coming to me as if she picked it herself. And maybe she had. I never knew I needed her as much as I realize this moment. She truly is my answered prayer.

"It's perfect." Dante's voice comes from my other side as he materializes next to the bassinet full of shadows, surrounding the emerald-green blanket of our little hellion boy. He and Kase were right about the baby being male, and they are so fucking proud of themselves, though I know Arabella already has them wrapped around her little finger.

"And what about this little beast? We can't just call him our devil spawn." Lucian appears across the bassinet, his hellfire lighting his body aglow. I hadn't realized he was here but seeing him raises so much love inside me.

"Mateo." The name whispers through my mind as I say it out loud. It's strange to already know with such certainty.

"They are both precious gifts, aren't they?" Cassius stands

beside Lucian, and I blink a few times, wondering where he came from.

"They will serve humanity well." Andre's voice draws my attention to where he and Zade stand on the other side of Arabella.

I can't stop the frown from crossing my face. There is something strange about this moment that I can't put my finger on. But it doesn't matter. I'm just so happy to be here with my babies and my devils. Life would be nothing without them.

"Life will be nothing without you." Micah's voice whispers through my mind, drawing my attention away from Arabella's light and Mateo's darkness. I still can't see their little faces in their bassinets.

"Please, don't take her from us. This isn't fair. I have done everything you have asked. I have followed the path you set before me even when it descended into Hell. I have served you with righteous intention. I have given my faith to you. Please, don't take her." Micah's prayer stabs at my heart, and I spin around on the balls of my feet, searching for him.

The other devils disappear, and I gawk at their absence. Where did they go?

My heart sinks into my stomach. Where are the brilliant light and calming shadows that were in the bassinets? Now they're empty and only blankets of pure white remain. This can't be right.

"Raven. Come on, pretty soul. Open your eyes for me." Dante's voice prods at me, shaking the world.

"My eyes are open. Where are you?" I ask, spinning around again.

"I heard her. Keep talking. She's coming to." Micah's voice echoes everywhere around me and my mind.

"You're doing so amazing. You're so strong. Open your eyes. You're about to meet our first baby." Dante's whispers trickle through the darkness now surrounding me.

What is he talking about? I've already met Arabella, my precious little angel. She's so full of Elias's light that I could bask in her presence and feel content for eternity.

"Arabella? It's a girl?" Micah's comment swirls through my mind. He's thinking them to me telepathically.

"How do you not know? I've been watching her sleeping for hours next to Mateo." I blink rapidly, trying to focus on the nursery again. "Where are you guys? You were just here?"

The darkness lightens, and I stare down at the bassinet once more. That was so strange. I know that things have been weird lately, and I wonder if I should sit back down.

Reaching into the bassinet for Arabella, I try to lift her tiny body into my arms, but I come up empty-handed. There's nothing within the light.

What? I don't understand. Where is she? Where did she go? She was right here.

Rushing the few feet to Mateo's bassinet, I reach into the shadows and once again come up with nothing.

Panic rushes through me in an icy wave, and I tremble. My breathing quickens, and I feel myself on the verge of a panic attack. I try to slow my racing heart, but I can't. I'm hyperventilating. I feel as if I can't breathe. I feel as if I'm going to die if I can't find the twins. I see their power before me. I know they're nearby. But where are they?

"Raven, damn it. Open your eyes. Please. You need to hang on." Kase's growl tugs at my being, but I still can't turn away from the power radiating from the empty bassinets.

"Her body is weak," Cassius says, his voice remaining even in tone.

"But she's strong. Raven, wake up. The baby is coming. Wake up! Don't give up yet! Don't let Heaven take you!" Dante yells the words, his anger and fear jolting me from my panic.

Pain swells through me, and I scream and snap my eyes open. What the fuck is going on?

"Push!" a feminine voice commands. It's my obstetrician.

"Raven, I know you're confused, but you're in labor. The first baby is coming. Just another push." Elias grips my hand, his fingers squeezing mine so tightly as if he's afraid if he loosens them even a bit, he might lose me.

Everything hits me at once. The babies are coming. He just

said that the first one is almost delivered.

My heart raps against my ribcage, and I can't stop the sob shaking my body. "Put her back! I'm not ready!"

Another hand slides into mine, and Zade leans in close. "Be brave, Raven. I know this isn't how things are supposed to go. I know..." Zade sniffles with a sob, his face glistening with tears. "I know you're scared. I know everything is so messed up. But we can't put her back. None of us are ready for this. Take my strength. Take everything you need from me. I'm going to help you through. Elias is not going to leave you. You will not be alone."

I cry, the pain and anguish overwhelming me. This can't be happening. How am I supposed to be brave when I know what lies in my future? I'm losing everything, and there's nothing I can do about it. It's as if I'm being punished for just loving the devils. I'm being punished for creating the most power-ful, breathtaking beings the universe has ever seen. I'm being punished for an angel falling in love with me in a past life I don't even remember. I'm being punished because of who I was before.

"This isn't fair." I gasp and turn my attention to the rest of my body, watching as the doctor wraps up a baby and hands her to Elias.

"It's a girl," Elias says, his voice cracking with his words. "Raven, our angel baby is a girl."

I already knew. Arabella showed me a glimpse of the future I will never have, as if she was trying to help me through this agony.

Dante and Kase move for Elias, and he sets Arabella on my chest. I look into her squished face for the first time. I've never seen an image so beautiful. So pure. So mine. She radiates with heavenly light even now, capturing the best things in the universe and bottling them up for me to savor in this moment. And then she squeaks out the softest whimper of a cry.

My heart breaks.

It shatters into a million pieces.

"I'm so sorry, Arabella. I'm so sorry that I won't get to know you how I want. I'm so sorry that I had to bring you into the world this way. You are so special and so incredibly powerful. I want you to know how much I love you. And how much I love your dads. They're going to take good care of you. I promise." My eyes burn, and my tears blur my vision.

"Raven, this isn't over. You're not going to make those kinds of promises. You're going to take care of our babies. I swear on everything that we will get you back. Heaven cannot have you. I will destroy everything!" Kase roars, his devil form stealing away his humanity.

I can't respond as another intense cramp shudders through me.

"Get him back. We need to deliver the second one," the

doctor snaps at the devils, and they kick into action.

Dante and Lucian envelop Kase in a hug, squeezing him until he returns to his mortal façade. Growls of frustration coming through the air make it hard for me to breathe. It's as if a heavy weight crushes my lungs.

The world turns dark.

I find myself standing in the nursery once more, but this time I realize it's only in my head. This isn't the future I get. The power in the bassinets isn't really there. This is my mind creating what I want from the future. A future I will never have.

"Please, let me in. Let me get her soul. You can't do this to me. You can't do this to us. I'm sorry for turning my back on you all those years ago. I'm sorry for not remaining as a savior. But you have to understand. This was our destiny. We were always meant to meet at this point. You can't take her from us now." Elias's voice drags me from the nursery and back into the delivery room in the mansion. The brightness of his wings silhouettes him as if his whole body is haloed in light, and he kneels in front of what looks like a ring of dim light.

"Try harder. We have maybe a minute. If you don't break through now, we're going to lose her." Cassius stands behind Elias. "You can do this. Concentrate. They can't lock you out."

"I'm fucking trying! It's not Heaven. Something else is cutting me off." Elias growls with his words, summoning an orb of heavenly light and shooting it at the fading portal.

"You're not! I swear if you don't break through right now, I'm going to cut off your fucking wings! This is your goddamn fault! This is all of your faults! You should've fallen the second you laid eyes on Raven again. You should've jumped. Had you done so, she wouldn't be dying. We are going to have to raise those babies without her. What are we going to fucking tell them? How are we going to explain that we failed their mother? That we failed them?" Dante hollers with his words.

The room heats up with hellfire, all of the devils on edge.

A strange peace washes over me, and it's as if my body numbs to the pain. The doctor shouts commands at me, telling me to push, but all I can do is stare in silence as the world crumbles around me.

"Elias, Dante. I need you. I need you to stop. I don't want to die without you by my side. It's over. It's up to you...all of you to ensure that all of this wasn't for nothing. Don't let the angelic army destroy humanity. Now, please. Come hold me. I'm scared." My voice whispers the words, my whole body cooling, and my eyes continuing to stream tears.

I can't leave this world knowing that my devils and soulmate will go to war with each other. I need to know that they will stand together always. I need to know they will take care of our babies and everything we have worked so hard to save.

Eight pairs of hands touch my body, and just the pressure

of everyone touching and holding me, surrounding me and pouring their love and strength into me brings me a peace I never knew existed.

It's in this moment that I know everything will turn out how it's intended to be, regardless of where I land in the universe. This was never supposed to be about me. This was always about them. About their power and what they can create in the universe. This is about the balance of humanity. I have served my purpose. I have reunited them and brought the brethren back together.

"Almost there, Raven. You should see all of this beautiful hair." Cassius's voice remains soft as he rests his palm on my knee.

"Must take after me," Dante teases, a smile crossing his mouth despite the tears shining in his green eyes.

"You fucking wish. That's all me." Kase grins and shakes his shoulder.

"You two are both wrong. That little devil has to be Andre's. He's a fucking knotter. I bet it was him to knock our soul up. It would make sense." Lucian wags his eyebrows at Andre, the anger fading from his expression.

"As long as it's not yours is what matters." Zade chuckles with his comment, making Lucian growl.

"It doesn't matter. They belong to all of us. We are their family. They are created from the best of all of us through

Raven." Micah rubs his hand over my leg. He cradles Arabella in the crook of one of his arms. I hadn't realized he had taken her from me. And seeing her so quiet and content, radiating with light that doesn't burn him fills me with something indescribable. "Isn't that right, you sweet angel Arabella?"

"One more push. Give me a big one, Raven!" The doctor turns to the devils. "Almost there."

As if the devils and Elias fill me with their strength, I manage to push one last time. The world stills around me, and I blink a few times, staring at the gorgeous dark-haired baby boy being held in front of me.

"Mateo," I whisper, reaching my hands out to take him.

I didn't expect to survive him leaving my body. I have never felt so much relief seeing his scrunched little face.

Kase roars, and red power bursts through the air. "Raven! Raven, no!"

Mateo and Arabella both cry.

Silence fills the room.

Silence fills my very being.

19

Hell to Lose

DANTE

"**I**F YOU STOP, I will take your fucking soul to Hell." I clutch Raven's cold hand, staring at her face, her eyes open and glassy. I never expected to see her like this, but I can't look away. I refuse to let her go. I can't.

She's gone. I know she's gone. What remains on the bed is just a body.

But she's still mine. And I refuse to just accept the fact that Heaven has won. I refuse to believe that Hell has lost to the fucking angelic army.

"I don't know what you expect from me, Mr. SaTan. I've done everything I can. She's gone. You need to focus on your two beautiful twins. They need you right now." The doctor shuffles back, fear lining her eyes, but she doesn't give in to my demand.

Andre steps between us and motions toward the door. "You may leave. You will be heavily rewarded for everything you have done."

I hiss and flash my fangs. "Everything she has done? She has done nothing! Raven is dead!"

Two hands latch onto my shoulders, and Kase spins me around, forcing me into a hug I fight. He ties his tail around me and refuses to let go until the door slams.

"Dante, the doctor is right. Raven's soul will not return to this body. If we are going to get her back, we need to strategize a different plan. Elias will get her." Kase loosens his hold on me and touches my face, his eyes flashing red with his power. "This isn't the end. She would not want you to waste time doing the impossible."

I heave a couple of deep breaths. "She was proof that anything is possible!"

If the soft sound of one of the babies crying didn't capture my attention, I might have spit venom in Kase's face. I'm just furious. I don't want to stand here and do nothing. I can't just hope that Elias can get his act together and get Raven back. He already struggles to break into Heaven. What if he falls? What if the veil slams closed on him forever?

"Come here, Dante. Come hold Mateo. It will help. I promise." Lucian nods his head, motioning to our son in his arms. I can already see the power growing with every passing second.

Slumping my shoulders, I shrug away from Kase and do as Lucian says. It isn't fair for the twins to see us like this. I don't want them to assume that Raven's death lies on their shoulders, even as these tiny, precious beings. It is not their fault, and I will suck up my grief and show them that no matter what, I'm here. I will protect them as Raven wanted. I will give them everything I have inside me.

I bring Mateo to my face and snuggle into the blankets around him. His scent smells like powder and something sweeter like caramel, and I can't help wondering if it's possible to bottle up his scent to carry around. Something about holding my son brings me such relief. The warmth of his body fills part of the gaping hole left behind the moment Raven took her final breath.

Tears cloud my eyes as I relive the worst moment of my eternity over again. My shoulders shake as I silently cry and clutch onto Mateo.

"I promise, Mateo. I will bring your mama back even if it's the last thing I do. I will give up my place in the universe so you can have her always." My voice hitches, and I scrub the back of my hand into my eyes, trying to stop the tears. I'm a fucking devil. I shouldn't feel such agony. It's my job to torture those bad souls and not feel as if I am the one who deserves such torture.

"Dante, man. Raven would never want to switch places if it meant losing you. Don't think like that, my brother. We must only think about things as if we are not going to remain lost. We will rise again." Lucian squeezes my shoulder, staring at Mateo in my arms.

I grimace and whip my attention to him. "Who the fuck are you? You're not Hell's most notorious devil. Raven would be fucking shocked by your words."

"No, she would be dropping on her knees to suck my cock from how hot she finds me treating you with such kindness. She would even tease that I might have wings." He blinks his eyes, clearing the glossiness away.

"Fuck! Come on, Elias. We are going to fucking get into Heaven. Now." Kase grumbles with his words, grabbing Elias from the spot on the floor where he has been in this meditative state since the moment Raven lost the light in her eyes. He hasn't said a single word to any of us, nor has he even looked at Arabella. Zade holds her in his arms, rocking and singing softly under his breath. And now that I see Elias on the floor, anger rages through me.

"He's right. You've spent enough time speaking to those who refuse to listen." I stride closer to him, adjusting Mateo in my arms. "Get up. I want you to look at the twins and remember who this is about. You need to remember that they're who are the most important and why you were fighting to bring Raven home again."

Still, Elias doesn't move. He doesn't respond. It's as if he is in a trance and looking at something we can't see.

I stand in front of Elias and spread my wings, trying to intimidate him until he looks up. But it doesn't work. He continues to press his hands together in silent prayer. It's as if he doesn't want to deal with anything anymore, losing himself to the loss of his soulmate.

"Elias. Look at me. You need to be here with us and not wherever the fuck your mind wanders." I nudge him with my boot.

Again, he ignores me.

This time, I drop to the ground in front of him and hold Mateo out. His wings expand and flap, the light shining from them suddenly fading. Snapping his eyes open, Elias jerks his attention to Mateo. Something indecipherable crosses his face, and he automatically opens his arms and takes our son in his embrace.

I rest my hand on his shoulder. I should be taking my own advice and kicking myself for the fury coursing through me and for my behavior in front of the doctor, but I need to focus on something else. I need to focus on Elias and get him to pull himself together. His ability is more important. He is the only one that can access Heaven like we need. "Raven would want you to at least acknowledge their existence. I know this is hard—"

"Raven would want me to fucking be there with her. I was supposed to go, but I can't get back in. I'm trying everything. I'm praying to the Higher Power. I'm begging for forgiveness. I'm trying to thin the veil to blast through. But nothing's working. It's as if Heaven has been walled off from me. I'm failing Raven. I'm failing my soul and my mate. She will spend eternity grieving if I can't find her. I need to focus. I'm no good to any of you guys. I have failed over and over again, and I don't want the twins to think of me as a failure for the rest of eternity. So please, take him and Arabella and show him what a powerful and amazing king of Hell you are. Let me figure this shit out." Elias breaks, his wings sagging, and tears spill from his eyes and splash across Mateo.

Shadows glow from our son, wrapping around Elias as if the power embraces him. Zade brings over Arabella, slowly settling on the floor beside us. He holds the beautiful angel baby to her biological dad, and I can't help thinking about Raven. She looks just like her with hair as dark as midnight. Even their pouty mouths are the same, and I know that I'm going to have to send a whole bunch of asshole mortals to Hell on her behalf if they even manage to get within a foot of her.

"Perhaps Heaven isn't closed off to you, Elias. Have you considered that it is your daughter who keeps you here? Feel her grace. Feel the power coursing through her. Focus on her and see for yourself. It's not your fault. If you just look at Arabella and give her the attention she wants from you in this moment, you might be able to access Heaven again." Zade holds out Arabella to Elias, his voice remaining even. "And you know what?"

Elias shakes his head as he takes Arabella and cradles her in the crook of his other arm, holding the twins together. "I don't know anything anymore."

"Have you considered that you can't get through right now because maybe Raven wants you to stay here? She wouldn't want you to leave the babies to be with her. It was important to her that they had all of us." Zade rubs his fingers on Elias's shoulders, kneading his muscles and getting him to look into his eyes.

The others surround us, taking spots on the floor until all the devils of Hell sit around our last angelic brethren as he holds the two most precious gifts Raven has ever given us.

Elias squeezes his eyes shut. "It isn't fair. I should've ignored her wishes and accepted the deal with Mikail. It should be me facing an eternity of isolation. Not her."

I narrow my eyes at the others, making sure they don't agree with him despite if they actually do or not. I hate to admit it, but if I were Elias, I would've done just that. If I had to spend eternity by myself in Hell, damn straight I would to ensure Raven was on Earth and with the twins. She is their mother. It should've always been her here.

"We can't change what we feel we should've done. We need to focus on the new path before us and figure out what comes next. What we want to do next. Arabella and Mateo need us." Cassius clears his throat, scrubbing his hands into his hair. "It's important that we see what the angelic army is up to now. They're not going to just pretend we don't have the twins. Because we refused their deal, I'm sure they are going to be striking again."

I hate agreeing with Cass-hole. But he's right. They're going to know we're not just giving up. It's not in our nature. They will expect us to come at them hard, and that's exactly what I plan to do. If we can get them here, then we can get back into Heaven. Without its guards, the plane will be open.

Ruffling my black feathers, I push to my feet, drawing every-one's attention. "There's no fucking way I'm letting them attack. I'm not going to stand around here and just wait. If Elias can't ground himself to the heavenly plane even with his angelic light, I'm going hunting. I will get a bastard who can."

"Fuck yeah. I'm in." Kase holds his hand up to me, silently asking me to help him to his feet.

I pick him up and instead of letting him stand, I catch him

in my arms and hug him, burying my face against his neck. I knew he would agree with my plan. I knew he would stand by my side in my strategy to get into Heaven.

Someone has to risk it, and I feel like showing these angels what kind of Hell they're going to pay.

"You fucking bastards can't have all the fun," Lucian says, summoning his fire chain. "There's enough of us to split up. Four of us will stay with the twins, and four of us will go after the army." Turning to Cassius, Lucian holds his hand out. "What do you say, brother? Do you want to learn what kind of power lies in being a devil?"

Cassius raises his eyebrows, and I expect him to deny Lucian because of their eternal rivalry, but he surprises me and clasps Lucian's outstretched fingers. We'll have two flyers and two earthbound. It's a perfect mix. The perfect balance. That's just what Raven needs from us.

"Micah, will you take Raven's body to the center of all our kingdoms where Purgatory will rise? I want her where she belongs until we can reunite." I take a deep breath with my words, my heart fissuring and aching at just a thought. As much as it hurts thinking about not seeing her in the bed, being able to pretend she's just asleep, I know it must be done. We can't just leave her here. She needs to be home where our power and love are the strongest.

"Yes, and I'll be ready to do what is necessary. I want Mikail's wings splayed out in my foyer. Bring him here so we can destroy him together." Micah waits for me and Kase to carefully wrap Raven's body in the blankets.

Tears burn my eyes, and I snuggle my face into her hair, inhaling a breath of her scent one last time. Her time as a mortal is over. Her life as my pretty soul has ended. It's time to embrace our eternity. Just because she's no longer with us in her body means absolutely nothing to me. For the first time in a long time, I have faith that I'll get her back. She was never intended for Heaven. I know that with every fiber in my being.

The angelic army will see.

They will pay.

Kase kisses Raven's forehead before meeting her lips. He whispers something despite us knowing that she can't hear him. Her soul has been gone for a while. She was alive because of the babies. We all knew that they would have to come at some point, but if only it wasn't so soon. If only Mikail hadn't induced her labor.

But it doesn't matter.

I kiss her next, hugging her one last time before letting Micah take her. We watch in silence as Lucian, Cassius, Andre, Zade, and finally Elias say goodbye. The twins remain quiet and resting in his arms, and I think we manage to hold ourselves together for their sake. They might be young souls, but they are so much more than that. They have been truly blessed by the most magnificent woman in the world. We won't let them down.

I clear my throat and look at Kase. "Are you ready?"

"Fuck yeah. These halo heads are going down. They're going farther than that. We are going to wipe them out of fucking existence." His eyes flash red.

Damn straight.

This is what Raven would want.

This is what we need.

We were so close before, but I know we can do it again.

This time, we won't fail.

Hell will rise. Humanity will win.

It's as if the light just left the Mortal Realm. I should be relieved. I should celebrate that I can't sense a single damn angel. But it pisses me off. Those chickenshit bastards have left this realm completely. They knew we would come after them, so now they hide behind the heavenly veil that now struggles to keep a devil out.

"We need a sacrifice." Lucian cracks his knuckles, staring around the empty apartment complex that was known to house angels. It was where Cassius, Andre, Zade, and Micah all holed up while they were trying to protect Heaven.

But every infuriating reminder of the angelic army has vanished.

"A sacrifice, Lucifer? Are you fucking insane? We can't take the life of a pure soul." Cassius uses Lucian's heavenly name, and I think it's to remind him that despite being a devil, he was the morning star and the brightest angel apart from himself.

"Don't be a dipshit. I fucking know that we can't...but I know at least a hundred locals within a half a block who can." Lucian wags his eyebrows at me, the thought of sticking a dark soul onto one intended for Heaven thrilling him.

He's always been a twisted son of a bastard, and his plan might just work. Someone will have to come and collect the soul. That's what the guides are for. They watch over humanity, and when a soul's time comes, if they were pure and good, they would send them to eternal paradise. If their life was cut short, they'd still have to guide them to cycle again. Either way, some featherhead will come. Most likely someone weak. Maybe even one of those pure ones that just got into the heavenly realm.

I flash my fangs. "You deserve a fucking blow job for that idea."

Lucian rubs his hands together, chuckling. "I'm going to hold your ass to it. You've always been fucking excellent at sucking my dick."

I almost tell him that he's going to have to wait for Raven so we can give her the show she loves, but then reality hits me hard. It feels as if life itself treats my nuts as a punching bag, wanting to send me to my knees, curling in on myself.

"Like hell you are. Dante won't be sucking your dick or anyone else's. His mouth belongs to Raven, and she prefers that he only takes the mightiest cock between his lips, which is fucking mine. Now, get your shit together. You're going to find a fucking dirty soul." Kase whips his tail around, stroking it along my chest and getting me to look at him. "Do you want to help me pick out a good one? We have to make sure it's one that is already on its way out."

"What about me?" Cassius spreads his annoyingly vibrant wings. "Shouldn't I be the one? I am still close to Heaven."

I hiss at him. "But you're still a fucking asshole, so no. You're going to prep for the sacrifice. We need to keep the pure soul contained. You know what you have to do."

Cassius closes his eyes for a minute. "I do. This must be done. For Raven." He doesn't say the words to any of us but mostly voices his thoughts out loud. I can't blame the asshole. What we're about to do is fucked up. But the world is fucked up, and we're going to set it right again. Sacrifices must be made.

With a sigh, Cassius scoops up Lucian, launching into the air to drop him off where he needs to be to collect the vile soul.

I turn to Kase, fidgeting with his tail. The fucker strokes it out of nerves, and I jerk my hand out and lock my fingers around it, squeezing it.

"Now is not the time to lose your shit. I know this is going to suck, but it must be done for Raven. We need the angel." I try to keep my face expressionless. I just have to remember that the pure soul we choose will be someone unattached. We're not that fucked up. I'd prefer it to be a man, because I don't know what kind of dark soul Lucian will pick up. I can't agree to put a woman through anything that the fucker could come up with. I might be the devil, but I do have morals. I will make sure everything goes quickly and painlessly. The soul we choose will be one who had a long life, and it might take a bit of time. It would be what Raven would want.

"Come on. I know where to look. There's a hospital around the corner." Kase cracks his knuckles and rolls his shoulders. "This is for Raven," he says, mostly to himself. "This is for the good of humanity. If this is your intention and your plan, send us a sign for fucking once. You know I don't want to do this." Tipping his head back, Kase stares up at the sky. I don't think I have ever heard him speak to the Higher Power since he jumped. Something about this moment and hearing his words...I love this guy. He truly is my greatest companion.

A horn blares, drawing our attention to the crosswalk at the end of the block.

I raise my eyebrows and look at Kase. "If that's not a fucking sign, then I don't know what else is. Look, he's even coming our way."

The old man shines so brightly as he shuffles in our direction. He might pass at any second.

Shit.

I pull out my phone and dial Lucian. "Hurry the fuck up. We have a pure soul."

Hanging up before he can respond, I puff out a breath. The sacrifice bullshit is about to get real.

20

Sacrifice

KASE

"**I**T'S BEEN NEARLY two decades since a man as muscular as you held me in his arms." The elderly guy wraps his arms around my neck, whispering the words into my ear.

I chuckle and shake my head. I expected him to put up a fight or question what the Hell was going on. Instead, he just stopped right in front of us, seeing us through our Hell power, and said he had a dream about his end. He said we would bring him peace.

"Is that so? What about handsome?" I keep my voice light, carrying him down to the end of the block where we are meeting Lucian. Dante wanted to fly, but the old guy said he was afraid of heights. Carrying him was the least I could do, considering he volunteered, knowing that his time in the Mortal Realm has come to an end. Some mortals are just more perceptive of things. I wouldn't say that they've been blessed, but it's very possible that this guy is on one of many soul cycles. He's probably been through the Mortal Realm a couple of times. It has given him a better sense of things.

"I'm blind, so I can't tell." He sniffs me. "But you smell nice. Will you buy me dinner first before I finally shed this aching meat sack of a body?"

Dante tips his head back and laughs, his deep voice echoing through the quiet neighborhood. "I'm sure we could hook you up with someone to give you a blowy as well if you want."

The man wheezes and coughs, his attempt to laugh cutting short. "Maybe the reaper you've chosen can."

A blip of sadness courses through me. It's been a while since I've been around a pure soul who wasn't Raven. It's as if the Higher Power put this man before us to remind me exactly what we are now fighting for. We are fighting for humanity, despite the anger I carry toward almost every other soul. Raven would appreciate the humor this old guy finds, even knowing that we're going to have someone murder him.

It'll give him a choice about whether to start a new cycle or to finally enter Heaven. I don't ask him which he'll pick, because

I don't want to influence him. I don't want him to worry that there might not be a Heaven to go to soon enough.

"I'll even pull his teeth out, so you get one hell of a gummy. He's a vile bastard with no chance of redemption. He's headed straight for the bowels of Hell." Dante grabs the man's shoulder and gives him a little shake.

"Well, when you say it like that...fuck no. I don't need that kind of honor. Serving the greater good is the only thing I truly need apart from the constant agony finally coming to an end." The old man's voice softens with his words, and his face slackens as he loses himself in his thoughts. I can't see his eyes behind his sunglasses, but if I didn't know any better, I'd think he could see through the veil.

Picking up my pace, I carry the old man until I spot Lucian restraining a man within his fire chain. It looks like duct tape covers his mouth, preventing him from screaming, and I'm sure he stuck something else on his tongue to torture him while he waits.

And damn. Lucian really knows how to pick a dirty bastard soul. Looks as if he is a murderer, cannibal, rapist, and animal abuser. He's going down.

The old man gasps from my arms, jerking his attention toward Lucian. "The rebellious son. It seems you have proven yourself worthy."

I scrunch my face, a bit annoyed that he deems Lucian to be

what sounds like the only devil in his eyes.

"Perhaps you've learned from your companions," the old man adds, squirming in my arms until I finally set him on his feet.

Okay, he's off my shit list.

I grin and punch Lucian in the arm. "Bow down to our pure sacrifice, you fucker. Show him you appreciate what he's doing."

Lucian pushes the evil bastard mortal forward, tripping him and forcing him to kneel on the ground. "I don't bow to anyone except Raven. This guy will have to do." Growling, he rips the tape off of the guy's mouth.

I knew it. The guy coughs and spits out what looks like some sort of appendage. Maybe a ball sack. But it doesn't belong to him. He would be sobbing and screaming if it did.

"I caught him right in the act. He was filleting someone right on his kitchen table. Disgusting." Lucian links his fingers through the guy's hair, jerking his head back. "I have the perfect place in Hell for you. You're going to love it."

Lucian flashes his devil façade, and the guy hollers and sobs, showing just how truly pathetic he is. Sure, he's a fucking bad guy when it comes to hurting people weaker than him or catching them off guard. But when he's face-to-face with the devil...it always shows the truth.

"I'll do anything. Tell me what you want me to do, and I'll

do it. Just don't hurt me." The man tries to dry his eyes on his shoulder, but Lucian doesn't allow him to move.

A smile widens across Lucian's face. "You're going to do what we say regardless. Don't worry. It's right up your dirty bastard alley. You're going to end this old man's life."

The murderer bastard sniffles and frowns. "What? What do I get for it?"

I whip my tail at him hard enough to slash his skin open. "You get the perfect place in Hell. That's it. Do it and do it mercifully. You will not cause him any pain. He is going to be humanity's sacrifice. Let's make it a good one."

The door to the building behind Lucian creaks open, and Cassius pokes his head out. His eyes flick from the asshole on the ground and to the old man. Blue light shines in his gaze, and he ruffles his feathers.

"The circle is ready. Are you guys set?" Cassius asks, opening the door wider to show off the shithole apartment. It looks as if he found an old safe house used by angels. Hell, he probably used it himself.

"Fuck yeah. Let's catch ourselves a feathered bastard. They can ride to Hell together." Dante grins and reaches down, grasping the dark soul's chin. "Whichever bastard who comes could ride your ass down. What do you think about that? A dry pounding might be just the way for you to go."

The man begins to sob again, and I growl, flashing my devil

form as I drag my claws through the front of his shirt. Cassius barely has time to open his arms before I toss him toward the empty building into his arms.

He only holds him for a second, scowling at me before dropping the dark soul to the ground in disgust. "The world will be a better place with you gone."

Damn. I like this side of Cassius.

Dante whacks me on my back, offering me a weak smile. Now that our minds are no longer focused on getting a sacrifice ready, it's hard not to think about why we are doing this in the first place. An ache squeezes my chest, and I wish that it would yank my heart out for me. I can't stand knowing that Raven is gone. I believe that we will get her back, but every second that passes is like a century without the woman I love most in the entire universe. And I can't stop thinking about what happens if we do fail. I don't want our children to know that their fathers have broken their promise to protect their mom always.

I blink my unexpected tears away, channeling my rampant emotions into my wrath. I'm pissed. I just want to fuck shit up. I want to destroy everything that comes in my path, starting with the guardians. I'm going to destroy the veil after that. Heaven will be no more. Once we get Raven back, we'll figure out how to make Elias finally do what he was supposed to and jump. We will have everything that we have fought so long to get.

"Please, God. Forgive me for everything I've done. Don't let them do this. Please." The dark soul gasps with his breathing, his voice choking with every step toward the angel trap. It's intended to temporarily capture our sacrifice's soul, drawing the angel out of hiding.

"The Almighty has already answered our prayers. This is your way of redeeming yourself. Your actions will save humanity. It will not be forgotten. But still, it's not enough to save you in the end. Maybe you will learn and end up somewhere else in Hell." Cassius tightens his jaw, acting as if that's even possible for this guy. I think he only says it to get him to shut up. There's no way he's going anywhere other than the pits.

"You think so? I can get into Heaven?" The man stops blubbering and looks at each of us.

Lucian cackles, transforming into his beastly form, his horns jutting toward the ceiling and scraping the paint off. "He's just fucking with you. You're going to be my bitch. Now, it's time."

The dark soul shakes his head. "You can't make me."

We all look at each other, a smirk mirroring across our faces.

The old man groans, wobbling on his feet.

"You want to bet, fucker?" Lucian manifests a blade, slapping it into the guy's hand.

In a moment of desperation, the guy swings his arm, trying to fight Lucian. But it's pointless. Lucian moves out of the way and gets in front of the old man. Groaning, the dark soul lunges at the same time Lucian moves out of the way. The dark soul can't stop himself in time, colliding with the old man.

All it takes is our sacrifice to swing his arm and slap the dark soul across the face. It happens so fast that I don't even get a chance to brace myself for the blinding heavenly light exploding from the old man's body. The angel trap ignites in blue fire, set off by the old man's soul now escaping his body, dead from a stab wound right through the neck a second before he was going to die from old age.

I never like to give credit to miracles, but this was one if I ever saw it. A true miracle without influence from divine intervention.

Tipping my head back, I stare at the ceiling and whisper a silent thank you.

The dark soul pushes himself off the ground and spins around, realizing he's within the angel trap and surrounded by fire. The world shifts and moves, and I watch as a figure materializes within the bright haze created by the trapped soul.

I crack my neck, gathering my red power in my palms. I can taste the sweet revenge already.

The dark soul sees the angel and cries out, grabbing him and latching on as if the angel could even save him. This couldn't get any better.

The angel's so distracted by the dark soul tainting the air

around him as he tries to grab the pure soul that he doesn't see Dante come up behind him. Lucian opens a portal to Hell, knocking the evil soul in, ending his life as he deserved.

The angel gawks in surprise. "Heaven, help—"

With a swing of his Hell sword, Dante cuts off one of the angel's wings. I can't let him have the honor of doing the other one, and I summon my own blade and beat Lucian, slicing the angel's other wing off, sending him to his knees.

"Your sacrifice will never be forgotten. May your choice to cycle or to enter the heavenly plane be as magnificent as you are." Cassius uses his blue power to open the angel trap, releasing the pure soul. It disappears, choosing to go through another lifecycle.

I knew the old man was a smart bastard. I hope to one day see the fucker again. Maybe next time, he'll do something to end up in my kingdom, and we could throw a fucking party. Hell doesn't have to be torturous for everyone. He'll make a fine demon.

The angel jerks his attention toward Cassius, his eyes widening as he gathers heavenly light in his palms. I summon my ruby energy and thrust it at the angel, winding him. He can try as hard as he wants, but we've won. This bastard is going to Hell...after he opens Heaven.

"All right, fuckhead. You obviously know who we are, so instead of resisting or trying to defend the wrong side, why don't you make the right decision for once? Think with your damn head instead of being a follower to Mikail. You're new enough to have living relatives. Do you truly want to destroy them?" Dante hisses, flicking his forked tongue with his words.

He's damn convincing. If I were an angel, I'd be on my knees and swearing allegiance already.

The angel groans, bowing forward, his back a mess with blood and chunks of his wings still hanging. "Please, I'm following my path. I'm not a warrior. I'm a guide. Please, you have to let me go to heal."

"We don't have to let you do anything," I say, gathering more power in my palms. I chuck it at him, wishing with everything in me that the world would just open up and allow us into Heaven to get Raven. We know it's possible now. That's probably why only low-level angels such as this douche get to shift the worlds, considering that we can't find any of the warriors around.

"The only way you're going to make it out of here without being chained to the bottom of my fire pits is if you cooperate. Open the fucking portal to Heaven. You have a soul there that doesn't belong to you. It belongs to us. Open it, and you will have a good place by my side." Lucian flashes his devil façade, his horns curving up from his forehead. He looks sexy as hell, but I'd never admit that to him.

"That's not my place to go." The angel turns to Cassius.

"You must understand. I know that you've only forsaken Heaven recently. Please. Make them release me."

I snarl, transforming into my Hell beast. Launching from the ground, I pounce on the angel and shove him back, sending fire bursting around us. "Last chance. This is not open for negotiation. The guardians have fucked up everything, and we're trying to save humanity. We are trying to save the woman we love. The Higher Power would not have brought you to us had it not been its plan. Open the fucking portal."

"And take us to Raven. If you can do that, you will be a prince of my kingdom. You will serve us better than you could ever serve Heaven. You could guide souls from one level to the next until they finally have learned enough to move on from Hell. It's what we've been trying to do for all of existence." Dante stands next to me, resting his big palm on my shoulder blade, stroking it over my heated skin until I sit back on my haunches. I don't transform back. I need to remain powerful. I need to be prepared for the second he gives. Because I can see it in his eyes. He believes us. He's going to do it.

"So all I have to do is open the portal and guide you?" The angelic man asks, looking at each of us in need of confirmation.

"If you can do that, you will rise. You will have done the Almighty's work." Cassius keeps his voice low and reaches his hand out, offering to help the angelic man up. "Feel it with your entire being. You know we're right. You know this is what must be done. Please, Gabe. Do this, and everything will be righted. The universe will find its balance again, and we'll have peace. Isn't that what you want? Peace instead of war? Because if you don't, your existence will end here and now. The entire heavenly plane will fall. There will be no home for pure souls."

Of course, Cassius knows the angel's name. I guess I should've asked the dickwad first. It's easier to connect with someone on their level if we know something personal. I tuck away my annoyance to unleash on him later once we get Raven back.

The angel, Gabe, tips his head back and stares at the ceiling. He closes his eyes, listening to his emotions, seeking guidance without asking it. "Okay. I'll help you. But my path must remain on this course until you fix this. The pure souls still need me to guide them. Heaven needs the power." The angel tightens his jaw as if we might lash out at him.

But I raise my hands to Lucian and Dante, knowing that they want to argue. Cassius remains stoic and silent, letting me take control.

"It's a deal. You may continue to guide pure souls until the seven sinners take their thrones and hell rises with the creation of Purgatory." I finally manage to get my boiling blood cool enough to stand before him as a man.

"Fuck yeah! Let's get you back to our place. You're going to open a portal where we can control what comes in and out."

Dante surprises the guy by scooping him into his arms. Cassius grabs a hold of Lucian and me, lifting us from the ground and carrying us to the door as if we can't even walk. I try not to smack him upside the head. But he smiles at Dante, and my heart skips a beat, and I feel hope for the first time since watching Raven take her last breath.

"Lucian, call Andre and let them know we're coming. We're going to need Micah to return from Hell. We're going to need fucking Elias to get ready to join us. He's our safest bet." I stare at the hellfire flickering in Lucian's gaze. He looks ready to take on the universe by my side.

We've had our ups and downs, but we are finally coming together as one, just how Raven always wanted and needed. She will have a future. She will not remain trapped against her will for eternity.

We're going to get her back.

Purgatory will rise.

My heart and very being will be complete soon enough.

This isn't the end. This is only the beginning.

Rise

ANDRE

I STARE AT Arabella, picking out the features familiar to Raven. She'll have the same beautiful shade of midnight black hair like her mom, and I'm sure her eyes will be the same, though right now, they're more gray than blue. She has petite ears and is smaller than her brother by two pounds. Even so, her wails are louder, and she shines so brightly that I'm sure she can banish a demon away.

"I heard the others land. Want me to take her?" Zade rubs his hands together, stepping in close until our arms touch.

It takes me everything inside me to nod my head. I don't want to let her go just yet. It feels as if I don't hold her for the rest of eternity, I'll lose the best part of me. The part of me that Raven took with her.

"Her brother could use her right now. You know they're used to being close. Tamia would also love to hold her. You haven't even let her get within a few feet, Andre." Zade pats my shoulder, waiting patiently for me to finally shift Arabella from my arms and into his.

As much as it hurts me on a deep-seated level not to hold her, the expression Zade gives makes it worth it. His eyes light up, and his whole face smiles with his happiness. He hurts on the same level, if not more because he is empathetic to every emotion coursing through the room. My sacrifice, giving away my time of just cuddling with Arabella and loving up on her as our daughter brings me relief. It makes it easier seeing how it gives Zade strength.

I clear my throat. "Be careful with her, you two. She radiates with heavenly light."

"You're not going to hurt your cousin, are you now, baby girl?" Tamia wiggles her fingers, holding her hand out to Zade. "You're going to save that for all the assholes that try to hurt us, aren't you? I bet you could merge your powers with your brother's and just blast all those pesky, lying angels away, right?"

Zade chuckles, and I shake my head. "They're going to be so powerful. I can already see it."

"Damn straight." Dante struts in the room, cradling a familiar angel in his arms as if he's practicing for holding the twins. Gabe looks miserable, his face scrunched in pain, but he doesn't scream or fight.

Kase comes in behind him, stretching his arms out already, heading straight for Tamia and Gia. "Give them here. I need to cuddle the fuck out of them. It's been a long day."

I expect Tamia to argue, but she holds Arabella out alongside Mateo as Gia holds him out as well. I'm thankful for it. I know that Kase struggles. His eyes fill with tears, and just the sight of his pain stabs me deep in my chest. It's easier for me to shut things out, to carry faith, and to carry hope, but he and Dante—Lucian too—they've been so far removed from Heaven for so long that I'm sure it's not easy for them anymore.

"Where is Micah?" Lucian's voice booms through the room. His eyes flash with firelight as he strides into the room with Cassius right behind him. He looks ready to start a war, and I savor the power radiating from him. I haven't been planning this for my entire existence as he had. He probably feels wronged because Raven was so easily stolen from us.

"He's ready and waiting in the basement. He doesn't want the babies to be so close to the Hell circle." Zade kisses Arabella on her forehead and returns to my side. "We are good to go."

I look toward Elias, quietly sitting in the rocking chair, staring off into space. I know his thoughts wander to the heavenly plane, and he might even still be trying to access it. "What about you, Elias? Are you ready?"

It takes Kase nudging him with his tail to get him to even look in my direction.

"What?" he asks, scrubbing his hands into a scruffy face. "I mean, yeah. I'm ready."

He doesn't sound so sure. I know it's going to take a miracle to pull him from the darkness of his thoughts. He carries the blame for Raven's death. He carries the blame for not being able to access Heaven again as well. He refuses to share the weight of the universe on his shoulders, so it's up to us to grab it from him to show him that even though he is not a devil, he is still one of us. He is one of Raven's loves and the reason that her soul was angel-kissed in the first place. He never made a mistake, sharing his light with her. He never even made a mistake when the two of them decided to cycle again. Everything that has happened in existence has happened for a reason. I know that we'll get Raven back. I know that this moment of time, and her absence, will only make us stronger.

That's how I keep myself together. I can't believe anything otherwise. I'll not stand the thought of her being imprisoned in Heaven forever. The Almighty doesn't work like that. We were not given the ability to turn our backs on his plans for nothing. I believe with every fiber in my being now that this was what it wanted. The Higher Power is not our enemy.

"We will be with you the entire time," Cassius says, draping his arm over Elias's shoulders. I think it's the first time I've seen him show that kind of affection toward Elias, and it doesn't go unnoticed.

Elias flutters his wings, light radiating from his being. Cassius squints, but he doesn't pull away. Instead, he pulls in closer and hugs him.

"The only thing I regret in my existence is not opening my heart sooner. I wish I could look at the world like you had when you found Grace. I'm sorry for trying to take her from you. I'm sorry that I also tried to take Raven. I hope you can forgive me. All of you." Cassius swallows, his Adam's apple shifting in his throat.

This is the man that I would follow anywhere. He has finally overcome his pride, and even though it is his kingdom, I know that he will not go back to how things were. He knows now how to listen.

"Yeah, yeah. We can fucking celebrate later. We don't have much time. I'm sure the angelic army is going to notice something is up." Kase claps his hands together, turning to the angel. "You're up, Gabe. Don't let us down."

"If you do, our deal is off," Lucian adds, muttering.

Instead of asking about the deal, I quietly follow behind the others, kissing Arabella and Mateo on their foreheads as we pass by, leaving them with Tamia.

Because Raven needs all of us.

So does the rest of the world.

"Everyone brace yourselves. There could very well be an army on the other side of this portal." Kase tightens his grip on his blade, preparing to charge into a portal not intended for us.

"I'll go first and shield you to the best of my ability." Elias swivels on the balls of his feet and looks at each of us. "I'll be able to sense Raven's soul immediately. Once I do, we should be able to manipulate the realm. You guys fend off the angels, and I'll get her. If I'm not back—"

"Your next words better not fucking be to take care of the twins on our own. You can't stay, even if you want to. Raven will kick your ass straight to Hell if you try. So just get our pretty soul." Dante hisses with his words.

I nod my head, silently agreeing with him. He's right. I know Elias wanted to go with Raven even if he couldn't bring her back so she wouldn't be alone. But we all know that the twins need him. They need all of us. We don't have any other options.

"I don't think the angelic army will be waiting. They're confident in their ability to keep you out." Gabe rubs his lips together, tensing as if we'll blast him with hellfire.

It looks like Micah wants to. He gathers flames from his kingdom, growing them in his hands as if he plans to blast anything and everything from his spot in the summoning circle. He's not going with us, but his power and tether are what will give strength to us in this moment. Because we're going to need it. Heaven hurts my very being to cross into.

"We're about to prove them wrong. So open the portal. I'm ready." Elias unfurls his wings, straightening his shoulders. For the first time all day, he looks as if he's channeling the strength of Hell despite being blessed as a reincarnated angel.

Gabe lifts his hands, tipping his head back. For a moment, I'm afraid he's not going to be able to access Heaven and that he's already been forsaken by making a deal with us. Everyone shifts, our nerves rippling with our muscles. Shifting my gaze, I glance at Zade. He tightens his jaw, gripping his sword tighter. Purple electricity dances across his gaze and I force myself to smile at him. This is like old times, standing together. But we are stronger now. We are better. We see things more clearly.

Bright light flashes through the air, stinging my skin, but it doesn't burn me. It's as if Elias absorbs the sacred air coming through the portal. Gabe groans, his whole body shuddering. I realize he currently stands in the middle between angelic light and Hell power, and if he isn't strong enough, he could be destroyed in the process.

"Move!" Elias charges forward, not letting the pain stop him. He flaps his wings, rushing into the heavenly portal first.

He jerks to a halt, and Kase nearly plows him down, using his tail to stop him from crashing to the ground.

Then I see them.

We were right. There has to be at least a hundred guardians in formation, gathering heavenly light in their palms.

"Everyone, fall back!" Elias shouts, gathering his own heavenly light. "I don't feel her. Raven's soul isn't here."

Shock rushes through me, and I gape at Zade. What does he mean that Raven's not in Heaven? We all know her soul was there. We could sense it before. It was being imprisoned deep within the sanctity of the heavenly plane. A soul doesn't just vanish. Raven was the only one I've ever seen to be able to manipulate a soul into new energy.

"What?" Kase growls and shoots Hell power at the front line of guardians. "She has to be!"

Elias spins, spreading his wings wide, creating a wall between us and the guardians. "She's not! Now go! They're going to crash through."

I intake a sharp breath and swing my arm out, grabbing Zade and Lucian. I drag them as I flap my wings, launching us back toward our summoning circle in the safety of our home.

"Seal the portal. Now!" Elias demands, growling as he faces Gabe, still holding open the portal.

"Please, forgive me. I did as you asked, but I could never betray Heaven." Gabe leaves his hands up, keeping the portal open.

Rage cuts through me like a tidal wave, and my devil form breaks free. Whipping my tail over my head, I stake the bastard angel through the chest and swing him toward Micah. Gathering Hell power, Micah blasts the angel before he can even get within reach, burning his skin.

The portal shuts, and the room dims.

But this isn't over.

I see what the angelic army is now preparing for. If Raven is not there, then they think she's with us. They weren't hiding. They were calling every angel in existence to war. They're coming not for us but for the twins. They still believe that they are a gift to Heaven.

They're going to learn how wrong they truly are. I'll destroy the universe alongside my brethren to protect our children. The angelic army is done for. We will bring Hell not only to Heaven, but to Earth. There's no other way. The angels aren't the only beings that can reset humanity.

The universe is about to go dark. Maybe then, we will find Raven.

Only her soul will shine. She is the center of our existence. We will get her back from wherever she is. She will be Purgatory's queen.

22

Isolation

RAVEN

I STARE AT the fog surrounding me. It's as if I'm everywhere and nowhere. My soul aches and tears cloud my eyes. I can't believe this happened. I never thought how heavy the realization of dying would be until I shifted from the Mortal Realm and into this heavenly prison. The image of my babies is imprinted into my mind, and they're all I can imagine.

There is no peace in this prison.

There is no light or love.

Fuck. I haven't even seen an angel yet. They're probably avoiding me because they know I'll rip every damn feather from their wings.

"Don't be afraid. I won't try to hurt you. Just show yourself. You can't leave me like this. I don't deserve this imprisonment." I try to gather the strength not to break down. I focus on my devils and what they must be going through in this moment. They are probably blaming themselves. I hope they're not fighting. I hope that they just love up on the gifts that they helped me create. I hope that they can figure out how to come to me.

In this moment, I realize that my soul hurts on a deep-seated level as if I've been broken into a million pieces. I can't be put back together again with the huge chunks of my soul gone. I didn't think I'd want Elias to come to me, because he deserves to have an existence with our children, but now that I'm alone...fuck. Am I selfish? Maybe. I'm just so fucking angry. I'm furious. How could the Higher Power believe I deserve this? I have done nothing immensely as bad as the angelic army. There are monstrous souls out there that even though they suffer, they don't face this type of torture.

The unfairness of it burns through me.

"Goddamn it! Show your fucking selves now!" I shout the words, but I'm not even sure if I'm able to hear them. I can't tell if I'm pure energy or not. I can't manifest anything. I can't focus enough to distinguish the difference between what is in my being and what is outside of me.

I think about closing my eyes until the haze disappears, leaving me in darkness. I try to shut the world out completely. I need to think. I need to meditate. I need to see if I can summon the devils to me even though I no longer have the power given to me by our babies. I'll have to try.

I can't just exist in this world of nothing. In this world of utter despair.

"Please, God. If I'm in Heaven, then I have to be more connected to you than ever, right? Please, help me. I can't truly believe this was a part of your plan. I think that your warriors have fallen off their paths so much so that maybe the plane for good souls has been turned into one of punishment. I can't believe you would consider the idea of souls growing and learning to be anything other than something you would want. You created this universe with the idea of souls recycling, right? But they were destroying what you put in place. And the devils only wanted to fix things. They might have unconventional methods but look at everything they have done. They want nothing more than to keep the balance of the universe. They don't want to take over. So please, hear my prayers. Give me a sign. Give me answers. Show yourself." My very being buzzes, and I snap my eyes open and stare at the fog again.

No one answers. No one materializes in front of me. Whatever the Higher Power is, I know it isn't going to show itself. But the buzzing grows. It's as if electricity sizzles from my core to light up the world around me. The haze dissipates, and I find myself standing in the nursery of my home.

I gasp and cover my mouth, my eyes spilling tears at the sight of my devils standing around the twins opens a dam inside me. I can't believe it. They're so close, yet a wall of impenetrable glass stands between us. It's the veil.

Holy fucking shit. This isn't Heaven.

This is the plane that the twins created.

What this means? It means that I have a fighting chance. Heaven couldn't contain my soul like they had wanted to. And maybe...my sweet, beautiful, powerful children. They had to have been responsible for this. Maybe they were the ones to answer my prayer. They helped my soul move from its imprisonment in Heaven and to the safety of their perfectly balanced world. If this is the case, it means that I should be able to communicate and let the devils know I'm okay.

I slap my hands to the invisible barrier, sending strange sparks around me. "Hey!" I yell, wondering if there's any way that I can just break the veil.

No one looks at me. The devils stand in a circle, muttering under their breaths. I can't hear them clearly, the energy humming through the air as loud as the sound of an imaginary heartbeat pounding in my head. It's strange how even in this state of energy without my body, my being still holds onto what it was like in my physical form. It's like with Hell and how

I could still feel pain and pleasure. It's not that I'm mortal, but my soul feels more of a transfer of energy.

I inhale a deep breath, calming my nerves the best I can. I suppress the sound of my own energy in this plane and concentrate on listening.

If Dante hadn't thrown his arms out and shouted, "Gather the armies. We are opening Hell. We're going to unleash our power on this realm," I wouldn't have heard him. It's his fury that allows me to figure out what's going on.

And oh, no. The angelic army knows that I'm not in Heaven. They're probably coming for the twins. They have been back-and-forth about them all this time, and I know they believe they have a right to these two precious beings and had expected they would eventually get them, but now they're going after them immediately. I can't let this happen.

"We're going to break the plane. If we all use our power, we can bring Hell to Earth. We already know it's possible. The angelic army will fucking regret ever messing with us. They will truly see what it is like to know eternal torture. If they want to reset humanity, they're going to fucking have to destroy it first." Lucian cracks his knuckles, summoning his fire chain. He stretches it out before him, looking as if he's going to open the gates of Hell right in the nursery.

"Mikail is mine." Elias says, his voice is deep with his anger as he adjusts my gorgeous little girl on his shoulder, rubbing soothing circles on her back.

I can't help thinking about the fact that they're so young and already facing so much. I don't even know how much time has passed. It could be weeks. I don't think it's been months though. They're still so little.

"Like fucking Hell he is. We're going after him together. We're going to shred him piece by piece and feed them to the hellhounds, wait for them to shit him out, and then we're going to do it all over again." Dante hisses with his words, flashing his fangs.

A phone ringing sounds through the air, and Lucian pulls out his cell and brings it to his ear. "Everything is ready. All we need to do is head out and blast the fucking portal as wide as possible. Once we crack the foundation, our legions can come through."

My eyes widen. The devils are going to be in so much trouble if they take the twins into battle already. I trust them with my life, but this is teenage stuff. Our babies need a chance to know life with pure love and not utter destruction.

I smack my hands to the veil again. "I swear, you guys are going to be in so much trouble if you even think of strapping on a damn carrier and taking the twins to war."

As if Elias hears me, he cocks his head in my direction, staring right at me. But he doesn't react as if he can see me. His jaw remains tight.

"Is Micah ready with the protection circle?" he asks, adjusting Arabella in his arms again. "We need to stay on complete guard. I can hear the battle cries already. They're going to come straight here. We might have minutes."

"He's ready. All the earthbound contracts are gathering, ensuring that we have enough time." Cassius speaks for the first time, expanding and closing his wings.

And then I remember what he taught me about crossing planes. If I can just manage to connect on a spiritual level, I might be able to get in touch with them. What could he possibly do? I have no idea. I know that they have bigger priorities at the moment. Our children come first.

But damn it. This fucking sucks.

No one has a chance to respond, because the world explodes, shaking the foundation of the mansion. It's as if a tornado hits the place, sending debris and smoke raining through the nursery. But it's not a natural disaster.

One second, I'm watching my devils, and then the next, I'm outside and staring up as the sky cracks open, sending blinding light to the world.

What the fuck?

Something buzzes, like a fly getting close to my ear, and I swing my attention to look around. This can't be happening. What the fuck is the angelic army doing? I spot several bright souls floating through the air, acting as if they're being sucked into the heavenly plane.

Fear crashes through me, and I rush back toward the mansion. But I don't make it inside. The ground cracks beneath my feet, and I scream, watching as fire explodes from the earth. I fall back and hit the ground, staring in shock as the mansion crumbles and disappears into a Hell portal.

Pushing to my feet, I run toward it, trying to summon everything in me to jump. This might be my chance to connect with the devils. It's as if the universe crumbles before me, now exploding from below as Heaven reigns from above with me trapped in the middle. This isn't how I imagined Purgatory to be, but right now, this battle is destroying the Mortal Realm.

I launch from the ground and toward the crack, bracing myself for pain that never comes. I smack into an invisible barrier, staring down at the lava lakes and the dark cloud of souls swirling and growing as it prepares to launch from Hell.

It's just like it was before when the angelic army was trying to free their warriors from the pits by unleashing Hell on Earth. But this is different. This is controlled by the devils themselves.

"Stop!" I scream, pounding my fist to the invisible barrier. "You're better than this. You're going to steal the realm we've been fighting for." My voice falls flat, the realm around me not allowing me to even break the barrier an inch.

Fog swirls around me, stealing the sight of the Hell plane beneath me, and I yell out in frustration. What is happening?

It's as if something drags me away from my spot, and there's nothing I can do about it.

Flashes of light and shadow crash around me, and it feels as if I'm being dragged at high speed with nothing to hold onto.

"No! Fuck!" I don't know what else to do, so I just give in to the pull and allow the world around me to drag me from the place I wish I could be with my devils.

I don't know how long the world zooms around me, maybe minutes. Maybe an hour. Time doesn't move here in this realm. But the sensation suddenly stops as the fog stills. It's like someone hit the pause button, and now I'm trapped within a glass box with nothing but my own thoughts to keep me company again.

Tears pool in my eyes. I can't live like this. I can't spend eternity so out of control. I'd rather just watch my devils and not be able to talk to them ever again than be in this isolation. This fog.

"We need more energy." Mikail's deep voice shocks panic inside me. What the fuck? I know he's close, but I can't see him. I can't feel his disgusting present either. "It's time to call every pure soul to Heaven."

Holy fucking shit. Is he going to rapture everyone he can from the damn Mortal Realm?

"Gather the guides. We must all stand together. It is finally time to bring Heaven to its intended glory." The female voice snaps through the air, but I don't recognize it. I can't see her either. All I know is that these assholes are going to destroy eternity for my children.

I can't let it happen.

"No. You can't do this. This will not help Heaven to rise. It'll destroy everything." I say the words despite knowing that they can't hear me. It's as if I'm alone and watching. This is exactly how I imagined ghosts feel like, but at least they can mess with the realm. They're not completely isolated from it. Their energy can do crazy things, including possess people.

I feel as if I've lost all my power, and I'm utterly hopeless and helpless to what the angels plan. Think, Raven. Think. They can't get away with this. If you can just return to the devils, maybe you can put your energy toward the veil. Maybe you can make them aware that you're here. If they know you're here, you can...

The world shifts. The hum of the angels' voices and their light fades, and I find myself standing in front of the men I love and the children I would do anything for. They're so close that if I close my eyes, I can feel as if we're on the same plane. I have to do something. They need me. They've always relied on me to help them. I was supposed to be the one responsible for helping Hell rise. I refuse to be its downfall. I refuse to do anything other than use my entire being to see to it that they succeed. That is my purpose. I know it deep in my very being as if the Higher Power handed it to me with a blessing to make things right.

I feel it's as if I was given Elias to consume and absorb everything he is as a powerful angel and let it grow inside me. I feel the same about the devils. I wouldn't have ever been able to conceive such power had it not been my purpose and my path. But now, I must prove that I was worthy of such a task. I am the queen of Purgatory. I am humanity's last chance. I can save the universe. I never believed that such a task would fall onto my shoulders, and in my past life, I wasn't strong enough. I wasn't dedicated enough. I was too lost in the light. But the devils' darkness helps me see. They help me grow.

"I summon you into my world." I press my hands to the barrier, imagining manifesting the tethers of light that bound us together. "You're mine, and I'm yours. We will not be kept apart. No plane. No army. Not even the Higher Power can keep me from you. We're intended as one. We will rule together and ensure the souls get the eternity they need. The angelic army is not getting in our way. We'll create a future for our children. But you must come to me. Hear my call. Feel my soul. Remember who I am and what I can do." The words resonate through the air around me, and I feel it deep inside my essence. If I can just push harder, gather their strength, then I can reach them. I don't have to be trapped in this world of isolation, a mere onlooker to a world that I deserve to be a part of.

"There has been a sighting." Lucian's grumbly voice cuts through the veil to me, and I imagine it vibrating across my skin. I imagine the heat of his Hell power cascading through my very soul, lighting me up.

"We need to hurry. Take the twins and go. You have to protect them with your life. They're gathering the purest of the pure before their time." Cassius unsheathes his sword, swiveling on his feet to look toward the gaping hole between worlds.

I notice they stand in front of a portal connecting Hell in the Mortal Realm. And beyond that...blinding light. He's right. The angelic army gathers all the pure souls for their purpose to use them to bring Heaven to Earth just as the devils have brought Hell.

"Just kick their fucking asses. I want all of their wings." Dante hisses with his words, holding the twins in his arms as he unfurls his wings. "You're our last chance, brothers. Fight for Raven. Fight for the twins."

Kase hugs Dante and gathers his ruby light, striding to the line where the other devils wait. I stand frozen, pressing my palms and my nose to the veil, wishing with everything in me it would snap open already. What the fuck do I have to do to get through to them? What the fuck do I need to do to bring my world into theirs as they have done to the Mortal Realm?

"Go, Dante! They are here!" Andre explodes into his devil

form, using his wings to launch his hulking body forward and toward the blinding angelic light growing and growing like a tidal wave about to cascade into Hell. And with that blinding light comes complete annihilation. The blinding light eats through the fire protecting the devils. The souls are powerful enough to send them back to their kingdoms.

It's enough to make way for the angelic army.

"No!" I scream, my whole body igniting with fear and utter despair at the sight of the wave of light crashing into Andre, devouring him as if he isn't a devil of Hell and just a shadow of darkness. He vanishes before my eyes, and while I know he's not gone, he leaves the other devils to fight on their own.

"Fight!" Zade shouts, shooting his purple electricity toward the raging hurricane of pure souls stolen straight from mortal bodies before their time. "Don't let them in."

He charges toward the portal entrance alongside a wave of pure black from the darkest souls in all of Hell. They eat through the light and shake the world. But the light steals away the darkness, leaving him exposed until it swallows him whole.

"Everyone, attack at once! On my command," Kase snaps, his voice booming through the air. "Don't let these fuckers close the portal. Keep pushing. We have to break the realm. If we don't, they will get in."

Kase, Cassius, Lucian, and Elias stand together, each gathering their own power. I watch as Elias charges forward first, expanding his wings and creating a light shield for the devils. He hollers, and I gasp at the sensation of his pain stabbing through me as if it's my own.

He vanishes in the light, and I scream out. It's as if Heaven claimed him, and he can't escape the pure souls.

None of my devils can.

I stand frozen, screaming for them to fight, but there's nothing they can do.

The pure souls crash into them.

All I see is pure light.

23

Worlds Collide

RAVEN

THE SHOCK OF electricity strikes my middle, and I watch it bounce back to the invisible barrier, separating me from the men I love. The world quakes as a crack crawls up the veil, sending the light through to me.

I gasp, my eyes widening in shock as it spills out from me. I expect to turn into pure energy. I expect for it to devour me and instead of relocating me, I feel as if my end is here. Heaven has won.

But pain doesn't swell through me.

Peace does.

The pure souls fill me up unlike anything I've ever experienced, washing away my pain and anguish. My grief and desperation. The energy crackles across my skin, sending my hair floating in static. It gives me the strength to push against the veil harder. Swinging my arm, I punch my fist against it, and the plane explodes in light and shadow.

I hop back at the energy swirling like a tornado, gathering and moving toward me as if I'm drawing it in.

My whole body buzzes as the first wave hits me. It's as if it's water and I'm a sponge. I absorb the pure light of the souls and fill my very being with them. But that's not it. I gather my courage and take a step forward, crossing from my plane into the Mortal Realm. I stand between Hell and the angelic army. The first line of angels gather light in their palms, their features sharp and angry as they see me for the first time.

They want me. I can see it on their faces. They're going to try to take me this very second.

My rage gets the best of me, and I hold my arms out, summoning power from my very core, built from the pure light of souls and the pitch-black energy from Hell. I thrust the power at the angels, and shouts and wails fill the air. Their figures implode in crackling white light that sparkles through the air like glittering confetti. But it doesn't hit the ground. It catches on an invisible wave of energy and crashes into me, knocking me to the ground. The intensity of the power burns over my skin and lights me up. I become a vessel as if my soul turns tangible and sucks up every bit of the divine energy. It flows through my core, tingling across my skin, and I close my eyes and embrace it. I imagine gathering it up and filling my heart with it. I imagine it tethering me to this world, so I never leave again. I imagine it tethering me to the devils and Elias. To the universe and everything in it.

A shock of electricity steals my breath away, and my body arches as I float in my form created by my angel-kissed soul and the energy I have siphoned from all of existence.

The world turns white again, and I stand in absolute purity. I should be afraid. I should try to cast the light away with the darkness lingering inside me, but something holds me back. This place isn't Heaven. It isn't the Mortal Realm or Hell either. It's a plane created for me. It's made from the energy and from everything that life has taught me, manifesting a sanctuary that protects me instead of imprisons me.

And then I feel it. I feel the light wrapping around me and pulling at my center, dragging me forward, connecting my soul. It's hard to explain, but it feels as if I'm being guided in a specific direction like I'm intended to follow this path now materializing before me. The holographic rainbow road leads into a wall of pure prism light, the colors so beautiful that it's all I can think about in this moment. I've never seen something so spectacular in my life apart from the moment I laid my eyes on my twins.

This particular light, sparkly and full of colors beyond the human spectrum, reminds me of the love I carry for my babies even though I haven't had time with them in the living world. It reminds me of what we fight for in Hell. It reminds me of how beautiful the world can be with balance. It's not about light or dark or black or white. It's not about gray. It's about the vibrant color of every emotion and every feeling. Every life and every ounce of energy created from coming together as one.

A figure stands within the light. Its silhouette a striking darkness as it spreads its wings. But it doesn't scare me. I recognize it. It's me. The silhouette is my reflection shining back at me from the rainbow world.

And holy fucking shit.

Stretching out my arm, I graze my fingers over the silhouette of my angelic being, and energy ignites inside me.

The world jostles and I feel myself flying, but I don't know how I'm doing it. It's as if my soul travels through time and space and existence only to throw me out in the Mortal Realm. It sets me down in the place where Heaven and Hell collide in the mortal world.

I land in a crouch, digging my fingers into the soft grass. The universe breathes life back into my very being. All of my pain and anguish vanish, and all I can think about is humanity. All I can think about are the worlds colliding in an unnecessary war.

I gather power, spinning to look at the angels staring at me in utter shock. The ground shakes beneath my feet, and the angelic army suddenly vanishes in a flash of light.

Fucking cowards.

They know that they have fallen on the wrong path.

They know that their time is coming to an end.

"Darlin'...I don't believe my eyes." Elias's soft voice sounds from behind me, his shock filling me with a thousand emotions. "You're here. You've been blessed."

I slowly swivel, staring at him and his beautiful eyes. "I've been given a new path. It led me right here."

Elias rushes to me, engulfing me in a hug and lifting me off my feet to spin me around. Tears fill my eyes as we both cry, our light enough to blind the world around us.

"I was so scared I lost you forever." Elias kisses my cheeks, smearing my tears with his in the process.

"I was too. I was so isolated. I thought that the angelic army had imprisoned me and was just going to leave me without ever confronting me. But then something happened, and I could see through the veil. I could see...Elias, take me to the twins. I need to see them. I need to meet them and hold them and kiss them and love them. Please." My whole body shakes with a sob as I imagine my world disappearing again. I don't want to waste another second without seeing the two most precious and loved beings to me in the universe.

"They're the most amazing little souls I have ever seen. They're just like you." Elias rubs his hand over my spine, touching my feathers in the process, exploring my wings as if they're the most mesmerizing things to him.

I rest my head to his shoulder, closing my eyes and sucking in breath after breath of his scent. I feel like if I even move an inch, the world will explode. I know that's not the case, but the lingering fear still weighs heavily on my shoulders. The angelic army is still out there. Those cowards are still going to plot the Mortal Realm's destruction. And it sucks. All I want to do is go to my devils and love up on them and hold my babies and act as if nothing else is happening in this life. I just want to embrace my future as the devils' love and as the mother of the universe's most powerful gifts.

But I can't ignore my wings. I can't ignore the strange pull that still strikes me to the core. I know that my path doesn't end here. This is not my destination. Not yet at least. There's still so much I need to do.

But I want to breathe. I want to rest. I want to savor every second I have in this moment because I thought before was my last. I thought I was spending forever alone.

"Raven!" Kase's familiar voice rings through the air, and I whip my head up from Elias's shoulder and spot my handsome feline devil standing tall in his monstrous form.

I wiggle in Elias's arms until he sets me on my feet, and I rush toward Kase until my wings flap and launch me from the ground and at him.

He squints through the brightness of my angelic form, and his jaw slackens in shock. It's enough to make me stop short. I don't know if it's his expression or if it's the strange new darkness I see radiating from his burgundy eyes or what, but I realize he might need a second to prepare.

"What the fuck? Get your bubble butt over here before I fucking spank you." Kase whips his tail at me, encircling my waist and dragging me into his arms.

I cry out and cling to him, peppering his neck with kisses as I work my way up to his mouth. He groans and slides his tongue between my lips, not even wasting a beat to kiss me with enough passion to send my body singing and my soul glowing with the brightness of Heaven.

"I still might fucking spank you. You're an angel. What the fuck? I don't understand." He holds me up with one hand while cupping my cheek with his other. "This is...a damn weird-ass miracle. You're fucking burning me, but I love it. I would face being scorched for the rest of eternity as long as I could bask in the presence of everything you are, my real angel-girl."

A soft cry sounds from behind him, and I inhale a sharp breath at the beautiful melody of one of my babies crying. It's as if my whole being screams at just the sound.

Kase realizes what's going through my mind, and he whips around and faces the other devils, now gathered and staring at the two of us in anticipation.

The way they look at me...I'm surprised my clothes are even still on. They look like they want to devour and ravish me in the best way. No angel form or heavenly light will stop them.

"Get your asses over here. I need you." My voice cracks with my words, and Kase sets me on my feet, but he doesn't let go of me, keeping me bound to him with his tail. "Let me see the twins. I need to feel Arabella and Mateo in my arms. I think I'm here because of them."

"You are. You never made it into Heaven. It's as if they pulled your soul from imprisonment to protect you. And now this...Raven, this was your purpose." Cassius keeps his voice low. He's afraid the other devils will lash out at him for even suggesting that my death was my destiny.

But he's right. I can see it now. I was supposed to die a mortal so I could ascend as an angel. Everything is so clear. I don't think Elias could have ever jumped from Heaven to create his level of Hell unless I was an angel too. It's how Purgatory is supposed to be made.

I don't know how I know, but the thought is deep-seated. It's the only thing I'm certain of apart from my love for the devils and my devotion to the world we want to create for humanity.

Dante steps forward, his black wings flapping and sending a stinging breeze over me. We are on opposite ends, our power wanting to battle each other, but our hearts love the sensation. My body tingles like crazy the closer he gets. I can imagine the pleasure that comes with his punishment.

"Arabella and Mateo, look who it is. Mama is finally here. And you did this. You saved us all by bringing her." Dante's voice comes out hoarse as tears spill from his eyes.

I blink, trying to clear my gaze, but it's as if my tears are never-ending. "Hi, my sweet babies."

I take each baby from him, cradling them together in my arms. Leaning forward, I kiss their foreheads and just breathe in the scent of their skin. I bask in the power radiating from them. They are perfect. They're everything I imagined them to be. And I am so blessed to be their mother. I'm so blessed to be able to be here to raise them alongside their dads. Their family.

"I love you. I love you so much. I had no idea I could love anyone this way. I'm so sorry I wasn't here for you when you came into this world. I tried everything I could to stay, but I just couldn't. Please forgive me." My body trembles with my comment. I don't know why I say it or why I ask, but I just need to let them know how incredibly important they are to me. I wouldn't purposely abandon them. I never wanted it to be this way. I didn't want to die. But I had to.

"You don't need to ask for forgiveness, Ray. Never ever." Lucian comes up beside me, wrapping me in his arms, careful not to squish the babies.

"I know. I just...I'm so happy to be here. I'm so thankful and relieved." I swallow and lick my lips. The devils all surround me, each taking a moment to hug and kiss me and tell me how much they love me and how important I am.

I could bathe in their love for me forever. I plan to.

"We are too. So let us take care of you. Let us give you everything you deserve. I can't wait another moment." Elias kisses my shoulder.

"We're never letting you go again. We're going to bring the world together. We don't have an option. The angelic army wants to reset the universe, but we are going to fight for it. Even if we must give up every realm and coincide on one plane." Andre speaks for what feels like the first time, the sudden closeness of him igniting something wild in my being. I can feel him on every level. He's starving for power. He's starving for me.

"How are we going to do that?" I ask, my nerves bunching my muscles. "Are you sure that's a good idea? We can take the war to them again. They can't keep me out of Heaven."

"We're going to send every damn dark soul through this portal. Heaven has rejected so many that they don't stand a chance." Lucian growls deep in his throat, his power flickering across his skin.

The world rocks under my feet, startling me. I don't get a chance to react before Dante and Andre lunge for me. Scooping me up, Andre cradles me in his arms as Dante gathers the twins in his. Kase joins him, hanging onto his side and preparing to fight.

"The fuckers had the same idea. We have to move." Cassius grabs Lucian and Elias lifts up Zade.

Hellfire cascades through the world behind us, and I spot Micah launching a wave of dark souls toward the light flashing around us.

"Move!" he hollers, transforming into his beastly form.

Bending his knees, Andre launches us into the air. My skin buzzes, my new angelic form responding to the intense light of another wave of angelic warriors. Expanding my wings, I force Andre to release me and spin in the air. The warriors don't stand a chance. Their very beings call to me.

I gather power in my palms and blast it toward the front line of angels.

Silence falls over the world as they crackle and pop like a firework show before us. Their energy steals my breath.

Andre snatches me from the air, diving down.

He drags me into Hell.

24

Together Forever

RAVEN

"LET ME GO!" I shout, wriggling and kicking in Andre's arms. "I can fight. It has to be me!"

Andre runs across the black onyx path outside his palace. It takes me a moment to realize it, but his orgy tornado is nowhere to be seen. What the fuck? It's quiet as well. Screams don't rip through the air. It's unsettling.

He sets me on my feet, folding his wings on his back. I could easily jump up and fly away, but it's as if something draws me to stay. I know it's Andre and his desire to protect me. But it is something more than that. I want to find the missing souls.

Except...I know where they are. It's so strange.

"Raven, look at me." Andre touches my cheek, drawing my attention to him. "Let me take you inside. We need to wait this out."

"Where are the others? I thought they were coming with us." I spin on the balls of my feet, kind of missing that weird-ass tornado orgy. It was entertaining to watch, to say the least. If I were a normal soul and ended up in Hell, I think I would be okay being punished by Andre in his kingdom. I'm a freak like that.

Andre hooks his arm around me. "They had to go to their kingdoms for just a bit. Don't worry, little hellion. I will take good care of you until they get here. We chose my kingdom for a reason. We weren't kidding when we said we wanted to be with you. Losing you and your mortal form was the hardest thing I've ever faced in my existence. It was even harder than when I fell from grace."

His words set off something wild inside me. He hits me with a wave of his lust pheromones, turning me on with the simple idea. My brain decides that it will not allow me to think of anything else besides getting pounded by the devils, and I get wet thinking about it. Who knew I wanted it so badly? I thought angels were pretty chaste. Except for Elias. I suppose I did give Andre a blow job when he was an angel. I guess being so close to the mortal world gives them mortal desires. And me? It's so much more than that.

I've always used sex with the devils as a distraction. What better way than to improve my mood with a fucking fantastic time? And the way Andre looks at me now, I might as well be naked. Slowly nodding my head, I turn back toward him and away from where the orgy tornado usually swirls. Without saying a word, I close my wings and tug at the front of my shirt. It is the weirdest fucking thing to have it easily come off and not get caught on my wings. It's hard for me to remember that I am manifesting myself and my clothes in this moment. I have complete control. Andre looks as if he's about to take it away from me though. And I want him to. I want him so badly that I can't wait a second longer.

I rush him and link my fingers to the hem of his shirt, ripping it off his head. Our mouths crash together as lust explodes through me, sending tingles between my legs. Andre growls deep in his throat and lifts me off my feet, breaking from my mouth to kiss my neck and work his way down to where my bra suddenly burns away with his lustful power here. I suck in a breath at the heat crossing my nipples, and Andre takes each one into his mouth, sucking hard enough to send a burst of energy to my core. I arch my back and stretch my torso, wanting him to work his way lower. As if he reads my mind, he lifts me up higher until he positions me with my thighs around his neck. I use my core strength to stay upright and comb my fingers through his hair, holding myself in place as he buries his mouth against the apex of my legs, licking his tongue hard and fast, just needing to get me off. I moan every breath of air. I gasp, squirming and making it a challenge for Andre.

I scream out in ecstasy as Andre brings me to my peak, and I squeeze his head between my thighs as I orgasm. And holy shit. He growls as I light up like a fucking star, but he doesn't complain as his skin reddens.

"That's your punishment for being such a good devil," I say, not letting Andre get me off for a second longer. The vibration of his growl strikes me right in the clit, and I moan, my body and my muscles relaxing, allowing him to bring me back down. He's going to fuck me right now, and I know it. I will be stuck to him for however long, and I don't even care. All I want to do is please him and feed his desires, turning him into the powerful devil I'm so madly in love with. The other devils will figure things out. We all know that I have enough holes to go around. Who knew that the idea of getting stuffed with all of their cocks could be so thrilling? And I'm stronger than ever. I'm a goddamn angel. I'm about to bring the devils to their knees. They will worship me as they always do. I will be their queen and we will change the universe.

"You naughty girl. I thought that I would be a bit romantic, because you deserve all of my love and affection, but I'm going to fuck the Hell into you that you'll be walking funny for eternity. And even longer than that. Just wait until the others arrive."

Damn. I don't know what has gotten into Andre, but it's as if he's channeling Lucian. And his new hot intensity gets me off already. I want more. I need more.

"I think you're all talk. If you weren't, I'd already be..." I moan with a scream as Andre aligns our bodies and thrusts his massive cock inside me, the pressure and power of his pounding zinging to my very core. I stab my nails into his shoulders, clinging onto him as he guides my body back-and-forth, going as deep as he wants. I swear I can feel him in my stomach, and he purposely rearranges my damn insides just to fit his long, girthy length into me.

His balls slap my body in a way that makes me moan and squirm. I'm not going to make it easy. If he wants to fuck my brains out, he's going to have to work for it. I know that by the sensation of pressure building between my legs that he won't even be able to pull out now.

I tighten my muscles. "You're mine now. You're going to be the one walking fucking funny for days."

"Fuck, angel-girl. Talk to my ass like that." Kase's rumbly voice draws my attention away from Andre, and I lean back and stare as he and Dante hold the twins in their arms. Cassius, Lucian, Zade, and Elias land beside them. Micah materializes in a wave of flames, smiling.

I should care that they arrive and are holding the babies while

I'm basically putting on a show for them, but I have no shame.

"You were supposed to wait for us, dickhole. Your ass should've fucked her last. Now we're going to have to wait fucking eternity for you to release her." Lucian glowers, but it doesn't stop him from coming forward. He reaches into his pants and pulls out his hard cock, stroking the length as he strides closer. "I'm taking your ass, Ray. Going and turning your sweet ass into an angel makes me want to punish you to no end. I'll make sure to reach around and flick your clit as I pound you. Come here. Andre, spread her open for me."

I gasp with a laugh, and Andre spins me around protectively, not letting Lucian have his way just yet. But I know it's coming. I want it. I want him. I want all of them.

"I think Andre's enough devil for me right now. Why don't you watch the babies, Satan?" My hair cascades down my back, and Andre continues to rock his body over and over again, not even stopping as I talk.

And I love that about my devils. They don't care. We are all in this together. They are mine, and I am theirs. Always and forever.

"Yeah, Satan. Hold the twins. We're about to tag-team our girl. If you're nice, maybe Raven will allow you to have some fun with me while you wait your turn for her." Dante summons a bottle of lube, squirting it in his palm already.

I'm so used to Dante and Kase fucking around with each

other while they fuck me that the moment that he mentions letting Lucian have at him as they take turns with me turns me on more than I expected. I knew that he had cut Lucian off the second he decided that he was mine and I was his, but this isn't anything other than a bonding experience between them. None of them are in love with each other like they are with me. This is about our deep-seated need to get off. To have fun.

"That's so hot," I say, wiggling my fingers at Dante. "You are so thoughtful and considerate. He doesn't deserve your precious offering of that sexy ass of yours, but damn. I want to see it. Let me be the conductor of the ass train for once."

Dante tips his head back with a roar of a laugh, tossing Lucian the bottle of lube. Kase adjusts the twins in his arms, and the rest of the devils follow behind Andre as he leads the way inside the palace. And holy shit. His bedroom has changed since the last time I was here. There's no bed. The room is a bed. The entire expanse of the floor is a mattress and there are toys everywhere. It's as if he just summoned Dante's entire collection and brought it into his kingdom.

"The twins are fed, changed, and already asleep for their nap. They won't be disturbed by us. Look, I've ensured it." Kase motions to the corner of the room with two bassinets. My mind was wandering too much over the upcoming adventure that I hadn't realized.

And his actions and thoughtful gesture gets to me good. I

want him so badly. I want them all.

"Let me taste you, Kase. I want to give you the best fucking blow job of your existence." I flick my tongue.

Andre lowers himself to the floor with me still on top of him, and the other devils surround us as if Andre has turned into an altar for me, and they're about to worship my body.

"I want you all to have whatever you want. I just want to forget everything, even if it's just for a little while." I balance on Andre, managing to split my focus, and he links his fingers to my ass, spreading and closing my cheeks in the process, teasing the others as they hesitate. They're waiting for me. "But first, I want you to fucking get out of your clothes. Give me a show." The lust kingdom strikes me, turning my love into complete filth, and I'm ready to just act on my dirtiest desires. I have few boundaries with the devils. I have learned that I enjoy pleasure on every level. They know my limits. They know what I like and what I need from them.

"Keep fucking talking like that, and you're going to get a damn cum shower." Lucian continues to stroke his cock, aiming it at me as if his orgasm is some sort of threat. I reach out and whack the side of his cock, making him jump. He loves when I play rough with him.

"Don't tell me what to do. You're my devil. Now take off your clothes and be my good boy." I grin with my words, my voice light, and he play-growls at me.

"Fucking fine. Just this once, I will be a switch, and only this once. You have three minutes to boss me around." Fire lights his eyes, and he strips from his clothes, coming closer.

I hold my hands out to Dante, curling and uncurling my fingers to get him to come closer. "You and Kase did have first claim on my ass. So come here. I want to give you pleasure." I hold my hand out to Zade. "If you ask Andre nicely, he might make some room for you to join him. He makes me extra bendy."

I wasn't joking when I thought about them having their way. I'm strong enough. There's nothing they can do that won't bring me extreme pleasure.

"It's a good thing we've been working on your stretches," Kase says, kicking his pants off as he stands above Andre, fully prepared to squat so I can take him into my mouth.

"To give her what she desires, she needs to be in the splits." Micah's soft voice sounds on the air, and I turn my attention to him as he stands beside Elias. He's totally devouring every single one of my dirty thoughts, his lust clear on his face and on his rock-hard body as he jerks himself off as if he can't wait.

And maybe he can't. They're all tense and ready to really come together as the sinners of Hell.

I shift my legs, stretching them completely, feeling the ache of my muscles as I expose myself. Andre automatically reaches up and rubs his thumb over my clit, loving seeing me on him like this. Zade squeezes between me and Kase, and he pulls one of my legs up just a bit as Andre helps brace my body. I don't know how they manage it, but Zade slips into me, keeping his movements with Andre's. It's a tight fit, the stretch both filling me with pleasure and good pain, my body adjusting to the intensity.

Cool lube spills across my ass, and I gasp as Dante comes up behind me and kisses my shoulder, lifting my hair from my neck to sink his fangs just a little into my throat, sending a wave of pure intoxicating bliss through me. It sets me off, and I orgasm, screaming out in pleasure. He glides his cock into my ass, moaning with every inch I take, and I tip my head up and stare at the mirrored ceiling.

And fuck. The view? I can't take my eyes off Lucian as he prepares to take Dante from behind. The cocky bastard glances up and smiles at me in the mirror, his eyes lighting with hellfire. They look so hot getting pleasure while giving it. I hold my hands out, waiting for Elias and Cassius to join our side. Lube pools in my hands, and they each curl my fingers around their bodies, fucking my closed fists as Kase kisses me passionately and whispers how sexy I am before he repositions himself and guides his cock into my mouth, his jewelry hitting the back of my throat. Micah stands close, stroking his cock, watching the show and Elias surprises me by reaching out and jerking him off. Talk about a real friendship and bond. I can't get enough, and they all know it. They do it for me and because of me.

I lose myself to the pleasure and love radiating from the devils. I act as a vessel for their lust, just opening myself completely and letting them have their way with me. My body shines brightly, lighting the room around us, and they tease me with their Hell power, the nine of us together as one, sharing each other as one until that's what we are—one entity of power that can take on anything. This is how it should be. No more worrying. No more war. Just power and pleasure and the ability to set things right. To bring hope where it feels as if there is none.

The world shifts, my body practically floating as Andre uses his power to manifest restraints to keep me in place. I moan, my voice vibrating over Kase's cock until he comes into my mouth. Lust weighs my eyelids, and I close them and just savor the sensations coursing through me.

With every orgasm we all have, Andre's hold on me loosens, and he slides out, and lets Kase take control. Micah takes Kase's spot, and Elias switches places with Dante. It's as if everyone fucks everyone, and I love every second of it, the scent of our passion like a sweet fragrance that keeps me dripping wet and slippery, so all I feel is bliss.

I don't know how much time passes, but one by one my devils get their fill until we lie together in a cuddle pile with me sprawled out across all of them. My body trembles in the best way, and I listen to the sound of their hearts beating in unison. It's in this moment that I know we are going to make it through this. We will set things right. We will get everything in order for the future we desire, even if we have to wait for the planes to crumble so we can rebuild the Mortal Realm.

And maybe that's the plan. Maybe it was always supposed to be this way.

But we're not resetting humanity. We're only rebuilding from the destruction that light and dark have done. It is time to find the perfect balance. And we will create it. I know it. I can feel it in every fiber of my being. It is my purpose.

I'm both angel-kissed and devil loved. There is nothing greater in the world than that apart from the children we created from our devotion.

The babies suddenly start fussing, and I pull myself away from my guys, even though they all get up at once to go to the twins. But I want so badly to comfort them. It's something I need to figure out how to do. This is all so new to me. It's also new to the devils but it's like they already know. It's like it is deep-seated inside them. Kase follows behind me, wrapping his arms around my waist from behind. He kisses my shoulder, and I lean into him and stand between the bassinets. Light glows from Arabella and shadows radiate from Mateo. It's the first time I've really seen their powers manifest outside of myself, and it's the most mesmerizing thing I've ever seen.

And then the ground begins to rumble beneath my feet. I quickly scoop up Mateo, and Kase grabs Arabella. I spin and look at the rest of the devils with wide eyes. Something's happening. The world shivers around us, and I watch as the world cracks open, sending in both light and dark.

No one has to say anything for me to know what's happening. This is it. This is what we've been waiting for. The universe is falling apart, so we can put it back together. Hell is about to completely morph with the Mortal Realm. And as Hell morphs with the Mortal Realm, that means Heaven will as well.

I rub my hands together, manifesting clothes. The other devils surround me in a protective wall of pure muscle and power, and Elias cuts between Dante and Lucian, opening his arms to take Arabella from Kase.

"You're far superior at fighting, brother. Let me and Raven protect the twins." Elias nods his head, ensuring that Kase knows that he's only taking Arabella because he doesn't trust himself enough to really fight by their sides while he is still an angel. There's only so much he can do to fight against the guardians.

As for me, I'm ready.

They can't do anything to me now. My soul is not on the line. They have far more to lose. I have already hit the lowest point in all of the universe, and I can only rise from here. I will succeed.

The devils and I will make this right. The angelic army is going down.

<h1>25</h1>

End of Times

RAVEN

"**E**VERYONE HOLD ONTO Raven. This is going to get fucking messy." Lucian rests his hand on my shoulder, gripping me tight enough to make my muscles ache.

The others each touch a part of me as the world crumbles completely. I've never seen such a sight. It's so strange watching as dark souls and pure light whirl and collide, sending fire and debris through the world.

And then there are the bodies.

I have never seen so many dead lying on the ground. It's as if something just grabbed their souls and ripped them away, leaving them as empty shells in the rubble.

"Holy fucking shit," I mutter, hugging Mateo tighter. "Are they all dead? Like dead-dead? The whole world? I thought you said..."

Cassius squeezes my elbow. "We're going to fix this. We no longer have the same laws in the Mortal Realm. Heaven and Hell have collided with the realm, opening it up to the power never intended to be unleashed here. Those are bodies, yes. But look closer. Their souls are still anchored. It's only those that rip free that will never be able to reunite in their mortal physical form.

"What do we do now?" I bounce on the balls of my feet, staring around, realizing that we stand within a protective circle of fire. Our worlds might've collided, but the devils still have immense power. So do I.

It's enough to give me the courage to step forward. I can't help wondering what this would be like for a mortal who knows nothing about the realms. This is so crazy to wrap my mind around. For the first time in a long time, I think about my parents. I wonder if they're dark or light. I wonder about the rest of my estranged family. About my old friends. Fuck. It's been so long, but I don't even know how to contact them. Tamia was always the one who stayed in touch. I was so isolated because of Joel, and now...they don't deserve this kind of fate.

The world quakes with another shift in the realms, and I stare as the ground fissures open and several demons crawl from the depths of Hell, moving and shifting along with the souls. It's not over. The worlds are still coming together. What happens when it's over?

"If the realm shatters completely, there might not be any humans left," Micah responds to my thoughts in my mind.

I spin and look at him. I turn my attention to the other devils as well. "What do we do?" I ask again. "Everything is ruined. Where is the—"

Pain rips across my back as if someone cuts me open with knives. Feathers from my rainbow wings dance in the air, and I don't even get a chance to move as Kase launches over me.

He roars, his voice is booming through the air, and Dante hisses and charges next. Lucian swings his fire chain over his head and lashes it. But I can't turn to move. My body hurts so badly that it feels as if I might be dying. But I can't die.

"Fuck, Raven." Elias takes Mateo from my arms and hands him to Andre.

Gathering heavenly light in his palms, he sends the beams over my skin, the sensation enough to wash away the blistering agony threatening to send me to my stomach.

"Destroy him!" Lucian yells.

Destroy who?

I gasp a breath, swiveling my body to look at the fight unfolding. I expect to see Mikail and the angelic army, but they are not here. There are demons lined up and waiting for someone's command.

And then I see Vincent. Kase stands on top of him, impaling him with his claws. Vincent can't order the demons to attack because Dante spit venom in his face, melting his lips together. This fucker was supposed to be in the fire pits. But I guess it's not enough anymore. The fire now cascades from the ground, eating away everything in its path, destroying the mortal world.

"Stop!" I yell, managing to use Elias to push to my feet. He takes my hand, sprawling out his wings beside me, and we stand together now completely focused on the bastard demon that should've stayed away. "Restrain him for us. You guys are not getting the satisfaction of destroying him. We are."

I drag Elias closer, and Vincent writhes and bucks, trying to escape Kase's restraint. But he can't. He is nothing but a bad soul. He might have been promoted as a demon long ago, but I'm taking that away from him. He will be the source of our power now. I will annihilate him.

Gathering angel power in one of my palms, I grow it bigger and bigger, mirroring Elias as he gathers his own. And then Lucian, Dante, and Kase join in, summoning their own power. I don't get upset that they feel that they must help even despite me demanding to serve justice. It is supposed to be this way. Us together.

I turn to look over my shoulder. "I need all of you. We're going to fucking show him what it means to betray not only the kings of Hell and their queen but also all of humanity."

The others join our sides, and we circle Vincent and blast him with power, turning him into complete energy that we all absorb as one. Our powers now combine with our bond. My whole body zings with excitement, and I know what must be done. This is how we end the angelic army. At least, those who refuse to stand down. Because I don't want to destroy everything pure and light in this world. I don't want to condemn everything dark either. I just want fucking balance. I want humanity to be able to live and learn and grow and better the universe as a whole. It is my duty to see it through.

I heave a couple of deep breaths, the energy sending static electricity zapping across my body. "We need to find where Heaven has collapsed. I know that is where we will find Mikail and the angelic army. He's going to be hiding. He knows he's lost."

Kase purrs under his breath, circling me and sticking his big head between my legs to lift me off the ground and onto his back. I hug him with my entire body, letting him launch forward, where we see a beam of bright light radiating through the air.

"The only way this is going to end is if we take his essence as well. We need the power to stop this!" I dig my fingers into Kase's back, snuggling close yet yelling out loud enough that I know the other devils can hear me.

But we don't have to look hard.

A giant entity of pure, Heaven-bound souls grows in a tidal wave, not even a block away. Mikail and at least a few hundred angels stand before us, looking as if they're prepared to go down as long as the universe falls with them.

I can't let that happen.

We can't let that happen.

"Surrender and we will not destroy you." Cassius flies ahead with Lucian, acting as a barrier between me and the angels.

Mikail ignores his words and expands his wings. Thrusting his arms out, he shoots angelic light at them both. The force of so many angels acting at once sends them skidding across the broken pavement.

The bright light envelops them, and I scream out when it fades with nothing left behind. I don't know where they went. Usually, they would've gone back to their kingdoms. But now? Fuck.

"Keep going! They'll be back!" Dante shouts, using his wings to fly forward faster than Kase can run in his devil form. "They are going to fracture the entire universe if we don't stop them."

I knew I was right. This is what the angels want. With their lack of hope comes their desire to just destroy everything. They will go down with the universe instead of realizing that they have gone so off path even the Higher Power has turned its back on them. That's why I'm here.

"Hit them from the left, Andre. Kase, keep moving forward. They want Raven the most. She needs to be our bait." Zade gallops up beside Kase, his equestrian-like devil form rippling with muscles and fire as if he is supercharged in this moment. And he is. I can feel it as if his power is my own. He has never felt as exhilarated as he does now, knowing exactly what needs to be done. He is fighting for humanity like it was intended.

"Like Hell—" Kase slows, gathering his ruby power in his clawed paw. He stands up on his hind legs, forcing me to squeeze his body with my thighs. He walks forward while he chucks his power. It's rare that I see him on his hind legs like this, and damn. He's so incredibly sexy all protective over me.

If only he wasn't about to get pissed off enough that he might try to unleash his wrath on me next. Because Zade is right. The angelic army wants me. They want the twins. If I can distract them even for a couple of minutes, the other devils can attack at full force.

I climb up higher to Kase's head and kiss him below his ear, stroking my hands around two of his horns in the process. "I'm so sorry. You can punish me later."

He doesn't get a chance to try to grab me with his tail before I launch into the air above him and out of his reach. He yells out for Dante to grab me, but I blast Dante with enough heavenly light to get him to go where Zade instructed.

"Give them everything you got!" I shout, gathering my power in my palms.

And then something happens in my hands. Fire erupts within the brilliant light, and I stare in shock. I had no idea I could still summon Hell power, but it's as if it blends with my heavenly light, creating the most beautiful white, blue, and orange orb of energy. And it's all mine. I can feel it inside me that I'm not channeling it from the devils. I'm channeling it from the plane the twins created for me. The plane I know now is intended to be Purgatory.

"Mikail! Stand down! I have been blessed and given such a gift by the Almighty. You are to stand down or face the consequences!" I slow down, gliding through the air with my wings spread, staring at the angelic army.

Mikail materializes from within the middle of the mass of angels, using them as a fucking barrier like the coward he is. I realize that it's not him I need to command. It's the others. If I can get the angelic army to listen and call the pure souls back, it'll stop the universe from collapsing.

I can stop this war.

"Again! Don't listen to her! She is a sinner of Hell." Mikail holds up his heavenly sword and points it at me, glaring as he silently threatens me. "Take her down! She will show her true self!"

The angelic army is so distracted by his command that they

don't see Dante and Kase coming up on them. Their eyes are trained on me in the sky. Dante stays close and prepares to spit his venom over them. Elias flies up on the other side, carrying Micah in his arms. They prepare to blast them in unison.

Andre remains behind, protecting the twins as he flies and stays as close as he can without getting in the line of fire if he's afraid to leave us. He's in his devil form and can fight with his piercing tail alone.

"Attack!" Mikail hollers, throwing his angelic energy in my direction.

The second the others release their heavenly light, Kase launches right into the middle of the angelic army and spins around, slashing his claws and knocking at least a dozen of the angels away in the process.

Zade shoots his blue electric light, frying another couple of angels before he gallops over them, his huge form not allowing them to escape.

Nosediving, Elias shoots heavenly light across the angelic army, blinding them long enough that he can drop Micah without them automatically blasting him away. He sends orange flames across another dozen angels, causing them to scream in agony.

But it's not enough. There are just too many angels and not enough of us. The demons and Hell's legion remain fighting the pure souls, tangling and twisting through the air, destroying all of the realms.

"Attack!" Mikail repeats, aiming his sword again. He doesn't try to blast me with light. Instead, he goes after the devils, commanding his angelic army to hit them instead.

Bright light from the pure souls rains around me, and Mikail uses his heavenly power to manipulate them into another wave that crashes over Zade. He yells in frustration for only a second before he vanishes, getting sent to wherever his kingdom now lies among the crumbling universe.

"We need to separate them. They're too strong together." Dante grabs my hand, pulling me to him to kiss me. "Get the twins. I want you to take them to the highest peak of Heaven. Elias can be your guide. I don't know how much longer the universe is going to last. I can already feel some of the dark souls vanishing completely. They're just gone."

My heart pounds with his words.

"I can't leave. You and Elias take them. I'll follow." My mouth dries as I say the words. Just the thought of leaving my children ignites pain inside me like I'm dying all over again.

"You can leave, and you will." Dante hisses, spitting more venom across the angels trying to fly up toward us. He jerks his head and looks at Andre. "Bring them here."

Andre flies forward, holding out the twins, and he doesn't give me a chance to refuse them, putting them in my arms. I automatically snuggle them close. I have a fierce need to protect them in this moment, and it's enough to get me to pull away from Dante. Elias comes up beside me and takes Arabella. My heart cracks at knowing we are leaving. We're taking the twins and hiding from the war that started because of us. And now it's going to end with us. It has to. I cannot see the universe destroyed because of me.

Elias grabs my hand. "We're going to be okay. All of us. We must trust our family to take care of things. This way, the angelic army will split up. We can attack better."

A wave of light grows as a dozen angels come together. Anger explodes through me, and I blast my power in their direction, channeling everything in me to stop the wave of pure light from crashing over us. It only stops them for a second.

But it's all we need to get away. I know if we don't leave now, they will keep coming harder and more seriously. This is our chance. I know the devils fight with a vengeance that can destroy all of the heavenly plane. They won't be concerned about protecting me or the babies.

I can focus on doing something else. I need to figure out how to stop the universe from crumbling. I know I can do it. I don't have a choice.

Elias flies beneath me, protecting me from below as we ascend, darting through the swirling souls fighting just to exist. I watch as dark and light souls collide and explode into sparkly stars that vanish, the energy having no place to go. My entire being weeps at the sight. How could the angelic army be so callous to think that any soul deserves such a fate of never existing and never learning and growing is beyond me. It isn't fair. Why are they like this?

"Raven, to your left," Elias says, pointing out an angel heading in our direction. I gather the darkness inside me and blast them with my new light made of Heaven and Hell and everything in between. The angel explodes, turning into a brilliant lightshow like fireworks igniting to light the world in color. And then I see something strange happen. The angelic energy leaves a hazy barrier. It's healing the universe. This is what needs to happen.

"Elias, take Mateo. I need to be the one to defend us. Did you see that? Did you see how the angelic energy seemed to heal part of the realm?" I extend my arms, holding out Mateo until Elias cradles him in his other arm.

I flip midair and get beneath him, creating a wall to sandwich the babies between.

Elias gets ultra-close until I can feel the babies brushing my wings. "Darlin', I know you are afraid to not help out. I know you want to get revenge for everything that the angelic army has done—"

"This isn't about revenge, Elias. I don't want revenge. Sure, I do want to get justice for what these bastards have done, but not revenge. I want to save humanity. I want to put a stop to this madness and I know how." I drop lower, gathering more angelic energy in my palms. Another angel flies up from below, and I demand they stay back, but they don't listen. So I thrust the power, annihilating them. Their energy lightens the world, separating the pure souls from the ones Hell-bound. It's such a mesmerizing sight that I gather more power in my hands. I nosedive, leaving Elias with the babies. He doesn't follow me. He lets me descend and shoot another wave of light and dark at the angels trying to chase us, those who abandoned the devils.

"Raven, Elias!" a familiar, agitating voice booms through the air.

Mikail has a lot of fucking nerve to follow us.

My vision darkens with the depths of Hell, now flowing through my veins, pushing away the goodness blessed into me by the Higher Power. I jerk up, spotting him flying in front of me to block our path. He wields his sword, sending sparkling light over the blade. His face twists in a scowl, and two guardians stand by his side.

"It's over. If you choose to stand by our side, we won't wipe you out of existence. We know that you have been manipulated by the devils. They have played on both of your mortal rationales. If you come with me, we can build a brighter, better universe than the creator could've ever done. We have the experience and knowledge to succeed." Mikail waves his sword around the crumbling realms. "Do the right thing. There is a reason you two have been given grace despite being undeserving."

"Fuck off!" Wrath ignites inside me, and I can feel Kase through our bond. And Dante. Cassius and Lucian. Zade and Andre. Micah. Elias. I can feel all of the men I love most in the world crash into me at once, filling me with everything I need to stand up to this bastard.

Gathering light in my hand, I thrust it at him. Mikail dodges out of the way and bolts toward me. The angelic soldiers follow his lead, surrounding me.

Elias shouts my name.

I ignore him.

I brace myself for the final battle.

26

Final Battle

ELIAS

MY HEART SINKS into my stomach, my whole body turning cold as I watch Mikail and two angels gather light to blast at Raven.

I should be protecting her. I should be the one fighting for her. But she is so damn stubborn that all I can do is hold the twins closer, using them to keep myself from intervening.

Raven summons a sword, and the blade ignites in brilliant flames created from Heaven and Hell power. She swings, keeping the angels away, but they blast her again, trying to blind her and incapacitate her.

I inhale a sharp breath, the sight of Raven screaming and me hovering in the sky, feeling utterly helpless, stabs my very core.

"Arabella, Mateo. Please, my sweet, powerful babies. Mama needs you. She needs your help. Daddy needs your help." I whisper the words, trying my best to keep my distance but also be aware of the surroundings. More angels could come at any second.

Raven shrieks, dropping ten feet as Mikail jabs his sword into her wing. Light seeps from the cut, blinding Mikail enough to give Raven a chance to counterattack. She uses the moves Micah taught her, spinning and slashing her blade again. She doesn't let Mikail come at her. She takes the offense and forces him back.

Swinging her sword, she manages to slice across the front of his shirt, getting his skin. He hollers in pain and can't guard himself well enough to block Raven from attacking him again. She shoves her sword deep into his belly, twisting the blade and sending his skin scorching. The weight of his sudden fall drags her down with him, and the guardians chase after the two of them, trying to attack Raven from above.

She won't let Mikail go. I know she is going to persist until she's too hurt to fight or he is annihilated.

I've never been so proud or scared in my life. She is so powerful that I have faith in her, but I want to help her more than ever. I want to fight by her side.

Arabella and Mateo fuss in my arms, their soft whimpers

turning into full-blown cries. I readjust them in my arms, catching sight of the brilliant power gathering in their chests, their hearts glittering with magic born from Raven and love. Born from me and the devils.

They want to fight by her side too.

Things have never been clearer.

"Don't worry, my sweet babies. We're going to help Mama." I summon angelic light, tying and wrapping it around Mateo and Arabella, ensuring that they are never going to be any-where near Mikail or the other angels. There's no way anyone can get through the chains of light I use to bind us together. And they continue to radiate with power, creating a shield that wraps around me protectively.

Closing my wings, I nosedive a few feet until I glide in Raven and Mikail's direction. The angels don't even see me coming, and I blast them each on their wings, sending them spiraling back to the earth.

Raven's screams rip through the air, her agony penetrating me at my very soul. Her pain is my pain. Her weakness is mine. But my strength and her strength combine and make us unstoppable.

I will destroy Mikail for everything he's done. He stole my soulmate's soul and started this. He took power that didn't belong to him when the other saviors abandoned their grace to follow Raven. He has done cruel and unusual punishments to other angels all because of his twisted faith and for no one other reason than what he felt was right. But after all of my existence, after living longer than a millennium and going through a soul cycle to understand what it's like to be a mortal and an angel and even Hell-bound, I know that there is no right or wrong answer. There's only what is best for everyone. Everyone must be able to learn and grow. They must be able to give back in love and justice and grace and strength, and so much more. It's okay to make mistakes. But consequences must be accepted. Accountability must be held, and I plan to do it with Mikail. If he cannot in good morals coincide with humanity without trying to completely control it and ruin it and just destroy it if it doesn't go his way, then he will give back to humanity by giving it the power it needs to not only survive but thrive.

"Elias, stay back!" Raven shouts, thrusting her hands at Mikail, burning him again with her blend of Heaven and Hell power. Her new abilities are intended to go both ways because she is destined to create Purgatory.

"No! We are in this together! All of us!" I aim my sword and watch as glittering power bolts from Arabella and Mateo in the most magical chain I have ever seen. It winds around my wrist and climbs up my blade, sending it aglow in a color my eyes can't even comprehend. It's iridescent and rainbow, almost like my wings but even more breathtaking. It looks like Raven's wings and her new being as an angel. It shines as brightly as her soul. Even the purest of souls in all of Heaven can't outshine our children.

Our new light shines brighter than everything in existence, hazing the world in a way that even Mikail and the angelic army can't clearly see through. Our light is only blinding so that it will make a path for all to see.

Raven uses Mikail's distraction to her advantage and flaps her wings, stabbing him right through the heart with her blade. He opens his mouth in a silent scream and light shoots from every orifice on his body, cracking his very essence into a million pieces, sending bursts of light raining through the air. And it doesn't stop there.

Our light devours every angel standing against us, turning them into pure energy to cycle them back into the universe. I don't know if they are gone forever or if they will eventually become whole again, but none of that matters.

What matters is that the realms need to be put back together. We need to summon all of the energy we can to heal it before it's too late.

Raven shouts, her back arching as power zings through her very being, turning her into a light show. My eyes widen as her very essence glows like the sun, sending all the pure souls and the ones bound to Hell flying away from us to clear a path.

My chest tightens at the sight, and panic steals my breath. Flapping my wings, I fly toward her, shielding my eyes as the light stings my skin despite it being made of Heaven and Hell. Despite it being made of the love born between us. Raven is the most powerful being I've ever seen alongside our children, and it reminds me of the moment I laid eyes on her crying over her sister's gravestone in a past life when she was Grace and she had lost Hope. I knew that very moment that she was my world. I knew that I would do anything for the soul. I knew I'd give up everything to be with her, and I know why now. She was always going to be humanity's saving grace. Even in this life as Raven, she is intended to bring together the realms to make the perfect existence for all of us. Angels and devils. Demons and humans. Animals and plants and everything that pieces together to make this eternity worth living.

I live for Raven. I exist solely to stand by her side. We are soulmates. Forever.

Stretching my arms, I fight through her building energy and manage to grab her wrist and catch her as she begins to descend, her wings drooping as she loses consciousness.

Carrying the weight of the universe alone hurts her deeply. It is my duty to bear some of the weight when no one else can. The devils are busy bearing the weight of the destruction caused by those who refused to see past the light and into the beauty of the darkness. The darkness that allows us to see things clearly from the outside.

"Darlin', please. Open your eyes," I beg.

Raven dangles in the air, only my strength keeping her from falling to the ground of the broken planes.

Raven doesn't respond to my voice, and the twins cry out, their voices wailing louder than ever. I can feel it in my core that they know something is wrong. Destroying Mikail and turning the wayward angels into energy to recycle hasn't fixed the crumbling planes. The universe still falls apart.

Squeezing my eyes shut, I reach out to Micah through our telepathic link. I need him and the other devils more than ever.

"Micah, what's happening down there?" My thought sends my head pounding. Micah doesn't respond right away, and my whole body trembles. What if something happened to my best companion? What if something happened to the rest of the devils?

Silence greets me for another moment, and then finally, Micah swears through my mind, the F-bomb a surprising relief, considering he rarely ever cusses. "Are Raven and the twins safe?" he asks, his telepathic link prodding into my mind as he tries to search for answers. "I can't hear her. It's as if she's walled off."

"Raven couldn't handle the amount of power it took to stop Mikail. She's knocked out." I say the words out loud, my voice hoarse with the admission, and my mind doesn't think the words any better.

"Not only him, Elias. She obliterated them all. Every single angel that didn't surrender was taken by the wave. It has left the realms too far gone. There's not enough balance to keep the universe from collapsing. We're going to try our best to hold it together for as long as it takes you, Raven, and the twins to get to the highest point in Heaven. You should be safe there." Micah's words are like a knife in the gut. He's not saying what I think he's saying. I can't possibly leave him to face the collapse of existence.

I frown, tilting my head to look at the blurry world below, the haze too thick to see anything happening. "No—"

"Take her now!" Micah hollers, his voice booming through my mind, making me wince in pain. "There is nothing more to be done. It is your duty to save them. Protect them. If you come back here, it'll all have been for nothing. Do not let all of this have happened in vain."

He's right. I have to get Raven and the twins to the safest place in the universe. The same place that Lucian, Kase, and Dante jumped all those years ago to create Hell.

I never thought I would see it again, but here I am, flapping my wings and listening to my companion and his instructions, surely coming from all of the devils.

"I will not let anything happen to them. I promise. I will not fail you. Not now. Never again." I ascend higher, flapping my wings and launching through the haze, dodging around the blurring light trying to drag us back down.

Raven remains limp, her body swinging with every movement, but she's safe. I'll never let go of her. The twins ensure it as their light continues to bloom and grow and wrap around her until she floats in front of me, carried on a beam of light as if they hold her in their loving embrace despite them being so new to existence.

The higher I fly, the more peaceful I become. I feel as if someone pours warmth, hope, love, and faith over me, bathing me in the emotions I remember so clearly surrounding me in Heaven. But this is different. These emotions come from those I love the most. It comes from my devotion to not only Raven and the devils but from the twins and from my devotion to humanity. I will not let the world end. None of this will have been for nothing.

And as I reach the brightest, highest point in all of existence, I see my path again. I know exactly what my purpose is and what I'm supposed to do.

If only my heart didn't hurt at the thought. There is only one way for me to help Raven, our children, the devils...our family. I do not belong up here in the brilliance of grace. I belong fighting beside the devils, helping them keep the universe together. It takes seven sinners to join Lucian in creating Hell so that Purgatory can rise. If I don't jump, everything will be lost. Raven has always been my path, and she has taken me right back to here, where everything began so long ago.

"Elias…" Raven's soft voice breaks through the pounding in my head, and I lick my lips and meet her blinking eyes, her legs heavy and her body still weak as she hangs, tangled in the light radiating from the twins.

"Darlin', we're safe. We're almost there. Just take a couple of deep breaths. I'm sure your whole body is out of whack, and you're in pain. Mikail hurt you." I try to keep my voice even despite the rage burning through me, thinking about the bastard angel.

"Where are—" She groans and covers her eyes, her body trembling and shaking.

"Breathe in and out. Please. You're weak. You used an enormous amount of power and blasted some fuckers into a new existence." I can't stop smiling with my words. Damn. I can't believe how lucky I am to have such an amazing woman love me. I'm so fucking lucky that we have children. A family. Before I fell for Grace, I never imagined such a thing possible. And now it's the only thing I know to be possible. The world could end, but we never will.

The haze in the air clears, and I find the highest point of the Heaven realm, the pure white nothingness of the world shifting to match what I envision it to be in my mind just as I saw it the last time I was here. The massive cliff overlooks a layer of clouds that go on forever. I fly the dozen feet it takes to get to the cliff and land on the edge, setting Raven on her feet.

Without waiting for her to do anything, I hold out the twins for her to take. I know that if I don't do what I need to, I might not have the courage. I have to do what is right for us and not what is right for me. I have been greedy for far too long, wanting everything my way and wanting Raven to myself. But her love is too powerful to only be reciprocated to one being. Her love is greater than anything I have ever been blessed to encounter.

I expand my wings, feeling the cool breeze touch my iridescent feathers. The air is sweeter up here, lifting Raven's hair and wafting her scent over me. I inhale a deep breath, wanting to capture it forever, allowing it to imprint in my mind.

I touch her cheek, and she leans into my hand, pressing my fingers harder with her skin. "You're doing great, darlin'. You've always been so amazing. I want you to know that. I love you no matter what happens now. The other devils all love you. And we love these two beautiful beings we've created with you."

Raven's eyes water, and a tear slips on her cheek. "Elias...why are you saying that as if this is goodbye?"

I swallow, my own eyes burning with tears. Because it could be. I don't know what's going to happen next. All I know is that I need to jump. I need to join the other devils. It is my time.

I slowly drop my hand and take a step back. "I will never say goodbye to you, Raven. I just want you to know how much I love you. How I do everything for you, and it's time for me to do this for them."

Her lip trembles, and she flicks her gaze from me and to my feet. "Elias, what are you talking about? Get away from the edge."

I don't respond to her.

I caress her cheek once more and bend down and kiss Arabella and Mateo on their foreheads. "I love you all so much. You are my existence."

Turning my back on Raven, I fold my wings.

I close my eyes and whisper a prayer to the Almighty under my breath.

"Elias," Raven snaps, her voice turning desperate.

I turn and look over my shoulder at her, tears dripping down my face. "Be brave, darlin'. I love you. Always and forever. But it's time."

Raven rushes closer, snatching my wing. "Elias, no!"

27

The Fall

RAVEN

"ELIAS, PLEASE. PLEASE, you promised you'd never leave me. You can't just jump. Not now. Not after everything." My heart aches with my words. But I know he's right. This must be done. The universe crumbles around us, and I know that if he doesn't help the devils, all is lost.

But where does that leave me? I have the twins to think about. They are my top priority, even if that makes me selfish. I choose them over the world. They are my everything. But so are the devils. So is Elias.

Elias steps away from the ledge and engulfs me in a hug, pressing the twins between us because I can't lift my arms. He brushes his lips to mine, kissing me softly, his light warming my skin. And then I realize what he's doing.

"I'm never going to leave you, Raven. I'm giving everything to you. I'm giving you my heart and soul. My essence and light. I'm giving my life to you to hold always." Elias doesn't let me pull back, and his very essence as an angel pours into me and fills me up.

"Elias..." My voice fades. I don't know what to say or what I can do to convince him otherwise. It's not in me. He's following his path even if it means turning his back away from me. Even if it means he must give me all that he is to do so.

"I love you. I love you so much, and I know things will work out as they should. Be brave. You are the most powerful, strongest woman in existence, and this is why you have been chosen by the universe. That's why the twins chose you to be their mother. That's why the devils chose you to be their queen. You will get through this. I promise." Elias kisses my trembling lips once more. Turning around, he strides to the edge of the cliff and expands his wings, flapping them once to send a breeze through my hair.

It's now that I see he's changed. His beautiful rainbow wings dim into a dark gray color. He morphs before my eyes, his body shifting and cracking as he takes on a devil form. He has given me his light and his grace. He gives me everything so he can abandon Heaven to finally jump and take his throne.

But where will he land? I have no idea. There's no more Hell. This is the only part of Heaven as well. And as for the Mortal Realm? It's barely hanging on. The devils are the only ones keeping it together. What if when Elias jumps everything just collapses? What if it turns out to be just me and the twins for the rest of time?

I shove the thought away. I can't think like that.

Elias transforms into a canine-like beast, his body bowing forward until he's on all fours in a form I want so badly to touch. Fire sprouts from his skin, shifting and moving as if it's fur but made of flame. Horns grow along his back, protruding across the spine until the base of a burning tail. His triangular ears twitch and move and he releases a growl, the noise reverberating through my bones.

He is magnificent and so incredibly fierce. He is exactly how I imagined him to be as a devil. Cunning and strong. My perfect man. My perfect devil. It's not his greed to make him jump. It's his selflessness. It's what he needed to do to finally descend.

I bounce on my feet and turn the twins toward him. "Look at Daddy. Look how powerful he is. He's going to protect us and humanity now. He's going to help the universe."

Elias stretches his body, his sleek devil form preparing to launch from the cliff.

"We love him so much. He's going to help your other daddies. He's going to make everything okay. I promise." The twins remain quiet and calm, settling down for the first time since I've landed with Elias on this cliff.

I hold my breath, my whole body stilling and tensing. I can't move. I can't speak. All I can do is watch as Elias launches into the air and jumps from the edge.

A sob racks my chest, and I rush forward, watching as the clouds break open and flames ignite the world below. Elias spins midair and looks up at me, his wings open and now capturing the color of the flames around him.

The ground rumbles as fire cascades over him, and he disappears completely.

I gasp and drop to my knees, hugging Arabella and Mateo close, wrapping my wings around them as I sob into their little bodies. It feels as if a part of me has died. The absence of being away from Elias and my devils cuts so deeply through me. This isn't right. This isn't how it was supposed to be.

I kneel and tilt my head back, staring up at the white world above me. "What do I do now? This can't be it. You did not put me through all of this just to have me end up like this."

Silence greets me, but it's not the silence I'm used to. The silence that came with no one listening. The silence is heavy and blankets across the world, muffling the noise of the fires burning far, far below.

A sense of peace washes across my very being, and I open my

eyes and stare at my beautiful babies as brilliant power radiates from their hearts and crawls across my arms, working its way to my shoulders and down my chest. It fills every molecule of my being, setting me aglow in everything good given to me from both Heaven and Hell. It fills me with everything humanity taught me and everything I've been fighting for. The twins give me the strength to get back to my feet, and I clutch them close, resting them against each of my shoulders.

I stroll to the edge of the cliff and peer down again, watching as flashes of light and dark swirl through the air. The souls are still flying around carelessly, unable to do anything as they're trapped in a universe where there's only one plane.

Whatever happens below doesn't stop the universe from continuing to crumble. It's not only Elias that must jump. I know it now. I know it with every fiber in my being that it's my time. And I'm not doing it alone. I have the strength of the devils and the hope given to me by my babies. I must jump for them. I must make Purgatory to bring the universe back together.

"I love you both. More than I knew possible. We're going to be okay. Mama will protect you just as you will protect Mama. And you're going to protect your daddies. You're going to help Mama bring balance to the world, aren't you?" I toe the edge, expanding my wings to feel the chaotic wind shooting up from below in bursts of hot and cold.

Nerves bunch my stomach, and I inhale a couple of deep breaths. I can do this. I know I can do this. I have faced far worse things in my life. The sinners of Hell need me to take my throne. This has been the plan all along, and it is now time.

Before, it wasn't right. I needed to create the perfect balance from Heaven and Hell with the twins. It's now that I know it was in my fate to die. I would've never been able to claim Purgatory as its queen if I wasn't an angel now. If I wasn't given the strength of Heaven and Hell. Because it's not only the world that needed balance. It was me.

"Are you ready, Arabella and Mateo?" I ask, forcing my voice to remain strong. It takes everything in me to shed my human rationale. It's hard to shove away my fears. Because with this jump doesn't come the end.

I must jump to create a new beginning. To rebuild what had been damaged and broken. I need to jump to create a new path for the universe to follow.

It is my destiny.

I must see it through.

Arabella and Mateo continue to glow with power. Arabella's so pure and beautiful while Mateo's flows in dark, hypnotic tendrils. Their powers merge in the most spectacular braid until it winds around me, and the three of us are bound together.

Kissing each of them on the tops of their heads, I bend my knees and launch from the cliff, expanding my wings to glide. I fall through the mixture of souls and haze, light and fire as I make our way down toward the Mortal Realm. My eyes burn with tears, but I manage to blink them away. The closer I get to the destruction, the lighter my soul feels. It's as if something draws me in, refusing to let me go. But I'm unafraid. I feel freer than ever. My stomach doesn't soar to my throat and my heart remains steady with its even beats. I keep my wings open and continue to glide until sparks of power flicker across my skin and my wings set ablaze with the most mesmerizing rainbow light that casts iridescent beams through the air, lighting everything up.

My wings tingle with the power, and a force bunches the muscles in my back. I can't stop myself from folding my wings close to my body. The world spins around us, and I clench my jaw to keep myself in control. This is it. This is how things are supposed to be. Every one of the devils had to jump from grace. And while I might be jumping from Heaven, I'm not jumping from the Higher Power. I'm jumping to humanity. For humanity. With the Higher Power guiding me and the devils waiting for me somewhere below.

The edges of my vision darken as I plummet with the twins, unable to do anything except whisper a prayer. I don't pray to be saved. I don't pray for the world to stop. I pray for strength, and I pray for humanity and that I can succeed. I pray for love. I pray for the perfect balance in the universe.

Suddenly, the world stops.

The realm shakes under my feet. I exhale a breath, my muscles relaxing as I shudder. The world around me is nothing as I remember. Everything is destroyed. Bodies lie on the ground, no longer working because their souls aren't here. They're still flying through the air.

"Kase? Dante?" I call out, spinning on the balls of my feet, clutching the twins tighter as my heart slides into my stomach. "Micah? Zade? Andre?"

I close my eyes, trying to listen for their voices. I try to feel for their essences. They're not here. The only thing left here are the bodies and broken buildings and the souls flying around. It looks as if the world has really experienced a true apocalypse. Flames eat away at everything, and there really is no life. If there's no life...

"Lucian! Cassius! Where the fuck are you guys?" My voice rings in the air, and I take a few tentative steps forward. This can't be right. I wouldn't have jumped from what was supposed to be the safest point in the universe to land in the middle of a wreckage. Something's wrong.

"Elias! Elias, please. We need you. We're here." My voice cracks with my pleas, and I once again close my eyes to listen.

No one responds.

No one comes running.

It's just me and the twins and this broken realm around us.

I need guidance. I need something, someone to tell me what to do. I have to do something. I can't just accept that we were wrong. I know we weren't.

"Please," I whisper, adjusting the babies in my arms. "Please, show me."

As if Arabella and Mateo understand me, they begin to fuss and their power breaks from my body to lash out at the world around us. I stare in shock and awe. Wherever our power touches, rainbow light remains in its place. I know what to do. I need to channel all of my energy and strength and pour it back into the realm to heal it.

I must manifest everything as it should be. As I want it to be. I need to absorb the chaotic souls and return them to where they belong.

"Give me the strength." My body buzzes with electric shockwaves as power cascades from me, turning the desolate world around me from grays and browns and blacks and reds. From fire and smoke and ash, changing everything to pure colorful light. I've never seen anything like it.

I watch as the light blooms from the ground, healing the earth. The broken structures rebuild, coming back together. The fire disappears and the cracks in the ground turn solid.

And then I watch as the souls begin to return to the bodies. It's not over. Humanity is returning to what it was once before. But it will be better. The universe will be better and balanced.

There will be no divide between Heaven and Hell. There will only be the Mortal Realm and...I guess, the Afterlife. Because each devil will have their throne, and I will have Purgatory. From there, souls can finally have a chance to either go through another cycle or turn into the energy that keeps the universe going around. It is how it was always intended to be. I know that. I feel it deep in my bones. It is not about testing souls as they live. It's about teaching them, nurturing them, and helping them to grow and thrive as they continue on for the rest of eternity.

The realm changes around me, and I watch as glittering rain pours from the sky, washing away the world around me until I stand in a familiar meadow. Colorful flowers stretch on for miles, and a glorious sunset shines pinks and purples across silvery clouds as if they're now made of cotton candy.

"My babies," I whisper, kneeling among the flowers. Without even having to try, I manifest a blanket and sprawl it out, setting them on it. "Look at this place. Isn't it magical? We created this. You and me and your daddies."

I lay down between them, staring up at the sky, just wanting to take a moment to breathe and exist, enjoy this newfound peace. This is Purgatory. I know it deep inside me. Our power healed and rebuilt the Mortal World and in doing so, we created the perfect place of balance and peace. The perfect place for those ready to serve not only humanity but the entire universe.

A shadow casts over me, and I can sense Andre's presence before I even look up at him.

Tipping my head back, I smile at his handsome face, watching as he stretches his black leathery wings out. I blink my eyes and they suddenly turn white and like they had been before he jumped and claimed the throne in the lust kingdom. Just as quickly, his wings return to the dark shade I'm used to.

"Andre..." My voice fades with my words. I don't get a chance to think about things before he bends down and scoops me into his arms, hugging and kissing me a dozen times, spinning me around.

"Little hellion. You must open the portal to let us in. The others are getting anxious." Andre's voice vibrates across my throat, and I jerk my head back to meet his beautiful eyes. "They all want to see your amazing kingdom."

My kingdom. I was right.

Setting me on my feet, Andre vanishes from the world in front of me. I realize he was projecting himself the same way he had done so a dozen times while I was asleep.

A blip of fear tightens my chest, but I know that this isn't a dream. This is real. He's real. And they're all waiting for me.

With the thought, the world before me opens up, and I stare at the eight silhouettes of the men I love most in the universe. I don't get a chance to move from my spot as they all step forward in unison and spread their gigantic wings.

I cover my mouth in surprise. I can't believe it. They have been given their wings again. Yet, they still embody the Hell power from their kingdom. Not only has the universe found balance, so have they. They look a little bit angelic and devilish, and incredibly sexy.

"See, I told you that you had fucking wings again. You didn't believe me but look at those things. They're bigger than your damn ego." I grin as Lucian launches into the air and flies at me.

The others do the same, each trying to race each other until I find myself engulfed in their arms. Elias picks up Arabella and Kase and Dante grab Mateo, holding him together. It's such a sight that I want it forever in my mind.

They each take turns passing the twins around, hugging and kissing them and loving up on them. I've never felt happier. I've never felt more complete in my life. We did it. The sinners of Hell and me.

"Comment again about my wings, and I'm going to bend you over my knee and spank you until you beg for forgiveness. Don't think I won't smite that ass." Lucian grins with his words, fire still lighting his eyes.

"Fuck off, asshole. You know her ass belongs to me." Kase pulls me away with his tail and twirls me toward him until he hugs me in his arms. His white wings sparkle with red tips, and I reach out and caress my fingers over their downy soft feathers.

"Damn, these are fucking sexy," I say, stroking my fingers along his shoulder. "I didn't think it was possible."

Dante chuckles from beside him. "Neither did I. If you like them enough, I can wrestle him and pluck some free to add to our collection."

I bite my bottom lip between my teeth. "A little sensation play, huh?"

"Anything for you, pretty soul." Dante kisses me softly, only pulling away because Arabella cries. Mateo joins her, and I open my arms for them.

"You mean, anything for us. Look at this place. Isn't it amazing?" I ask, smiling as I look around.

"It's perfect," Cassius says, his face softening into a cute smirk instead of the brooding sharp features I'm used to. "It's everything I imagined it to be."

I nod my head. "Me too. This is exactly as I saw our future. Together, always."

Elias smiles. "Forever."

Purgatory

RAVEN

I CAN'T STOP staring at my reflection. I look like me but different. I don't know if it's because I just haven't thought about it since I've been too invested in creating the Purgatory kingdom or what, but it takes me stepping into Dante's massive bathroom in our new palace for me to take notice of myself in the mirror. He combs my hair, using extra care to ensure every strand is exactly how he wants it to be so he can mess it up later.

"You know, we don't have to do this now. Fuck, you don't even have to get dressed to do it. All you have to do is sit that cute ass bubble butt of yours in your throne and we'll bow at your feet to worship you." Dante leans over and grazes his lips to my ear. "I'll worship you now if you let me. Come on. I just spent all of that time shaving you the way you like. Let me feel how soft you are."

I smile at him in the mirror. "Maybe if you beg me and apologize."

He lifts an eyebrow at me. "Apologize?"

Laughing, I spin around, grab his hand, and guide it into my robe so he can slip his fingers into my panties. "I already have to change. Do you see what you've done to me?"

He moans deep in his throat, sliding his middle finger between my legs. I hum softly as he puts pressure on my clit at the same time that he dips inside me before slowly pulling out and popping his finger into his mouth. "I will never apologize for this. But I can help."

Dante offers me a wicked grin, grabbing me by the front of my panties and pulling me to him. He snaps the band against my skin, and I startle at the lash of pain radiating through me for a moment before turning into pleasure.

I pat my hands against his chest, trying to put space between us. If I don't, we'll get carried away. Because I know I'm on the verge of letting him stretch my leg up to fuck me.

"You might want to tone it down, Andre. They're not going to leave the bathroom if you can't control your desire." Zade's voice hums through the air, attempting to snatch my attention away from Dante, but he grabs me by the back of my neck and laces his fingers through my hair, stopping me from even trying to look.

"Shut up and come in. Everyone can wait. Just don't let Andre participate. He can watch." Dante lifts me up and sets me on the sink.

I laugh and slide back down. "No, Dante. They're right. It's time. I don't want the universe to think we're going to just fuck for the rest of time."

"But it doesn't think. It knows." Dante tries to pin me against the sink, and I cup his hard-on through his pants, jolting him with a shock of my power, making him gasp in pleasure.

I shake my head, grinning. "I promise I'll let you smear my lipstick later."

He groans. "You make a hard bargain, pretty soul, but deal."

I wink at him. "It better be."

Keeping my hand on his hard cock, I tease him as I stroll around him and don't let go until I have a clear path to rush from the bathroom. I'll never get used to the fact that we built this palace together in Purgatory. The devils each have their own in separate kingdoms, but they stay with me. This is our home. At least, it's the home we stay in when we are not in the Mortal Realm. But we cross there whenever we want. None of us are bound to this realm because we are bound to the universe.

I never imagined that there would be no more Heaven or Hell. When I jumped with the twins and created Purgatory, it connected the kingdoms together as one. The levels are not all full of torture and never-ending punishment. They are intended for souls to grow and learn. Well, except for the worst of the worst. Lucian still gets to be his notorious asshole self. And he wouldn't have it any other way.

But me? I have complete control over what I like to call the gateway. Souls that reach me can either stay in Purgatory for however long they want in a world where no one has to be pure light or dark. They just have to understand balance and what helps the universe. It's through Purgatory that they can cross and cycle into the mortal world again. We are purely just the Afterlife. There is no good or evil. There is just existing and growing. It's exactly how I imagined things to be. Nothing has ever been so perfect. This might not be Heaven, but it is paradise. It is eternal.

"Look, you two. There's Mama. Doesn't she look so pretty?" Tamia's voice hums through the air, soft and musical just as I remember her as a mortal. And now...she's no longer a demon. She's no longer bound to Lucian to hold any sort of power. Tamia is what a true guide is supposed to be like. She is a soul who has decided to stay and help other souls cross from level to level when they're ready.

As much as Lucian wanted to keep angels in his fire lakes, I've granted them all mercy. Those who weren't obliterated and put back into the energy of the universe are now among the souls. As they help teach and guide, they can grow and learn themselves. Because they were never bad. They just...m ost of them were lost in the light. Just like half of my devils. Even sometimes me.

I hold my arms out and scoop Mateo from Tamia's arms, snuggling my nose to his. She holds Arabella out to me next, but a tail sneaks in and captures her first. Kase smiles, his handsome face lighting up. He hugs Arabella in close, and she opens and closes her little mouth, sucking on his nose and giving him the most slobbery kiss. He cracks up, loving the affection from our little girl. He loves her and Mateo and all of us just as the rest of the devils do.

"Keep up with the slobbering, and you're going to put out my hellfire, baby girl," Kase says, teasing Arabella as if she understands. And she might. I know that the twins carry a strange awareness that I've never known possible. They are still young infants but being in Purgatory and how the time runs differently here makes them absolutely unique. They're not on any level I'm familiar with except their own. They truly are the universe's gift to me. To my devils. Even to humanity.

Bright light flashes before me, and I spot Lucian and Elias land a couple of feet away. I never thought they would work together, but Lucian has been helping him set up his own kingdom while the others have been helping me tend to Purgatory.

"Let's get this fucking party started," Lucian says, racing Elias to scoop me into his arms first.

I squeal and hug Mateo as he spins the two of us around and sets me back on my feet, only to smack my ass like the perv he loves to be.

"Party? You mean worshipping. As soon as I sit on the throne, I'm going to prop my fucking feet up on your back. You're going to look so hot bowing before me, Satan." Teasing him will never get old, especially with how much he enjoys it.

"I plan to worship every fucking inch of you, Ray, starting with that pussy. You will be truly divine when I'm through." He growls with his words, grabbing me by the waist to pull me as close as he can so I can feel his hard-on against my pelvis. If I let him, he'd probably lift the skirt of my dress and crawl under.

All my devils would. And the thought excites me so much so that I force myself to pull away. They are far too good at distracting me. But it really is time. I can feel it deep in my very essence. It's time that I sit on my throne. It's time for me to officially claim Purgatory and set everything back into motion. The earth has healed, and it's time for things to begin a new cycle. A new beginning. It'll be so perfect. I just know it.

Micah and Cassius materialize in front of me, coming through portals from their kingdoms. We're all here together. I know that once I sit on my throne, we will officially connect, and I will get to welcome the souls for the first time ever.

A part of me is nervous, yet a bigger part of me is so relieved. I hate that I ever doubted myself. There was a point that I never believed this to be possible, and now that it is...I will enjoy it.

Tipping my head back, I stare at the brilliant blue sky with beams of rainbow light cutting across and leading into the horizon. "Thank you. Thank you for giving me this. Blessing me with the devils. For Purgatory." It's strange to say a prayer in front of my guys to the Higher Power, but I feel as if I must thank my lucky existence.

Lucian comes up beside me and drops his arm over my shoulders. "The Higher Power is the one thanking you now, Raven. None of this would've been possible had you not had faith in yourself and us. That's what it's all about. I hope you know that."

And I do. I just won't admit it to him. "You forgot these awesome powers." I smile with my words.

"I didn't forget. I could never. But it's more than just the power of Hell and Heaven. This is the power of us." He takes Mateo from me and holds him up in the air, smiling and flashing his devil horns. "Isn't that right, little spawn. Your mama needs to accept credit where credit is due."

Cassius comes up on my other side and laces his fingers through mine. "Don't worry, Raven. I'll keep my bastard brother in line. He will be the last one to give fatherly advice. You know how it was. Rebelling."

"Better than having a stick up your ass for a millennium." Kase play-growls and whips Cassius with his tail.

I love hearing them fuck around with each other. It fills me up with such warmth and love that I never knew was possible. They're not only the devils. They are brethren and kings. And I'm so thankful to be their queen.

I get between them and press my palms on each of their chests. "That's enough. Come on. My throne awaits."

Dante flaps his wings, launching into the air and over my head. Lucian follows his lead, carrying Mateo. Kase cradles Arabella and runs forward, choosing to stay on the ground. I don't think he thinks about his wings so much, but I do. They are just as amazing as he is.

I stretch my arms into the air, silently daring the devils to race to grab my hands. Andre and Zade beat everyone and each take one of my hands, pulling me into the air. Elias follows us, and Cassius finishes our line with Micah. I break away from Andre and Zade and dive down, grabbing Kase by the back of the shirt and pinning him to me.

He chuckles as I carry him with my strength.

"You like this don't you?" I murmur, kissing his throat.

"I swear if you summon a strap-on you're going to have Hell to pay, angel-girl." He grumbles under his breath, stretching his neck to nudge my head with his.

"You know how much I like that. I might wear you down eventually and claim your ass as mine." I bump my pelvis to his ass, making him practically cackle. I wouldn't do it though. Not with him holding Mateo. But it doesn't stop me from teasing the fuck out of him.

Rainbow light glows from me, lighting the realm in prism colors so beautiful that my soul can barely contain itself. Each of the devils blasts power in the distance, creating a huge hill with a beautiful crystal throne on top, overlooking the entire realm.

My smile widens, my whole body humming and zinging at the sight of the power created by my devils. It is just for me. For us. And I am now here to share it with the rest of the universe. I will be their vessel for salvation and mercy. To teach and help them grow.

I land at the base of the hill, joining the other devils. They all surround me and envelop me in their arms, showering me with kisses and hugs and love and everything amazing we've created together in this universe. In this realm, we have rebuilt and put it together from the rubble left behind by an imbalance between good and evil. But as it turns out, good and evil is more subjective than I ever knew. It's not about the light or dark. It is truly about the beauty of color.

"Our beautiful queen," Micah says, kneeling on the ground first and taking my hand and kissing the back. "Forever you may reign."

I take the twins and carry each of them on my shoulders, allowing the rest of the devils to follow Micah's gesture. They all kneel before me in their beautiful angelic devil forms, radiating with the power given to them by the Almighty and the universe. The power given to them—given to us— by our beautiful children.

"We swear our love and loyalty to you and humanity, angel-girl." Kase kisses my hand next.

"We vow to protect you and our children for the rest of time." Dante takes my hand from Kase and teases me by nipping my fingers.

"Everything we do will be for our kingdoms, our family, and the universe." Cassius bows his head and dramatically kisses the toe of my stilettos.

Fire sparks and Lucian gazes at the sight. "We promise to bring you strength and power from our very beings." The competitive bastard kisses both of my feet.

"You are our queen and the love of our existence. We will never take that for granted." Zade smiles at me, his blue eyes sparkling.

Andre bumps him with his shoulder, grinning just as widely.

"And we will always bring happiness, pleasure, and everything you could ever desire to our lives."

"We promise never to let you down or leave you. We bind ourselves to you and our children for the rest of time. You are our soulmate. And we are yours. Eternal paradise is ours." Elias expands his wings, blowing sweet air around us.

I hold the twins against me with my power and draw my fingers over each of my devils, whispering how much I love them. "And I promise to never let you down. I promise to help you all thrive and be the most powerful, caring, amazing men in all of the kingdoms. And all of the realms. I vow my very soul to you. To humanity. Forever and ever."

My devils get to their feet and all combine their strength and power, each adding a beautiful gemstone to a crown. As the first devil, Lucian sets it atop my head, and the whole world flashes with colorful sparks as if fireworks explode around us.

My heart races as I climb the hill with the twins and stand in front of my crystal throne, glowing with the light from the three of us. One angel, one devil, and me born from humanity. This is how purgatory was intended to be. This is how it'll be always.

Turning around, I stare at the vast beauty of my realm and kingdom. I never imagined such a sight. Its breathtaking beauty fills me up as I take a seat on my throne and a beautiful, rainbow portal cracks open and flashes of light and dark pour in, the souls who have already ascended to Purgatory ready for guidance from me.

"Welcome home," I whisper, spreading my arms wide. "Welcome to the Afterlife. May your souls find everything they need."

Eternal Paradise

RAVEN

I MOAN, MY voice vibrating across Dante's cock as he thrust deep in to my throat. He grips my hair, watching as I take all of him. Kase kneels behind me, fucking my ass as Lucian lies beneath me, keeping in sync with Kase, hitting me exactly in all the right places.

"Damn, I need another fucking turn. You are so sexy, darlin'. I can't get enough of you." Elias reaches his hand between me and Lucian, feeling around until he can rub my clit.

He uses a shock of power against my ring, and my whole body tenses with what feels like the millionth orgasm today.

"None of us can," Cassius says from my other side, stroking

his fingers across his cock. Micah, Zade, and Andre all lay around us, watching the show, their bodies sparkling with lube, toys scattered around the bed.

If I didn't know any better, I think we've been at it for a century at least. It might have just been a day or so. The amazing thing about our love for each other and how bonded we are is that no one is ever left out and we can rotate. But right now? The twins are hanging with Tamia and Gia. Their relationship has grown into something amazing, and I love having them around to help. The devils appreciate it too.

I gasp, another orgasm shocking me. Screaming, I arch my back as a wave of power and light illuminates my room, shaking the foundation of our world.

The act alone is enough to set all of the devils off at once, and I feel warm liquid splashing across me.

"Damn, angel-girl. When did you learn how to do that?" Kase asks, resting his cheeks against my spine, sandwiching me to Lucian.

I relax my body and just feel the sensation of both of their hearts pounding against me.

Dante slides his cock from my throat, and I lick my lips, the taste of his intoxicating cum sending tingles over my body. "She's been holding out on us."

I laugh and snuggle my face into Lucian's throat. "You can thank Andre for that. He taught me how to channel his energy.

Now all of your cocks are going to feel what it's like to come as much when I do."

Elias laughs. "Are you sure you want that kind of mess, darlin'?"

I grin and nod my head, closing my eyes and manifesting all of us into a giant tub with bubbles and hot water like the devils enjoy. "Hell yeah. It means more bubble baths. I could live in this tub forever."

Micah hums under his breath. "So can I. Come here. Sit on my lap."

I laugh and splash him with bubbles, knowing if I even get close to any of them, it could be another couple of days before we make our way back to the Mortal Realm. "Next time. I miss my babies."

Elias shoots power around us, shifting the plane until I find myself squished in a tub between him and Micah with the rest of the devils sitting on their asses, dripping wet on the tile floor of his bathroom in the Mortal Realm.

I cackle, clapping my hands, loving seeing everyone naked and hard and soapy. It's so fucking hot.

If I didn't hear the most musical laughter, I would launch myself out of the water and on top of them, continuing our fuck pile the way everybody likes.

Micah reads my mind and wraps a towel around me, picking me up to carry me over the other devils. We dodge around them, making it from the bathroom and to his room.

My heart races as a second bout of the sweetest laughter I've ever heard chimes around me.

The devils follow behind us, not even bothering to get dressed. I remain in a towel, and Micah rushes to the nursery in our mansion.

He stops in the doorway, and I wiggle from his arms and watch as Arabella and Mateo sit before Tamia as she covers her eyes and flashes them the demonic façade that she can still summon. They clap their hands and giggle, loving every second of this game, and I stride forward, sneaking up on them from behind.

"She's so funny, isn't she?" I say, smiling at my cousin as I kneel behind them.

Arabella stretches her chubby arms first, squealing at the sight of me. Tamia ruffles her fingers through Mateo's soft hair, and she winks at me before vanishing.

I whisper my thanks, and scoop up the twins, snuggling close. "Did you miss us? We missed you."

I let both of them slobber me with kisses, loving every second of their affection. The rest of the devils join us on the ground, now dressed by their power.

The twins wiggle away from me and latch on to Zade next, kissing him first and setting his whole body aglow with their light. It crawls through the rest of us, and I savor the warmth they bring.

"They are so perfect, aren't they?" Dante asks Kase, leaning in and kissing the top of Mateo's head.

"Just like their mama," Andre says, kissing my shoulder.

"Don't forget they have a part of you all too." I smile, looking at each of my devils in their beautiful gazes.

I never expected my eternity to begin like this, but I couldn't have asked or prayed for anything better.

This truly is eternal paradise.

The most perfect place we could ever be.

The End

Author Note

Thank you so much for traveling to Hell and back and finally finding the perfect balance with Raven and her devils. This series was incredibly fun to write, and I hope to one day explore more of the Seven Sinners of Hell's Kingdom world. And who knows, maybe Daddy Dante will return as my muse for more Kink Express adventures. See you in Purgatory!

XOXO,
Ginna Moran

Other RH Books

OMEGAVERSE SERIES

Saint Vista Pack Regimes

Bonds of Steele Omegaverse

PARANORMAL

The Seven Sinners of Hell's Kingdon

The Pack Mates of Lunar Crest

The Wolfpacks of Shadow Moon Island

The Fated Mate of the Dragon Clans

The Divine Vampire Heirs

The Royale Vampire Heirs

The Academy of Vampire Heirs

La Vega Vampire Showstoppers

Rise from the Flames

About Ginna Moran

GINNA MORAN IS the *USA Today* Bestselling author of over seventy novels including the popular Knotty Lessons and The Seven Sinners of Hell's Kingdom novels.

She always carried a fascination for all things paranormal and wrote her first unpublished manuscript at age eighteen. Her love of the supernatural grew stronger through her adult life, and she now spends her days with different creatures of the night. Whether it's vampires, werewolves, dragons, fae, angels, demons, or mermaids, Ginna loves creating and living in worlds from her dreams.

Aside from Ginna's professional life, she enjoys binge-watching TV, crafting and design, playing with her daughter, and cuddling with her dog. Some of her favorite things include chocolate, mermaids, anything that glitters, learning new things, cheesy jokes, and organizing her bookshelf.